Mindfi

L D Houghton

Copyright © 2023 L D Houghton

All rights reserved.

ISBN: **9798851977077**

Contents

1	4
2	13
3	20
4	32
5	36
6	45
7	59
8	66
9	81
10	87
11	95
12	100
13	114
14	123
15	129
16	141
17	150
18	157
19	165
20	171
21	179
22	183
23	191
24	198
25	205
26	213
27	220

28	226
29	233
30	241
Epilogue	252
ABOUT THE AUTHOR	257

1

An agent must always be aware of his surroundings, both physical and metaphysical.

Agency Handbook, Section 1.7

There were two bodies. No sign of the girl, just two charred bodies.

Nestor Grey stared through the night's gloom as the rain poured down, soaking the bare, cracked concrete and the crumpled bodies sprawled out upon it. The sound of the large, heavy raindrops rattling the corrugated roofing of the rusting warehouses far behind him rolled over everything, while around his feet puddles spat and jumped, reflecting the dull, cloud-shrouded moon above.

A man and a woman. Middle-aged, from what he could tell, but it would be difficult to know for sure even if there were more to see by than the light of the single distant, flickering electric light post at the entrance of the nearest warehouse.

It looked like the two of them had been heading away from the warehouses, though Grey couldn't imagine where they were headed *to*. Beyond them concrete gradually gave way to nothing but the Waste, desolate, lifeless soil and earth extending into the darkness, towards a vast wilderness given over to shrubs and roaches where few other things survived for long.

That, or they'd come *in* from the Waste, which was equally difficult to believe.

He stood in the gloom, dragging on the e-cig glowing fitfully in his mouth, sparking in the drops the brim of his hat couldn't block, and stared at the dark, vague shapes of the corpses.

Two bodies. No girl. But the scorch marks told him there *had* been a third person, a dark patch of burnt ground surrounding a conspicuously paler vacant area of rough concrete, exactly as burn marks surrounded each of the bodies.

Mindfire. Someone had used Mindfire on these two, frying them from the inside out, forcing their bodies into the pained, curled positions they now lay in. Their skin was charred, clothing burnt off until only blackened scraps remained.

Could the girl have learnt to use Mindfire so soon? But she was surely too young, and the chances of surviving her first use of

Mindfire low.

Then could someone else have done this?

The empty patch of concrete lay there mocking him, rain slowly pooling to form a smooth black layer that would in short time render it indistinguishable from any other strip of soaking ground. Which meant this must have happened recently.

A metallic clattering came from somewhere nearby, a feral coyote or rad-cat knocking aside a derelict pile of sheet metal as it stalked its prey. Grey tutted at the distraction.

What really stood out to him was the way the bodies curled in towards each other, each with a single hand outstretched. As if, even in the throes of their agony, their thoughts had been of reaching for the other.

A second clatter of metal, followed by a sudden hush; a hush that told Grey someone was trying very hard not to make any noise. The silence seemed particularly loud towards the narrow space between the two nearest warehouses, a strip of darkness the weak moonlight failed to penetrate.

Turning slowly away from the bodies, Grey stepped quietly but steadily towards the darkness, his hand slipping below his coat and grasping the pistol holstered at his waist. At the same time the moon emerged from a gap between the clouds, its light increasing the contrast between the open concrete and the darkness of the gap beyond.

He was only a few steps from the space when there was a sudden noise, the sound of someone trying frantically to be at once quiet and to make a hiding place amongst the old iron sheets piled haphazardly against the walls of the warehouses. They were failing at both.

The reflection of moonlight on metal gave a glimpse of the source of the sound and made Grey pause. Releasing his grip on his weapon, he took his hands from his pockets and held them out wide, palms spread to show he wasn't a threat.

It was a boy. Grey thought he couldn't be more than twelve or thirteen, though children weren't really within his area of expertise. Young, anyway. Young, pale, with mousy brown hair, his wide eyes reflected the cloudy night sky above. He was sat with his back against the metal warehouse wall, pushing futilely with his feet as if trying to force himself through and into imagined safety. His ragged breathing could be heard just above the rain.

"Hey kid, it's ok," Grey said, keeping his arms wide open and taking a slow, measured step forwards. "It's ok. I'm not gonna hurt you."

The child pushed harder with his feet, sliding sideways along the wall and against the iron sheets stacked against it. He looked up at Grey from a face grimed with dust, ash, and a dark material that looked worryingly like blood. Grey spoke in a slow, flat tone, trying to counter the panic coming from the kid.

"It's ok, it's ok. I can help. Just… just calm down, alright?"

Grey had never gotten used to talking to children. They didn't fit any protocol, and his standard methods were hardly suited to the easily startled. In his line of work, it was best that those who couldn't defend themselves were kept well away.

At least the child seemed to have stopped scrabbling quite so much in the pause as Grey tried to adjust the situation. Now the boy was sitting almost still, fidgeting slightly as he looked up at him. No, not fidgeting… shivering. The kid was clothed in some kind of thick white cotton top and pants combination, devoid of logo or pattern. These were soaked through, the cold rain rendering them useless as protection from the chill despite their thickness.

"Here, kid," said Grey, swinging his coat from off his shoulders and holding it out towards the child, trying to avoid any sudden movements. "Put this over yourself. It's waterproof, so you won't get any wetter, at least."

The child looked from Grey to the jacket twice, hesitation vying with cold until, decided, he snatched the jacket from Grey's hands and pulled it over his body like a blanket. He was so small it practically *was* a blanket.

"So, you got a name or anything?" said Grey, over the sound of rain.

The child didn't reply, but once again met Grey's gaze. Grey found the look disconcertingly direct. He'd thought the kid was crying at first, but realized now it was only the cold and rain making him sniff and shift around. The eyes were steady beneath the grime, as if challenging him to try something.

"Not talking then? Ok, well, let's get you out of the cold first, anyway. Here, let me help…"

Grey's words were cut short by a short, sharp crack somewhere behind him, followed by a piercing buzzing that got louder as it came rapidly closer. Only years of experience and trained reflexes let Grey do what he did next.

Spinning to face back out the alley, Grey flung out two outstretched hands and *focused*. The buzzing suddenly filled the air, a screech that emanated from a small glinting cylinder held, frozen in the air, before him. Grey grunted with effort, the air in front of him seeming strangely thick, raindrops making odd curling patterns as if a gel filled that small patch of air.

Letting out a long breath, Grey lowered his hands. The glinting cylinder fell to the ground, buzz cutting off when it hit the concrete.

A fizzer.

Grey instantly knew two things. One, he needed to get somewhere safe. Someone had just taken a shot at him. Two, that someone had some serious resources if they had access to fizzers.

Fizzers were bullets with nanoscopic, flexible 'fins' along the sides and a compact processor within, able to make small but significant corrections to their trajectory every microsecond. They practically guaranteed a kill-shot.

Practically, unless the target had access to... *unusual* countermeasures.

Still, no matter how unusual the countermeasure, it wouldn't stop the next few rounds tearing a hole through him if he didn't get behind cover *now*.

The leap Grey took couldn't be described as graceful, but it did the job. Throwing himself forward, he grabbed the boy as he flew over him, curling his body to protect them both as his back smashed into and through the thankfully flimsy rusting warehouse wall. Still, sharp barbs of rusted metal tore through his clothes and bit at his skin.

Grey's wild somersaulting left them sprawled amongst old industrial piping, a cloud of dirt and dust rising around them. Taking no time to regain his bearings, he staggered to his feet. He grabbed the child by the shoulder, coughing as he pulled him along to make their way deeper into the warehouse.

Unfortunately, the vast space was essentially empty aside from sparsely-spaced stacks of heavy steel pipes like those that they had crashed through the wall and landed amongst. These mostly lay stacked against the warehouse sides, piles of them tied together with cables. In places these cables had snapped, allowing their loads to roll haphazardly across the cold floor, but other than that only a few anonymous-looking crates took up any space at all, emphasising the emptiness rather than consuming it.

Two rows of metal support struts and connecting girders held the high roof up, a number of strip lights fixed along them. These still gave a fitful glow despite the sense that this place had been abandoned for several years. Grey headed towards the cover of the nearest strut.

Grey knew the fact that they had light to see by was a good thing, though the boy at his side was obviously looking around for a darkened corner to hide in. If the person hunting them had access to fizzers, darkness would hardly be a hindrance to their aim; they would certainly have decent target-assistance hardware that required little light. In fact, Grey was sure his own body heat and the heat of the boy would be easily visible through these walls to any semi-decent gun-cam. All they could do was keep moving, making use of what little cover there was.

He knew there was no way he could draw enough energy to stop a second fizzer. Frankly, he was still unsure where he found the power to stop the first. The area seemed far too abandoned for there to be anything like enough Aether for that, so Grey prayed to anyone that might be listening that they were moving fast enough to keep ahead of those hunting him.

It appeared that there were events more interesting to deities going on elsewhere, however, as his prayers were answered only by a second sharp crack. A dark round spot appeared on the wall near where they had crashed in, the screeching bullet curving straight for the kid.

Somehow in that split second Grey managed to twist and force the boy sideways behind him. The bullet curved to follow but was deflected just enough as the air thickened around it. Instead, it tore through Grey's left arm and continued on, exiting through the opposite wall.

Grey let out a gasp at the sudden pain, reaching up to cover the wound with his right hand. Blood poured through his fingers, but through the pain he could feel it was only a shallow injury. Nothing to slow him down. Yet.

That's two strokes of luck, he thought to himself. He didn't think he should count on a third.

If he got out of this, though, he was going to dine out on tonight's events. *Two* fizzers. Most Far agents fail at one, and that kind of failure meant you didn't get a second attempt.

Perhaps it was hubris, though, because something seemed set on disabusing him of any such optimistic thoughts the instant they crossed his mind. There were tall, wide doors at each end of the warehouse, and the one at the far end, in the direction they were heading, had just begun sliding open.

Grey spun on his heels, grabbing the kid again and pulling him back, accepting the fact that the blood from his arm would just have to flow for a while. The boy spun round, and they began hurrying towards the opposite end of the warehouse. They were practically in the centre of it now, equidistant from any exit.

The problem was, however, that this was the end the fizzer shots had come from.

Which means there's more than one of them.

In fact, there were several. The door ahead slid sideways to reveal six large forms silhouetted against the outside gloom, each figure bulky with the padding Grey knew must be body armour. Each also held a long, metallic something that glinted in the light, a glint that spoke to Grey.

It said, *assault rifles.*

Spinning again, the futility of their situation became clear. Another set of figures stood at the now-open far entrance, identically equipped. They were raising the barrels of their weapons.

Well, there's no getting out of this one, Grey thought to himself.

He did what little he could, though, grabbing the boy and shielding him with his body. Even as he did so, he knew this was an empty gesture.

"Clean this up," came a voice, electronically dulled to contain no identifiable tones. Standard comms equipment for most armed groups these days, private or public. Even Far agents had been known to use them, though Grey never did. Anything he said, he took ownership of.

With that final inane thought, an explosion of rifle fire. He closed his eyes.

…and opened them again.

Something was wrong. The rifles had sustained fire for what felt like several seconds; he should be riddled with bullets by now. Not still standing, hunched over the child.

Instead, there was a strange silence, followed by a gentle tapping sound. The first tap was followed by a second, then a third, then suddenly a shower of them as if the rain had suddenly begun to fall inside the warehouse.

Something rolled to a stop by his foot. A small, cylindrical thing.

Bullets were dropping to the floor all around him.

"What the f...?" came the neutral, flat voice. No way to tell if it was the same speaker as before, with every trace of inflection removed. Still, Grey sensed the shock in the words.

Grey straightened up slowly, looking down towards the boy. The boy's chin had been resting on his shoulder, and his head didn't move as Grey stepped back. His eyes were focused on a bullet in front of him, floating in the air as if held by a vice.

It was a standard bullet, of course. None of the attackers would have wasted a fizzer on such an easy kill. It rotated and spun as the child looked at it, head tilting to examine it as it moved.

Had the kid just stopped *every* bullet fired by twelve assault rifles? That was impossi...

Suddenly the child's head snapped up, the bullet dropping to the floor as if a string had been cut. Now, he looked at the men by the far door. They had rifles raised but stood frozen. Grey assumed that beneath their darkened visors they each wore similar expressions of surprise.

"Fire!"

This time Grey could definitely hear panic, even through vocal filters. Rifles spat in front and behind them, causing him to flinch.

None of the bullets came close this time. Each became a flattened, coin-shaped disc almost immediately as if hitting an impenetrable wall shortly after leaving the barrel. They dropped to the floor after a brief pause.

Impossible, thought Grey. *There's not enough Aether in a city, let alone out here...*

He could see the armour-clad forms turning towards each other, looking for orders or ideas. Eventually the one in the middle of the rear group, who Grey now saw was holding a screen-mounted rifle modified to fire fizzers, raised a finger and pointed towards them. Both groups advanced towards them.

"We need to run, kid," said Grey, placing both hands on his

shoulders, trying to gain the child's attention. The boy didn't move though, staring now at the group containing the modified rifle. The cold, hateful stare made the group hesitate for a second before they resumed their advance.

Loss of blood was making Grey lightheaded, and because of this he would never be *exactly* clear on what happened next. It seemed like the whole world turned in on itself for a second.

A sudden light filled the expanse of the warehouse, chasing shadows from every corner and drowning out any definition or contrast. Grey's eyes burned even through his closed eyelids.

Once the initial, spectacular brightness died down, however, light still remained. The crackling sound of burning came from somewhere over his head. Grey slowly opened his eyes and looked up.

A dragon. An honest-to-gods' dragon.

Grey wondered if the blood loss had been worse than he thought.

It floated above him, a form of pure golden fire that smouldered yet somehow gave off, instead of scorching heat, only warmth. Huge wings with long, curved talons curled over a body larger than a carbon sequestration unit, and a broad neck rose to a long-snouted head with serpentine eyes. Details such as the leathery, scaled skin and veined, powerful claws were somehow clearly visible despite the whole creature being made of pure, crackling flame. It stood upon the air as if on solid ground, towering over them, head almost touching the high roof.

The dragon roared silently, a tongue of flame pouring from its mouth into the air, and at the same time Grey became aware of movement beneath his hands.

His palms rested on the boy's shoulders, frozen in the moment of pulling him away from danger. The boy still stared at the attackers in front of them, but now his head was craned forward, eyes bulging and lip curling upwards. His teeth were showing like some primeval beast, and he was almost growling as the narrowed slits of his eyes focused on one figure than the next. Above, the flaming form moved in sympathetic reflection.

The boy moved as the dragon moved, Grey realised. Which meant...

His thoughts were cut off as the boy jerked his shoulders forward, and above the dragon curled in on itself and, in one graceful, curving arc, dove straight towards the armoured attackers.

A couple of them had time to drop their guns and begin turning away, trying to flee, before all six figures were engulfed. The flame passed across and through them, leaving them unable even to scream as heat and fire poured out from their lungs, charring them to cinder from the inside out.

Mindfire.

Grey felt panic rise in him, forcing aside the pain of his various injuries. That much Mindfire was impossible - nowhere had the population density to sustain such a burn. Especially not some abandoned warehouse district.

And Mindfire couldn't be *shaped*. It couldn't be *controlled* in the way he was seeing.

The form of the blazing dragon as it turned and arced over his head, plummeting towards the second group, begged to differ.

This time, Grey noticed that even though the blazing creature appeared to snap its jaws shut around the attackers, it didn't actually matter whether they were caught within that gaping mouth or not. The flaming dragon's form enveloped the armoured figures wherever it touched them, leaving them visible, dark and solid, within the partially transparent inferno. It wasn't really a dragon at all, but a flowing mass of energy, and it would surround and consume any living matter it touched.

As suddenly as it had appeared, the creature was gone. It passed across the fleeing group and left them behind as they fell, flowing into the wall beyond. If it had been truly the conflagration it appeared to be, it should have charred or melted the thin metal as it passed through. Instead, the wall was unmarked and the warehouse fell silent, save for the rhythmic sound of rain upon the metal roof and the soft thuds of carbonized bodies collapsing to the floor.

After waiting, frozen, for a few moments, Grey began to feel confident enough that the creature wasn't going to return that he could turn his eyes to the boy. Whatever had been going on inside the kid's head, it appeared to be over. The boy looked almost as shocked as Grey felt, blinking repeatedly at the charcoal forms fallen before him as if disbelieving his own eyes.

"Come on, kid," said Grey. "Let's get out of here before someone comes asking questions."

He stared at the charred remains lying in front of him.

"I don't know what we could tell them anyway."

2

The global population crash following the Sudden War was unprecedented in recorded history. The population boom that followed, however, was not. After just a handful of generations, humanity is well on its way to equalling its previous numbers despite being confined to half its prior range. We now have proportionally the youngest population the planet has ever seen, with commensurate risk of societal unrest that such a ratio brings.

Agency Handbook, Section 5.2 (Society & Group Dynamics)

The journey back into the city proper felt like an aeon. Grey knew the warehouse district was no more than a few tens of kilometres from the inhabited zones of the city of Albores, and he'd had reason to come out this way before, but it had never felt so distant. Sitting in the auto-cab beside the shivering child with the rain hammering on the vehicle's roof, he had to struggle to hide his own trembles. Only his were not due to the temperature.

Getting the kid into the city and up to his office was achieved without event, at least. The boy just sat there, staring out past the empty front seat of the automated vehicle with its gently glowing and generally obsolete dashboard, and into the dark, rainy streets beyond the windscreen. Despite his shivering, the child seemed hardly aware of the chill from his soaked clothes, fixated upon the glowing, frenetic vis-boards and ad-screens that flashed by one after the other as the car sped along the highway, kinetic images that revolved to follow them, screaming their lurid, exaggerated messages of brands and bargains in the Spanish-English fusion known as centra-English, the dominant language of the Reclamation. A clever trick of light projection, Grey knew, as each image would appear to focus on and follow the passengers of any and every vehicle passing, simultaneously.

When the auto-cab finally stopped directly outside the double doors leading into the tower block containing Grey's office, Grey let out a deep breath he hadn't realised he'd been holding. He jumped out of the door and into the street, running around the cab to the other side and swinging the door open for the child. A small buzz from his jacket pocket indicated confirmation of payment, and the taxi pulled away almost before the boy had stepped out.

The boy mutely followed Grey into the building, the two of them dripping rainwater onto the tiled floors of the atrium that made up the entrance. He led the boy straight across the tiles to the nearest elevator, call-sensor already triggered and displaying a car travelling down to meet them, while the boy looked around with wide eyes.

The building had never really been much to Grey, the atrium nothing more than a long, narrow hallway overlooked by the balcony-like walkways of the floors above, rising to the roof. The walkway of each floor formed a circle around the hollow inner circumference of the building, with a number of rooms available for use as offices or apartments on the outer side. Most of these rooms were empty – as with so many areas of Albores, this section was still relatively underpopulated, with immigration and settlement concentrated in the north and east of the city. The seclusion of the area was one of the reasons Grey had chosen to settle here.

There was a single grimy glass skylight in the roof, eight or so floors above, but it let in little light, leaving the LED strips lining the walls to do the work. This was a place where people stayed only temporarily, if at all, moving on once they found (and could afford) a more desirable location elsewhere. The boy, however, seemed fascinated by it.

With a chime, the door to the elevator opened, a slight rattle suggesting a lack of proper maintenance. The touchless controls registered Grey's keypass in his pocket as he stepped in, and the doors closed behind them.

Grey's apartment office was on the third floor, just two doors left from the elevator. He was almost at his door when he realised the kid wasn't behind him anymore. Spinning around, he saw the boy leaning over the railing and looking down to the ground floor where they had entered, the rainwater on the floor tiles marking their passage.

The railing was a solid metal bar above a waist-high concrete wall and had always seemed reliable to Grey, but he felt a slight quickening of his pulse at the sight of the child leaning over, feet lifting off the ground. Grey walked hurriedly back and hesitantly pulled the child away by the shoulder. The boy looked up at him, not blankly, but with an expression Grey couldn't read. It felt as if he were some strange creature the boy had never seen before, and the child was simply waiting to see what he would do.

"Come on, let's get some dry clothes and some food, yeah?"

He settled the boy in what, for the want of a better term, was his living room. It held little more than a worn-out couch, lining frayed and with deep indentations where the filling had given out under years of use, and a thin wall-screen in front of that. All of this was coloured a pale yellow by the full-spectrum lighting, supposedly effective at countering the lack of natural sunlight most Albores inhabitants suffered from living under constant grey clouds.

The wall-screen turned on automatically at their entry, declaring the latest products and medicines for a longer, better life.

"Volume down," said Grey aloud, the volume on the screen immediately dropping to a more tolerable level. "No, in fact, home screen."

The sound cut off immediately as the wall-screen switched to displaying an array of icons, everything from controls for lighting, heating, and water pressure for the apartment to news, media, and games for passing the time, and more. Most of these Grey had never bothered with.

The boy was staring at the screen hungrily.

"Here," said Grey, reaching out to slide the screen from its bracket on the wall. "Knock yourself out. I'll try to find you some... hell, I don't know, something dry, at least." The boy was still leaving damp footprints on the floor.

Passing the screen to the kid, Grey turned around with a calmness he didn't feel and stepped through the doorway to his office. As soon as he was through the door, and had slid it shut behind him, he collapsed back against the wall. His breathing came shakily, ragged as he tried to keep quiet enough that the boy couldn't hear. A wave of tension and fear washed over him, allowed to finally break.

Through the wall he heard the tones of the wall-screen responding to its user's commands.

That kid is a damn bomb.

Grey was having trouble believing his memory. What he had seen couldn't have happened.

But it *had* happened. The child in the next room had murdered twelve heavily armed, heavily armoured mercenaries, or whatever their attackers had been. And he'd done it in a way that shouldn't... *couldn't* have happened.

Mindfire doesn't do that. It doesn't... dance for you. It doesn't fly *for you.*

Grey had been dealing with incidents involving Aether and Aether users since the day he graduated from the Academy and became a Far agent. There were very few times at the Agency, however, that he'd had to deal with Mindfire. And since he'd... *resigned* ... he hadn't expected to ever have to deal with it again.

And now he apparently had the most powerful user he'd ever heard of sitting using up his bandwidth in the next room.

Grey was almost relieved when he realised there was someone in the office with him.

"Bringing strays home now?"

The voice was strong, feminine but deep, with the same air of command Grey knew it always carried. The speaker matched the voice, short cropped hair framing a square face, hard features almost unchanged in the years since they'd met last save a few new lines around the eyes. Broad shoulders told of a lifetime of unforgiving training and exercise, and a career just as unforgiving.

"So you're just overriding my locks now, huh?" said Grey, putting on a thin smile and trying to keep his state of mind out of his tone.

"It wasn't locked," came the reply.

"What do you want, career?"

That struck home, Grey saw. A small grunt of annoyance, and a flash of a piercing stare.

"I've asked you, *several times*, not to call me that."

"Fine. Sorry, Ritra, it's been a long day."

Ritra Feye.

She'd been his mentor in his early days in Far, back when she was barely out of training herself, and they'd known each other even before that. It wasn't long before she had far outstripped him, though, moving up the ranks at a pace that surprised her co-agents, and often her superiors.

She had a way of forcing herself onward to greater heights, and a drive that crushed anyone foolish enough, or just unlucky enough, to stand in her way. Grey was sufficiently aware of his own skills to know he'd been no slouch as a Far agent himself, but he had never been on the same level as his one-time mentor.

They'd maintained a kind of friendship even after she'd risen too high in the agency for them to have much professional interaction, and after he'd suddenly left it was her who had come to ask why. His explanation hadn't been enough, but still, they'd stayed in touch, and this wasn't the first time she'd shown up at his office. In fact, she'd probably been one of his first clients - "a little outsourcing for the agency," she'd called it.

"A long day? Looks like a long year from where I'm standing. You look awful. What happened to your arm?"

Grey chuckled, a genuine reaction this time, and rubbed the bloodied bandage wrapped around where the fizzer had torn his flesh.

"Just a difficult case. Not even sure I'm following the right path, to be honest. Things got a little complicated."

She stared him up and down, taking in his damp, bedraggled appearance.

"And the kid?" she asked.

Grey paused as he went to respond. Whatever the kid was, he wasn't sure he wanted to discuss it with a Far agent, no matter how well he knew her. For a start, there would be some awkward questions about how he found the boy in the first place.

"Just a kid I found. Some runaway, maybe. I'm working a case, but he's not even a part of it as far as I can tell."

He pushed himself from the wall and walked over to his desk, stepping around Ritra where she sat in the chair for clients and collapsing into his own seat opposite. Reaching down and opening a drawer, he pulled out two tumblers with one hand and a hip flask with the other.

"You're a walking cliché, Nest," said Ritra. She accepted one of the glasses, though, and he poured a liberal amount into each one.

They both knocked their whiskies back in one, sitting in silence while the alcohol did its warming work. Eventually, though, Ritra spoke.

"So, I'm hearing that you turned up in the 8th district this morning. Any reason in particular?"

Damn... thought Grey.

Still, he'd known it was going to get back to the agency. As soon as the two field agents had walked in he'd known something was going to go wrong, and when it did... Well, he hadn't held back.

Anyway, he still didn't believe he'd done anything wrong. He just hoped Ritra saw it that way, too.

Knowing it was fruitless, he tried to *Read* Ritra. How much did she suspect?

He got nothing.

Ritra's mind had always been a wall to him. She was one of those who thought in sensations, not words. Reading someone who operated without an inner monologue was always difficult, and Ritra was basically impervious to any mental intrusion. It was one of the reasons she had got so high in the agency.

Still, it also meant she was completely oblivious to any attempts to Read her, too.

It was always a two-sided coin, Reading. Those who could be Read could learn to tell when someone was Reading them, while the more resistant to Reading a person was, the less they could detect any mental assault.

Grey felt kind of bad for the attempt anyway. He liked Ritra, respected her. But he did also find it annoying that she kept trying to step into his affairs as if he were still an agent, and her subordinate.

"The 8th?" he said, giving no indication of what he had just attempted. "Ah, yeah. I was down there this morning on a case. Bumped into a couple of your boys, I think."

"You think?" She threw back her head and let out a short, barked laugh. "From the way I hear it, you almost threw one out of a window. There was going to be a *lot* of paperwork on that one."

She locked eyes with him, face serious. And suddenly, a knowing smile.

"But I cleared things up. Explained… who you were. Our friendly freelance agent, out on sabbatical."

Grey didn't give her the rise she was obviously hoping for.

"It's not a sabbatical, and you know it. I'm done with the agency. Have been for years." He spoke firmly, and Ritra waved her hands in mock supplication.

"Yes, yes, I know. Still, we can but hope our star agent shall one day return, can we not?"

Her grin *almost* got the rise she wanted out of him. She'd always enjoyed teasing him, right from the first time they'd met, him lost and frightened but trying to hide it as he found himself in a world he knew nothing about. She had been assigned to look after him. Look after *them*.

"I think the star agent is sitting across from me, no?" he replied.

"Oh, I'm *much* more than an agent now. You know that, Nest. I do miss the old life, though. Out on the streets, working the districts, making a *difference*. You know. Like this thing on 8th." She leaned forward, folding her hands together, serious again. "Why were you there, Grey?"

"You know I can't tell you that, Ritra."

"This ridiculous 'client privilege' you always talk about?" She leaned back in annoyance. "Come on Grey. You assaulted one of my agents. The least I can get for covering your ass is an explanation."

"Assaulted? That's what they said?"

"Well, not in so many words. There's male pride involved and all that. But the report *did* imply you were rather... out of hand. You can't mess with Far agents like that."

"I can if they're being stupid *pendejos*."

She sat silently, staring at him.

Goddamit... thought Grey. He was going to have to tell her something.

"Look, alright, I'll tell you what I can..."

He'd just have to be careful not to hint at what he was leaving out.

3

Of all ideologies proposed or enacted across human history, only one has consistently proven itself. That is the ideology of strength. All other social structures are viable only when those enforcing them wield sufficient power.

Agency Principles and Practice: Section 8, 4.21

The request to get down to a medium-sized residential build in the 8th district hadn't come directly from anyone. It was simply a ping on his thin-screen, triggered by a set of parameters being fulfilled during one of its repeated network searches.

The mid-morning notification came because it was the sort of thing his clients liked him to investigate. A possible Aether-incident, images and clips appearing online suggesting property damage and perhaps criminal intent. A lot of insurance companies who had him on the payroll would be thankful for prompt information. So he'd grabbed his jacket and headed out.

The 8th wasn't far from his office. A couple of autobuses got him there in about the same time it would have taken him to summon a taxi, for much cheaper. Then it was just a short walk down some narrow streets and round a few corners.

The subdistrict the incident had been flagged in was a standard residential sector, grid-arranged streets dividing square apartment blocks built of self-repair concrete and breathe-brick. All of them had that same stripy, grey-on-white pattern to their walls that the calcite-producing bacteria made, filling and repairing any cracks with every rain. It wasn't attractive, but it was cheap and easy to maintain.

The carbon drains and pollution pumps that always covered the roofs of such buildings provided a background hum as he walked, with only a few solitary pedestrians hurrying about their day. A heavy rain warning had been pinged for the area, and thankfully that was keeping the crowds away. For all the atmospheric cleaning that had been done in the past few decades, it still wasn't a good idea to be caught in a downpour if you could avoid it. Stained clothes could be the least of your worries.

Still, he was irritated to find that, upon rounding the final corner, the warning hadn't kept *all* the crowds away.

A small crowd was gathered around the base of the residential block he was heading for, looking up and murmuring amongst themselves. A set of steps was built into the front of the building, zig-zagging upwards to the top with a landing on each floor. It seemed like the crowd was reluctant to go up these, preferring to spectate from afar.

That reluctance didn't stop them from holding their thin-screens up towards whatever it was that was drawing their attention, though, screens flashing or glowing as they took their videos.

The fact that the first instinct of any person sensing trouble these days was to record and share it would have annoyed Grey, if it weren't for the fact that it made his job a whole lot easier.

As he got closer he was able to see what had got their attention. Well, to hear it, actually.

The loud bangs and thuds came from what must be an apartment a few floors up, hidden from view from where Grey stood on the ground floor, but he recognised the sounds of breaking furniture and what occasionally seemed to be the walls themselves. Someone was screaming, a cry of anger and frustration rather than fear. They sounded young, and it was hard to tell if they were male or female.

There were adult voices as well, Grey realised, lower and more difficult to hear. These were gradually rising in volume, becoming more frantic as the crashing sounds grew louder and more frequent. The edge to their voices made Grey begin to push against the crowd, fighting to get through.

A sudden booming sound, and glass came flying out and over the crowd from above. Each apartment on the ground floor had two small windows to the side of their doors, and Grey assumed it was the same pattern on the floors above. Which meant, he figured, that something had just blown out the windows of the apartment in question.

The glass at least had the fortunate effect of thinning the crowd somewhat, enough for him to make it through to the stairs. As he made his way through people now frantically brushing shards of glass out of their hair, their clothes, and, in a few unfortunate cases, their eyes, Grey congratulated himself on the cover of his wide-brim hat. Always a good idea to have one in case of…

"Yes, yes, I get it, Grey. And we both know you only have that hat so you can smoke in the rain."

Anyway...What Grey saw when he got to the floor the noise had come from was, essentially, what he'd expected. Maybe a little more... energetic... than he'd hoped, but nothing he hadn't encountered before.

There were indeed two small windows at the front of the apartment, and the glass that had once been inside those windows was now scattered on the walkway beyond, and the people below. The door had also been blown outward off its hinges and leant sideways against the chest-high wall and guardrail that separated the walkway from open air, opposite the now-empty doorframe.

Grey noted the splintering to its wooden surface, a deep indentation in the centre as if a giant's fist had smashed into it with great force.

So, almost certainly an Aether user. Grey didn't know anything else that could create enough percussive force to blow out two windows and a door without any trace of explosive, heat, or fumes.

Grey *reached*, trying to sense anyone nearby, especially anyone drawing on the Aether. Nothing. If someone was there, they were deeper inside the apartment.

It seemed like blowing out the door and windows had been the end of it, at least for now, because everything was silent save for the murmurs and occasional pained exclamations of the crowd below. Grey leaned warily forward and poked his head through the doorframe.

The entrance to the apartment was a small hallway leading into a slightly wider unit kitchen. Beyond that, Grey could see what was probably the living area, though it was difficult to tell. It *looked* like the scattered pieces of cloth and wood on the floor could have once been a sofa, and the glittering shards of plastic and electronics were likely once a pretty big wall-screen. The unit kitchen, at least, was obvious, even if the microwave oven and half a food processor lay bent and crushed against the wall as if smashed by an enraged elephant.

Of course, there hadn't been any elephants since the Fall, so unless someone was being *very* liberal with cloning laws, this was definitely an Aether incident.

Grey called out into the silent apartment and waited several seconds. No response.

"I'm coming in," he called, and carefully stepped inside, avoiding the broken glass and debris scattered all around.

The living area was framed on two sides by wide doors and the third side by a large set of blown-out windows overlooking the street outside. Across the street another residential block filled the view, identical in design to this one. A cold breeze blew in through the now glassless window frames.

The doors on the left side had tumbled outwards into the living room, Grey saw, lying split amidst the broken shards of family life. The doors on the right side remained standing, though tilted on bent hinges into whatever room lay beyond. It was the left room that drew his attention first, however. Or at least the bloodied feet within, visible where they jutted from the detritus of a collapsed-in ceiling.

Grey hurried over to the fallen form, though he knew it was too late. No one laying that still, under that much weight, was alive. Still, he did his best to drag the broken rebar and concrete lumps from off the woman as quickly as possible.

There were two of them, in the end. The fallen woman, and a man lying crumpled in the corner, hidden from sight of the living room. Both of them had been killed by a single, massive blunt force trauma, smears of blood under both their noses from the pressure exerted upon them, limbs at strange and unnatural angles where they had been thrown.

Grey checked for breathing or a pulse, knowing it was pointless but doing it anyway, then stood and turned back to look into the living room.

Whatever had happened, it had been centred *here*. This room. The bedroom, he could tell, the remains of a wide bed smashed against one wall. A wave of pressure expanding in all directions from a single point, a sphere of destruction spreading outwards and smashing everything it touched.

A classic compression-release technique, then, forcing the air in a given space down into a single, nanoscopic point before releasing it in an instant, sending a powerful shockwave through anything and everything nearby. But why here? His background search hadn't turned up anything out of the ordinary about the family living here.

Family.

His information request, made and fulfilled on the way here, had said they had a teenage girl.

Grey felt a sudden chill of understanding.

"Hey - the daughter, right?" he called out towards the doors on the other side of the living room, closed and still standing. "You're in there, aren't you?"

There was the sound of someone beyond. Someone crying.

Ah, crap.

In an instant, Grey knew what had happened, and it wasn't a pleasant story.

Coming into the Aether was never easy. Even if you were prepared for it, if the psych-docs caught it young and you had all the familial support and understanding you could wish for, it was still a lonely and terrifying experience. The sudden ability to hear echoes of people's thoughts, to cause things to move and jerk without consciously wanting it, or just to send animals into panicked fits from the emanations you were barely aware of emitting, can really mess a child up. Those with the rarer talents, like Dreamwalkers, had it even harder, and Grey couldn't even begin to imagine how Erophists handled it. But if you were ready for it, you could be guided. He himself had been caught very young, among the first of those students whose potential was identified *before* it manifested.

The worst thing that could happen, though, was for someone to come into the Aether without warning, without understanding. Without someone to guide them.

Despite being lauded in message boards and media as the world-changing 'greatest discovery of the post-Fall era,' the majority of people still had little to no understanding of Aether. It was just too rare, the chance of encountering even a single user lower than winning extra rations on the citizen's Requisition lottery.

To some, it was the domain of the elite, an ivory-tower science that occasionally brought new efficiencies and new gadgets, but had little relevance to their day-to-day existence.

To many more, the Aether was just another tool of the Reclamation Authority, and the Far Agency an extension of this. Especially in recent years, Aether-trained agents represented yet another way for the Reclamation Authority to maintain order in an unruly society.

To others yet, it was simply magic.

And if a powerful Aether user was born into a family, a

community, which had no experience of it, things could go very wrong, very quickly.

He found the girl sitting on her bed, arms wrapped around legs pulled up to her chest, rocking gently back and forth. Tears fell from her unfocused eyes as she gazed forward into space, staring at something only she could see. Soft sobs continued unabated as he stepped into the room.

"It's not your fault, ok?" Grey said, almost whispering, as he stepped carefully into the room. Games and gadgets, clothes, and the brightly-coloured trappings of a teenager's existence lay everywhere. "It's not your fault. You couldn't have known. You couldn't…"

A sudden lump in his own throat made him stumble over his words.

"This wasn't you, ok? It just… just happened. The rage has a way of getting to you, taking you over if you're unprepared. But, if you'll let me, we can teach you to make sure it never happens again."

The girl didn't seem to hear him at first, continuing to stare into the middle distance. Slowly, though, she became still and turned wide, tear-streaked eyes towards him.

She couldn't have been more than thirteen or fourteen, with dusty brown hair and a small build. She looked lost, as if she had no idea where she was, or why this strange man was here.

"My name is Grey, okay? Nestor Makhno Grey. I know, I know, unusual name. My family has Ukrainian in it somewhere, came over from Europe in the Great Migration, after the Fall. Same story for most of us, right…?" Grey knew he was rambling, but he was desperate to say anything that might distract the girl.

Confusion appeared on her face, though still layered under shock and fear.

"My parents," she said, almost whispering. "I… They…"

The girl held her shaking hands in front of her, eyes widening in horror as she remembered.

"I killed them!" she squealed. "I…I…I… I did this. I was so angry, and then everything just…"

She trailed off, uncomprehending.

Grey almost reached out and put his hand on her shoulder. Almost, but not quite. He would never be at ease around children; bad memories he'd long buried, and a way of life that meant they just didn't figure into his world.

Instead, he stood awkwardly slightly to the side, torn by a desire to make things better without having any idea how. All he had were weak, feeble words.

"What's your name, hey? Can you tell me that?"

He almost couldn't hear her response.

"Blane," she breathed.

"Ok, Blane, well look. I'm going to stay with you for a while, ok? Until the auth... until help arrives. Is that ok with you?"

Grey gently lowered himself until he was sitting at the foot of the bed, still separated from the girl but at what he hoped was a comforting distance.

In the silence that followed he *Read* the girl, but found nothing helpful. Her mind was racing in ten different directions at once, a cacophony of fear, regret, pain, and horror, questioning what had happened, and what was going to happen.

He could also hear, in one corner of her mind, a simple repetitive thought.

Please come back, please come back, please come back...

But Grey knew there was no way her parents were coming back. He also knew the girl knew this too. That wouldn't stop the mind from begging, though.

"Listen, Blane," he said. "Do you have any family I can contact? Anyone you want to be here?"

She didn't respond, but the thought-image *grandparents* flashed across her mind.

"You got grandparents?" he asked.

He didn't think asking this would be suspicious, not to a child. Hell, some families *did* still stay in contact with each other over multiple generations, old-fashioned as it might seem.

"'n," she nodded in affirmation.

"Can I get in touch with them for you? Do you have their contact?"

Shaking, the girl reached into the pockets of her pants, pulling out a thin-screen. The display lit up as she held it out.

A sudden voice from the living room made them both look up. Grey saw two men standing there, both in matching dark uniforms of steel-grey shirts and pants under black jackets. Thin lines glowed faintly under the lining of their suits, monitoring and recording the wearer's vitals and their surroundings at all times.

Far agents.

Grey knew it was going to go wrong from the moment they opened their mouths. The agents were too cocky, too sure of themselves. One was tall and hard-faced, the other short but stocky. Both looked young to him; they probably hadn't been on the job for more than a couple of years. This could even be their first incident without a mentor supervising them.

So, inexperienced, with something to prove. Worse, they moved into the room like they were entering a stim-den, not the room of a child.

Grey was up and blocking their path before they got to Blane, but not before one had started demanding the girl stand up.

"It's ok, agents. She's ok. In shock, but…"

"And you are?"

The agent looked Grey up and down. It was hopefully obvious that Grey wasn't involved in this, even to green agents, but the agent was clearly wary of him regardless.

"Commercial Inquiry Agent. Here in my role as insurance analyst on behalf of my clients. Look, the kid needs a little space, ok? She …"

The agent held up a hand, cutting him off. "A snoop? What, you didn't have what it takes to make the force?" he said, derision in his voice.

Some Far agents considered private investigators below even the regular police force, Grey remembered.

He felt the tall one try to Read him and saw his expression change when he couldn't. Grey kept his own face steady, as if he hadn't noticed anything. All the agent would be getting was disjointed flashes of unrelated words and images, and a fair amount of pink elephant.

'Do not think of a pink elephant.' A fairly standard trick for agents who'd been career for a while, but one these guys probably hadn't even begun to learn.

The tall one said nothing about the block, though. No doubt the same male pride Feye had noted. Afraid to look weak, so keeping information from even his partner. *That* was a habit a few more

Aether incidents would burn out of him.

"Listen, the girl's attuned now. She's stable, at least while everyone *keeps calm...*" Grey hissed the final part through gritted teeth.

He tried to keep himself between the girl and the agents, hiding the sight of them for fear of scaring the girl.

Short and stocky, though, had other ideas. He suddenly pushed past his partner and Grey, careless of where he was walking as fallen pictures and toys crunched underfoot, and strode up to the girl.

"Right, stand up. You're coming with us," he said, reaching out to grab her.

Grey was ready for the blast, though only just. The agents weren't, though the speed at which both raised a pressure shield as the shockwave boomed outwards moved them up in his estimation. Their reactions were well-developed for handling violent Aether users, at least.

Though that was the crux of the problem. These two only knew how to handle violent users, not those who just had no control.

Grey was first to his feet, his shielded roll almost a single movement that took him from standing to floor to standing again.

"What the hell are you doing?" he spat, glaring at the two agents dusting themselves off. Both had been thrown back into the living room.

He turned to where the girl had been sitting. Where she had been there was now only the wreckage of the bed, newly added to the debris already scattered everywhere. A massive hole in the wall behind led into the apartment next door, where she must have bolted.

Damn it...

Grey dove through the hole and raced after the girl. He tore through rooms the same layout as the apartment he had just left and was just in time to see the door at the entrance slam closed. Smashing into it himself, he forced it back open and looked both ways down the walkway outside.

No sign of the girl. Just the broken glass, the broken door, and the sound of running feet somewhere in the distance.

"That kid is *fast*."

The two Far agents came jogging up behind him, the short one's words sending a spike of anger through Grey.

"What the hell were you thinking?" he snarled.

Short and stocky held up his hands.

"Alright, alright. But you didn't say she could do *that*," he said.

Grey growled, a low throaty sound of annoyance.

"The state of the apartment should have told you what she could do," he snapped.

"Yeah, well, now we've gotta find her. Can't have a wild user running around the streets, let alone a goddam kid." This was the tall one.

"She's a dangerous one, alright," concurred short and stocky.

Grey span on them.

"She is *not* a dangerous one. She's a scared and confused *kid*. And you better remember it."

The tall one met his stare.

"Yeah, scared and confused enough to murder her own parents…"

The words had barely got out of his mouth before it was shut for him by Grey's fists.

"So you assaulted one of my men because, what, you were concerned for a girl who wasn't even there?"

Back in the present, Ritra Feye poured herself another drink, topping up Grey's without needing to be asked.

"I *reminded* him to watch his mouth around emotional, unstable Aether users who might be listening in from wherever they had run off to," replied Grey, leaning back. "I guess I could have reminded him a little too forcefully, though."

"And you didn't find her, I assume?"

"Nope. And neither did your agents, judging by your questions."

Feye nodded.

"Nothing. We've already sent people out to her socials and relatives, online and off. I don't *specifically* remember anything about grandparents - I'll check that out later. We'll find her."

Feye paused, turning her head to the doorway that Grey had entered by.

"Either way, I still don't see how this story ends up with you rescuing a *different* kid," she said.

"I spent the day searching the area, asking around, you know. Figured I could find a runaway. And I did, in a way. Just a *different* runaway."

"And he's here because…?"

"Because I want to make sure this one gets home safe. I don't need any Far agents chasing another one on to the streets."

"Far agents? This kid's an Aether user as well?"

Grey cursed himself for his slip.

"Uh... no. You know what I mean. Far agents, bio-feds, street cops; authorities. Too many of them too willing to use their power at the drop of a hat. I just want the kid to have a chance to calm down, figure things out before I pass him over."

Grey needed to change the subject. To buy time, he drew out his cigarettes.

"You really still smoke those?" asked Feye, raising an eyebrow.

Grey had almost forgotten – she *hated* these things. Most people did, these days, though he was sure the fashion for them would swing back around soon enough.

Pushing down on the switch to the side, Grey gave her a grin and waited for the inner element to heat up enough to make the thing smokeable.

"Those things will still kill you, you know. Doesn't matter what they say about e-filters or cell-therapy – they'll get you."

He gave a curt nod, remembering the countless times he'd heard the same speech.

Still, it seemed to have successfully steered the conversation away from the boy in the next room. They moved on to other topics - old colleagues, new ones, old frustrations, new ones - and it wasn't long before Feye stood up.

"Well, don't be a stranger, ok?" she said, swinging her dark jacket on. She stood almost a head taller than Grey, and most others, and used it to her advantage when establishing a pecking order in which she was very much at the top.

Grey gave her a tired nod. "You too. You ever need any outside help, you know where to find me."

"Yes," Ritra replied, giving him a suddenly sober look. "I do."

She left quickly, out the door and on to whatever business she had next without waiting for Grey to react.

What was that? Grey thought. Something in the way she had fixed him with her stare in that last moment, like she knew something he didn't want her to know.

Did she know he was lying? Well, not lying, but being less-than-truthful. And if she did, why didn't she say so?

Grey drew the small thin-screen from his pocket. He had… acquired… it from the tall Far agent during their altercation. Standard issue to all Far Agency staff, and shockingly not bio-locked to its user, only pass-coded.

Disappointing, is what it was. Grey couldn't remember a time he was so naïve that he could lose track of his official thin-screen. He certainly would *never* have kept its loss quiet from his superiors.

Pass-codes were easy to override for anyone with the skills of, say, a former high-level Far agent. And once you had access to an agency thin-screen, you had access to the agency report-stream.

In fact, Grey probably had more access than the agent he *borrowed* it from. Someone somewhere had forgotten to erase his clearance upon his departure from the agency - easy enough to understand, perhaps, when so few with his kind of clearance chose to quit - and he was able to access a few of the higher-level reports not ordinarily accessible to agents on the street.

So *of course* Grey had used the thin-screen to search for any news regarding runaway youths. And *of course* he'd moved quickly when he came across a report of a possible teen Aether user in the warehouse district.

He probably should have checked the details of the report a bit closer, though. It had been marked with an unusually high-security grade, after all.

Still, just because it hadn't been the kid he was looking for didn't mean it was something he was going to regret. He hoped.

4

"Secrecy is the first essential in the affairs of the Agency."

Agency Handbook, Section 2.2 (Public Relations)

There is a river that runs beneath us, its currents flowing deep and strong. Most people walk far above it, never knowing what runs below their feet. Some dip their toes in it, and feel the hint of something greater without ever understanding what. Some even wade through it, and shape the world with its power. But a very few swim in it, submerged in its essence until they themselves are something more than human.

At least, that was how they told it at the Academy. There was far more to it than that, and there were classes upon classes over the years trying to explain the Aether with a scientific rigour that left most students sweating or slumped over their desks, but Grey had always liked the poetic way it had been explained to him and his peers on their introductory course.

And it *could* feel like you were bathing in the Aether. When you performed that strange mental reaching so difficult to describe to those who couldn't, and felt it flow around something inside you that until that moment you hadn't known existed, the Aether could feel like a fast-moving river. And, occasionally, a bottomless ocean.

The first Aether users had appeared in the decades following the Sudden War, during the Fall that proceeded it. Some theories suggested it had been caused by the genetic mixing brought on by the Great Migration that accompanied these events, the mass of humanity shifted and shuffled across the face of a scorched globe as if an angry, losing god had thrown their game pieces across the board. No genetic markers had been found to suggest any sudden change in the general population, however, and the human genome was such an open book to modern science that these theories were falling out of favour.

No other theory, though, stood strong enough on its own to offer an alternative.

Whyever the first users appeared, it wasn't long before the newly reformed governments, kingdoms, theocracies and federations of now greatly-reduced populations realised this was something new.

Even in a world where bio-terrorism and phage-manipulation threatened to finish off the work the Sudden War had begun, the abrupt appearance of testable, verifiable, and reproducible psychic powers demanded to be addressed.

So the Far Agency had been set up.

Modelled after Pan-Fed, the first multinational and supranational body of the new era, the Far Agency carried legal and executive authority within all habitable zones of the Reclamation, and technically the Waste too. Where Pan-Fed was designed to detect and counter the dangers of gene editing technology and germline engineering techniques now easily accessible to any wannabe-creator of the next great pandemic, the Far Agency was designed to detect and counter the dangers of people who could affect and alter matter and energy without, it seemed, any regards for known physical laws - classical or quantum.

The key difference, of course, was that the cat was already out of the bag for Pan-Fed. All they could do was keep ready, watch, and react. The Far Agency still had a chance at keeping the lid on their particular harbinger of the second Apocalypse.

Grey had joined the Agency young, 'talent spotted' by Far Academy scouts while still in a state residential home. He had graduated barely out of his teens and spent almost all of the first three decades of his adult life in the organisation. During that time, his world expanded as the purview of the agency expanded, from dealing only with specifically Aether-related incidents to dealing with incidents that only Aether-trained agents could handle.

It was when the Agency became involved with street-level law enforcement that he knew he had to get out. He even came close to blows with other agents more eager to put their abilities to use than he thought appropriate. Several times he was brought in front of his superiors for conflicts with his peers, though nothing ever stuck.

Somehow, though, he thought he'd always known that it wasn't the place for him. Despite his aptitude for the trade, his quick grasp of what was possible for him and, more importantly, what was possible for other Aether users he encountered, he'd never quite *felt* the way an agent was supposed to feel. Certainly not the way agents such as Ritra Feye seemed to.

He had always marvelled at Feye's drive, but perhaps more so her commitment. She seemed to understand what the Reclamation *was* to a depth he never could. In his early years at the Academy he'd witnessed her engage in fierce debates with their teachers about the technicalities of RA protocol, and win - even when she was pointing out inconsistencies or contradictions in the system, something that would get any other student summarily punished.

When Feye pointed out these flaws, however, it was always extremely apparent that she was proposing methods for fixing them, for resolving the contradictions and thereby strengthening the Reclamation Authority. By the time she entered the Far Agency there were few who could match her knowledge and fervour.

Grey, on the other hand, often thought he was there because he had nowhere else to go.

The Agency was, at the end of it, a hard place. It was run almost like an old-world special forces group, militaristic and harsh. The abilities of self-reflection and empathy were considered, if not weaknesses, hardly strengths. So while Grey had an - if he did say so himself - *incredible* record of success when it came to bringing in wild Aether users without incident, he was never invited in on the decision-making processes.

He was, he told himself, a maverick.

And so one day, after a superior implied that perhaps Grey could Read a witness - just to, you know, confirm their statement - he quit. The writing had been on the wall for a while, but this carved it in with a chisel.

If there had been anyone to report this to in the Agency he would have, but he'd practically alienated himself from those around him by this point. Feye was the only person he even considered talking to, but she was going career and he wasn't going to be the one to jeopardise that.

Anyway, setting up his own commercial inquiry agency had felt like returning to his roots. He even enjoyed the fact that he could call it 'his own CIA,' a reference to a pre-Fall covert organisation based on this continent that few even remembered now.

He'd always had a certain fascination for the world before the Fall. It seemed like such a... *contradictory* place. They'd had it all, everything they could need, and they'd thrown it all away in a sudden fit of radioactive fury.

All that land, all that ocean, all that life and world and promise. Yet they'd still failed to make it work. They'd still made war and death and famine. In a time of plenty, they'd made the Waste. It was enough to make you cry, if it wasn't so laughable.

5

Occulta Lex

Unofficial Agency motto

With Ritra Feye gone, the room filled with an uncomfortable silence. Grey tapped at the 'borrowed' agency thin-screen as if willing it to ping something to take his mind off what he had to do next. There was nothing of interest in the report-stream, though. The streets were quiet. A few arrests of possible seditionists, a couple of fraudulent Requisition claims and one potential bio terror threat; no reports of any runaways.

No reports of anything happening in the warehouse district either, he saw, which was unsettling. If someone was able to keep the immolation of twelve heavily-armed and armoured people from being discovered by the agency, they were either extremely lucky or extremely powerful.

Grey tapped the portable thin-screen against his palm. He was putting off going back into the living room, and he knew it. He took a deep breath, slid the thin-screen into a pocket, and forced himself to stand and walk in.

The boy was perched on the couch, legs curled up beneath him in the same manner as Grey had found Blane in the distant morning. This time, however, there were no tears. The boy was staring avidly at the wall-screen Grey had given him, balanced on his legs, a screen designed for residential use and much larger than the agency thin-screen now in Grey's pocket, though essentially the same technology.

"You hungry, kid?" said Grey, stopping in the doorway.

The boy looked distractedly up at Grey for a second, shook his head, and returned to watching the screen.

No, burn that, thought Grey. He shouldn't have to ask - the kid must be starving. It was almost midnight, and the boy probably hadn't eaten all day.

Grey turned around, returning a few minutes later with two ready meals steaming on a tray. *This* got the boy's attention. The screen slipped from his lap and to the floor as the kid raised his nose, breathing in the smell like a dog.

Grey chuckled, feeling some of the knot inside himself loosen. "I knew you'd be hungry."

He passed the tray to the boy, who took it and held it in front of him as if unsure what to do with it.

"Go on, eat," said Grey, gesturing to the fork fixed to the side of the package. "Just break it off. Whole pack's biodegradable. Never had a ready-pack meal before?"

Grey wasn't too surprised. He wouldn't have expected so, anyway. Ready-packs were very much the meal of those expecting to eat only by themselves. Quick, cheap, and no-fuss no-frills.

"What is it?" asked the boy, tearing off the fork and poking at the food. His voice was surprisingly deep.

"Uh... fish," replied Grey. "Actually, I'm not sure what kind. Pack just says fish-meal."

The boy continued to poke at the slab of unidentified marine life atop a small mound of steaming rice.

"Is it good?" he asked.

"Is it...? What, fish? You've had fish before, right?" said Grey, grabbing the only other chair in the room and swinging it down opposite the couch to sit facing the boy.

The boy shook his head.

"I don't know."

Grey paused halfway through breaking off his own fork, looking up in question. The boy continued poking at the fish curiously, before using his fork to break off a piece and popping it into his mouth.

"You don't know?"

The boy said nothing, chewing the fish for far longer than was necessary before finally swallowing.

"Maybe? It tastes familiar. I think. They never told me what it was I was eating."

The boy picked up the rest of the fish with one stab of the fork and shoved the whole thing into his mouth. His voice was thoughtful, and mature in a way that made Grey up his estimate of the boy's age.

Grey waited to see if the boy was going to say anything else, but apparently not. As soon as the fish was gone, he started on the rice.

"Ok, kid, let's start from the beginning, shall we? I'm Grey. Nestor Grey. I know, I know, unusual name. Great Migration and all that. So, who are you?"

The boy seemed to think for a moment.

"Um... The doctor only ever called me 'subject,' but I don't think that's a name. A caretaker called me Fen, a few times. She was nice." He stared into the middle distance. "I think she got found out, though. She stopped coming one day. They're not meant to talk to me, and I'm not allowed to ask where they go."

Grey sat frozen with the fork halfway to his mouth. The boy... Fen? ... had spoken all of this in an empty monotone, all the while forking rice into his mouth at an unbroken, steady pace as if aiming to finish the food in as efficient a way as possible.

What was Grey supposed to do with that?

"Ok, uh... Fen. Maybe that wasn't the beginning to start from. Where exactly are you from?"

The group of rooms in which he had lived for as long as he could remember were a uniform collection of pale, cream-coloured walls and sparse, utilitarian furnishings. A bedroom with a small bed and a desk, a shower washroom, and a separate living space containing only two things: a tablescreen slightly larger than the bedroom desk, and a non-flex thin-screen fixed to the wall.

The door to the outside was kept locked at all times, except when guards came to take him for exercise sessions or other... excursions, or when whitecoats came to ask their questions.

Food was brought to him three times a day, always a thick, reduced paste that it was impossible to identify as being vegetable, fish, or meat-based. It took Fen a long time to realise that the consistency and flavour of the paste would change depending on the condition of his own body. If he appeared to be gaining or losing weight, or muscle mass, or some other criteria set by unknown figures for unknown reasons, his diet would change.

It took him a lot longer to realise that this was strange. Learning hours, which took up most of his day, did not include information on the outside world until he was old enough to notice his body beginning to go through puberty. He couldn't say when with more accuracy. That was really the only measure of time he had.

He was allowed to exercise when he liked but was required to do so at least once a day. A small open area was made available to him, a square of brown, dusty dirt located in what he thought was the centre of the complex, surrounded by tall walls and overlooked by two high towers upon which stood, at all hours of the day or night, at least two figures clad in thick body armour holding powerful-looking rifles.

"Like those people who attacked us back at the warehouse?" Grey asked. The boy nodded an affirmative.

Life was a dull routine of exercise or mandated learning hours in front of the thin-screen, except for when the whitecoats came, or he was taken to the tests.

He knew only three types of people: the caretakers, the whitecoats, and the armed and armoured guards who inevitably accompanied them both. The caretakers would come to his rooms to clean and sanitize, always with an armed guard watching, observing silently from the entrance. The caretakers rarely interacted with him, and those that did he rarely saw again.

The whitecoats, on the other hand, were full of questions. Questions and instructions.

Stand here. Focus on this. Close your eyes. What do you see? What can you *feel?*

They were of all genders, all ethnicities, some speaking centra-English, some one of the other dialects, some wholly different languages. He knew a few of the whitecoats by name and was taught to speak with all of them. He couldn't say which of the several languages he grew up speaking was his 'mother tongue,' and over the years - though time meant little in this place - he learnt others.

Other times they would come to him without words, forcing something over his head that rendered the world a dark and muffled place. It could be minutes, hours, even days before his senses returned, and he would find himself somewhere new.

These were the tests. He never knew what to expect during these times. Only that it would be *bad*.

He'd found himself naked and defenceless in overgrown forests where things moved in the undergrowth or growled in the distance. He'd been left cold and alone in deep snow drifts in some mountainous crag, or caged in rooms slowly filling with water, or noxious gas. Sometimes he'd wake still in his room but hunted by some wild creature that stalked through the hallways beyond.

Doctor Caldwell had explained it once - he only ever explained things once. He had been very clear. Fen had only himself to rely on during these 'survival tests'. He *would* be allowed to die - there would be no sudden rescue upon failure, no hand from the heavens to grab hold of. Caldwell said that would defeat the purpose of the experiment.

So Fen had learnt to survive. And to wait.

And then, one day - today - they'd made a mistake.

Fen had spotted the first hints of what he'd been waiting for a few weeks ago. A new caretaker, with a new escort, less careful than previous pairs. The caretaker was a woman, pale, with white-blonde hair the colour of which stayed somehow in Fen's mind, and the guard a dark-skinned man, tall and square-jawed, though most of his face was obscured by the dark visor of the helmets all the guards wore.

It was extremely unusual for a guard to actually enter Fen's accommodation rather than take up a post by the entrance, and even more unusual for such a pair to behave the way these two did. In fact, Fen thought, when he returned from the exercise yard to find them there the first time, he could swear the guard almost spoke, and the woman almost *reached out* to him.

The three of them had paused, Fen in the doorway, the two frozen in his living quarters looking at him in a way he didn't understand.

A low grunt from the guard, and the caretaker went back to sanitizing. Fen stood there a second, then went on as he always did at times like this, acting as if no one was there. He voiced on the thinscreen and went to shower and change, assuming they would finish their business and leave without a word, as usual.

These two stayed longer than normal, though. A standard UV clean and spray should last only a handful of minutes, but the two were still there by the time he stepped out of the shower unit and sat himself down at the tablescreen.

He could *feel* their eyes on the back of his neck as he stared down at whatever he'd been given access to today. Papers on Europe, it seemed, and discussion on the possibility of further reclamation of habitable zones. Addendums detailing realigned predator-prey relationships in the battered ecosystem, lists of potentially pan-level pathogens detected by remote surveys. A few of the predators in the images Fen thought he recognized from some of his live-or-die excursions.

Even if he had been interested in the material, though, he couldn't concentrate. The two were hardly bothering to hide their attention from him now, the room silent except for the sounds from his screen.

He turned in his chair, to find them standing next to each other by the door. He fixed his gaze on the guard.

"Is there something you want?" he said flatly.

Again, the woman made as if to step towards him, and again the man gave a warning grunt. Pausing, the woman gave herself a shake, and the two of them abruptly turned around and left.

They were back the next day, however, and every scheduled sanitizing shift after that. Though not once did they behave as they had on the first day, Fen was still aware of their eyes on him whenever they were there.

They moved differently to previous caretaker/escort pairs, less impassive, more given to fleeting glances and displays of the personality underneath. Sometimes he thought he even heard them whispering to each other, brief snatches of sentences cut off almost before they formed. They were even less careful than the one who had called him 'Fen,' long ago.

They were a question.

Tonight.

He saw it at the top of both their minds: the guard's and the caretaker's.

Tonight.

The thought-image was so clear when he Read them that Fen could almost believe they *wanted* him to Read it.

The general staff at the facility were almost invariably impossible to Read, and the whitecoats who could be Read responded with harsh punishments whenever he attempted to do so without permission. Only the strangeness of the pair had made him even try it on them, without any expectation of success.

And there it was, the same thought-image on the surface of both their minds.

They were an opportunity.

They'd come for him so early in the morning it was probably still last night. He'd been feigning sleep, wall-speakers whispering a steady stream of facts, moral statements and ethic-work in multiple languages just as they did every night, a background night-time noise he'd known all his life and could tune out without thinking.

The 'sensory dampener' pulled tight over his head before he had time to react. Well, that's what Doctor Caldwell called it. For all Fen could tell, it was just a bag of thick, dark fabric. Only the strange numbing sensation it sent down his entire body told him it was something more.

That, and his inability to reach the Aether. It was as if a soft, elastic net had been laid between him and it. He could stretch out towards where it flowed, feel it even, but something resistant and rubbery prevented him from drawing on it.

Through the numbness he felt himself being lifted. His vision was completely blank, and only muffled sounds came to his ears. His sense of smell was completely gone. Again, nothing out of the ordinary.

What *was* different was that he seemed to be being carried on someone's shoulders, rather than strapped to a gurney as was most common. Still, he was ready for slight variations. It changed nothing.

He felt himself, through that peculiar sensation of movement but not touch the sensory dampener allowed, carried for some time – definitely enough time to be outside the complex in which he was *imprisoned*.

Imprisoned. He focused on the word in his thoughts, repeating it over and over. Readying himself for what he was going to do.

He was a prisoner, and he would be free.

They were in a vehicle, some kind of large van from the feeling of space around him, rattling gently as it moved. He could hear the whir of the motor and soft hissing of tires on tarmac as he pushed the sharp blade from the back of his mouth. The taste of blood filled his mouth where it had cut him, once more nicking him as it had several times in the night as he lay, waiting for them to come.

Somewhere towards the front of the vehicle he heard soft voices, almost inaudible. He didn't know what they were saying, but they didn't sound like they were facing his way.

He used his tongue to move the razor blade into position, biting down on the flat so that the sharpened edge pointed outwards from between his lips. He began slowly moving his head to the side, then back, rubbing the blade on the material taut against his face.

The sharp pain of the cuts to his mouth and lips had another side-effect, one Fen thought the doctors back at the site didn't know about. Pain brought the Aether nearer, even when hooded. He had discovered this the times when they had hooded him, injured or hypothermic, following whatever their latest test was. The sensory dampener always felt less effective when he was hurting, something he had been very careful to hide from his observers.

His sense of the Aether changed as the blade cut into both the hood and his mouth, as if the energy were somehow drawing closer, the net preventing him from reaching it becoming more porous. He could feel a trickle of its charge flow into him.

Guiding the current of this thin stream, he used it to *Push* the fabric of the hood against the blade as he moved his head. *Now* he felt it begin to tear, a hole appearing in the fabric and a dull light seeping in. Feeling returned to his body.

Reading. Pushing. Flare, Thoughtscreen, and Slowtime. He'd learned them all, developed them all under careful teaching and observation.

They'd prodded and poked him all his life, testing the limits of what he could do. They thought they had the measure of him.

They thought they knew what he could do.

That was their mistake.

In the end, it was only two lives he had to take. The guard and the woman, oddly enough. They'd had no one else with them. Still, Fen didn't know how many people were usually assigned to take him on these outings. Ordinarily, he would only regain his senses once he was very firmly where they wanted him to be, isolated and alone.

He *Pushed* the fabric from his head as soon as he felt the Aether in full flow beneath his thoughts. The sensory dampener blew apart in all directions, thin filaments rippling and glittering between the flying fabric. He expanded the Push to his limits, a bubble of force expanding outward. A moment later he was diving out the side of the vehicle, the metal frame in front of him bending and tearing open, exposing the rushing ground beyond.

Fen bounced and rolled just millimetres above the concrete, Thoughtscreen catching his weight where he projected it beneath himself, rolling over and over until his momentum died. He heard the squeal of tires behind him as the vehicle came to a sudden, automated emergency stop.

The man and woman had been thrown from the vehicle by his Push, slammed out the opposite side of his own dive to freedom. Somehow the man had managed to catch the woman even in the abruptness of Fen's Push, and she lay atop him where they sprawled.

The woman was already recovering by the time Fen got to his feet, but she seemed concerned for her companion, glancing in panic from the fallen man to Fen and back again.

Fen ran. He even thought he'd escaped, for a time.

He didn't know how they caught up to him. He had told himself there was no way the man, at least, would recover in time to follow his trail, but somehow they found him and kept on him as he raced through the giant, empty buildings all around. Fen didn't know where he was, all he knew was he had to get away.

If they had just given up...

But they didn't. Their relentless footsteps stayed always somewhere behind him, sometimes closer, sometimes further away, but always in time returning. Wherever he ran, wherever he hid, they followed. Sometimes they called out, to each other, to him perhaps — but he didn't have a name to call.

It felt like hours before he finally stopped running. He would have to face them. He had prepared himself for this anyway, though he had never thought it would be this curious, enigmatic pair he would have to deal with. He'd imagined the men in the tower, the ones who always seemed ready to point a rifle at him or poke him with a barrel when he was slow to do what he was told. Since escaping the car he had even begun to believe that, maybe, he wouldn't need to use it.

The whitecoats didn't know what he'd found, didn't know what he sensed, curled up like a beast in a cage. Didn't know that he held the key.

He could feel it, like a frozen sun, a power in the Aether waiting to be unleashed.

He hadn't even known its name until Grey named it for him.

They'd come for him, and he'd let them see.

Mindfire.

6

The history of humanity is a song. Each nation, each creed, each people follows the same beat, yet hears a different melody. The triumphant crescendo of one is a descending arpeggio of sadness for another. We must be the conductor.

Agency Principles and Practice: Foreword

Grey's food was cold by the time Fen finished his story, cold and untouched.

"That's, uh, that's quite a lot, kid," he said in what, he was sure, was the understatement of the new century.

Fen said nothing, staring at him as if waiting for Grey to add something more. Oddly, this made Grey feel so awkward he was compelled to do so.

"Ok, so, uh… why the dragon?"

This seemed to surprise the boy. Fen leaned back, swinging his feet up and onto the couch and reaching for the wall-screen where he'd placed it down beside him.

The movement drew Grey's attention to the fact that both of them were still in the same outfits they'd been wearing all day. Though the climate control had mostly dried them both out, Grey was hardly comfortable and Fen must be less so. Now he knew to look for it, he could see the bloody marks around the boy's collar, stains he had assumed were mud and soil that the rain had failed to completely wash away.

He reached into his pocket for his personal thin-screen, reaching past the borrowed agency one. It unrolled in his hand, and he quickly put in an order with Requisitions for a few sets of generic but functional clothing for the kid, guessing his size. It would use up a significant portion of his monthly allocation, but he rarely used this all up anyway. The clothes would be here by morning, providing conditions were clear enough for the c-drones.

Once he had completed his order, he looked up from his thin-screen to see Fen holding out the larger display towards him. On the screen was an image of fangs and talons, a growling red lizard-like beast with huge leathery wings hovering over a burning town, flame curling from its mouth as it stared at a point just beyond the reader's shoulder.

It was clearly from a comic. Some kind of pre-Fall, print-based edition, rendered into digital format. It was also, clearly, the same dragon Fen had formed to burn and rend the attackers back in the warehouse. Only redder.

"They let me read them when I was good. Comics, I mean. This just seemed like… the right shape."

Grey stared from the image to Fen and back again as the boy spoke. He wanted to say *but Mindfire doesn't work like that*.

But he held his tongue. Clearly Mindfire *did* work like that. At least for this kid. Just because it flew in the face of everything he'd been taught at the academy, just because it correlated with *nothing* he'd experienced in all his years as an agent…

"They were having an affair, right?'"

Fen's words broke Grey out of his reverie. He blinked twice, train of thought not so much derailed as dynamited off the bridge.

"…n?" he said, mind racing to work out what Fen could possibly be talking about.

"Those two," said Fen, waving his hands as if gesturing towards whoever he was talking about. "The caretaker and guard. The ones who were taking me to my next survival test. The one's I…"

Fen stumbled over his words for a second, hesitating. Then, he looked down, cleared his throat, and looked up again at Grey with renewed firmness.

"The ones I killed first," he finished.

Actually, that explanation was what Grey had been leaning towards as well. Nothing else made sense, though as everything he knew about them came from the boy's account there was surely plenty of detail missing.

"Who knows? But that would explain a few things, like how you could *read* them. People without a strong inner monologue have to stay focused to prevent being Read, and trying to hide an office romance in a top-secret laboratory under constant surveillance could understandably lead to losing some of that focus, I guess."

Fen nodded, clearly gratified that Grey shared his conclusion, at least in part.

"So, do you have any idea why they were holding you? Or who?" asked Grey.

Fen shook his head.

"No idea. I didn't even know I was *being* held for more than half of my life. I only found out about the world outside when my 'education could proceed no further without the necessary knowledge to progress the study.'"

The last Fen said in a deep, exaggerated accent.

"This 'Doctor Caldwell' you mentioned?" asked Grey.

"Yes. He was the only constant in my life. Visited me at least once a week, usually. I think he was in charge of whatever they were doing to me. But not *in charge* in charge. I definitely saw him getting shouted at by men in suits from time to time. Usually when I'd been 'obstructing the progress of the research,' as he called it."

"Do you know what they were studying? Did they ever say what their goal was?"

Fen looked at Grey without speaking for a long moment.

"Well, I mean, they were researching… me. I think they want to know, when someone pushes me, how hard I can push back."

Fen stared down at his hands, fingers knotting with each other as some thought made him clench them together.

"Doctor Caldwell told me once," he continued. "He said they taught me about the world outside so I would know what they were doing to me wasn't normal. So that I would resent them. So I would get *angry*."

Grey talked with the boy for a while after that, until the boy began to yawn. It was only then he realized how tired he was, and how exhausted Fen must be.

Grey had a room off the side of the living room he kept specifically for those times when he had a client in difficulty. It was small but functional, with its own en suite. He set Fen up in there and left him quickly. The kid had gone from awake and alert to practically asleep in the space of a minute.

Grey went to his office and threw himself down at the desk, swinging his feet up and pouring himself a drink.

He sat that way, ashtray filling as his hip flask emptied, until the light from between the slats of the blinds told him the sun had risen.

Then he went to work.

"Mr. Nestor Grey?"

"That's right. And you are Mr. Majid Ayad?"

"That I am. And I am told you can help me, *in sha'Allah*."

This was the first time Grey had had a client from the Crystal Caliphate. Though international travel was not impossible, it was much rarer than in earlier eras. The threat presented by pandemics both natural and artificial meant major restrictions on intercontinental travel, and major expense.

Majid Ayad was a thin man with a short, well-kept beard that was running to grey. He must have once been tall, but age had begun to reclaim some of that height. He wore a plain grey suit that looked expertly tailored; clearly a man with resources.

"And what is it you hope I can help with, exactly?"

They were meeting in a cafe a few streets away from his office. It was a quiet place where he often met prospective clients, with sound-proofed booths designed for remote workers who were looking for a place where the only thing that would disturb them was the automated vendor rolling over with a constant supply of caffeinated drinks.

Outside the grey clouds promised more rain and inside the menu promised coffee; but Grey had tried the real thing once or twice, and while the bitterness of the drinks sold here was the same, little else about the taste or aroma was. Still, with coffee beans running to almost a month's salary for a kilo, it would do.

Not for Mr. Ayad it seemed, however. He took one gulp of his own brew and returned it to the table between them, wrinkling his nose in disgust.

"You know, we have reclaimed enough of my homeland that we rarely have to resort to this anymore. Reminds me of my childhood, though not a memory I look back on with any fondness."

Grey took a large gulp of his own, the drink burning as it passed down the back of his throat.

"Well, it's the best they can do here. But you didn't want to meet to discuss coffee, I think. So…?"

Majid looked around once as if making sure no one was listening in. The cafe was essentially empty at this time, the few other customers hidden in one or another of the booths further down.

"I have come to ask you for help finding someone. My son."

"Your son?"

"Yes. My son, Salim. He came with me on this trip, and now he has disappeared. I do not know how, or why. But I need you to find him."

Another lost kid. Grey stifled a sigh. He rarely had any business involving children, and suddenly he was dealing with three of them.

"How old is Salim, Mr. Ayad?"

"He will soon be 16."

"And do you believe he left of his volition, or...?" Grey didn't know how to finish that sentence in a good way, so left the question hanging.

"It seems like he left by choice. I mean, the rooms we were staying in are secure, and no one has been in or out without my knowledge. But I cannot imagine why he would leave. There is no reason for him to be going out into this city without me. He gave no sign of such a thing."

"No sign at all?"

"None. If anything, he seemed less interested in the place than I had hoped. He has been... tired, recently. I hoped this trip would raise his spirits."

"And you are staying where, exactly?"

"The Meridian."

"Hmm."

Grey nodded, pulling out his thin screen.

He'd heard of the Meridian, uptown and practically in the centre of what was becoming the diplomatic quarter. Apparently it was a nice place, the kind of place his wealthier clients liked. The big insurance execs stayed there when they were in the city, but Grey had never had call to visit them there. High security, and very private. The place was ringed with walls and guards, a holdover from when the city was a much less secure place. The only location in the city more secure was probably the Far Station itself, and the soon-to-be-completed Central Tower.

"And what do you do, Mr. Ayad?"

"You did not guess?" Ayad replied, glancing down at the cup in front of him. "I am an exporter. Of coffee."

That tracked. Export was still a fledgling industry in the post-Fall world, especially of luxury goods, and those who worked in it both made and needed money.

In the Reclamation and beyond, advances in automated machineage and Silicon Isle-donated Fabricators, along with the annulment of old-era copyright laws, allowed highly efficient factories to be set up anywhere they were needed, and led to the local manufacturing of much of the technology needed for regional populations, while avoiding the need for transportation across unclaimed and untamed Waste.

This was the manufacturing of non-organic consumables like vehicles and thin-screens, however, not things that needed to be grown. Hence why a citizen of the Reclamation could afford to have all the toys they needed flown in by drone only a few hours after they ordered them, but had to enjoy them between meals of processed, vit-enhanced meat-substitute. *Real* food needed to be brought in from the African continent, least hit of all by the Sudden War, and its price reflected this.

"And you came from the Caliphate on business, then?" Grey asked.

Majid nodded.

"Business, and politics. It has taken longer for this continent to recover than my own, but we feel that now the time is right for such a thing. Despite your ruler's, shall we say, *antipathy* towards organised religion, and even without the Miracle of Makkah, you have found a way to rebuild."

Grey knew the term. Despite suffering the same conflagration that most of the world had, when humanity had decided in its moment of madness to sear itself from the face of the earth, Makkah had somehow been spared the radioactive scars that rendered many other areas uninhabitable. The *Hajj* was able to continue even during the worst of the Fall.

This was the Miracle of Makkah, as followers of Islam discovered their holiest city remained open to them in stark contrast to the cities around it. Even the name of their new nation was a reminder of this contrast: The Crystal Caliphate gained its name from the glassed remains of the ancient pyramids of Cairo, turned slick and dark by the intense heat they had been subjected to in the Sudden War. *That* city was yet to be reclaimed.

Grey had heard there were other cities, scattered across the globe, that also exhibited this lack of radiation despite being completely destroyed. Yet no plausible explanation for any of these had been forthcoming, so perhaps it really was a miracle. He didn't think too much about these things - life was complicated enough already.

The son, Salim, had left his rooms two nights previously. His father's own rooms were adjacent, but separate – a 'present' from the parent to acknowledge a child on the verge of becoming a man. Door logs and security footage registered him leaving via the front entrance unescorted, a small pack slung over his back. Inside it, according to his father, must be the clothes and accoutrements of travel they had brought for their stay.

Also, cash.

For Grey, that made things more complicated in one way, yet simpler in another. The fact that Salim was avoiding using auto-pay meant he wouldn't be able to track him that way, but conversely cash was such a rare form of currency these days that he *would* hear about it if he asked around. Most high-end places refused to deal with it at all these days, citing issues from logistical problems to the potential for physical cash to be a viral vector.

Which left the less… salubrious places. Places preferred by people who didn't want to leave a digital trail.

Grey knew how to move through these places, and knew they weren't as bad as the sensationalist, state-controlled media made them out to be. For every shady fraudster there was a wife escaping her abuser, and for every dealer in one kind of illicit substance could be found… well, a dealer in another kind of illicit substances, but these ones were ok, you know, like *everyone* does it these days, and it's only on the weekend…

Grey had also always found the essential hypocrisy of people to be exceptionally helpful to his work.

So Grey headed downtown.

Downtown was literally that: the southern area of the city, where a few decades ago the first returnees to the area had settled. Like so many of the cities of the Reclamation, Albores was begun with industrial quantities of steel and concrete, forcing the land back under human control with little in regards to aesthetics or urban design. As more and more people arrived from the crowded camps of the equatorial region, and as the seed of the city germinated and grew, it expanded northwards, reclaiming the Waste and abandoning the southern areas to those who lacked the means or motives to follow. Now, this worn-out old end of a city sometimes called 'the nascent capital of the Federation' lay largely neglected and forgotten by its leaders, and by the majority of its inhabitants.

He started at *Methuselah's End*. A lot of people passed through here, and a lot more information - for the right price. Usually, this price was more information: gossip on pre-Fall sites uncovered by passing dust storms, dates for the release of the next migration permits for the Carib-Federation, details of the latest Aether incident, and so on.

Unfortunately, Grey didn't have much to pay with this time. Most of his recent jobs had been standard background checks on prospective candidates for sensitive positions, and the details of his last case weren't something he wanted to make public - he was still set on finding Blane before the Agency. Besides, a parricide, no matter how unfortunate or unusual, wasn't going to be of much interest to anyone here.

Still, he had people who would talk to him now, on the understanding that he would make it worth their while later. Jeder Francisco, sat in a booth close to the bar at the far end of the room, was one of those people.

"A kid from the Caliphate? *No he oído nada parecido.* Someone like that comes around here with *dinero*, many places they might go. Many people they could find for help. But not many people who will keep quiet, I think."

Grey had worked with Francisco a number of times. The man was old, old enough to remember the early reclamation attempts inland of the North American continent. He also must have a line on anti-geriatric drugs from somewhere, Grey knew. Though the wrinkles of his skin and slight greying of his hair betrayed his age, his lithe movements and clear, uncracked voice matched Grey's own. Anti-geriatrics were banned on the mainland, of course, but rumours abounded of a pipeline of the drugs channelled from the laboratories that supplied them to the ultra-rich of the states beyond the shore.

One result of this was that Francisco spoke as a bilingual, with clear distinction between the Spanish and English tongues. Very few centra-English speakers today even realised the language they spoke was really a creole of two older tongues, more really, and if they did think about this it was rarely for more than a moment. Even the old pre-Fall movies Grey liked to watch would be instantly translated to modern if he didn't specifically instruct otherwise.

So speaking to Francisco was always a curious experience, akin to a speaker of twenty-first-century English encountering a traveller from Shakespeare's time, or a Spanish speaker meeting a compatriot of Cervantes.

Curious, but rewarding. And, because Francisco had worked with pretty much everyone there was to work with at one time or another, often leading to unexpected outcomes, such as what he said next.

"But some news will probably turn up soon. Everyone is looking for that other kid, anyway, and when you search for one thing it turns up another, *es cierto*."

Grey struggled to keep from letting the sudden quickening of his pulse show.

"Other kid?" He said, keeping his tone low and level, as if it was only mild curiosity that made him ask.

"*Si, el otro niño.* Not from the Caliphate, so not your boy, but apparently big news. Someone offering a *lot* for information on some missing kid, and even more if they find him."

"Really? What's so special about this kid?"

"Nobody knows. But the men who came asking, they weren't the usual types who come down here. These were *big*. Big and serious, like some professional *soldado* or something. Showed up yesterday, busted up a few places demanding answers. Don't think they got any, because then they began offering big money instead. Now everyone is out looking for him - which means they're likely to turn up your kid, too."

Worried that the cold sweat he felt must be showing, Grey steered the conversation back to his own stated search for Salim. All the while, though, his mind was racing.

Fen. Someone was looking for Fen.

"Ok, Jeder. *Gracias por todo.* I've got to get back to work, but I'll come back tonight or tomorrow to see if you've got anything."

Francisco's face broke into a wide smile.

"And you'll bring me something good in exchange, *si*? You scratch my back, you know?"

Grey nodded, tapping his thin-screen to the charge point on the table and clearing the bill for both of them. As always, Francisco had somehow slipped a few extra drinks onto the tab without Grey noticing, and as always Grey said nothing. Trying hard not to let his haste show he stepped out into the street and a light, cold rain, already thumbing the cab-call function. Which is why he didn't notice the hulking man until he bounced off him and nearly went sprawling.

There were two of them, both clad in dark uniforms with the label 'Pan-Fed' in bright white letters on the chest and back[1], but there was no way they were typical Pan-Fed employees if they were Pan-Fed at all. The one Grey had collided with must have stood close to seven foot, with a square jawline and shoulders broad enough to block out the dim sun behind him. The beady-eyed man next to him was smaller, but radiated a barely-contained violence that if anything made him more imposing.

The first man turned his head downwards to look at Grey, as if noticing him only after a delay for the sensation of the collision to make its way up to his brain and register. Raising his arm, which Grey had to restrain himself from flinching away from, he placed a hand on Grey's shoulder and *shifted* him to the right. The strength in the arm was such that Grey couldn't have resisted if he tried. Instead, he stepped smartly sideways with the push, and breathed a sigh of relief as the men stepped past him and into *Methuselah's End*. He saw his auto-cab approaching.

"What's an ex-Far snoop up to here, then?"

Grey paused, closing his eyes and muttering a brief swear. Then, taking a deep breath and reminding himself to stay calm, he put on a big smile and turned.

It was the beady-eyed one who had spoken. Grey saw a thin-screen in his hand, a picture of Grey on the display next to reams of scrolling text. His bio-file.

So beady-eye at least had some high-level access to RA records. The data on the screen wasn't just low-level, public stuff, but included his history in the Far Agency. He must have packet-grabbed Grey as they passed, pulling details from the various cards, screens, and chips Grey had on him to run through the database and identify. The kind of thing an actual Pan-Fed official was permitted to do.

"I was wondering the same about a couple of germ-chasers," Grey replied.

Well, I handled this about as well as I usually do, he thought to himself as he saw anger flicker across the men's faces. Pan-Fed did *not* like that term.

"What are you doing here, snoop?" demanded beady-eye. The hulking one next to him offered a grunt that Grey supposed was support for this course of action.

---

[1] Officially titled the International Genomic Monitoring and Response Organisation, the section based in the Reclamation still used the old name for the group, when it was simply the Pan-Federation Viral Response Unit.

"Business," replied Grey, spreading his hands out and broadening his smile. "Things to do, people to see. Gotta keep an ear to the ground in this line of work," he said.

Beady-eye seemed about to respond sharply when suddenly he paused, biting down on whatever he was going to say and hand stopping with pointed finger held half outstretched.

As if a thought had just occurred to him, beady-eye turned to his partner and spoke.

"No, no, wait a minute. We could *use* an information broker. Especially an ex-Far agent." He turned back to Grey, expression taking on an insincere friendliness that didn't make it as far as his snake-like eyes. "What do you say? Willing to help out a fellow agency? Well, a *former* fellow agency?"

The way the big guy shifted his weight told Grey he didn't have much choice, at least not if he didn't want to make a scene. Of course, Grey thought he could take them; so long as they were in a populated area like this, and as long as these two weren't Aether users themselves, there was not much they could do to threaten him now he was aware of their presence. But using Aether for any reason, even self-defence, always resulted in a large number of questions even for an ex-Far agent, and using it against Pan-Fed officials would likely result in far more than that.

Besides, he could use this to his advantage. He needed to know exactly who was looking for Fen, and why, and it looked like he was about to be taken right into the belly of the beast. If he played this right, he could learn a lot about what was going on just by listening to the questions these two asked.

"And look, a cab just when we need it," said beady-eye, as the auto-cab Grey had called pulled up alongside. With a grin that made Grey uneasy, the man gestured at him to get in.

It took a lot for three people to make an auto-cab feel cramped, but they managed it. Big Guy, as Grey had taken to calling him in his head, sat directly across from him in what was still sometimes called the passenger's seat, though the ability to spin and face backwards wouldn't have been found in old models requiring an actual human driver. Beady-eye sat in the seat to Grey's right, forcing him to turn his head when he wanted to look at one or the other.

Big Guy didn't speak much, at least, though even so Grey couldn't stop himself from repeatedly looking his way. The guy seemed even more massive within the confines of the cab. He even *breathed* big, a discernible draft in the cab forming with each deep exhalation.

Beady-eye had thumbed a destination request into his own thin-screen without comment, so Grey had no idea where they were headed. He could check on his own thin-screen, of course, but that would feel like a victory for beady-eye somehow, so Grey made do with the 'time to destination' display projected in the smartglass of the windshield.

Less than 20 minutes, so they weren't going far. The rain had begun falling heavily now, the thudding of droplets and the cab's wipers providing a constant background noise to their silent cabin. Grey sat back, waiting mutely to see what their first move would be.

"You got your lock ready?" said beady-eye to Big Guy suddenly.

Big Guy grunted an affirmative, and gestured to a square bulge in his side pocket.

At that, beady-eye reached into his own jacket and pulled out his own stun-lock, turning it over in his hands to check the battery charges and the safety.

Grey knew they were trying to get a reaction from him, but he very carefully showed no change in his demeanour.

So, stun-locks. These ones looked like they would fire standard 9mm HEMI rounds, but appearances could be deceiving. Rounds designed to incapacitate could be easily overcharged to guarantee more permanent damage, or set to pulse to cause muscle spasms powerful enough to break bones. The standard shock charges could be deadly enough in their own way when misused.

Stun-locks were essentially guns from which each individual round, when fired into a person, could deliver an incapacitating charge up to three times when a secondary trigger was pulled. Even if the target was able to withstand the impact of the low-velocity needle-tipped rounds and keep moving, a quick pull on this secondary trigger would drop them to the floor. And if they tried to move again, well, there were always a couple more charges to knock them back down.

The name itself came from a time when branding was a thing, before localised mass-production, but it had stuck, and now any of the variations on charge-delivering firearms found the world over were generically known as stun-locks. They were favoured by many branches of law enforcement for their effective, non-lethal stopping power, though they could easily become lethal when fired at close range, or charges were overzealously applied.

Grey was conscious of his own stun-lock pressing into his side from the inside of his jacket. It was little comfort.

The time to destination display counted down to zero, and the cab pulled to a stop.

They stepped out into the rain and a grey, empty street. On one side stood some kind of open-air work-yard, glimpsed behind coiled fences of barbed wire. Grey could make out the forms of cranes and heavy-lifters outlined in the gloom, and the shapes of what seemed to be masts and hulls beyond, though the rain made it hard to be sure. A boatyard, then, which meant they were near the river. Practically as far south as you could go in the city.

On the side they had stepped out on to stood rows of abandoned-looking buildings, built from the same self-repair concrete as found elsewhere in the city only this time betraying far more lines of scarring, white and grey almost indivisible, telling of either age or a lack of care and maintenance - even self-repair concrete needed some protection from the elements. This must be one of the oldest areas of the city, landing pad for the first industrial-grade construction equipment of the Reclamation, and the militias before that.

The building directly in front of them was covered in graffiti, rising to the roof of the building some six or seven stories up. Numerous tags in various styles overlay one another, some displaying a certain amount of skill, others nothing but vulgar scrawls, but the rain and the scarring of the concrete underneath made it hard to make any of them out clearly.

"Do your thing," said beady-eye abruptly. It took Grey a second to realise he wasn't talking to Big Guy.

"My thing?" Grey asked.

"Yeah. The snoop thing. Or the Far agent thing. Whichever."

Grey raised an eyebrow.

"And what exactly do you think I'm going to do?"

Beady-eye locked him with a stare.

"Well, we can't go exactly go in there, can we? Not with our uniforms making us stand out like this and all. But you should be able to have a look around without much trouble."

Beady-eye looked from Grey to the building in front of them.

"And what do you think I should be looking for?" Grey replied.

"Well, you're looking for a kid, we're looking for a kid. Figure you can help us out while helping yourself."

Shit.

So it hadn't been a coincidence that these two had bumped into him outside the *Methuselah's End*. They'd... what? Bugged the place? Paid off someone to keep an eye on anyone asking around about a missing child?

Beady-eye and Big Guy grinned.

"And why here?" Grey asked, sighing. He knew he was on the back foot.

"Not a very good snoop, are you?" said beady-eye. "This is where all the runaways end up. One of those anarchist's retreats or something. They think they're building a utopia, and end up a bunch of dead bodies through cults or drugs or whatever. Always the same story. These ones call themselves the *Forever Fallen* - hell knows why. Of course, Pan-Fed keeps an eye on them. Never know when the next suicidal crazy will decide to take the world along with them."

The rain lessened and a pale light broke through the clouds as if to emphasise beady-eye's point. Grey could suddenly see a massive mural beneath the fresher graffiti tags and scrawls, a solid, closed fist that ran from the ground almost to the roof. The dark image of the fist towered over the street like a warning.

Forever Fallen? *Awake, arise, or be forever fallen...*

Grey knew there were still plenty of communities out in the Waste that kept themselves vehemently apart from the ponderous but inexorable rebirth of national and global society, and he'd had cause to deal with plenty of those who thought they could ignore the laws of the city, but he hadn't realised there were separatist groups large enough to take over a whole building in downtown Albores. He certainly hadn't encountered anything like this back when he was working as an agent.

Still, if this really was a place where runaways ended up, then he had a chance of not only finding Salim but also Blane. And he already knew the object of the two goons' search was lying on the couch back in his apartment, probably still devouring whatever words and videos his trawling online found. Grey had set an age-appropriate lock on his thin-screen and left Fen to it.

Shrugging, he affected a resigned air as he looked at the two Pan-Fed goons.

"I'll see what I can do."

7

"The purpose of the Agency is to predict and counter Aether incidents. It is immaterial whether facts exist to substantiate a charge of Aether misuse. If facts are present it aids in the fulfilment of our duties, but we may fulfil our duties without them."

CP Grover, First Chairman of the Far Agency, Address to Graduates

The ground floor of the building was hollow, or had been hollowed out, so that only a number of support pillars took up any of the wide, bare space. Grey could see where walls had been torn down to create one large open area. The room, if it could be called that, extended maybe ten or twenty metres to the back of the building, and maybe a little more than that from side to side. Unpainted walls enclosed the space, and the tiled floor was a dirty brown, covered in scuff marks and dust.

The dust and dirt marked the passage of a number of people, almost all footsteps heading directly from the entrance to a stairwell near the back on the left wall. At the very rear stood two half-closed elevator doors, but the loose cables hanging from what should be the call buttons told him all he needed to know about what would happen if he trusted that corroded machinery.

This was an *old* building, maybe one of the first to go up when rebuilding began, and it showed. Cracks ran up the walls and, alarmingly, the support pillars, with chunks of concrete fallen out onto the floor to be crushed to powder underfoot. Grey felt an urgent need to get out.

Which told him two things. One, he was losing his touch; and two, there was an Aether user here.

Grey stopped where he was, several paces into the room, and closed his eyes. Drawing a deep breath, he drew down into the Aether and *wrapped* it around his mind. At the same time, he forced himself to confront the anxiety rising inside of himself.

There is no danger, he said to himself. Even the earliest structures of the era of rebuilding would be standing long after he was dust; they were designed for function over form, and their function was to weather the generations of poisoned rain and apocalyptic storms forecast by predictive models of the battered, abused climate.

Grey forced the fear aside and pushed away the influence he was now aware of. Someone was here, and trying to keep him out.

"I know how Unsettle works, thanks. But nice try." He called out to the empty room. "The lumps of concrete and damaged cables are a nice touch, though. Now, why don't you come out and talk? I'm only here to ask a few questions."

Grey's chest loosened as the feeling of anxiety lifted, and he cursed himself inwardly for being lax enough to allow someone to *Unsettle* him - a simple enough technique that stimulated the amygdala and cortisol production, among other things. Whoever had used it on him was barely more than an amateur, though. The fear he had felt was definite, definable, and logical. Nothing like the gnawing, suffocating existential dread the best users could induce.

Grey suddenly became aware that there was someone standing next to the stairwell, and that they'd been there all along. So, not so amateur, but concentrating on two techniques at once.

"I know how Distraction works, too, thanks."

But he had to admit this woman was good. She'd used Unsettle to complement Distraction, inducing anxiety about the building with the former to enhance the minor sensory hallucinations of the latter. There was no way Grey would have failed to notice her if not for that added layer of deception.

The dark-haired woman was middle-aged, he guessed, but with eyes that seemed much older. Some of the hardness around them reminded him of Ritra Feye, though it would need many more years of tough decisions before she could truly match such inner strength.

"We don't like agents coming in here," said the woman in short, sharp tones.

Grey met the hostility with a smile.

"Then it's a good thing I'm not an agent, isn't it?" he replied.

"You're not?" Narrowed eyes showed her disbelief. "Not many people outside Far who talk about Aether like a box of tricks with individual name tags."

That was true, now Grey thought about it. Categorising and naming techniques was only something you would encounter at the Academy. But then how could this woman be so adept at Aether use without proper study?

"You got me," he said, holding up his hands with feigned chagrin. "But it's *ex*-agent. I left Far a long time ago. Now I'm an… information broker. And I was hoping maybe someone here could help me."

"A snoop?" Grey winced at the term - he was getting tired of the sneering way people had been saying this all day. "And... yes, I see... you're looking for someone, right? You wouldn't be the first snoop to come here. And you won't be the first one we've sent packing, either."

Two more figures appeared, though this time because they stepped out of the stairwell where they must have been concealing themselves. Both were male, well-built, one much younger than the woman who seemed to be the leader and one older, but both wore an expression no less hostile. The bearded older one, especially, gave off an aura of knowing how to handle himself. He carried a solid-looking carb-fibre bat, and the other a few feet of heavier and no less solid steel pipe.

Grey let his smile drop.

"Well," he said. "It sounds like those other *snoops*..." He rolled the word on his tongue. "... those other snoops weren't quite as persistent as I can be. And, also, I severely doubt they were trained former agents armed both mentally and literally."

The two men's expressions flashed uncertainty for a moment as Grey shifted his weight to reveal the stun-lock at his side, and looked towards the woman for direction. Her gaze, however, never faltered, but Grey could tell she was recalculating.

"What exactly are you looking for? Or should I say *who*," she said reluctantly.

The two men drew up to stand just behind her but advanced no further. Grey let his jacket fall back to cover the stun-lock, and held his hands to his sides. Besides, the stun-lock wouldn't be his first resort here. He could feel the Aether flowing strongly enough, should he need it. Plenty of people in the downtown area to maintain the flow.

"Look, I'm not here to cause trouble," he replied, adopting a conciliatory tone. "I'm just trying to help a worried parent. Well, and actually I'm also personally concerned for the wellbeing of someone else."

"So you're looking for two people?" asked the woman.

"Right. One's a boy from the Crystal Caliphate named Salim Ayad. About sixteen years old. The other's a girl named Blane. She's a few years younger. This set off any pop-ups for you?"

The woman didn't reply, but behind her the younger of the men gave a look towards his counterpart that told Grey at least *one* of those descriptions had meant something to them.

"A kid from the Crystal Caliphate around here?" The woman raised an eyebrow in surprise. "How does that even happen?"

So it was Blane. The woman's curiosity about the one betrayed her familiarity with the other.

"I'd like to know that myself. His father's extremely worried for his safety, as am I. No obvious reason for him to take off - no red flags where his dad's concerned. Could be a case of a kid taking off to see the big city, could be something else."

"And what makes you think he'd be here?"

"A... tip-off. Heard runaways sometimes end up here."

The woman looked thoughtful.

"No, no one like that has come here. I'll have some of my people keep a look out, though. Can be a dangerous city for someone who doesn't know their way around."

My people. An interesting choice of words. Grey made a mental note of it.

"And if you find him?" he asked.

The woman's eyes returned to their narrow, wary state.

"Well, we'll see. It depends on what he has to say."

Grey nodded. That seemed to be all he'd get for now.

"And Blane?" he continued. "She's here, right?"

The woman let out a deep sigh, realising what she'd revealed.

"Could be... but if she was, she'd have told us who she'd want to know. And I doubt you'd be on that list."

"Well, if she *were* here, would you at least deliver a message to her? Theoretically, of course."

The woman smiled.

"We might. If she were."

"Fine. Well, if she *were* here, please tell her I'm the guy who met her first after the... incident. And I know what she's going through. Well, at least, I understand, and it wasn't her fault. Tell her that. And tell her those two Far agents were jerks, but that there are still people out there to help her, and... and..."

He realised he was rambling. What *did* he want to say? He suddenly wasn't sure.

"Just tell her... tell her if she ever needs help, I'm here. Name's

Nestor Grey; hopefully she remembers me."

He trailed off, feeling lost.

The woman seemed to pick up on this, putting on a real smile for the first time. It was small, and there was still that hardness behind the eyes, but it was genuine.

"Nestor, was it? You seem like a good guy, Nestor. At least, for a Reclamation Authority dog, former or not. I'll see what I can do. But for now, you should get out of here. We're not as helpless against you as you might think."

The smile was gone in an instant, and Grey was convinced her words weren't empty bravado. Was she seriously implying they could take on a trained Far agent?

His eyes flicked from her to the two men behind her. Was it possible the weapons they carried were a diversion? Could they be Aether users too?

The temptation to Read them was almost overpowering. However, something told him that even if he did manage to Read one of them, the woman would know what he'd done. And the response would be... less than tolerant.

The taller, bearded man seemed about to step forward, gripping his bat tighter, until the woman held up a hand to block him.

"It's alright, Uriel," she told the advancing man.

"Look, I'll go," Grey said, taking a single step backwards and drawing out his thin-screen. "But could you contact me if Blane wants to talk? Or if Salim turns up?"

The woman stared at him for a moment, as if weighing him up on some scale he couldn't see.

"Fine. But only *if...*" she said, leaving the sentence hanging.

She drew out a thin-screen of her own, almost certainly an anon-spec model to prevent tracking, and accepted his ping. He looked down at the acceptance message on his screen.

"Raphael?" he said. "Someone in here's a big fan of Milton, then."

The woman, who was apparently using the pseudonym Raphael, raised an eyebrow.

"Well done. Unexpected for an agent to know the classics."

"Former agent. And I like what I like. There's a lot we can learn from before the Fall."

"There's a fall in *Paradise Lost*, as well."

Grey had never thought about it that way.

"Huh. And the whole 'Forever Fallen' thing?"

"Can't you see what has happened to us all since the Sudden War?" She gestured around her, taking in the building, taking in the world outside. "This isn't the fresh start we were supposed to make. This isn't revival. This is a return to what struck us down in the first place. Not light, but darkness visible."

She suddenly looked far older.

"Now go. We might be in touch."

There wasn't anything else Grey could think to do, so he did as she said.

It was still raining outside.

"So what'd you find? Any sign of the kid?"

Beady-eye and Big Guy were waiting where he'd left them, standing beside the auto-cab still idling at the side of the road; they must have used a priority override to prevent it driving off in search of fresh fares.

"Which kid are we talking about?" replied Grey, refusing to make their job any easier by taking the initiative.

His deliberate obtuseness did the job he hoped, with beady-eye shooting him a glare.

"Is the kid we're looking for here? I know you got the details from that fossil back in the bar," beady-eye growled.

Actually, Grey hadn't got anything from Jeder Francisco other than the fact that somebody was looking for a kid, and the Pan-Feds hadn't offered any information themselves. He said as much, watching beady-eye grow red with frustration and Big Guy clench and unclench his fists.

"...but as far as I can tell, no, the kid you're looking for isn't there. Not either of them – that one, or the one I'm looking for."

Grey was almost tempted to insinuate that Fen *was* with the Forever Fallen, to send the search in the wrong direction, but decided against it. No point in causing trouble for them, not with guys like this, and not while there were potential benefits from contact with them.

"Alright then, snoop," sneered Beady-eye. "Well, if you *do* hear something, you will of course contact us as soon as possible, won't you?"

Grey met the man's stare.

"Well, of course. Always happy to help an agent, Pan-Fed or Far," he said, knowing his tight, false smile would be read for what it was.

Beady-eye continued to stare at Grey for a while, then blinked and turned to his partner.

"Well, we've lost enough time going down this path. It was worth a try. Let's head back."

Saying that, and without looking at Grey again, beady-eye swung open the cab door and climbed inside. Big Guy followed close behind, and the cab pulled away almost instantly. Grey watched it until it turned a corner and disappeared from view.

"Well," he said to himself. "A pleasure."

He pulled out his thin-screen to call a cab of his own. There was someone he needed to see.

8

Since the early modern period, the nation-state has been the most persistent of all social structures. Other models have been imposed both above and below the level of the nation-state at various times and in various places, yet none have endured, not even the ancient model of empire. Nationalism remains a potent force even in a world of scattered peoples and broken borders, and can be harnessed for good or ill by both state and non-state actors.

Agency Handbook, Section 5.3 (Society & Group Dynamics)

It had been years since he had last had reason to visit the Station, and Grey would have preferred to keep it that way. But he had questions he couldn't answer, questions he couldn't even quite form, and he needed to speak to someone who thought about these things for a living.

So Grey headed to Albores Central.

Something about the architecture of the Far Station meant it dominated the skyline of this area of the city, despite the fact that a number of nearby buildings stood taller. He stared through the rain as the thick stone facade grew to fill the windscreen, and the cab pulled to a stop on the street outside.

Stepping out, he avoided the sweeping, cobbled courtyard leading up towards the collonaded main entrance with its faux-classical designs, and went around to the side door.

The auxiliary access point, as it was technically known, was nothing but a solid steel door with a barred view window embedded in it, set into the side of a bare, windowless wall towards the back of the Station. Most agents called it the side door. It led into a cramped waiting room with a single processing desk hidden behind misted, impact-resistant glass. Flaking white walls and stained floor tiles gave the impression of a run-down hospital emergency room, and the atmosphere was heavy and oppressive. It was usually deserted, as it was now, and felt abandoned.

This entrance was, however, no less secure than the wide hall of the main entrance. It was through this side entrance that agents would bring detainees that they would rather not be seen by prying eyes, hustling them through for processing and interrogation.

It was also an entrance he hoped could allow him to get in and out without too many people noting his visit. It may have been years, but plenty of those he had worked with in the past would still be based here - the Station was the centre of Far operations for the whole city and surrounding Waste, after all. He kept his head down; he didn't have the time or inclination to handle awkward questions.

Grey headed straight for the processing desk, staring at the small, circular holes set in the misted glass at head height to carry his words to whoever was on duty behind.

"I'm here to speak to Agent Chau. Tell him... tell him it's the discount detective."

Grey gritted his teeth as he said that. He'd never let on how much it irritated him when Chau called him that, upon learning of his plans to retire from the agency, but he also knew Chau would know who was doing the asking. Sure enough, after a few minutes a junior agent appeared from the door to the interior and gestured at Grey to come through.

The escort said nothing as he led Grey down the narrow hallway, bare white wall to his left and short-term holding cells and storage racks to his right The layout hadn't changed in the years since Grey had last been here, but mysterious marks and stains now lined the walls. A huge dent in the ceiling of one cell caught his eye, and a mass of cracks running the length of the left wall hinted at a heavy impact – or possibly multiple ones.

Detaining an Aether user was never easy, and the pressures of interrogation could lead to... significant incidents, but Grey had always done his best to keep the number of these incidents down. He didn't like to think about what it meant that they appeared to have increased since he left. Just another reason to be glad he got out when he did.

This hallway led further on and into the main section of the Station, but Grey wouldn't be going that far. A stairway set into the side led up a few dark flights to another narrow passage inset with a number of doors, each a plain, extru-wood thing distinguishable from the other only by the figure set into the side. Chau's door was numbered 101. The man had always found that funny.

Grey's escort left him at the door without a word, turning back and heading about whatever duties he had been pulled away from. Grey paid him no more heed and knocked on the door with three clean raps.

"… in," he heard, muffled through the wood. Grey pushed the door open.

The room beyond the door was a mess of books and paperwork. A small office, smaller in size than Grey's own back at the apartment, was almost completely filled by a large, heavy desk with an unseemly amount of draws, and bookshelves that ran from floor to ceiling, filled to bursting with various texts. A single LED strip in the ceiling provided an uncomfortably bright white glare that made everything contrasting shades of dark and light. There was no window.

Chau was sat at his desk, eyes locked on the pile of papers spread in front of him. He continued to read them for a second, as if searching for something, then looked up at Grey. His face broke into a wide smile.

"Well now, the prodigal son returns," he said, pushing the papers away. "And what could possibly bring our independently-minded investigator to my office?"

Grey gave a small smile back.

"I was wondering if you were ready to pack it in and come work for me yet," he replied with a low chuckle. "Could use someone who does his research."

Chau threw back his head and laughed.

Grey stepped toward the desk and retrieved a small stool, the only other chair in the room, from beneath a pile of loose papers and note books. Chau had always been curiously analogue, preferring the feel of paper and pen to thin-screen. Inefficient, and inconvenient for anyone hoping to refer to his notes, but Chau maintained a good enough record with the Agency that it had never caused him problems.

"I could use some help with a case," Grey said.

Chau's eyes became serious.

"Rare for you to seek help from Far."

"Well, actually I was hoping we could treat this as me receiving help from an old friend and co-worker, rather than from the agency itself."

Chau steepled his fingers and looked thoughtful. Grey knew what he was saying was as close as he could safely go towards asking Chau to keep their meeting from official records, and Chau would understand this.

"An old friend, eh?" Chau said, eventually. "Well, when you put it like that... How can I help?"

Grey let out a breath he hadn't been aware he was holding in.

"I need some... insight... into an Aether technique. Specifically, what is theoretically possible."

Chau's expression became puzzled.

"A technique? I'm surprised *you* would ask such a thing. After all, you were the star incident handler for a long time. I'd say *you* have more real-life experience with wild users than almost anyone here."

"I'm as surprised as you," replied Grey. "But I've come into some, uh, information that I don't know how to make sense of. Accounts of a way of using Aether I can't explain. And *you* are the one who devotes all his time to figuring out how this stuff works."

"Accounts?" Chau said, raising an eyebrow. "And what do these accounts say, exactly?"

Grey held back, reluctant to say too much.

Chau obviously saw this, letting out an exasperated sigh.

"*You* came to me, remember? No point getting hesitant now."

"Ok, ok, you're right," said Grey. "It's a... I'm hearing things about a new way of using it. A way of shaping it in ways that shouldn't be possible, making it *fly*."

Chau's lowered his hands, and he fixed Grey with an intense look.

"Be clearer. What technique are you talking about?"

Grey took a deep breath.

"*Mindfire.*"

Chau watched Grey for a time, saying nothing. Then, he leant back in his chair exhaustedly, stretching his arms out behind him and rolling his neck as if to force out some stiffness

"You've been away from proper investigative procedures for too long, I'd say," Chau said eventually. "I don't know where you've been hearing these *accounts*, but you must know that makes no sense. That's not how Mindfire works."

Grey nodded inwardly to himself, remembering how he had told himself the same thing repeatedly even as a bright, burning dragon of the stuff hovered over him, glaring down.

"I know, I know," he said, making an expression that implied he agreed. "Like I said, it doesn't make sense. But, you know, I need to look into this for a client. Need to humour them, if I want to get paid. So could you humour me?"

Chau seemed to buy this explanation, and his smile returned.

"Of course, though I still don't know exactly what you want to know."

"I just… need to check my understanding of the facts. I'll need to be clear on them when I speak to my client next, and simply telling them that what I'm hearing is impossible probably won't be enough. So, can we go over exactly what Mindfire is? *Why* isn't it possible?"

"A remedial class for Nestor Grey?" Chau chuckled. "Well, you really *have* lost your touch since you left us. But worry not, I can help. I happen to know a great deal about many of the abilities found in Aether users all across the Reclamation and beyond…"

Grey listened with half an ear as Chau got this out of his system. He'd thought this would work, gambling that Chau hadn't changed too much in the intervening years. Research into the Aether had always been his primary passion, but a close second was telling anyone who would listen about it.

And Chau did know his stuff. Sure, Grey had more experience with the *reality* of Aether use, but it was Chau who could put it into words that wouldn't have sounded out of place at a symposium.

"So, what do we know about Mindfire…"

To understand Mindfire, you had to understand the Aether, and there was still debate over if this were truly possible. Chau, of course, was on the side of the debate that said it most definitely was.

The Aether was believed to be a form of energy produced by non-apoptotic, non-necrotic organic matter. By life, in other words. It was generated in negligible amounts by even the smallest single-celled creatures, but only on a level detectable by the finest of specialised instruments. It was complex, multicellular organisms that were the powerhouses of Aether generation, the various interactions of mitochondria, organelles, and nucleus producing it as a by-product of the biological processes of survival and reproduction. And it was humans who produced Aether in the greatest quantities, though the reasons for this were still unclear.

For aeons, since life first crawled out of the sea, this energy must have gone undetected, unknown and unaffected by man or nature, in amounts too small for evolutionary benefit. Perhaps, and it was a very strong *perhaps*, there was something to the idea that the old stories of the supernatural, the divine, of sixth senses and ghosts and psychics, *perhaps* these were attributable to some early perception of the Aether, but it was unlikely this could ever be proven.

And then... a population explosion. A mass of humanity spreading across the continents, breeding and expanding and conglomerating in dense cities of tens of millions or more. And below them, the trickle turning to a flood, the stream into a torrent.

Until one day, an errant gene or a single misread strand of DNA enabled an evolutionary change that allowed humans for the first time to truly channel that energy.

But with limits. The Aether wasn't energy in the same sense as light or electricity. It didn't conduct, or travel across significant distances. It was more akin to magnetism; a fixed field around the living cell that produced it.

Hence why Aether "techniques" were almost exclusively limited-range ones that affected another living being. From Reading, which allowed one person to see the shape of another's thoughts, to Distraction or Unsettle or Flare, Aether use was primarily a way of interacting with or disrupting another person's cognition.

The only techniques to defy this pattern were generally classified as Thoughtscreen or Push, though both were really variations of the same thing. A near-physical barrier created by concentrating the energy just beyond the body, forming a field that could stop sound waves, light, or, with a talented enough agent and enough Aether available, something like a bullet - though this had only ever been demonstrated in a controlled environment.

Grey thought back to the two fizzers he had *Pushed*. Then to the uncountable number of bullets Fen had.

And then there was Mindfire.

What made Mindfire truly special, and truly terrifying, was that there was no defence against it. It was the perfect first-strike weapon, instant and unstoppable. If used against you, there would be no warning, no way to counter or limit the damage. You were simply... done.

Mindfire was the release of a living creature's Aether all at once, each cell pouring out it's stored energy in an instant. Where this energy would usually dissipate outwards only gradually, Mindfire started an explosive chain reaction in its victim. Mindfire *was* an explosive chain reaction, a release of Aether so intense it actually released heat and light - a flame that burnt everything around it.

Very few wild Aether users ever learnt to use Mindfire, or rather, very few wild users learnt to use it more than once. Because, lacking an understanding of what they were doing, most users who discovered such an ability incinerated themselves before they knew what they had done.

However, if a person *did* learn to handle the technique, they were one of the most dangerous beings alive. They could torch you with a look, with a *thought*, and there was nothing you could do to stop it. It was the first instances of Mindfire use that led to the establishment of the Far Agency, just as designer-plagues saw the birth of Pan-Fed.

"But of course, that just confirms what you already know," said Chau, wrapping up what was practically a monologue. "Mindfire can't be *shaped*. It can't move around independently, because it's not a physical thing. It's a release of energy - a powerful, searing release, but it needs a source."

"But we've seen users who can smash holes in walls before, or send tables flying across the room." The thought of Blane, a lonely child sat in a destroyed apartment, flashed across Grey's mind.

"That's a form of Push. A release of energy across a small area just beyond the body, but powerful and sudden enough to cause a pressure change, an explosion, outwards. Similar to Mindfire in some ways, but on a much lower energy scale."

Grey nodded. Everything Chau had told him only confirmed what he already knew. But the fact remained. He knew what he had seen back at the warehouses. Fen had moulded and moved the burning flame of Mindfire in ways no theory he knew of could credit.

The beginnings of an idea formed in Grey's mind. Even he had managed to hold two fizzers in the air by himself, something he would never have believed he could do even in a crowded area of the city.

"What if... what if there was a massive amount of Aether available? Couldn't they extend the 'field' around themselves beyond its usual limits?"

Chau looked thoughtful, glancing down at his notes as if looking for an answer there.

"Well," he said after a long moment, "To be honest, who knows? But it would need to be a *lot*. Everything we know suggests an exponential increase in Aether necessary to extend its influence by even a centimetre. I can't imagine where you could find population density enough to stretch a field more than a dozen centimetres."

Chau's eyes narrowed.

"You seem awfully invested in this story," Chau said. "As if... do you know something beyond what you're letting on?"

Grey responded with what he hoped was a disarming expression.

"No, no," he said. "I just have to be thorough, you know? Ask the questions my client might ask."

"Hmm...," said Chau in a way that made Grey think he wasn't quite convinced. "Well, I hope I was of some small help. Is there anything else I can help you with?"

Grey declined. He had nothing more to ask, at least for now. Wrapping up with a few enquiries into the health of Chau's family, he made his farewells and left.

It was time to check on Fen.

The rain was finally letting up by the time Grey pulled up outside his apartment building, just in time for the dusk to give way to twilight. A fog rolled in as the light left. Not one of the old stingclouds that were still common even in his childhood, vapour carrying moisture-wrapped particles of whatever poisons the wind picked up from out in the Waste, but thick nonetheless. Once upon a time this kind of weather would have been unknown to this region, but the Sudden War had shifted the climate to the extent that no citizen of a previous era would have recognised it. Only the groaning, rattling filters stacked atop every roof prevented a return to a time when even stepping outside could be a risk.

A vehicle across the street caught his attention. The fog hid much of it, but from the outline it was large. The silhouette of a figure stood to one side of it; Grey could see them shuffling around, trying to stay warm as the temperature dropped.

Whoever the figure was, it looked as if they were waiting. Not waiting *for* someone, just... waiting. They seemed to be looking around - they turned to face the auto-cab Grey sat in as it pulled closer.

"Uh, a little further up the street, please."

The auto-cab chimed recognition of the spoken command and pulled out into the street again.

Grey had learned to trust his instincts when it came to certain things, and right now his instincts told him that whoever that was, they were on watch. And if someone was on watch, then there were probably already other *someones* around.

Ice ran down Grey's spine.

"Ok, stop here," he said aloud. He jumped out as soon as the door locks clicked free, the cab making a low electronic chime behind him.

He was several buildings down the street now, and the fog made it impossible to see back towards his own building. Someone could be walking towards him right now, and he wouldn't know until they were almost on top of him. He hurried down a nearby alleyway.

Could he be overreacting…? No, Grey knew a Rapid Reaction Vehicle when he saw one, and that had been one parked right across from his home. A group carrier, he thought, meaning at least eight or nine people. It would be armoured, made from lightweight, tough, and above all expensive alloy.

That's not good.

Maybe those Pan-Fed agents hadn't been as finished with him as he had thought. If they'd decided to check out where he lived…

The hiss of another vehicle pulling to a stop in practically the same spot his cab had just left caused him to press tight against the wall, hiding from view behind the collection point of a tall, grey refuse compactor jutting out from within the building behind him. It began to whir and rasp as someone inside threw their garbage into the machine for shredding, crushing, and storage, which covered any sound Grey was making but also meant he was equally unable to hear.

He leaned forward, peering around his cover to the end of the alley.

At least four more, he saw, and this time they were close enough for him to make out the same body armour as the assailants in the warehouse district had worn.

That's really not good.

They didn't seem to know he was there, at least. It looked like he had got away with his moment's hesitation outside the apartment.

No, they were clearly preparing for something, unaware they were being watched. They stood at the back of their RRV, huddled together and speaking in muffled tones while someone - *so, at least five then* - passed long, heavy objects from the inside. More rifles.

The group silently made a few hand signals to each other and moved out of his sight, moving quickly in the manner of a well-trained squad.

Pulling himself back behind cover, Grey stared at the concrete wall across from him and tried to think.

So, no way he was going out the way he came in, not when he had no way of knowing if anyone had stayed behind with this RRV to keep watch too. And the other end of the alley only led away from where he needed to be.

Which left... *up.*

Grey took in the alleyway he was standing in. Narrow, dark even without the twilight fog, with bare concrete walls on both sides. But if he climbed up the side of the out-jutting refuse collector *here*, then jumped across to that coolant box *there*...

He almost didn't make the jump across to the fire escape he'd spotted, running from the roof of the building down to the second floor, out of reach from the ground. It gave a nasty metallic rattle when he landed on it and he stood frozen, half-crouched, listening intently for any sign that he'd been heard. Nothing except the drip, drip, dripping of condensation falling from various surfaces to the ground below.

He forced himself to breath. Rushing would only expose both Fen and himself to more danger, so he took each step upwards carefully. Once he reached the roof, however, he took off, racing across the flat, open concrete towards his own apartment block.

Getting up on to the roof of his own building proved much easier than he had expected. Though it was another few stories climb, ladders of metal handholds had been set into the concrete wherever there was a rise in height, providing access to the entirety of the roofs on this side of the street.

In fact, Grey only realized now that the 'buildings' along the street were really only a single structure. Though from the front they presented different facades, each 'building' was really just an isolated section of a single, huge mass of sculpted concrete, design and function laid out and built long before people actually moved in.

The benefits of planning and building a city from scratch, he thought.

He spotted the skylight of his apartment building a few metres ahead, a weak light escaping through the grime that covered it. A glance through it showed little; just the inside edge of each floor's walkway, and the entrance hall far below. Grey couldn't see enough to tell if anyone was on any of the walkways, but the entrance hall looked deserted enough.

Beyond the skylight was a slightly raised square access hatch. He pulled it up to reveal a small set of steps down to a short, dusty passageway. It looked like no one had used this way for years.

He moved warily into the building, and almost instantly low voices from further ahead proved his caution justified. Two or three voices, again speaking softly through vocal suppressors that removed any trace of accent, gender, or emotion. It sounded like they were on the same floor as him, around the corner from where this access passage led onto the walkway of this floor.

Grey paused, listening. Nothing in the few whispered words he could make out told him much; they were waiting, that much he could tell.

So, whoever they were, they had people on point both outside, and on the upper floors. Blocking off escape routes. Which meant this was a capture operation, and Grey was in no doubt who they were here to capture.

He *Reached* out from himself, searching for that strange flicker of sensation that every person gave off, their slight effect on the Aether perceptible to a trained user, like the ripple of a fallen leaf on a still lake. Three of them, he confirmed, less than five meters away. All three felt alert but calm; unaware of his approach.

Which was extremely useful for Grey, because an alert but unaware enemy was extremely susceptible to Slowtime.

What happened next appeared very differently depending on whether the viewpoint was that of the three armed figures or Grey. For Grey, he stepped smartly out of the access passage behind the three figures and swiftly disarmed the first, sweeping their legs out from underneath while at the same time snatching their rifle from a strangely weakened grip. He then used the butt of this rifle to smack the back of the lethargically-turning second figure's head, knocking them down despite their helmet. Finally, he pushed away the slowly rising muzzle of the third figure's rifle and stepped smartly behind them, grabbing and putting them into a chokehold, forcing them down first to their knees, then to the ground, unconscious.

All of which was accomplished without hesitation and with the practised movements of a seasoned professional, but at a controlled, steady pace, unhurried and allowing no mistakes.

What the three figures saw was a blurred form appear out of

nowhere moving at a rate faster than the eye could keep up with. The first of them was down before they could process what was happening, while for the other two there was just enough time to feel as if they had been struck by a bolt of lightning.

The dulling of an opponent's senses with Slowtime never lasted long, though, so Grey was quick to put a single stun-lock round into the back of each sprawled figure before they could recover. That would guarantee they stayed down for the next half hour or so, at least, and he couldn't imagine whatever was coming wouldn't be resolved by then - though whether for better or worse he couldn't say.

He knelt down beside the closest figure and rolled them over. Their face was fully hidden behind some kind of thin, dark-green mask that was built into their helmet, eyes barely visible behind an almost opaque, plastic-like covering and a filter where the mouth should be. A woman, he thought, though steroidal rebalancing and osteoblast alteration meant most female enforcement agents were built no less heavily than any of their male counterparts.[2]

This close up, he could see the raised lettering of the official Pan-Fed initials on her body armour. IGMRO, black on black, perceptible only at close range. And below that, in slightly smaller lettering: RR. A quick check of the other fallen figures showed the same.

Grey cursed his luck. He knew who these people were. Or at least, he knew their outfit, though he'd never had reason to interact with them.

This was Pan-Fed's Rapid Response team: the first to go in when all the security checks and detector systems had failed, the first on the scene when eyeballs were bleeding and organs were melting.

This was Quick-Fix. So-called because, when a psychopath with a home-brew lab and a basic understanding of genome editing released an especially virulent pathogen out into the world, they were the only 100% guaranteed containment method.

After all, there really isn't a way for a virus to spread if everyone who could be a vector is already dead.

---

[2] Most children in the Reclamation received some form of osteoblast and steroidal treatment in infancy, or even in the womb. The extent of this was generally dependent only on parental decision, though there were limits on what was acceptable for those too young to offer informed consent. Further body-sculpting tended to occur in adolescence, resulting in the hulking brutes of both genders you could find in many security services.

What the fuck have I got myself caught up in?

Grey cursed to himself as he made his way quietly down the walkway. He kept imagining armed figures jumping out of the doorways to his right, or rappelling suddenly down on his left and riddling him with bullets as they descended steadily from the skylight to the atrium many floors below.

The Far Agency had always worked in cooperation with Pan-Fed when necessary, and Grey had worked with a number of Pan-Fed officials in his time. But Quick-Fix was something he, like most people, knew only from the Federation's propagandistic *New Patriot* movies. They were a small and elite group within Pan-Fed, operating in parallel with the wider organization but not in tandem, trained and equipped with only the best materiel.

Just as Pan-Fed was older than Far, and a lot of what Far became was based on lessons learned from its older sister organisation, so Quick-Fix was older than Pan-Fed. The difference was that Quick-Fix had been incorporated into the bureaucracy of the larger body when the times demanded it.

And demand it they had. Quick-Fix had gone by a lot of names in the years after the Fall, and reported to a lot of 'governments'- some of which lasted years, some of which lasted only months. For most of its existence, it was a paramilitary organisation in the most literal sense, changing leadership, membership, and allegiances time and time again yet somehow maintaining a core identity that could be traced all the way back to the chaos of the Sudden War.

Quick-Fix had, in more recent generations, been a key player in enforcing the stability and security that allowed the Carib-Federation to emerge as the regional economic and societal powerhouse despite the masses of refugees and migrants crowding up its shores, and as such it had received a considerable amount of legitimacy and support from the upper echelons there. However, it had also been quietly encouraged to find its place in the Reclamation, returning to the American continent where a great many of its ideological roots could be traced. An unlicensed and uncontrolled military was, of course, not something a newly-minted elite felt comfortable allowing so close to home.

And so Quick-Fix had been amongst the first to return to the mainland, its discipline and firepower an ideal match for the poisoned wilderness of the blasted continent. Few could deny its effectiveness in leading the charge to reclaim what had once been lost. But here too, the group eventually found itself a threat to the very system it helped create.

This time, however, there would be no moving on. Instead, one of the first actions of the new-born Reclamation Authority was to incorporate the group into the newly formed security forces, and soon after specifically into those forces tasked with handling the sudden profusion of crazies who had realised that a) a large number of historically significant viruses had their entire genetic sequence available online,[3] and b) hey, I can make that in my bedroom.

Through a series of incentives, threats, and outright bribes, the Reclamation Authority managed to get the main figures of the movement to announce their acceptance of incorporation into legitimate Federation structures, and the militant-but-totally-under-control Bio-Terror Rapid Response Unit was born. Quick-Fix. They even called themselves agents.

'For a better future' was their official motto. Most people knew it as *'When the cure is no better than the disease.'*

And now Grey was storming through a full team of Quick-Fix agents; in fact, he'd already taken down three, which meant he couldn't expect calm and even-handed treatment if he got caught.

Still, he told himself. *I've got the edge, as long they don't know that I'm here.*

There were no Aether users in Quick-Fix, or Pan-Fed as a whole. Aether, and agents trained in Aether use, were strictly the province of the Far Agency, and the limited number of potential recruits would keep it that way for some time to come. If Grey maintained a stealthy approach, he could get to his apartment before…

A massive blast of heat and light threw him off his feet and against a door to his right at the same time as a huge boom rattled the entire building. Blazing golden flame poured upwards towards the skylight, filling the open area that ran up the centre of the building. It writhed around itself and licked at the walkway rail as if exploring. Grey instinctively curled himself into a ball, though he knew that just a touch of that roiling Mindfire would end him no matter how he

---

[3] Some pre-Fall societies saw the free sharing of viral genetic sequences and clinical and epidemiological data as a noble goal, both for the advancement of science and for global society. Of course, this data remained available forever, to whomever. This was now widely considered a mistake, if not a crime.

tried to protect himself.

But the golden fire didn't come boiling over the rail. Instead, it snapped out of existence as quickly as it had appeared, leaving behind an abrupt, violent silence that hurt the ears.

Something fell somewhere in the building, a heavy thud that Grey somehow *knew* was a heavily-armoured, lifeless body. Several more thuds came swiftly afterwards.

Despite the unreal power of what Grey had just witnessed, though, Fen obviously hadn't got them all - because then the shooting started.

9

> *Understanding of Aether has much in parallel to understanding of language. Without specific neural pathways and cognitive processes, language is just incoherent sound. One who hears an unknown language does not experience anything close to the instantaneous connection of sound and meaning that comes from a known tongue. To those who come into an awareness of the Aether, it is as if an unknown language that has always been whispering in the ear becomes suddenly comprehensible.*
>
> Far Agency Academy, *Foundational Text*

One of the curious things about Mindfire was that it left inorganic materials (and sufficiently deceased organic material, for that matter) practically untouched. Oh, inorganic surfaces in close contact with a living creature flaring off its stored Aether might be scorched, but something about the effect of Mindfire meant that even typically flammable material often failed to ignite.

This was true of what had just occurred in Grey's building, too. If he hadn't seen the flaring of Mindfire fill the open space of the inner atrium in an all-consuming rising torrent of golden flame, he wouldn't have known it had happened at all. Everything was as it had been, save for the shots and sudden shouting below.

"Stop firing, idiots. You'll hit the kid."

The words reverberated up from the lower floors in the curiously neutral, electronic tones that vocal suppressors transformed even urgent or panicked shouts into.

"Stun-locks only."

The Quick Fire team were no longer trying for stealth, it seemed, as the click of ammunition-switching echoed upwards. Nor were they trying to hide their objective. But it seemed they weren't aiming to kill Fen, either. Had something changed since the warehouse?

A rush of footsteps came from below, the sound of reinforcements arriving from those who had been waiting outside. Grey sat with his back against the walkway wall, holding his stun-lock in front of him and breathing heavily, straining his ears for anyone approaching. Nothing that sounded close, though. It seemed all the activity had been drawn to the lower floors, presumably surrounding his third-floor apartment.

He *Reached* to be sure, but this technique really only extended a few metres at best and, as expected, he detected no one.

So, he needed to get down there *now*. The elevator was out of the question, of course, which left only the narrow stairs directly beside it. But if he was going to take that route all the way down he may as well announce himself by loudly yelling "shoot me" and making himself as large a target as he could. He needed the element of surprise.

Which unfortunately left him with only one option he could think of.

Grey made his way down four floors by the stairs and stepped out onto the circular walkway of the floor above his own, careful to check for anyone who might be waiting there. He sensed no one, though, and could hear hurried movements and the soft whisper of radio communication leaking upwards. Clearly all attention was focused on readying their next assault.

They need to surprise him, he thought to himself. *If Fen sees them coming, he'll fry the lot of them. They'll do one sharp, coordinated attack, giving Fen no time to react.*

A cautious glance over the walkway railing confirmed his prediction. Though he quickly ducked his head back down, it was enough to glimpse several RR agents arrayed along the walkway on the level of his apartment, rifles raised and trained on his door. The door itself was almost fully closed, though something seemed to be preventing it from shutting completely. The lock was clearly smashed in, so it must have been forced open and swung shut again sometime earlier; Grey would bet a Carib-dollar this was at the same time as Mindfire filled the atrium.

Five of them, two to each side of the door and one preparing to kick it open again. Which meant he had little time to think about what he was going to do - which was probably a good thing.

Taking a final, deep breath, adrenaline surging through his veins, Grey vaulted over the railing and threw himself through the air towards the walkway below. Though he knew it was only a few metres down at most, and less than that across, it still seemed as if he was falling through the air for an inordinate amount of time. With everything moving slowly - the effects of the adrenaline, not Aether - he managed to find the focus to use Distract.

It shouldn't have worked. You can't use Distract on five highly trained, highly alert soldiers. Even at his best, he thought he would only ever have been able to distract two at once.

But Grey could feel the Aether below him flowing in an inexorable tide that he only had to dip into for it to pour through him. It had been this way at the warehouse district, too. He *shouldn't* have been able to stop two fizzers even in a heavily populated district, let alone the essentially deserted forgotten outskirts of the southern city. He'd felt it at his apartment the night before as well; the feeling that with just a thought he could reach out and force his will on the entire world.

It was Fen. Specifically, proximity to Fen. The boy wasn't only able to use the Aether in ways that couldn't be explained, he seemed to *generate* it, at a degree that even a city's worth of people didn't. And Grey was able to tap just the slightest, most infinitesimal trickle of it, and feel it roar through his veins.

He wondered what it felt like for Fen.

Distract hit the five agents simultaneously. Grey had no way of knowing what it was they were each seeing, but the momentary hallucinations caused by the technique most commonly manifested as something almost like synaesthesia, a visual blooming of light and colour, and alterations to depth and temporal perception. The effects of the technique were usually compared to those of psychedelic drugs, a sensory overload that rendered the affected party confused, bewildered, and disorientated.

Most often, this effect would pass in seconds, the neural pathways snapping back into their old routes swiftly and completely, giving a skilled agent just barely enough time to make their getaway. This time, however, the effect was more pronounced.

The nearest two to Grey fell to their hands and knees still facing away from him, rifles clattering to the floor underneath them. The one closest to the door seemed to lose his balance too, only to reach for the door as if to catch himself but instead tumbling inside and out of sight.

The final two managed to keep enough of their wits about them to realise at least that something was wrong, turning to face the direction Grey was in. They wouldn't see him, though, because he was frantically trying to pull himself up and over the walkway railing before he fell to the floor below. He hadn't quite made the jump after all.

It took a good while for him to do so, and he was glad there was no one in a sound enough state of mind to see his inelegant efforts to haul himself up and over. Still, he managed it with enough speed that the RR agents had still not recovered by the time he flopped onto the walkway, rolled over, and got to his feet.

The immediate threat was the two agents still standing, so he moved for them first. A hit of Flare sent the first, then the second, Quick-Fix agent down as, for them, everything went white. A more simplistic but extreme version of Distract, Flare overloaded the senses of a victim so that to them it seemed as though they were assailed by an avalanche of noise and light. After what Distract had done to them, Grey didn't think they'd be getting up for a while, but he put two stun-lock rounds into their backs between joints in their body armour, then did the same for the other two, still crawling on the floor in a desperate attempt to find out where *up* had gone.

Then he stepped inside.

Grey's apartment was a mess. The first thing he noticed was the Quick-Fix agent who had fallen in, seemingly coming to his senses and slowly pulling himself to his feet. Grey put a stun-lock in the back of his neck, at the joint where helmet met armour.

The second thing he noticed was what had been blocking the door.

The bodies of two more Quick-Fix agents lay in the entrance hall, or at least what remained of them. They were now not much more than blackened, vaguely human-shaped lumps of coal wrapped in slightly singed anti-ballistic fibre. They appeared to be screaming, though Grey knew this was just what happened when a body went taut as it burned up.

The third thing he noticed was Fen standing framed against the office window, feral look draining from his face as he saw Grey entering, and the Quick-Fix agent outside that same window swinging in towards the glass.

Fen didn't even have time to turn as the glass splintered inwards and showered over him, the assaulting agent landing expertly on their feet behind him and instantly detaching their rappelling rope. Before Grey could do anything they had raised their gun and fired two quick shots, the distinct, dull sound of stun-lock rounds filling the room at the same time as Fen collapsed forward to the floor.

Fortunately, the Quick-Fix agent seemed just as surprised to see Grey as Grey was at the agent's sudden arrival. More so, in fact, because Grey at least was prepared for the possibility of further attacks, which was useful because it gave him the time he needed to hit this agent with Flare as well, and then use another stun-lock round to neutralise them.

Grey rushed over to Fen's side, kneeling down beside him. The boy was breathing but unconscious. Grey pulled the two stun-lock rounds out of his back, the needle tips drawing from the flesh they were embedded in easily but slick with blood. The holes, only a little larger than a pin prick, would heal easily enough, though the boy would have some extensive bruising from such close-range shots. For any of this to be a concern, though, they needed to get out of here as fast as possible. Grey grabbed the boy and flung him over his shoulder. He was surprisingly light.

Holding his stun-lock ahead of him, Grey ran back the way he'd come. He needed to keep moving, get out and away before more RR arrived. He sprinted out of his door and to the left, moving for the stairs at the same time as footsteps and neutral, emotionless shouts told him more were coming in from below.

The dash up five flights of stairs was one of the worst experiences of his life. There was something about yet *another* flight to climb that took away the frantic thoughtlessness of even a life-or-death situation, and by the time he reached the top he was cursing as he gasped for air. Somehow, though, he'd made it. He stepped out onto the roof...

And remembered that the last Quick-Fix agent must have been rappelling down from *somewhere.*

A team of five black-clad figures turned to face him as he stepped out, rifles raised and most definitely not set to use stun rounds.

"Put the boy down," said the central figure, voice masked as always.

I put Fen down and they shoot me, Grey thought to himself.

He was certain the only reason they hadn't fired yet was the risk of hitting the kid. The targeting system on the rifles would soon confirm a trajectory within an acceptable margin of error, he had no doubt, but either way Grey was hardly going to use Fen as a shield.

Lacking any other option, Grey knelt to gently place Fen on the ground. Tensing as he prepared to stand and face whatever was to happen, he barely had time to register the flicker of the boy's eyelids before the five figures ahead were suddenly enveloped in golden flame bright enough to turn the night into day. The flame curled around the writhing, screaming figures and poured upwards, twisting and spiralling into a huge column above them that slowly took on the form of a giant, scaled dragon.

The creature roared without noise at the night sky as the agents collapsed to the ground, jaw parting wide to reveal jagged fangs longer than a man's arm. Its leviathan head tilted back and stretched towards the heavens, the moon framed between the upper and lower jaw and shining through sharpened teeth as if with a single snap the dragon would swallow it whole. Though no noise beyond the hissing and crackling of the flame came, Grey could *feel* the creature's cry rattle his core.

The wings of the behemoth unfurled until they blocked out the stars, casting a baleful orange glow over everything, and its long, serpentine neck curled around for the monster to stare down at the fallen forms beneath its clawed feet.

Narrow, cat-like eyes blinked once, then the entire thing winked out of existence.

"Damn kid," said Grey, swaying with exhaustion and rubbing his eyes as the darkness returned. "Is it me, or did you add a few details?"

A flash of light and a sudden roar filled the night sky as something streaked across the city towards them, growing closer at an unbelievable rate. It reached its zenith what seemed like half the city away, yet tore down upon them before Grey could do anything but struggle to draw a breath to shout. With a boom louder than anything Grey had ever heard, it smashed into the building somewhere below.

The floor beneath him cracked and fell away in a tumult of heat and sound, and the world went black.

10

The pre-Fall industrially-developed society was populated by genius magicians. At the flick of a switch they could summon fire or light, and command great machines to do their bidding. With the touch of a screen they could access information that made them more knowledgeable than any of the ancient philosophers. And yet this still wasn't enough. Still they destroyed themselves.

Carlos Arthawan, *On Reclamation*

Everything hurt. Parts of his body he didn't even know *could* hurt, hurt. Which was strange, because there was no way he should be feeling anything at all.

Did I just get hit by a goddam missile?

"Oh *madre mia*, tell me the afterlife isn't just more of the same..." he moaned to whoever might be listening.

Eventually, he forced himself to open his eyes.

Well, if this was the afterlife it was a very disappointing one. In fact, he'd go so far as to say this appeared to be a pretty typical Albores back alley, down to the really quite shockingly large rat that was eyeballing him from atop the nearest power junction box fixed to one of the walls enclosing this narrow space.

The rat jumped down with an annoyed squeak and scuttled away, disappearing into some hole Grey couldn't make out in the gloom. Something moved behind him.

With a groan, Grey rolled over onto his other side. Fen was half-sitting, half-lying a little way away against a wall, soaked through with rain and stained with grey dust but apparently in much better condition than Grey. The boy looked up, noticing Grey was back among the living.

"Are... are you ok?" Fen asked. It was the first time Grey had heard something like concern in his voice.

"Nnng..." Grey tried to respond but found himself choking on gravel and dust. After a few moments coughing and spluttering, and then wiping the remains of his apartment building from his face, he tried again.

"I'm fine. What the hell happ... How are we alive?"

Fen looked at him with a quizzical expression, as if not understanding the question.

"I wouldn't let you fall," the boy said, matter-of-factly.

"You... you wouldn't *let* me fall? The whole damn *building* came down beneath us. We should be... wait, where are we, anyway?" Grey looked around, but nothing about the alleyway stood out to him.

Somewhere nearby, though, sirens echoed through the night.

"Damn it, we're still close, aren't we?" he said with sudden realisation. "How long was I out?"

"Not long," said Fen, worry tinging his voice. "We rolled quite far in the explosion, and then I got us into this alley. I didn't know where to go."

"It's ok, kid. You did good," Grey replied, wanting to reassure the suddenly uncertain child. "You did fantastic. I should be pulverised into ready-pack paste by now."

Fen smiled at that, pleased by a shared piece of knowledge about the world beyond his former prison.

"And you *will* have to explain how you saved us," Grey continued. "But right now we need to get out of here. That dragon of yours seems to have changed things from *find-and-capture* to *seek-and-destroy*. Besides, it must have been seen by half the city. God knows who's going to come check out this mess."

Grey lifted himself up by his elbows. Something inside his chest creaked, and a stabbing pain warned him of a badly-bruised rib, if not broken. He pushed the pain aside and stood up.

The squeal of tires from one direction made him turn to head the opposite way.

"Come on," he said, offering his hand to Fen. "Let's get out of here."

They ran into the night. It was once again starting to rain.

The first thing to do when being hunted was to get off the grid. This was easier said than done, Grey knew. Surveillance was *everywhere* in Albores - anything could be a camera, and usually was. Simple but effective facial recognition programs could scan and analyse live visual data anywhere in the city in minutes, so you had to keep your head down and keep moving. A notification on some anonymous agency screen could be informing on their whereabouts right now.[4]

---

[4] Ironically, objections that such all-pervasive surveillance violated the right to privacy meant that information regarding who actually had access to said surveillance, and what was done with it, was kept extremely private.

Fortunately, Grey knew something that wasn't generally broadcast to the general public. This was that, though surveillance was indeed everywhere, there were areas of the city where this surveillance was less than effective. The older parts of downtown were among these.

It wasn't that the cameras themselves were lesser in either quantity or quality, however. It was instead that, somehow, a large number of them found their functions impaired. An old piece of fencing stacked nearby, perhaps, obscuring the view, or an overly large decorative plant hung just below and growing in such a way as to cover the lens. Maybe renovations to a building meant a new awning sticking out just so and cutting off half the visual range, or some carelessly placed crates were stacked just where they would be in the way.

Oh, there was never any *vandalism*, nothing to attract anything more than a few questions which, if the authorities were even able to identify the responsible party, were inevitably met with profuse apologies and promises to swiftly resolve the unfortunate mistake, but there were an *awful* lot of these 'mistakes'.

It had gone on for so long that these days the local enforcement agencies didn't even bother trying to prevent it. Besides, everywhere needs a place to be a little less… observed, shall we say. Grey had spotted plenty of the city's more influential people there at one time or another. Sometimes even those who made the laws needed a place to avoid them.

So they made their way downtown. It took hours.

Grey had never really realised how large the city was before now. There had always been an auto-cab to take him wherever he wanted. To use one now, though, or to use anything that required payment via his thin-screen, would be tantamount to painting a very large 'we're right here' sign on his back and marching up and down the street loudly declaring the same thing.

So they walked, taking the side roads and back alleys as often as they could, and cutting through the many empty blocks that would one day, if metropolitan planning was to be believed, be thriving commercial areas.

They spoke little as they made their way through the silty rain, too exhausted and too wet to form words. At one point Grey realised that Fen, for all his quiet resoluteness, was shivering violently, and he passed his jacket to him. Its tail trailed on the ground behind the boy but seemed to warm him somewhat.

After a few hours of this they huddled beneath an old road-bridge, waiting for the rain to break.

The second thing to do when being hunted was to find help. The most difficult people for Grey to trace had always been the ones with contacts. Not family, not friends, but connections with the right inclination and right attitude towards law enforcement - the right inclination being absolute mistrust and the right attitude being one of complete and utter noncompliance. An Aether user with the right sort of contacts could give the Agency the run-around for weeks, even months.

It felt strange to be on the wrong end of a chase. Grey was used to being the one *doing* the chasing, but now he was going to have to try everything those he had ever hunted tried, only better. Grey had never let anyone get away.

So, they needed help. And to get help, they needed cash. This shouldn't have been a problem. Grey always kept a small safe full of the stuff in his office, for use on his trips to places like *Methuselah's End* where not everyone he talked with wanted to leave a digital trace. Unfortunately, said safe was now buried under several tons of what had been his apartment complex, if it had survived at all.

Which meant they needed an *envío*, and that was going to be a problem.

Envío had been around since the earliest days of the Reclamation, a time when only the strongest, most able of the millions of refugees crowding the beaches and ghettos of what would become the Carib-Federation were able to endure the struggles of the return to the mainland. This meant the breadwinners of thousands, hundreds of thousands, of families leaving their relatives to an uncertain fate. While there was a basic universal welfare structure established on the many reclaimed or artificial islands teeming with these families, this had been overwhelmed and underperforming from the earliest days of its introduction, and the vast camps and slums of the islands were regularly struck by storms both political and literal.

So there was an immediate and constant demand by those at the spearhead of the Reclamation to send what they could home, and it was *envíos* who did the sending. It was no small feat, moving goods and finances through the many layers that separated the emerging mainland society from the more established ones beyond the shores, and each layer added more and more to the 'costs,' both formal and informal, of these movements.

Added to this, there was soon the additional demand for the movement of not only goods but people. Initially, this was a movement of people seeking to move away from the Carib-Federation and beyond, into the Reclamation itself. Even with all the incentives and policies created specifically to hurry the movement of people out of the camps onto the mainland, bureaucracy and red tape made this a slower process than many could tolerate. And then, as the authoritarian realities of the Reclamation settlements and the harshness of the waste beyond set in, a parallel demand grew for *return* to the places they had left.

And so the *envío* made money. And more money. All of it in the shadows of the fledgling official economy. Yet shadows are often longer than that which casts them, and indeed *envíos* had at some points been as powerful, if not more powerful, than the purported authorities of new settlements and cities. Only with the constitution of state-controlled armed forces and law enforcement agencies had their power been severely curtailed, often bloodily.

Still, though, the *envíos* operated from their old shadows, moving people and products across the porous and ill-defined borders of the growing Federation-to-be, as well as dealing in other, less salubrious vocations.

As a Far Agent, Grey had only ever had an antagonistic relationship with these figures, and this history had carried over to his days as a Commercial Inquiry Agent. What little information he could procure from them always came at a far higher cost than it would for anyone else. Burning bridges had always come easier to him than building them.

Luckily, he knew someone who had been building bridges since before this city was even a city.

Contacting Jeder Francisco wasn't the problem. The problem was contacting him without betraying their location to whoever was currently looking for them.

It took the better part of a day, moving around the areas Grey knew Francisco carried out much of his purposely ill-defined business. Places where people gathered to share information and gossip without being seen to do so, bars and haunts like the *Methuselah's End*. There were plenty of these downtown, wedged between the more populated and developed north and the abandoned areas to the south; almost abandoned, at least. Grey now knew the *Forever Fallen* made their home there.

The thought of the *Forever Fallen* planted the seeds of a plan in his mind.

They finally cornered Francisco late in the day, and by this point both he and Fen must have looked for all the world like some pre-Fall itinerants, homeless and filthy. Both of them were bloodied and covered in dust that the rain had done nothing to clean away, and in desperate need of sleep.

"*Mierda!*" Francisco cried out in surprise as Grey grabbed him and dragged him off the street into the alley. Grey expertly knocked the youthful geriatric's hand down and away from the piece Francisco was instinctively reaching for, tucked into a holster at his side.

"*¡Tranquilícese!* It's me. It's just me," said Grey, spinning Francisco around to face him and releasing his hold on the man.

Francisco got halfway in reaching for his gun again before recognition showed in his expression.

"Nestor Grey!" he said with surprise. "You be more careful next time. I could have shot you."

"You'd have to be a lot faster with that antique than you are," Grey replied in quieter tones, a smile flickering across his face.

Francisco grinned back. He had carried the same handgun for as long as Grey had known him, and claimed it was a pre-Fall piece. For all Grey knew, that was true. It certainly wasn't a modern firearm but even had it been, Grey was a fully trained Far Agent. Few amateurs would get the drop on him - though Francisco had been surprisingly difficult to sense in the Aether. Grey put that down to exhaustion.

"*Claro, claro*. Still, if I did I'd make quite the days' worth, *si?* Plenty of people looking for you now." Francisco's eyes drifted to Fen, half hidden behind Grey, and narrowed. "*Para los dos.*"

"People are looking for me?" Grey asked.

"Since this morning, at least. Suddenly the whole town is talking about how there's good *dinero* on offer for some snoop and a kid he's with. Wasn't hard to put together, after the questions you were asking yesterday." Francisco held up his hands, showing they were empty. "But, you know, I've always liked working with you. *Me gusta tu personalidad*. Enough that I won't sell you out *right* away, at least."

"I'll owe you another one though, right?" Grey said.

Francisco's grin grew broader.

"They're offering a *lot* for you. Especially with the kid as well. You'll have to make up for my loss somehow."

Grey nodded.

"And I will. But first, I need your help."

"*El envío?*"

Grey gave thanks to whatever deity was listening for Francisco's ability to cut to the chase.

"Yes. I need cash, and I need it untraceable."

"*No será facile*. You'll need to match whatever the street is offering for your head. And don't think you can pretend to be someone else, or use your hocus-pocus tricks on them. Your face is all over the place. They'll know who you are, and what you can do. You think you have anything of value to trade?"

Grey had been ready for this. An inventory of his remaining possessions had led him to the disheartening realisation that all he now owned was in the pockets of the clothing he was currently wearing. Fortunately, in one of those pockets was something the seedier side of the city would pay handsomely for.

"How do you think they'd feel about an unlocked Far Agency thin-screen?" he said, drawing out the device he had 'borrowed' from the agents at Blane's home what felt like a lifetime ago.

Francisco's eyebrows rose.

"*En serio?* You surprise me again! *Sí*, that should be enough to get their interest."

Francisco's eyes narrowed again, this time at Grey.

"You are serious? Nestor Grey, Far trained and Far owned, selling stolen Far goods?"

Far owned? Grey hadn't been aware he was perceived like that.

"You didn't think people down here thought of you as one of them, did you?" Francisco said, reading Grey's expression. "You're a good guy, Nestor, and you've helped more than a few people around here. But you're still *agencia*. Still *federales*. You don't know half of what goes on down here." He glanced towards Fen again. "But, I am thinking you will learn."

11

There is very little that should be outright banned in the new order of things. It is the forbidden fruit that offers the strongest temptation. However, this does not mean such temptation should be cultivated. Supply chain limitations need not only be obstacles to overcome. Indeed, they can be a tool.

Attribution unknown, *Unspoken Founding Principles of the Reclamation* (Unsanctioned Digital Document)

Francisco brought them to what he called a "safe house" by one of his private vehicles. Grey hadn't even known he had his own car, let alone a number of them.

Let alone a whole floor of a building set aside to conduct "business."[5]

The place was *massive*, and furnished in ways that wouldn't have looked out of place in the high-rent areas of the Carib-Fed. A lot of this stuff was, if not illegal, still highly discouraged throughout the mainland. Public access to Fabricators only meant practically anything *could* be built, with the right raw materials, and raw materials were still at a premium even generations into the Reclamation. Beyond what were classed as necessities - things like thin-screens, clothing, furnishings, and entertainment systems - requisitioning or purchasing could be an exhausting slog through red tape.

And there weren't enough scissors in the world to cut through the red tape surrounding some of the stuff here. Grey was fairly sure that was real gold trim on the chairs and chests of drawers liberally scattered around the main living area, and some of the paintings hanging on the walls looked like they had been valuable *before* the Fall.

Grey had heard the word ostentatious before, but never really understood its meaning until now.

"*Mi casa, su casa*," said Francisco as he'd led them in. He seemed somehow taller in this place, with a swagger Grey had never seen.

"This place is *yours?*" Grey had been unable to stop himself breathlessly exclaiming as they stepped inside.

"Well, technically *desocupado*. But, yes, this is my place." Francisco said with a chuckle.

---

[5] Grey was coming to realise that much of the language used to talk about Francisco required quotation marks.

"You made me pay for your *drinks*," Grey said.

"And you got your money's worth from me many times. You think I got all this doing things *gratis*?"

It was a fair point. Still…

"You are wondering why I chose to spend my time helping out a small-time information broker?" continued Francisco, once again pre-empting Grey's own words. "As I said, *señor agente*, you are a good man. I like you."

Grey wondered what he'd ever done for Francisco to warrant this. He didn't think he'd ever done anything to help the man directly.

"Not me, Nestor."

Francisco interrupted Grey's thoughts again, and again with such eerie accuracy that for a moment Grey entertained the notion that Francisco was a secret Aether user, Reading him.

"I heard about you long before you heard about me, Grey. All the way back to when you were in Far. A *federale* who actually tries to help people? We don't see many of them around here. And especially not a *federale* who challenges his fellow agents when they are, shall we say, overreaching their authority."

It had never occurred to Grey that the various troubles that arose between himself and agents he'd worked the streets with could be common knowledge, but then again, he had also not been the most circumspect when he felt a fellow agent was being overenthusiastic in the use of their abilities.

"Wait here," Francisco said. Not waiting for an answer, he turned and walked out the way they'd come.

Which left Grey and Fen standing in the most luxurious apartment, no, *suite* he'd ever been in.

The main living space where they stood was larger than his own entire apartment had been, dark mahogany flooring contrasting with the rich whites of the walls and furnishings. A huge sofa of what seemed to Grey's admittedly untrained eyes to be real leather[6] took up the centre of the room, a wide glass table set in front of it upon which stood a bowl of actual *fruit*. There were peaches, for god's sake. Grey had only seen peaches in movies.

Both sofa and table were oriented to face what some would mistake for a blank white wall. Only the soft blinking of a small light

---

[6] Leather, and the cattle species that such materials came from, was almost entirely a thing of the past.

seemingly from within the wall told the observer that the entire surface was LEF - Light Emitting Fabric. Voice-controlled, Grey had no doubt. At a word, images at a fidelity more detailed than the human eye could see would appear from what appeared to be plain, though rather fine, wallpaper.

A framed oil-on-canvas hung on the opposite wall, a rendering of a wide river under the kind of blue sky you got before the Fall, before the atmosphere filled with dust and ash and the toxic fumes of a hundred thousand mass cremations to become a persistent dull grey. Wedged between the river and the sky was a building on fire, the flames that poured from it towards the heavens reflected dull red in the waters below. Dark clothed spectators crowded the river bank across from the conflagration, staring at it with a helplessness and futility that was unsettling.

Grey didn't know art, but it looked expensive.

There was a shelf running beneath the painting, filled with what Grey would have called Bric-a-Brac if not for the feeling that each of the small ornaments was probably worth more than he made in a year. He could identify none of it, save for the crystal-cut scale model of the Great Pyramid of Giza, a perfect depiction of the monument, blackened glass melted and misshapen by nuclear fire.

"Woah…"

Grey had never heard Fen say "woah" before, or anything like it. He turned slowly, worried by what exactly could stun a child capable of conjuring a blazing monster of instant death.

"Woah."

This time it was Grey.

It hadn't been visible from the entrance, but now they had stepped inside a small recessed area had come into view. And in that recess…

"Impossible…" Grey caught himself. He was beginning to get tired of saying that.

What they were looking at was most *definitely* not only discouraged in the Reclamation, but enough to get you imprisoned, if not disappeared entirely.

It ran from floor to ceiling, a tall, heavy grey monolith of smooth metal and plastiglass. The front was darkly opaque, revealing only murky silhouettes hinting at the complex nest of cables, valves, and extruders within.

It was a Fabricator. Not only that, it was a *Personal* Fabricator.

If you were to try to explain a Fabricator to someone from the pre-Fall era, you would probably start by asking them to visualise a 3D printer. Then, ask them to consider the abacus.

An abacus, you could then say, was to a supercomputer running simulations of nuclear fission as a 3D printer was to a Fabricator. That is, completely incomparable and barely useful as an example.

And a personal fabricator was like having access to all that from the comfort of your living room.

The invention and functioning of the machines known as Fabricators was shrouded in mystery, at least for citizens beyond the borders of the Althing Republic, or the Silicon Isle, as it was more commonly known. And, once upon a time, Iceland.

How the island nation had survived through the Sudden War and subsequent Fall was the topic of discussion and conjecture in halls and bars across the continent, and beyond for all Grey knew. Though most of the northern hemisphere above the 45th parallel was even today considered an uninhabitable hellhole of frozen waste, somehow Iceland, or the Althing Republic as its ambassadors demanded it be called, prospered.

It was the introduction of Althing fabricators, and the offer of their use under an extensive lend-lease agreement, that had allowed the Reclamation to progress at the pace it had. Without the apparently no-strings-attached usage of such machines, not even half the currently existing infrastructure and devices on which the population of the mainland depended could have been developed.

The Silicon Isle didn't even ask for payment, at least not much. Enough to cover costs, they said. Either way, the amount was negligible even for the disparate command economy of the mainland. Some theorised the price was so low because the whole of the Silicon Isle was now one huge geothermal power plant, a land of unlimited free energy where all could live like a king.

They laid only one condition on their offer: to be left alone. For access to their fabricators, for the usage of their tech, they insisted their borders be respected. And their borders were *closed*.

Grey had heard stories of amateur adventurers taking to the skies in an attempt to find out what lay behind that curtain of mystery. It was said no one ever returned. Of course, Grey knew the more rational explanation was that any untrained pilot attempting to navigate the tempestuous air currents of the icy Atlantic was likely to find themselves only a watery grave, but it made for a good modern-day ghost story.

The thing was, Fabricators were *huge*. As in, industrial-sized machinery needing staff and an entire series of warehouses to manage their input/output resources and materials. Hence the warehouse districts. These provided both storage areas for the huge amounts of raw materials the machines required - organic, inorganic, natural, synthetic; even refuse could be broken down and restructured - and for the refined products they produced.

Personal fabricators, on the other hand, were almost portable, and heavily restricted. They were worse than germline editing technology; of course, still able to produce any type of viral vector a crazed mind could dream of, but almost as a side show. Such a thing wouldn't even require much organic matter. Hell, get some radioactive material and you could make a thermonuclear bomb.

Pan-Fed would be down on this apartment like a meteorite on a bunch of unsuspecting dinosaurs if even a hint of its existence got out. *Every* government agency would be down on this place, from local law enforcement to Far to Quick Fix. Personal Fabricators were *not* something you just found in someone's apartment.

"You think it can make cheesecake?" asked Fen. "I've never tried cheesecake."

"Yes…" said Grey, not taking his eyes off the machine. *Who the hell is Francisco, really?* "I think it probably can…"

12

With the declaration and institution of the articles of Federation, the cities of the Reclamation are combined to enjoy all the benefits of a centralised state. However, until such time as the situation warrants, the Reclamation Authority maintains supreme authority over all issues regarding the resettlement of the continent.

Processes of Regulation and Order in the Reclamation (Sanctioned Digital Document)

Francisco didn't return that night. Fen fell asleep on the sofa surrounded by the final few crumbs of cheesecake, solitary survivors of an appetite Grey found hard to believe could exist in such a skinny frame. The kid had practically *inhaled* the cake.

They'd found packs of a flour-like substance in the kitchen and fed this to the fabricator, typing "cheesecake" in on the touch screen built into the side. A few minutes of mysterious whirring and hissing later, and a still-warm, freshly baked cheesecake appeared in the dispenser.

Grey waited for the boy to be soundly sleeping before returning to the machine and typing "ammo." After 10 minutes of scrolling through the frankly bewildering list of choices he still hadn't found what he was looking for. There were thousands of makes and models listed; it seemed like the designs for every weapon and firearm since the dawn of time were accessible on this machine, and this must be only a tiny proportion of the stored designs.

SHOW ME THE WEAPON.

Grey blinked twice, concerned that lack of sleep was making him hallucinate.

SHOW ME THE WEAPON.

The words remained on the touchscreen, bold and unchanging.

Trying not to shake, he slowly drew his stun-lock from his side and held it up to the screen. For several seconds nothing happened, except that he felt slightly foolish.

Something clicked in the machine, and again a whirring and hissing came from somewhere inside.

Three stun-lock bullets rolled out of a small dispenser near the bottom of the machine, and the screen changed again

INSUFFICIENT MATERIAL.

Fortunately, there was whisky in the kitchen. He grabbed a whole bottle and took deep swigs of it as he explored the rest of the apartment.

Aside from the main area, there were two expansive bedrooms and a second, smaller room that looked like a study. There were actual paper books on the shelves that again looked old enough to be pre-Fall. Behind them, a wide window showed the lights of the city stretching out below.

The thing was, none of this place looked lived in. The beds were tucked and folded like a hotel, the study a thing of straight lines and orderly storage, and there wasn't a speck of dust in the whole place. Of course, with apparent wealth like this Francisco could have just used hired help, but Grey didn't think there was any help in the world you could trust to keep a secret like the Fabricator in the other room.

He stood there, bottle in hand, staring out as the city moved through the night below.

"*Buenos días, señor Grey.*"

Grey didn't remember falling onto one of the beds, but he must have because the next thing he knew Francisco was standing in the open doorway of the room as oddly-bright sunlight streamed in through the small windows high up the walls.

"I am sorry to have kept you waiting so long, but these things require time, you know?" continued Francisco.

The man had a smile on his lips and a liveliness in his words that stood in complete contrast to how Grey felt. The past few days seemed to have caught up with him all at once, along with - now he noticed the empty bottle lying on the floor nearby - the whisky from the night before providing support.

"You sorted a meeting?" asked Grey, pushing himself groggily up and swinging his legs off the bed.

"*Sí*. But we have some time. For now, you should perhaps wash up and change, yes? There is a change of clothes already in the washroom for you. We will wait for you in the living room."

It was only then that Grey became aware of Fen standing just behind Francisco, glass in hand and drinking what appeared to be a fresh smoothie through a straw. The boy gave him a wave, then turned and headed back to the living room.

The sudden mental image of a towering column of Mindfire made

Grey's headache worse.

"*Gracias,* Francisco. I'll be there soon."

In the end, he took longer than he had meant to. The washroom was a thing of beauty, and the shower almost magically restorative. There wasn't even a restrictor on the water supply; no time limits or daily litre allowance here. Grey barely even wondered about his. After everything he had seen in this apartment, access to clean water beyond the usual limit was hardly worth thinking about. The Reclamation Authority projected only a year or two more of water restrictions for Albores anyway. Purification and detoxification programs were on time and, amazingly, apparently within budget, so this was the least of the mysteries of the place.

Francisco had indeed prepared clothing for him. In fact, he'd prepared *exactly* the right clothing, down to the slightly broader shoulders and collar Grey input when placing his own orders for clothing. Which meant either Francisco had an incredible eye for tailoring or he had access to Grey's Requisition history, which shouldn't have been possible.

Feeling the most human he'd felt in days, Grey went to the living room. Francisco and Fen were both sitting on the sofa, the entire wall in front of them showing an old, black-and-white movie. Some kind of giant lizard crashed through high power lines while old-world artillery and tanks blasted round after round ineffectively towards it. Grey tensed as the monster reared back and unleashed a stream of fire from its mouth and set a row of buildings ablaze. All the while, soldiers shouted in a language Grey was unfamiliar with.

He shivered. The idea of Fen getting any more ideas regarding giant, unstoppable fire-breathing lizards was not something Grey welcomed.

"Uh, so, what are we doing here then?" he said loudly.

The two didn't seem to hear him, or at least they took no notice.

"*Mira, niño.* See how they did this? Before any digital effects, before motion capture or even computers? *Increíble!*" Francisco sounded genuinely excited as he spoke.

Fen looked no less excited. In fact, he looked enthralled. He didn't blink as he watched, deep and dramatic orchestral music filling the room as the monster on the huge screen strode through the destruction it had wrought, pouring more flame into the buildings burning all around it.

Half of Grey's mind *knew* the effects were cheap, the buildings obviously hollow models and the flaming breath of the monster clearly superimposed over the film. Yet the other half of his mind worried if *Fen* knew that.

The chill that ran down his spine was becoming unpleasantly familiar.

Grey took another step into the room, coming around to stand beside the screen and into the sight line of the audience. Francisco at least seemed to notice him then.

"Ah, but maybe we finish this another day, eh, *niño*? I think to business now. Screen off."

Fen seemed to come out of his trance as the screen winked out, staring around him as if only just realising where he was. He registered Grey with a nod, and then reached down and grabbed an apple from the bowl. It was the last piece of fruit left - evidently, the boy had been enjoying his time here.

"Maybe we discuss this in the study?" said Grey, looking meaningfully from Francisco to Fen.

"No, no, *no te preocupes,*" replied Francisco, waving at Grey to sit in a chair that had somehow appeared there since last night. "My boy here, he is already very much involved, I think. He will need to hear what I say."

Francisco paused suddenly, a quizzical expression on his face. He turned to Fen.

"My boy, I am sorry. What *is* your name?"

Fen stopped halfway through a bite of his apple, looking lost.

It was only then that Grey realised that he'd been thinking of the child as *Fen* since he'd heard the story of the name his old caretaker had given him, but never used it with the boy.

"Fen," said Grey. "This is Fen."

Grey looked to Fen to check the boy's reaction. With a small smile and nod, the boy returned to his food.

"Ok, Fen, *encantado de conocerte.*" Francisco gave his own small smile, then turned back to Grey. "So, this was *not* easy to set up. I had to be *very* circumspect with the details, you see, and *envío* do not like uncertainty. Still, I found one willing to meet. The offer of a Far Agency thin-screen is a difficult one to turn down."

Grey felt a tightening of his chest at the mention of the thin-screen. In the fear and exhaustion of last night, offering such a trade had seemed... if not easy, then the only thing he could think of. It *still* felt like the only way. But it was also an incredible breach of trust, and, indeed, something that could put his former fellows in danger. Who knew what kind of person he would be making this offer to?

He glanced at Fen. It *was* the only way. Besides, the agency would *have* to notice a missing thin-screen at some point; then they could simply disallow its network privileges.

"When and where?" Grey asked, forcing confidence and certainty into his voice.

The *when* turned out to be later that day, as the early evening sun dipped below the grey horizon and the fuzzy grey of the blurred moon emerged high above. The *where* was underneath the broken ruins of a pre-Fall highway, a dusty and empty patch of Waste far outside the city. It would take hours to get there even in the over-sized 4x4 Francisco produced, a monstrosity of a machine that wouldn't have fit down many of the more narrow streets in central Albores.

"Who exactly *are* you, Francisco?" Grey asked after they clambered in, the car moving off as soon as Francisco keyed in their destination.

Francisco grinned and held a finger up to his lips.

"No, Grey, that I cannot tell you. A man in my line of work, he must keep his secrets."

"Keep his secrets?" replied Grey, heat rising in his voice. "You let me see a goddam *fabricator* in your place, and you talk about secrets?"

Francisco's face went hard at that.

"My place, *señor*? No, I think you will find there is no record or any trace of evidence to link me to that apartment, even if it were found. And of course, it *won't* be found, will it, Grey? Because if you ever need my help again... well, let's just say *when* you need my help again, you will want me in a friendly mood."

And that seemed to be that. Francisco and Fen spent most of the time chatting about old movies - Francisco seemed to be even more of an old-movie buff than Grey, with access to a selection Grey could only dream of getting past Reclamation censor algorithms - and watching clips of famous scenes on a thin-screen.

Grey watched the old man with the middle-aged form as the car drove itself. Before everything that had happened, he had not even entertained the thought that the man could be dangerous. Now, he felt an almost overwhelming sense of threat from the mysterious, ever-grinning figure.

The car abruptly juddered before coming to a halt, a loud beeping from the navigator system indicating unsafe terrain.

"Ah," said Francisco, rolling up his thin-screen and placing it in his pocket. "Now we are leaving civilisation, I must drive. No roads out this far."

With another of his smiles, he jumped from the car and went around to the back, pulling something out from beneath heavy blankets. Both Grey and Fen murmured surprise and Francisco held up what for all the world looked like a steering wheel.

"This car can go *manual?*" exclaimed Fen, as Grey stopped himself from asking the same thing. Francisco smiled wider and, without saying anything, moved around to the front.

The steering wheel slid into a hollow cylindrical opening to one side of the dashboard, and as it did so foot pedals snapped out below. Pushing a set of commands into the navigation console to disengage it, Francisco was suddenly *driving*.

Grey tried not to show his uneasiness at being inside a human-controlled machine. Of course, he knew how to drive himself, but it was a rare moment when he actually had to do so, and having someone else in control of the vehicle he was in was unnerving. The jarring and juddering as they moved off over broken rock and sand didn't help to make this any better.

In the rear window the low squat buildings of the Albores outskirts grew hazy with both distance and dust thrown up by their vehicle's passage, and everywhere else the broken world stretched out in cracked, weed-strewn desolation, the land somehow parched despite the near-ceaseless rain of a climate in turmoil.[7]

The meeting point under the broken highway came into view as Albores was fading, a cracked, jagged lump of concrete jutting into the air like a fallen giant's dagger. What once must have been an elevated road many metres above the ground had tumbled down and in upon itself, most of it now buried beneath the dirt and dust of

---

[7] The rain, filled with particulate matter and pollutants, provided little nutrition to that which it fell on. It could even be suffocating to plant life. Access to purified water was in fact one of the major limiting factors in the timescale of the Reclamation.

years past. This section, however, remained half standing, tilting upwards from the ground to form a dark overhang beneath which nothing could be seen. Bent and twisted metal hung from its edges, wind-battered signage littering the area with old place names Grey wouldn't have recognised even had the lettering remained legible.

The car pulled up some ways before it, Francisco turning to them.

"We walk from here," he said. "No one drives closer than this for these meetings. It is good to see who is approaching from afar."

They climbed out of the car onto the crusty ground, both Grey and Fen instantly raising their hands to shield their eyes from the bright sun and swirling dust. The tinted windows of the car had hidden the fact that a strong wind was blowing all around, clearing the grey skies so that a trace of blue could even be seen in them, making a rare passage for the sun. It shone down brighter than any of them were used to, though Francisco at least took it in his stride.

"Ah, fresh air," said Francisco, taking in a mocking long breath of it. How he didn't choke on the dust Grey couldn't fathom. "Good for the soul, eh?"

Francisco held out a cloth to the both of them, keeping another one for himself and wrapping it around his head to cover both mouth and nose.

"Still, can have too much of a good thing, right?" he said beneath his makeshift mask. "Use this. There's more dust out here than in your fair city."

Your city. Francisco seemed not to have noticed the slip, but Grey had. *Where are you from then, Francisco?*

There was no time to ask, even if he'd wanted to. Grey hurried after Francisco, who had swiftly turned and was leading the way, a hand planted on Fen protectively to help the boy over the rough terrain.

They made their way in silence, the wind seeming to pick up strength with every step they took towards their goal, trying to push them back. As they got closer, a solitary figure became gradually visible, a small blot standing in the shadow of the raised edge of the broken section of highway.

"My contact!" cried Francisco over the wind, turning back to look at Grey and pointing towards the figure.

As they continued moving forwards, Grey had less and less time to look forwards towards his companions and their destination. The ground underfoot became more and more covered by smashed debris, jagged lumps of concrete and spikes of old steel thrusting upwards as if designed to pierce the unwary traveller. A stumble at one point left Grey with a cut to his hand, and another a slice to his shin.

Which is why he almost fell over Francisco and Fen when they came suddenly to a halt.

He wiped dust out of his eyes and looked around. There was still one or two hundred meters to go to the figure waiting in the shadows.

"What did you say, *niño?*" Francisco said, over a sudden lull in the wind.

"I said, didn't you say no one drives here?" Fen said.

Grey followed the boy's gaze with a sense of foreboding.

"*Si,* boy, *si.* It's why we have to do this *maldito* walk every time." Francisco replied, impatient to keep moving.

"Then why are there vehicle tracks over there...?"

Grey could see them too, now. Perhaps as far away to their left as the figure waiting for them was in front, but visible. There were deep tracks in the areas where the ground was relatively free of rubble, with shallower tracks still obvious here and there where it wasn't. Whatever had come through here was *heavy*.

"No, no... That's not right. That's not... They wouldn't..."

Francisco saw the tracks too now, eyes flicking worriedly from them to his companions to the figure still standing motionless below the highway.

"*Puta.* They want you more than I gave them credit for," said Francisco, his expression suddenly grave. He looked Fen and Grey in the eye in turn. "*Escúchame.* You need to get back to the vehicle. But the moment we turn back, they'll know they're made. So..."

Francisco swiftly turned and waved his hand at the waiting figure.

"*¡Hola mi amigo!*" he shouted over the wind. *"Un momento!* My friend, he is not used to this climbing, yes?"

Francisco turned back to them, passing something to Grey.

"Take this. It's my thin-screen. It will give you access to my car. Try to get away."

"You're not coming with us?" said Fen, fear clear in his voice.

Grey's eyes narrowed, taking in the set of Francisco's shoulders, the tension building in the man's muscles as he prepared to run.

"He's not leaving with us, but he is leaving," Grey said. "He's leaving us to save *himself*. He knows it's us they want."

Francisco looked from Fen to Grey and back, leaning down to give the boy a firm squeeze of his shoulders.

"*Lo siento, niño*. The man is right." He straightened up, looking directly at Grey. "I *am* sorry, my friend. An *envío* willing to betray their client to the RA is a thing I could not imagine, *y yo he imaginado muchas cosas*."

"So why help us get this far?" Grey asked. The distant figure seemed to be stirring.

"There are greater things at work here, Nestor, than I can say. There are those who wish to help you as well as those who wish to do you harm. *I* wish to help you. But I must *not* be seen to be involved."

Francisco turned back to face the waiting figure, who seemed to be speaking into a comms unit at his breast. He waved once more, causing the figure to hesitate.

"Now, *run*."

Grey grabbed Fen and span back the way they had come, heedless of the biting rocks beneath their feet. The sharp edges cut through the soles of his shoes now, at the pace they ran, and he had to concentrate intensely to prevent himself from falling. Fen stumbled beside him, and it took all he had to catch the boy and not go over himself.

The treacherous terrain fought them at every step, and the vehicle they were racing for seemed unbelievably distant. He heard noises behind them, shouting, the yelling of orders, and the sound of something heavy shifting into gear, but spent no time looking back. Dust and dirt filled his mouth, the cloth around his face falling to his shoulders from the jolting.

"Faster!" yelled Fen, lighter on his feet and pushing ahead. "It's coming!"

That made Grey look back. The split-second glance was enough to take in the large group of dark-uniformed, heavily armed figures that had appeared out of the darkness, and emerging from behind the highway a massive, caterpillar-tracked personnel carrier. Mounted atop the vehicle was a long-barrelled machine gun, the operator protected inside a dome of what Grey knew was ballistic glass.

Bullets began spattering into the ground around them in heavy, dull thuds that spat up yet more dirt and dust. One whizzed past

Grey's ear so close he could feel the wind of its passing, but none hit them. He realised why as Fen stumbled and slowed.

Grey scooped up the boy without hesitation, allowing Fen to focus on *pushing* the bullets away from them, and kept running. He could feel the blood from the soles of his feet making each step slippery but allowed himself no time to feel the pain. There would be time enough for that later, if they got out of this alive.

They reached the car at the same time as *something* came whooshing overhead, from the opposite direction to their pursuers. Grey pushed Fen into the car and quickly jumped in as well, swinging up into the driver's seat in time to see what it was.

A sleek, black drone was tearing towards their assailants, metres across in wingspan but with a form so thin and dark it looked more like a lump of sky torn out of reality than an actual machine. No, not *towards* their assailants. Slightly to their right, where Grey spotted Francisco running at an angle taking him away from both the car and the Quick Fix team.

In a second the drone was bearing down upon Francisco, and in the next second was swiftly banking away and *up*. Another millisecond later, and Francisco was yanked into the skies, trailing behind the drone on a monofilament line too thin to see from this distance.

Grey thought he saw Francisco twisting to look towards them as he was born away at incredible velocity. That, or the powerful pull into the skies had snapped his neck. There was no time for Grey to decide which.

He slammed the car into gear, muttering prayers and thanks to nameless deities as the tyres spun and the vehicle jerked into motion. He slung the wheel right and the car span with it, turning them away from the assaulting forces.

Bullets thudded into the glass, sending thin cracks through the window panes but not piercing through. Francisco had once again spared no expense, it seemed.

They tore across the Waste in a cloud of dust, moving as fast as they could *away* with no regard for *towards*. What mattered now was they get as much distance as possible between themselves and...

More bullets smashed against the side of the car, and bursting out of the dust to one side came the APC, terrifyingly close. Grey pushed harder on the accelerator pedal, and the car jumped like a rad-cat on a leash. The roar of the engine filled his ears.

"You reckon you can do something to help us out, kid?" Grey yelled over the noise, not taking his eyes off the terrain ahead. No reply came as he swung the car wildly around, zig-zagging in an attempt to shake their pursuer.

"Kid?"

Grey was forced to take his eyes off the, for want of a better word, road. He craned his neck around to look into the back of the car. Fen was lying sprawled against the rear seats, hands clutching his sides. Crimson ochre was dripping out between his fingers.

"Oh shit, kid. Oh no."

More bullets cracked against the side of the car, and Grey wrenched the vehicle away from the attack. Fen groaned at the movement.

"It's ok kid, it'll be ok. Just hold on, I'll get us out of this…"

But Grey had no idea *how* he was going to get them out of this, or even if Fen could hold on for that long. No matter how fast he pushed the car, the APC behind them kept up, relentlessly pouring bullets into them. Though heavier and slower, its tracks meant it rolled over the rubble and debris that threw their own vehicle from side to side.

A fracture in the rear window became a crack, and the crack a ragged hole. The whole thing was clearly about to shatter, and that would be that. There was no way Grey could protect them from the guns of that APC.

A huge explosion rocked the car, lifting it onto two wheels and almost rolling them over. At first, Grey thought the car itself had exploded, some fuel line bursting and igniting and spelling their end, but then their car righted itself and tore on.

Looking back through the rear view mirror - a feature Grey had thought an affectation, and a redundant one at that - he saw something that made his heart leap.

The APC lay on its back, tracks spinning futilely in the air. Nearby, a huge crater that hadn't been there a second ago released thick black smoke.

"What the…?"

He was forced to swerve the car to avoid the sudden appearance of two other vehicles, tearing past on either side of them towards the APC. Two long jeep-style cars, rear sections open to the air. At the back of one stood a woman with a long, wide cylinder resting on their shoulder.

A rocket launcher. A goddam *rocket launcher*.

The newcomers bore down on the upturned APC where the first of those inside were attempting to climb out a buckled side door. Without hesitation, the woman fired a second rocket at close range. The APC exploded in a ball of fire and smoke that, when it cleared, revealed only shredded metal and a burnt-out husk of what had been there before.

Now what the hell was going on? There wasn't time enough for the *why* to matter to Grey, but definitely the *what* seemed important. Were these friends? Some of the mysterious allies Francisco had hinted at? Or was this some other group hunting them - or, more specifically, hunting Fen?

Fen...

The boy lay unresponsive in the back, arms hanging loosely and blood continuing to pour from his side across the seat and floor of the car in a dark, devouring pool.

There was no choice. Grey stopped the car.

Grey didn't wait to try to attract the attention of the new arrivals. He climbed straight into the back of the car and leaned over Fen, stuffing a wad of the cloth Francisco had offered them earlier over the wound. It turned bright red in an instant.

Grey looked frantically around for a first aid kit or something, anything, that could help. More cloth. This time, he maintained pressure on the wound to staunch the bleeding.

"Fen!" he called out. "Fen! Can you hear me?"

The boy gave a low groan.

Oh, thank gods... thought Grey. At least he was still conscious.

A loud banging on the side door split his attention. The vague form of a woman was visible through the tinted glass.

"Open the door!" came the voice.

"Ok, ok, but you've gotta help. It's this kid, he's bleeding out..."

Grey stretched with one arm and pushed open the door, not allowing the pressure to lessen on Fen's wound.

"Oh *damn*," came a female voice, which now the door was fully open Grey recognised.

The apparent leader of the *Forever Fallen,* who had called herself

Raphael, stood just outside the car. Several armed men and women of varying ages were lined up behind her, rifles held ready. More could be seen further back, monitoring the horizon for any more Quick Fix, along with two more of the strange, half-military half-civilian flatbed jeeps they drove.

"Weapons down, people," Raphael yelled, without looking back. "Medic! Get Serinda here now!"

A middle-aged woman pushed through from somewhere behind the group, pausing only briefly to gasp as she took in the child lying bleeding in the back of the car.

"Can you help him?" asked Grey as she forced her way past him.

The woman, whose name was apparently Serinda, ignored him. Instead, she looked first at the wound, then leaned in close to Fen's face so they were almost temple to temple. She closed her eyes, muttering something quietly under her breath. Grey felt the Aether *move*.

Almost immediately Fen's breathing calmed, the rising of his chest becoming slower and more regular.

"What was that?" Grey asked, trying to see past her. "What did you do?"

"Get this man out of my way!" Serinda snapped, moving away from Fen's head and returning to the wound.

"Out, Grey," said Raphael, gesturing for him to get out of the vehicle. "Serinda will do everything she can, and the sooner we get him out of here the sooner we can get him some proper medical care."

Grey stepped out of the car, at a loss for what else to do.

"What did she just do?" he asked again.

"She *Calmed* him. A slower heart beat means less blood loss," replied Raphael.

She raised two hands and pointed to the vehicle Grey had just got out of. Instantly, two men stepped forward from behind her and climbed up into the front seats, the one in the driver's seat taking hold of the wheel.

"Give him control," said Raphael before Grey could react.

"What? Why? Where are you taking…?"

Raphael glared at him and cut him off with a pointed finger.

"Grey. If you want the child to live, then we need to get him somewhere safe *now*. So give my men control of the vehicle, and they can get him where he needs to be."

Her gaze softened slightly as he passed Francisco's thin-screen up to the driver. The car ignition turned, and the car drove away without another moment's wait.

"Don't worry," she said. "We'll be right behind them."

With that, Raphael clicked her fingers at those behind her, not taking her eyes off Grey. The group suddenly broke apart, splitting into smaller numbers and rushing onto the nearby vehicles. The closest vehicle started up and, driving in a wide loop, came around to stop behind her.

"Well?" Raphael said, grabbing the side of the car and swinging herself up onto the rear flatbed. A rocket launcher lay discarded in one corner. "Get on. We've got to go."

Grey looked from the burning wreckage of the APC back the way they came. Dust obscured the old highway, somewhere in the distance. And somewhere in that dust, more enemies.

He got on the flatbed.

13

When every individual is involved in the running of the State, all action is limited. Flexibility is sacrificed for pluralism. Unrestricted participation leads to restricted outcomes. Citizenship must be conferred only on those who earn it. Nothing like the Sudden War can be allowed to happen again.

Articles of Federation: Article 17

"Can you really save Fen?"

They'd been driving for several minutes, but this was the first time Grey had been able to ask anything at all. For the intervening time he'd been only an impotent spectator as Raphael and 'her people' chattered on the radio, sharing sightings of pursuers and working out routes to avoid them. The vehicles had split up soon after departing.

"Safer apart than together, when the RA is hunting you," she'd said in explanation.

Grey didn't have the mental reserves left to do anything more than grunt in feigned comprehension at the implication that Raphael was used to being hunted by the Reclamation Authority.

"Can you save Fen?"

I should have stayed in the car with him. The thought ran through his mind again and again. *I should have demanded they take us to a hospital.*

Even knowing that a visit to any hospital was a guarantee Fen would be traced, Grey still couldn't shake the thought. Even despite knowing that, in this day and age, a trip to the hospital was only something you considered when the situation really *was* life or death. The virtual obsolescence of antibiotics due to the proliferation of strains of resistant bacteria, both man-made and natural, meant hospitals were not the institutions they had once been. Instead, they were where you went when all else failed, turning your fate over to dead-eyed orderlies and dark, compassionless screens repeating their dry requests to input symptoms[8].

"Can you save him?"

"I told you; we will do everything we can. Chances are better for

---

[8] As with most other industries of the RA, the medical industry was both deeply reliant upon AI large language models and deeply resentful of them, and as with all such models, they were severely restricted in both ability and scope.

him with us than any of the plague-houses, anyway," Raphael replied, using the derogatory nickname for the hospitals. It was an exaggeration, but not overly so.

Grey's mouth opened and shut several times.

"Calm down. You look like a fish," said Raphael. "What is the kid to you, anyway?"

Grey froze at the question, analysing his own feelings. She had a point. After all, he'd known Fen for, what, a few days?

The boy's face as he told the story of a life in captivity floated across his thoughts.

And then, unexpectedly, another child's face floated up, one he thought he had managed to long forget. A shard of pain cut into his chest, and he had to force the image away.

"He just... he deserves something better. Something better than all this," said Grey, gesturing as if to take in the whole world. "They all do."

"They?" Raphael's eyebrows rose in question.

"The... the kids, dammit. The next generation. They didn't do anything to deserve *this*."

"Huh, our little Far agent has a big heart, it seems." She paused, turning to mutter something into her radio in response to a squawked query. "It looks like we lost them," she said.

"We can't hide for long. They'll spot us the moment our IDRF trackers are within range of the city."

Raphael smiled at that.

"No, they won't. Our cars are scraped."

Grey nodded, inwardly scolding himself. He was thinking like an agent again, not someone who ran from agents. Of course they were.

The *Forever Fallen* having access to these kind of vehicles and weaponry was obviously not something Requisitions would have permitted. They could only be illicit, meaning they would also have had the ever-present tracking discs that were built into every vehicle removed. Or "scraped," as the process was commonly known.

This would of course come with its own problems, notably that if a scraped vehicle was spotted on the street, it would be impounded and its owners immediately incarcerated for that crime alone. Grey assumed the *Forever Fallen* rarely used these cars; he'd chased a few Scrapers in his own time, with clients or suspects attempting an anonymous exit, and it was relatively easy for law enforcement to spot these cars by their very absence from their ID-checking screens.

"Nothing compared to the car the Spaniard gave you, though."

He had to replay Raphael's words in his head before he understood them, spoken over the wind of the car's passage as they were.

"The Spaniard?" he asked. Could she actually mean...

"You call him Francisco, I think," continued Raphael, hair whipping in the dry, dusty wind. She didn't seem to notice. "It's the name he's been going by for some time now."

Grey gave a noncommittal nod. He needed these people, but he still couldn't be sure of their motivations, nor could he be sure who he needed more.

"He's not from here, you know," Raphael continued. "Well, of course he isn't, not at that age. But he's not a part of the Reclamation, never was. He has no record. He's not Federation, or Reclamation Authority, yet seems to have connections with both. And he's taken an interest in *you*."

"I buy information from him. Usually in return for drinks," Grey said over the wind.

"Yeah, well, I think by now you've realised he doesn't need someone to pay for his round. I assume the drone that tore over us on the way to you, whatever the hell model *that* was, was something to do with him, too?"

She seemed to be looking for some kind of confirmation from Grey. He was careful not to give it to her.

"Ha... well, we call him 'The Spaniard.' Not because we think he's from old Spain or anything, but because of the way he speaks. And he's got to be from *somewhere*. Turned up about two decades ago, and suddenly had his cables in every port in the city."

She caught herself, apparently wondering if *she* was saying too much. Shaking her head, she looked back to Grey and began again.

"But enough about him. I'm more interested in you and your companion. Now *he's* an interesting one."

"What do you know about him?" Grey asked, keeping his expression and tone guarded.

"Well, we know he's called Fen now, at least. That, and the fact that a whole lot of people are looking for him, and aren't afraid to break some pretty important 'understandings' to do so."

"Understandings?"

"The Reclamation Authority has never had a complete grip on the mainland, you know, and the new Federation even less so," she replied. "Building a 'community of cities,' as they like to call it, required trade-offs with a *lot* of groups. Some of whom you and your Agency friends might be surprised to discover even exist."

She paused to look out past the front cab, where the outline of the city was slowly emerging from the dust.

"But in the past few days, they've come storming through places they are very much *not* welcome."

"Like your building downtown, where we met?"

Raphael smiled at that.

"No," she chuckled, shaking her head. "They haven't been *that* stupid. Yet."

Her expression snapped back to serious. She really *did* remind him of Ritra Feye.

"I think, Mister *former* Far Agent, it's time you learn a little more about us."

They didn't approach Albores the way he thought they would, instead sharply curving away when it seemed the buildings and low towers of the outskirts were only a few minutes away. Instead, they curved south, tracing the circumference of the city without getting any closer.[9]

Eventually, Grey saw what they were heading for. An old manmade waterway appeared in the distance, presumably connecting at some point to the main river that ran near the *Forever Fallen's* building. Even this far away, Grey could see lumps of brownish scum floating on top of the water, symptoms of the poison, effluents, and waste from decades of industrial leakage. The stale, chemical smell of it wafted on the wind.

Ahead and to their right the waterway grew wide, terminating in a large, open area where dilapidated iron jetties stretched out into its waters, the remains of fallen cranes and heavy equipment dotting the sides. Several large rusting cargo vessels and container ships lined the concrete embankments surrounding the water, some listing to the side. This place must have once been an old inland docks.

---

[9] Another result of pre-planned city design, there were no suburbs, or satellite towns. There was just Waste, then city; the dividing line between the two was clearly visible.

So we follow this down to the river, he thought.

But instead, their vehicle drove all the way up to the water's edge, where a particularly large ship half-floated, half-rested, on the nearest embankment. Time, and the weight of the boat, had sent long cracks through the concrete around it. The top of it rose several metres above them, and rusted patches marked its sides. Once upon a time, it had likely plied these waters delivering the innumerable goods pre-Fall society thrived upon, goods that could have been manufactured anywhere in the world. Huge metal containers would have filled its wide, flat deck. Now, it was nothing but an abandoned, empty husk.

Or so Grey thought until a figure appeared along the top of the ship.

Raphael's radio squawked a query, and, upon her response, a ramp was lowered. Their car drove carefully up it, cresting the lip and pulling up onto a bare, open deck. The surface of the deck was so patchy with rust that Grey grabbed the sides of his seat reflexively, feeling as if they could fall through at any second.

Another moment, and a large section of the deck slid apart in front of them, groaning and creaking as an electrical motor whirred with effort. Slowly, the gap between the section and the deck widened, the floor beneath their car moving downwards into it; they were being lowered *inside* the boat. After a few seconds, the moving section they were carried on came to a stop, a patch of light from the hole above contrasting starkly with the darkness of the inner hull. The car drove off the pad, into the darkness, as behind them the section rose again and sealed out the light.

The inside of the boat was cool and damp, a wide open space broken only by steel support shafts spaced regularly along the length of the hull. The inner walls of the hull must have been cut out; even without the rust and decay of age, this boat would never be seaworthy again.

There *was* light down here, created by weak LED strips placed sparingly around the area. Grey's eyes gradually adjusted as the car pulled to a stop beside a number of vehicles, one of which he recognised from their wasteland rescue. Several figures stood around it, smoking and chatting in low, murmured tones. A pair of legs stuck out from below, metallic sounds indicating some kind of repair or maintenance work going on.

"Check our car next, Shiner," Raphael yelled towards the pair of legs as she stepped out the vehicle. "Can't see how they could've got a tracker on us, but check it thoroughly all the same."

A muffled affirmative came from under the car, followed by a loud clatter and louder swear. Laughter came from the people standing around it.

Grey stepped out after Raphael, wary and struggling to hold in a hiss of pain as he put his weight back on to the shredded soles of his feet. He was more injured from the dash across the Waste than he wanted to reveal in front of this group, whose motives he still didn't understand.

They were a real variety, these people. Men, women, a couple whose gender Grey couldn't place, ages varying from looking as if they were barely out of their teens to well past middle-aged. Each of them, however, carried a firearm with the ease of familiarity. No weapon was the same; Grey spotted two pistols at the sides of one, and an automatic in the hands of another.

He felt someone try to *Read* him, like a tickle in the back of his head. He shut his thoughts down instinctively, as he'd learned to do many years ago in the Academy.

"Whoever that is had better stop it," he said, the words bitten off, half-formed sounds that were typical for someone actively blocking a Reading, as if their mouth was filled with foam.

The tickle grew stronger, not weaker, like a spider's web gently wrapping around his brain, beneath the skull.

"I said, *stop,*" he snarled, giving up any attempt at counteracting the effect mentally. The room went quiet.

Glaring around, he caught the eye of one of the people near the other car, a tall, muscled man with dark hair and thick black beard; Grey recognised him as one of the men who had stood beside Raphael at their first meeting. As soon as they made eye contact, the sensation in his brain stopped.

The man grinned through his beard, a grin without warmth or welcome. It was a grin that told Grey the man was Reading him because he *could*, and there was nothing Grey could do to stop him.

Grey refused to be intimidated. Outnumbered, in this enclosed, rusting box, he forced himself to stand as tall as he could and to meet the gaze of each onlooker in turn.

'So this is where you hide from the RA?" he said, directing his words to each and every figure watching him.

Beard grinned again. His beard was tinged white, Grey could see now, implying he was older than Grey had first thought.

"Where exactly do you think we hide around here, Far?" the man said, gesturing expansively to take in the damp, empty hull all around them.

"This is where we store the vehicles," said Raphael to Grey, stepping up beside him. "We walk from here."

Beard turned away from Grey the next moment, as if suddenly he no longer held any interest to him. After a few more seconds, the rest of the group also returned to their previous stance, quietly talking amongst each other, waiting.

"Come on," said Raphael, stepping forward towards deeper darkness. The hull stretched away from where they had entered and quickly faded into darkness. "The others will wait here, make sure the rest of the cars get here safe. Which reminds me…"

Abruptly breaking stride and turning, she yelled once more towards the legs under the other vehicle.

"Shiner, I want you to look at the car we brought in today. The one this guy and his kid were driving. Make sure she's clean, and we can make *good* use of her. It's a Switcher."

Raphael began turning back almost before she finished speaking, striding off into the darkness. Grey followed, ignoring the fire in his feet, feeling like a wounded prey animal struggling to hide its injuries from the gaze of watching predators.

He hadn't known Francisco's car was a Switcher, a vehicle able to operate with IDRF trackers active or inhibited. *That* technology was extremely restricted; in fact, it was commonly taught that IDRF couldn't *be* inhibited. They were either always on or had to be 'scraped' off. Far at least knew Switchers were real, though so rare that very few agents ever had any dealings with them.

"We're keeping it, by the way," said Raphael as the light grew dimmer and dimmer. "A cheap enough price for saving your life. And the kid's, hopefully."

"Where is he?" replied Grey at the mention of Fen.

"We're going there now. Look, I'm sure he's fine. I would have been told by now if anything was wrong," she said, tapping the radio at her chest.

"*Where* are we going?" he demanded. He could barely see as darkness enveloped them, mainly proceeding by following the sound of Raphael's footsteps, metallic echoes on the floor.

"Patience. We're nearly..." her voice became abruptly strained, as if she were lifting a heavy weight. Something screeched, the sound of metal on metal. "... *there*."

Sudden light flooded Grey's eyes, forcing him to raise a hand to block it. The sound of running water filled the previously silent air, and the chemical smell of the river redoubled.

Once his vision came back, Grey could see that Raphael had opened a heavy iron door set into the side of the boat, obviously added after the boat had been rendered derelict. It swung open inward to reveal the outside world beyond, the same sloping concrete embankment they had driven in on. This section too consisted of cracked, grey concrete, weeds growing fitfully where they could. A short way down, though, he could see an old, steel wire fence. They headed to a gate whose creaking joints resisted being fully opened, a faded yellow sign hanging from it that warned trespassers away in old English. Squeezing through, Grey found himself surrounded by corroding machinery and empty metal crates, the detritus of a bygone world without Fabricators and Requisitions and localised manufacturing. These formed a maze that Raphael unhesitatingly led him through.

Eventually, after what felt like an eternity of painful footsteps, they came to a central section with a large, multi-story building from which jutted a broken chimney stack, one that must have once stretched high into the sky. Grey couldn't see where it had fallen, though it had surely smashed through whatever it had fallen upon. It looked like this had been a central building for the docks, perhaps some kind of processing plant.

"In here," Raphael said, glancing back to make sure he was following before stepping through an empty double-door frame, the doors themselves having long since broken off or been removed.

Grey bit down on his questions, and followed on behind her. He knew he wouldn't get any answers.

She led him through room after room of this building, some small, some hall-sized spaces stretching up to the very roof of the place, each littered with the accoutrements of pre-Fall businesses. Desks, computers, rotting papers and even wired telephones lay scattered across the floors almost everywhere. At first, Grey couldn't understand what they were doing here.

The next set of doors, though, led into the modern. The *extremely* modern, in fact.

Anti-sep plastic lined the clean white walls of the next room, sterilising spray coating him in a fine mist from the automated dispensers that registered his entry. The area was brightly lit, with rows of seating filling the room. Most of these were empty, but scattered around were people tensely waiting for... *something*.

A second pair of doors stood at the other end of the room.

"The surgery's through there," she said. "Uh uh..."

Raphael held out a hand to block Grey from heading to those doors.

"You don't think you can just walk in there, do you? Covered in the city, and leaving bloody footprints behind you? You'll kill the kid, and half the other patients."

"Patients?" Grey asked, trying to push past her, sparing only half a thought to wonder how long Raphael had known he was hiding torn feet. "So this is a, what? A hospital?"

"In a way," Raphael replied. "More of a free clinic. One for those who don't want to attract the attention of the authorities."

"In the middle of an abandoned docks? This place could be even worse than a plague-house," Grey said, throwing her words back at her.

Raphael just smiled at this.

"Oh no. You have a *much* better chance here. Here, we can still handle the outbreaks that make other hospitals such a hellscape."

"How? Is this like your cars and weapons? You have a line on some new antibiotics?"

Grey waved his hands around to take in the clean, sterile room.

"No, not antibiotics. We have something better."

"What?" Grey said, irritated. It felt like she was playing with him.

"You haven't figured it out, Far Agent? Here, we use Aether."

14

Corruption is the cancer in the roots of every form of governance. Pre-Fall systems from collectivism to autocracy to democracy invariably crumbled into chaos and disorder once the scale of governmental deceit became apparent to its citizens. They had neither the capacity nor the morality to solve the problem of social cohesion.

Processes of Regulation and Order in the Reclamation (Sanctioned Digital Document)

"It was close, but he's stable. Now his mind and body need rest."
Serinda was literally washing the blood off her gloves as she said this, before peeling them off and throwing them into a nearby auto-disposal. Grey and Raphael stood close by, within what Grey could only think of as an operating theatre.

More specifically, a partitioned section of the operating theatre, transparent walls dividing them from the main section of the room, where he could see Fen asleep on a raised gurney.

"He'll be out for at least a day," Serinda continued.

"Anaesthetic?" asked Grey.

"Anaesthetic, and my influence," replied Serinda, ablutions done and turning to face Grey.

A young man who seemed to be an assistant of Serinda's bustled past and through the plastic curtains covering the way into the theatre proper, where he began gathering the bloodied medical instruments from the surgical trays beside Fen. Grey watched him pick up the bullet that had been inside the boy and place it in a small blue disposal bag.

"Influence?" Grey asked, attention torn between Fen and Serinda's words.

"A little sleep-inducement. Non-atonic, but deeper than REM sleep. He won't dream, but he'll wake up feeling a whole lot better."

Aether for medical uses; Grey was still half in shock. He didn't know if this was because he hadn't known this was possible, or that no one at the Academy had ever implied that this *was* possible.

It wasn't only for calming patients, though that word didn't cover the medical potential for the ability to non-chemically control bodily functions such as blood pressure and hormonal balance. Serinda used Aether to *sterilise*. On top of standard sterilisation procedures, of course.

Serinda could essentially burn infectious organisms out, using low-level Aether inducement to release the energy of microbes all at once. Her assistant, the one now carefully spraying down various surfaces around where Fen lay, had used the same technique to sterilise Grey's feet before wrapping them in sterile cloth.

Upon first hearing Raphael explain what this technique was, Grey had the horrible feeling that this was *Mindfire*. It almost was in its effects on bacteria, but the difference was that it didn't propagate. It didn't *spread*. By using the technique on a localised area of the body, such as a bullet wound, Serinda could stop infection before it started to spread.

And apparently she and her assistant weren't the only ones. According to Raphael, practically everyone in the *Forever Fallen* was an Aether user to some degree, and many of those trained under Serinda - though Raphael had implied that Serinda was the most skilled. Hence the 'free clinic.' The *Forever Fallen* offered medical services unavailable elsewhere, for free.

Well, almost for free. Grey had a feeling he was going to learn about the price of their help at some point soon. A Switcher wasn't going to cover it.

"Are we safe here?" Grey asked. This was, after all, just a derelict building on the outskirts of the city. "You said the Reclamation Authority was looking for us."

Raphael and Serinda shared a look he couldn't read, before the leader turned back to him.

"For now," said Raphael. "Very few people know about this place, and those we bring here are always kept in the dark about where they are. I think *your* kind call it Closing."

Closing was indeed a term used at the Academy, one for the technique of shutting off another person's senses for a substantial length of time. It could make you feel like you were in an isolation tank, with no sense of taste, touch, heat, light, or anything else. It had very little practical use, however, because it was extremely easy to shake off even for non-Aether users. The senses *wanted* to be used.

Though if someone acquiesced to the effect...

"So, you bring people here on the condition that they accept being Closed when brought?" he said, half question and half statement.

Raphael nodded in response.

"... and we move locations every so often. Don't think I'm

showing you *everything* the Fallen have, Grey," she said. "We only rescued you because we were investigating chatter about some operation out in the Waste. I still don't know how far we can trust you. Just because you're an enemy of the RA doesn't make you a friend to us."

"Well, that's a problem, because I need a favour," he replied.

Raphael looked at him quizzically, as Serinda led them out of the theatre and down a long corridor.

"'A favour? We did just save your life," she said.

"And I owe you one. But *you* want to know what they want with Fen as much as I do, I think. So, in return for this favour, I'll share what I find out."

"And what exactly would this favour be?"

Serinda led them into what seemed to be a break room, with vinyl seats and, in one corner, a couple of roll-out beds: essentially the same as the gurney upon which Fen had been sleeping. Serinda rolled one of these out and unfolded it, falling onto it with a sigh. Raphael, meanwhile, gestured at Grey to sit on a chair facing the one she sat down in.

"I need to borrow a car," he said.

Raphael raised an eyebrow.

"Going somewhere?"

"Yes. I'm going to find out exactly where Fen escaped from. I know it's somewhere south of the warehouse district. According to Fen, it could only have been a few hours away."

"That's still a pretty big area," said Raphael, but her tone held curiosity.

"Which is why I need a drone," he said.

Raphael didn't respond.

"I know you must have some. Or at least, can get some. If you've got Scrapers, I know you can get me a decent-range drone." He continued, locking eyes with her. "I can find the site from on high, then drive down there myself."

"And then? There's a lot of people with guns out looking for you, and you're going to go looking for *them*?"

"I can take care of myself," he said with a confidence he willed himself to actually feel. "Listen, I *have* to go. I can't keep running, trying to keep Fen safe from the entire damn system. I need to know exactly what this is."

Raphael sat quietly for some time, thinking. Finally, she appeared to reach some sort of conclusion.

"Fine," she said, nodding to herself. "I'll lend you a car, and a drone. But you get yourself caught, and you will *never* find us again. *Comprende?*"

"I understand."

"And if you get yourself killed, well…" She trailed off, leaving her words hanging. "No one will come to help this time, ok? It will just be you."

Grey nodded back. "I work better alone, anyway."

And so the next day Grey found himself back out in the Waste, alone this time. He'd got some fitful sleep back at what he now thought of as the clinic, in one of the simple beds he'd first seen in the break room; relatives were occasionally allowed to come along with the sick, Raphael had explained, and were not permitted to leave until the patient recovered.

He had driven past the warehouses where he first encountered Fen, and the first two of the many bodies the kid seemed to leave in his wake, and continued out into the empty land beyond, with only the remains of the roads of a previous era to guide him. The car they had given him was a basic one, and struggled when the ground turned to dusty, broken rock. Still, he was slowly getting comfortable with manual control.

Eventually he pulled to a stop, almost randomly, and launched the drone. Palm-sized, it could nevertheless deliver highly detailed imagery directly to the similarly-sized screen that controlled it. The drone shot upwards, launching into the sky so high that it quickly became imperceptible to the naked eye.

He stared intently at the images the drone sent back as it slowly moved south on a sweeping path that took in as much terrain east and west as possible. The images showed nothing but gently rolling dirt and rock ahead, as expected. There were no settlements this way for hundreds of kilometres over treacherous terrain.

Spinning the drone around, he could see the warehouses and outline of the city behind him, somehow comforting even though it now offered as much danger as safety. He paused, taking in the buildings made shadow in the dusty air, then recalled the drone. He drove off again, always following a generally southern heading.

It took several tries, and several hours, for Grey to find what he was looking for. It was nothing but a dark blur at first, like a smudge on the screen, but there was *something* out there. A patch of order amongst the disorder, clean lines where all else was jagged and broken. A collection of low, huddled structures. The wind crashed against the sides of the complex and sent dust spiralling skywards.

Grey recalled the drone, and headed for the site. Details became more apparent as he drew closer, but it still took a few minutes more before he realised it wasn't just dust rising from the buildings. It was smoke. He pushed the pedal down harder, knowing already that it was too late.

It *had* been some kind of complex, he could see. The outline of what he saw, at least, matched with Fen's descriptions of the place he had grown up. The entire facility was enclosed within an almost unbroken chain-link fence topped with barbed wire, the only entrance the dirt road he drove in on, a road made through the regular passage of vehicles entering and exiting the site rather than deliberately laid.

The central area looked to have been surrounded by smaller buildings, with the remains of what must have been the watchtowers poking up at points amongst the smouldering ruins. Interestingly, the ash and rubble showed traces only of the building's superstructure itself. He saw no sign of equipment or electronic debris.

So, thought Grey. *They swept the place clean, then burnt what they couldn't move.* Which implied that, while rushed, they still had time to shut up shop properly. Everything they had on Fen, and who knew what else, was still out there somewhere.

Charcoal crunched underfoot as he made his way through the debris, allowing his path to be guided by whatever trail was easiest, casting around for anything that could give him a hint as to the nature of this place. Nothing spoke to him. This was now just another derelict site in a world full of them, with less to say about itself than even the pre-Fall sites with their semi-intelligible signs…

The thought made Grey stop in his tracks. Surely it couldn't be *that* simple?

But even as he looked back towards the fence he knew it was. If they weren't going to leave anything for him *inside*, then he should look outside.

He only had to walk a short while along the fence before he found the first warning sign, and a short while again to find two more. Each only confirmed what the previous one said:

> ABSOLUTELY NO TRESPASSING.

And below that, in smaller letters:

> Unauthorised entry forbidden. Lethal force may be used.

Below that, more writing, smaller again:

> *This area has been declared a restricted area under the provisions of the Reclamation Internal Security Act 161.2.*

And then, finally, in the bottom right a crest. A dull green circle with a thin red line around its circumference, two pale cream stars inside this at the upper left and lower right. Below this, in dark lettering:

> **Agencia Federal de Aether**

Better known as the Far Agency.

15

The social cohesion problem is a question of opportunity, and the perception of a gap between what is available to the majority, and the elite. The destructive potential of many modern technologies is as great today as it was before the Sudden War, and must be restricted. However, such technologies are also productive. Thus the majority will justifiably feel that those permitted access to such technologies are afforded rights and privileges they are not.

Therefore, the majority must be kept blind.

Unspoken Founding Principles of the Reclamation (Unsanctioned Digital Document)

"*My* damn agency."

"I thought you were an *ex*-Far agent," said Raphael. Now she was the one throwing his words back at him. He ignored them.

"For how long? Fen has got to be, what, thirteen? Fourteen? Even fifteen? Which means this was happening when I *was* an agent.'

"Maybe even before, considering how long it must take to prepare an operation like that; and who says Fen was even the first?"

This was Serinda. Grey had come to realise that she was more than just a medic in the *Forever Fallen*. She was always where Raphael was, listening, and very occasionally interjecting. And even when she wasn't directly participating in a discussion, Raphael was clearly paying attention to her. A simple nod of Serinda's head could make Raphael concede to someone's request where she had been reluctant a moment before, a shake make her refuse outright.

She clearly valued the other woman's opinion. At times, though, Grey thought maybe there was more to it than that. Raphael's eyes took on a certain softness when she looked at Serinda, a softness that wasn't there for anyone else.

None of which mattered at the moment.

"The whole time I was an agent they were experimenting on *kids*," Grey spat. "We're meant to help make the Aether safe for people, but we were turning kids who use it into *weapons*."

"The Far Agency is big. Lots of different sections and divisions doing different things. Maybe *you* made a difference," said Serinda.

Raphael flashed a glare at her, just for a split-second.

"Don't defend Far just because you feel sorry for him," she said. "You know what Far is capable of. You know what they're *all* capable of."

Serinda gave a tired nod, unwilling to argue, and closed her eyes again.

He'd returned to the *Forever Fallen* from the Waste a few days ago, and stayed with them since. Raphael he met only a handful of times after his return, with Serinda keeping him updated on how Fen was doing. The boy was recovering, but it would still be some time before he would be allowed to move. He was talking, at least, though Serinda insisted Grey only discuss his general health and other light topics when they spoke.

This was difficult, considering the boy's health currently included a gut-wound, and his life had been hardly an easy listening song. Fortunately, they had movies to fall back on.

On the morning of the third day, tired of being ignored, he marched through the building until he found Raphael. She was in another room of the clinic, one that looked out over the oily waters of the inlet the dock was built around, holding some kind of meeting with a number of people he'd seen before and a number he hadn't.

Serinda was half-asleep in a chair in one corner, listening with half an ear to the discussion that wrapped up almost the moment he entered. It seemed as though her life consisted of snatches of rest in between performing a never-ending sequence of medical procedures.

Raphael dismissed those with her, and it wasn't long before the conversation had turned to the topic of what Grey had found in the Waste, and what it meant. The conversation they were having now.

"What are you saying?" he demanded. "*What* are 'they' capable of?"

"The Agencies," Raphael answered. "Pan-Fed. Far. Requisitions. All of them, placing the Reclamation above the lives of those who live in it."

Grey opened his mouth to contradict her, then thought better of it. He needed their help, and besides, what he had found in the Waste had left him feeling lost.

"Say it," said Raphael. "Say what you were going to say."

Grey didn't.

"*Say it,*" she insisted.

"Fine," said Grey. "The roots of..."

"The roots of liberty are from time to time refreshed with the blood of those who tend them."

Raphael almost spat as she finished his words for him.

It was a maxim known throughout the Reclamation, born almost before the first groups crossed the waters from the Carib-Federation to resettle the mainland.

"A perversion of older words," Raphael said.

Grey nodded.

"But the situation and meaning is different to Jefferson's words," he said. "It isn't about revolution, it's about *survival*. The Reclamation *does* require sacrifice; there's just too much out there that could finish what the Sudden War started. We just have to ensure it is limited to what absolutely *must* be sacrificed."

Raphael snorted derisively.

"You must know what it was like," he continued. "This world was broken. Most of us grew up in the camps, or the deadlands..."

His voice hitched, throat closing upon words he hadn't expected to say.

Raphael didn't seem to notice, her anger getting the better of her.

"So you let the Reclamation Authority decide what those sacrifices are? Who has a voice? Who gets to *breed*, like we were cattle?"

Raphael was referring to the RA policies of population control, Grey knew. Immigrants were forced to accede to anything from libido-restricting drugs to enforced, though reversible, vasectomies upon arrival, only gaining permission to correct these measures when (and if) they achieved citizen status.

"I thought... The Reclamation doesn't work if there's no one to make the hard choices; the nation can't survive. In the Academy we were always told..."

"'Only following orders' is an excuse older than the Sudden War," snapped Raphael, cutting Grey off.

Grey's thoughts turned to Fen, lying in a surgical bed a few rooms away.

"So you're saying everything I've done, everything Far... everything the Reclamation Authority has done was wrong? That we should have allowed violence and bio-terror and Mindfire to run wild?"

Whatever Raphael was going to say in response was interrupted by Serinda, who opened her eyes with a loud sigh and pinched her temples.

"You're from the deadlands?" she said, staring at the ceiling.

So *she* had noticed the hitch, at least. He shook his head, not in denial but in refusal to respond.

Serinda pushed herself up from her chair.

"Come on," she said, gesturing to Grey. "There's someone for you to meet. Raphael, you're coming too."

Serinda wouldn't say where they were going as she led them to the derelict hull in which the vehicles were stored. Grey followed behind her and Raphael behind him, muttering about wasting time when there was so much to do. Nevertheless, she ordered a man apparently standing guard to transfer Serinda the e-key to the nearest car, a much larger and more powerful one than the one they had lent Grey.

The auto-drive took them back into the city at Serinda's command, a winding route that took longer than any direct path but was necessary to prevent any surveillance algorithms calculating their origin point. Even so, Raphael told him, she had given the order to clear out the dockyard. The clinic would already be being packed up and transported to a new location, Fen along with it.

When Raphael had given the order Grey couldn't tell, but this confirmed what he had begun to suspect; Raphael communicated with the other *Fallen* through a combination of hand signals and *Tell*, a useful Aether technique that, while not actual telepathy, could communicate intention to others. A well-trained team, familiar with each member and their methods, could achieve a level of synchronicity that appeared like true telepathy to a non-Aether user.

Eventually, they entered an area of the city Grey was familiar with. They were somewhere downtown, no more than a district or two away from the *Methuselah's End*. For the first time in what felt like forever, Grey saw ordinary people going about their business, uninvolved and unconcerned with Far or Quick Fix or the *Forever Fallen*.

Grey almost envied them.

A few minutes later they pulled into a basement car park underneath a high tower block similar, though taller, in design to Grey's apartment... his *former* apartment. He had to keep reminding himself that, when and if this was ever over, he was still down one place to live.

Grey shuffled uneasily in his seat as they pulled to a stop. There were other vehicles there, and that meant people. And *that* meant surveillance. Though he saw no one at the moment, there were undoubtedly cameras. He couldn't trust that they had all been blocked.

"Here," said Serinda, passing what seemed to be a piece of incredibly thin, shiny cloth to him. "Put this on your face. Just pull it flat from cheek to cheek."

Even as she spoke, she was doing the same with hers. As the cloth touched her skin, it stretched and stiffened, fading until it was no longer visible.

Grey saw a different person sitting across for him. Sure, their face shared much in common with Serinda, but the cheekbones were higher, the nose broader, eyes more sunken in. Just a few slight changes, but enough to trick the eyes into seeing someone else.

Grey looked down at the cloth in his hand. He couldn't tell what it was made from, only that it was cool and silky, a pattern of pale and dark browns that seemed to weave together on a level too fine for the eye to see.

"Spangle fabric," this new Serinda said. "Bonds to your skin when you put it on. No one will recognize you, especially not facial recognition algorithms. I think it's some kind of polyglycerol base, maybe polyglycerol sebacate."

"You don't know what it is?"

"No, but I've got some ideas. It resembles artificial skin used for skin grafts, at least."

"Where do you get it from?"

Raphael, who had been busy applying her own mask, smiled at that.

"No, no," she said, wagging a warning finger at Grey. "It's enough we're letting you even *see* it."

"Hurry up and put it on," said Serinda. "It'll start to degrade after a day or so; it will look like your skin is peeling. Comes off with too much warm water too, so try not to sweat much."

Raphael was also changed. Grey was amazed how much of a difference such a subtle alteration of facial features could make. The tone of her skin remained the same, as it had with Serinda despite their differences, but she looked... younger? No, not younger, but lacking the hardness that so reminded him of Ritra Feye. Her temple seemed higher, and chin less pronounced. If he hadn't seen the change, he could have been easily convinced that he was sitting beside someone who just resembled Raphael, rather than the woman herself.

The cloth felt positively cold when he pressed it to his face, and it sucked at and stuck to his skin like something alive. He felt it both stretch and tighten across his cheeks, his nose, beneath his eyes, until all of a sudden the feeling was just... not gone, but no longer noticeable.

Serinda chuckled at Grey trying to avoid making it obvious he was looking for a mirror. She held up a thin-screen, his image projecting back at him.

He looked older. At least, he thought he did. Maybe he just hadn't looked in a mirror recently. He certainly *felt* older, especially after these past few days.

Either way, the man in the mirror looked sufficiently unlike himself that he felt the tension in his chest relax. He didn't think even his own mother would recognize him, at least not from afar.

If she were still around, of course; she had passed when he was barely walking, a victim to one or another of the virulent strains that spread like wildfire through the crowded Carib-Federation camps of those who came over in the Great Migration. The loss of his one remaining family member was one of the reasons he had been able to cross over into the mainland so young, and one of the reasons the Academy had found him during their testings. Orphan centres were one of the prime hunting grounds for early-age Aether users.

Grey shook off the memories that seemed intent on rising unbidden as Serinda stepped out of the car.

"Come on," she said. "She's this way."

Blane was stood at the small railing-topped wall that wrapped around the edge of the roof of the building, leaning against it and staring out over the twilight city. She stood barely tall enough to see over it.

It was dusk, Grey realised, the sun already below the horizon but its orange glow suffusing the sky above where it had set. The wind whipped her hair behind her, and covered the sound of their approach.

"She's still… fragile," said Serinda. "But she has been asking about you."

"She has?"

"She has," said Raphael. "We told her you were asking after her when you first came to us. She didn't want to talk about you, or anything else that happened at first, but… well, you know, things change."

"She told me she had family. Grandparents."

"Now is not the time to contact them," said Raphael, firmly.

"You won't let her?"

"She agreed," said Serinda. "We can help her, but only if she stays with us. You can't have one foot in our world and another in the RA's. We gave her the choice: she chose."

"She's a kid."

"A kid who blew up her own home. I'm sorry," Raphael shot a contrite look at Serinda, who had flinched at her words. "…but it's true. We have to face reality; her childhood ended the moment her abilities manifested."

Blane finally noticed their presence, turning from the view of the city to look at them where they waited, at the entrance door back into the building. Her eyes widened slightly in recognition upon seeing Grey.

"How is she doing?" he asked.

"Ask her yourself," said Serinda, and with that strode over to the girl.

Grey noticed how a small smile appeared on Blane's face as Serinda greeted her, the older woman giving a single gentle stroke of the younger's cheek. They began talking softly, words inaudible from where he stood.

Grey felt as if something physical was holding him back, a hesitancy that bordered on fear. What was he meant to say to her? What *could* he say to her?

A firm push from Raphael unfroze him, and they both joined the other two near the walled edge of the roof.

"Hi," said Blane softly.

"Hi," said Grey. He felt foolish.

"Thank you for helping me, back…then," said the girl, words fading towards the end so that they were almost impossible to hear over the wind.

"It... uh, it was nothing. I hardly helped."

Serinda put a comforting arm around Blane's shoulders.

"Blane tells us you punched out two Far Agents in front of her apartment," she said with a smile.

"You saw that?" Grey said in surprise, staring at Blane.

The girl chuckled shyly.

"I was hiding. There's a little bit on the floor above that sticks out. You can hide there and see when mum and dad are coming home..."

Serinda squeezed Blane's shoulders as her words cut off. Grey could practically *see* the memory threaten to overwhelm her, but the girl took a deep, shaky breath and focused back on him.

"You held one of them over the side by his feet," she said. "I thought he was going to cry."

She'd been so *close*. Grey cursed himself. She'd been on the floor above the whole time. If he'd just searched a little more...

But then, if he'd found her would he have found Fen? Or the *Forever Fallen*? Or would he have led her into the hands of an agency he now knew would experiment on children like lab rats?

Sometimes you just had to focus on what *is*, not what could have been.

"Have they been treating you alright?" he asked.

"They've been teaching me," Blane replied.

"Teaching you? What?"

"How to use Aether. Now that I'm ... what did you call it? ... *attuned*."

"Agents do love their lingo," said Raphael, snorting.

"Didn't you just say Blane's abilities had 'manifested,' a second ago?" Grey retorted.

"Alright you two, enough." This was Serinda. Ever the peacemaker, Grey was realising.

And he was thankful for it. He found it hard not to react to every derisive comment or look Raphael made about the RA and Far, but he needed their help.

In fact, he thought, they were the only people he had right now. But he was going to work on that.

"I'm glad you're ok," he said, crouching down so that he was eye to eye with Blane. "You ever need anything, you just have to ask, ok? I'll be here."

Blane went a little wide-eyed at that, but after a second or so she nodded.

Grey stood up again, cracking the small of his back with his knuckles. He *was* getting old.

"Thank you for letting me see you," he said. "And thank you for looking after her," he continued, turning to Raphael. "But I think you've got one more person I want to see."

Raphael raised an eyebrow at this. "We do?"

"Yes. I think, by now, that you've found the other kid I was looking for. Salim. You don't seem like the type to leave loose ends."

"Very *good*, Mr. Grey," said Serinda, waving a hand to stop Raphael's reflexive denial. "He's here, too. Though I wonder if you've worked out *why* he ran away?"

"Well, if you found him, and he's still here, I think I have some ideas..."

Salim could use Aether. Grey didn't need to be told, because as soon as he walked into the common area it was obvious. Not only that, but...

"He's a Dreamwalker," said Grey.

The common area was a converted room a few floors down from the rooftop, a wide open room with thin-screens and gamepads scattered amongst a variety of tables and chairs. Grey also saw more analogue entertainments, like actual *board games*.

There was only one person in the room, and Grey knew immediately it was Salim. The boy matched the photos his father had shown him - except that this boy looked *extremely* tired.

The dark tones of Salim's skin had become pale and washed out, and the deep rings under his eyes were visible even from across the room. He was sat staring in the general direction of a thin-screen hanging on the wall, side-on to Grey, but his eyes were unfocused and half-closed, his mouth hanging loosely open.

"He's learning to manage it," said Serinda, "But it's hard. We keep this floor empty, and the ones above and below, but he still gets into the heads of people further away. Two or three floors, sometimes. And the less sleep he gets, the less he can control it."

Dreamwalkers. A rare form of Aether user, and one of the least understood. The Academy taught two potential explanations.

The first, and most widely accepted, was that they practised an extreme form of Reading, one that allowed them to see far deeper into the thoughts and feelings of others. Though "practised" was perhaps the wrong choice of word. Most were unable to stop the effect without concentration and focus, a concentration and focus that became harder the less sleep they got.

And a Dreamwalker was most definitely *not* sleeping when they were walking the thoughts of another. MRI scans of active Dreamwalkers showed an incredible amount of brain activity, comparable to a combination of PTSD and epileptic seizure. Manifesting with the physiological symptoms of severe insomnia, Dreamwalkers unable to take control of their abilities suffered a significant risk of psychosis and even death.

The second explanation, meanwhile, said that Dreamwalkers weren't actually Reading at all, but Projecting. While such a technique had never been demonstrated elsewhere, the descriptions Dreamwalkers gave of their experiences did indeed sound more as if they were literally trapped within the mind of another, rather than outside looking in. The idea was discounted by most, however, due to the lack of any noticeable change in the brain activity of those the Dreamwalker was experiencing.

That was what they called it: experiencing. And, just like Reading, multiple double-blind trials had proven the effect was real. Dreamwalkers really *did* see the deepest thoughts and images of those they experienced, most clearly when their subject was sleeping, but could do so at almost any time. It was also one of the only abilities to extend far beyond what was normally the range of an Aether technique.

But two or three floors… That was further than Grey had ever heard of. He knew he should have been more surprised, but Fen had already shown him how little he really understood about the limits of the Aether.

"Medication?" Grey asked.

"Benzodiazepine. But we limit that as much as we can. He's just a kid. Besides, it doesn't work well with Dreamwalkers. The brain seems to boot back up far sooner than it should," said Serinda.

"And he's chosen to stay with you?"

"No." This was Raphael. "He's in no position to make a choice like that. You should have seen him when we found him. Blacked out in an alley under a pile of old sheets."

Grey looked at her in surprise.

"He was that bad?"

"Worse. He was so dehydrated we had to put him on an IV. You wouldn't believe it, but the way he looks now is a whole lot better than when we found him."

"Why'd you bring him here?"

"This is where we keep the rescues," Raphael explained. "We control every floor above the fifth, and the other residents are, shall we say, *sympathetic* to our cause."

How they could have managed to do this Grey had no idea; Requisitions should have come down like a neutron bomb on anyone trying such a thing. Whoever it was that was helping the *Fallen*, they must be extremely influential.

"Can I speak to him?" Grey said.

Serinda nodded.

"It's thanks to you we even knew to look for him, so I'd say you earned it," she answered. "Gentle, though. You won't get much out of him, but like I say, he's finally getting at least some sleep. Which is why we can't stay here long."

Grey walked over to where Salim sat, pulling up a chair to sit nearby. The boy gave no sign he was aware of him.

"Hi, Salim. My name is Nestor Grey. I'm a... a friend of your father's."

At the mention of his father Salim stirred, his half-closed eyes opening slightly and head lethargically turning to look at Grey.

"My father?" he asked. "Is he alright?"

The boy's centra-English was far more refined than his father's, a polished accent speaking to an expensive education.

"He's fine. He's worried about you."

Salim looked pained at this, even through his evident exhaustion.

"Tell him... I'm sorry."

"Why don't you tell him yourself?" said Grey, forcing a hint of cheerfulness into his own voice. "He'll be so happy to know you're ok."

More strength returned to the boy's face, the lines of his cheeks and jaw hinting at the man he was becoming.

"But I'm *not* ok, sir. I'm... this is not right."

"Not right? What do you mean?"

But Salim settled back into his seat with a deep sigh, his eyes closing and breathing deep, slow breaths.

Grey looked up at Serinda, standing close by with Raphael.

"What did he mean, not right?" Grey asked.

"Damned if I know," said Raphael, cutting in over Serinda. "That's more than he's said to any of us. He wouldn't even tell us who his dad was, or how to contact him, and if we stay around too long our thoughts swamp him."

"Well," said Grey, standing up. "I *do* know who his father is, and I need to let him know his son is safe. Will you help me?"

Raphael and Serinda shared a look.

"We will," said Serinda.

"But," continued Raphael, "We really *do* seem to be helping you rather a lot. At some point, *you* are going to need to help *us*."

And that seemed to be that. Grey knew what he needed to do next. For the first time in a while, he felt the certainty of purpose.

First, he was going to get Salim back to his father.

Then, he was going to find this 'Doctor Caldwell' from Fen's stories.

Then he was going to get some answers.

16

By granting each member-state equal status, pre-Fall international organisations planted the seeds of their own destruction. A single nation could veto any action, lock up any resolution, when it was needed most. Bad actors soon realised that, to render an opposing alliance impotent, they simply had to ensure a single member nation was dependent upon them. Whether this dependence was financial or political, based on trade or energy, military or cultural, made no difference.

Coen Falwell, *Flames at the End of the World* (Sanctioned Publication)

It took the best part of another four days to organise a meeting with Majid Ayad, far longer than Grey had hoped. But it couldn't be helped; the *Forever Fallen* couldn't exactly walk up to him and say they had his son.

The pretext they used for trying to arrange a meeting with Ayad was that of a prospective buyer looking to make a large purchase. Even then, it took a lot of persuasion and demanding calls to get the man to agree to meet. The initial calls, set up through *Fallen* intermediaries, were rebuffed because Mr. Ayad was "indisposed." Though it was never stated why, Grey knew it was because the man must be focusing on finding his son. It took a day to even get a message passed on to him.

Eventually, though, Ayad gave in to the relentless calls. Through his office, he agreed to meet.

All of this Grey only knew second-hand, from updates given to him by Serinda, Raphael, or another of the *Fallen*. Grey had spoken to a handful of them during his time there, though Raphael kept the numbers who knew about Grey's presence low. Besides, they all treated him with evident mistrust. None of them were going to talk any more than they had to with a former Far agent.

At least Fen was back where he could keep an eye on him. They'd brought him here, hobbling but moving under his own volition, on the second day. When Grey had gone to meet him, the first thing the boy had done was apologise for "failing to protect them." Grey had done his best to disabuse the boy of the notion that he had failed anything at all, or that he had a responsibility to protect anyone.

"That's my job," Grey told him.

Fen had smiled at that, but it was a smile that worried Grey. It was a smile that said Fen didn't agree.

Now the three 'rescues,' as Raphael called them, were all in the common area together; Fen, Blane, and Salim.

It was odd. Fen's arrival had caused a change in both the girl and the other boy. Blane's at least, Grey thought, could be explained. The girl, upon hearing Fen's story, seemed to have taken it upon herself to look after him. Replacing dwelling on her own trauma with helping another recover from theirs, Grey supposed.

The change in Salim, however, was less easy to explain. Almost as soon as Fen had arrived, the older boy had fallen asleep. Not the broken, twitching rest that was all he'd been able to snatch up until this time, but a deep, sound sleep. No one had even noticed at first, until Serinda went to check on him.

"I can't see him," said Salim, upon waking. "The boy you brought - I can't see his mind. He's here, isn't he? As soon as he arrived, it was like everyone else became quieter. Not silent, but... more subdued. Enough that I can shut them out."

So they brought Fen to meet Salim. Blane had insisted on coming too, and the three had been hanging out ever since. Which was how Grey left them, as he went to meet Majid Ayad.

The meeting was arranged for an eatery on the other side of the city, a wealthier area that matched the image of a high-class prospective customer. It was set for late morning, as if Ayad's potential client were expecting to dine as they discussed business. Hopefully, nothing would appear out of place.

Grey wasn't alone as the auto-drive threaded its way across the city. Sat across from him was the muscular, bearded *Fallen* who had openly Read Grey upon his arrival at the clinic in the docks. He called himself Uriel, another obvious Milton pseudonym - Raphael seemed to like these, and had got quite annoyed at Grey pointing out that they called themselves the *Fallen,* but named themselves after the angels.

The restaurant was a large one, but styled so that each table was tastefully enclosed by low walls with carefully-placed, colourful flowers, the presence of such flora saying more about the wealth of the clientele and price of the food than any menu could. Small scaled-to-size rockeries and streams ran through the place, harking back to the extravagance of pre-Fall nature, with a number of caged songbirds dotted around and filling the place with song.

Following the instructions of the screen at the entrance, Grey made his way to a table a little way inwards where Ayad was already waiting. He wore the same tailored grey suit as he had when they first met, but it no longer looked smart or well-kept. His beard, too, had become less defined, with stray hairs curling outwards from it, and his shoulders were slumped forward.

He looked, in other words, like a father worrying for his son.

Grey saw no spark of recognition in the other man's eyes when he sat down across from him. The fresh layer of spangle fabric he had put on before departing was obviously doing its job, along with the well-fitted suit he himself now wore. The only item of his former outfit Grey had was his wide-brim hat, which he carried under his arm.

"Mr. Ayad," said Grey. "Thank you for meeting with me."

"Yes, yes," said Ayad, impatience getting the better of him. He seemed to realise this, however, and drew himself up. "I am sorry. Thank you for your interest in my coffee. Now, can I get you a drink?"

Ayad indicated the touch-screen built into the table, the menu slowly scrolling through the restaurant's offerings in gold font on black.

"Order anything you like, Mr. Ayad, and don't react. I'm here about Salim."

Grey could see Ayad stiffen in shock, but he did well to recover. As if nothing was out of the ordinary, he placed an order for two drinks. What these were, Grey couldn't say.

"Is that you, Mr. Grey?" said Ayad, keeping his voice carefully neutral as he looked up at the man sitting across from him. "Yes, yes it is. How did you...?"

"It doesn't matter now. What matters is that you keep calm, and keep talking like this is just a business discussion. I've found your son. He's ok."

Grey saw the light of relief behind Ayad's eyes, before being replaced by fresh fear.

"I didn't know what had happened to you. I heard nothing from you, and then those people came and asked me all those questions."

"People?" asked Grey. "What people?"

"They said they were from that organisation - the one with the very long name. I cannot say it in your language. The virus one."

"Pan-fed? The International Genomic Monitoring and Response

Organisation?"

"Yes, yes, the International whatever-you-said. They seemed to enjoy saying it at me. Two of them, a large man and one with evil eyes. They were quite persistent. You know, in the Crystal Caliphate they do not take nearly the same attitude."

So the two that Grey had met outside *Methuselah's End* had been following up on what they had heard, had they? Which increased the likelihood that they had been behind the attack on his apartment, too.

Grey hoped he got to see them again before this was over. He had a few things he'd like to say.

"My son, Mr. Grey."

Ayad's words snapped Grey back to reality.

"We finish our drinks, without rushing, then leave. We don't know if you are being watched. If they've already spoken to you once, it makes it more likely they're keeping tabs on you, so it's important you act like I'm just another potential client."

Their drinks arrived as Grey spoke, wheeled over on an auto server that beeped softly to them as it arrived. Ayad picked up both drinks and passed one to Grey. They chinked their glasses together as the auto server backed away.

"To business," said Ayad, loudly. Grey did the same.

"Now," said Ayad, lowering his voice again. "My son. Where is he? What is he involved with? He is a good boy, a good son. I cannot see how he can be caught up in some Federation problem half a world away from our home."

"He's... He's not, Mr. Ayad. Look, this is because of, well, because of *me*."

"Because of you, Mr. Grey?" Ayad eyed him suspiciously.

"Well, because of another case I'm dealing with. Your son ran away, yes, but that's not why Pan-Fed are questioning you. They are looking for me."

"I see," said Ayad, though he gave Grey a look that told him he would expect much more explanation later.

The drink was some sort of non-alcoholic cocktail, Grey found as he sipped it.

"I am a Muslim, Mr. Grey," said the older man as he watched Grey eyeball the drink disappointedly. "And I am also a representative of the Caliphate. I did not travel across this poisoned world in a personal capacity only. Reopening trade with your

Federation is as much a diplomatic issue as it is economic, and if your leaders think that their issue with *you* is more important than relations with us, then you must be involved in something very serious indeed."

Grey nodded dejectedly,

"More than I think I yet understand," he said.

"And I am sorry for that. But you will not bring my son into this," Grey nodded again, this time more resolutely.

"Right. So, let's go get him," he said.

Uriel input their destination the moment Grey and Ayad got into the car. Only the *Fallen* knew where they were going; Raphael was wary of letting even Grey know, when there was a possibility that his meeting with Salim's father would be monitored by those looking for him. The *Forever Fallen* had not managed to survive for this long by sharing information with those who didn't need to know, she said.

The journey took a tense hour, with Ayad growing visibly more uncomfortable with each passing minute. Grey could see what he was thinking without the need to Read him; was he really right in trusting this investigator? What did he really know about Grey, aside from the fact that he was, by his own admission, being hunted by his own government?

The tension only grew as their destination became more apparent. The ubiquitous vis-boards and ad-screens of most of the city's roads slowly gave way to static, painted signs warning that they were entering a restricted area. Residential and commercial buildings began to give way to large, hulking storage areas. They were entering another warehouse district, but this one was very much in use. In fact, Grey gradually realised they were closing in on one of the city's Fabricator districts.

Uriel refused to answer when Grey asked exactly where they were going, telling him only to wait and see. This served to unsettle Ayad even more, to the point that Grey considered attempting to use the calming technique Serinda had been teaching him on the man.

Before he did so, however, their car suddenly pulled to the left and entered a narrow road leading to a large metal gate. In front of this gate stood a small guardhouse, two armed figures sat inside and clearly visible through its wide windows. They wore uniforms typical of the security guards of any of these sites, thin-brim Pershing caps and pale blue shirts, holsters wrapped around their waists with stun-locks hanging in easy reach. Grey didn't need to see the logo on their patches to know that these were Requisition staff.

So, they were at a Requisitions site. As in, they were pulling into a carefully monitored, secure Reclamation Authority asset. Why the *hell* were they doing that?

Grey's surprise only grew as Uriel rolled down his window and nodded towards one of the guards. As if there was nothing out of the ordinary, the guard turned back to his console and pushed something on his screen.

The tall metal gates before them gave a metallic screech and rolled sideways. Grey sat in silence as their vehicle drove through, the gates rolling shut behind them.

"We have sympathisers everywhere," said Uriel. Grey could tell that was all the explanation he was going to get.

They pulled up in front of a large warehouse, the same basic design as the ones where he had found Fen all that time ago, a thin metal shell covering as large an area as possible. It was designed to protect whatever was inside from the elements, and not much else; a storage place for the vast quantities of materials both consumed and produced by a voracious Fabricator, which must be located somewhere nearby.

The lot outside the building had several vehicles already there, but far fewer than its capacity implied was usual. Uriel stepped out of the car without saying a word, indicating for the others to do so too.

"My son is inside?" asked Ayad.

He was looking at Grey, but it was Uriel who gave a short nod.

"You'll see him soon," said the *Fallen*. It seemed his distaste for Grey did not stretch to those he was with because Grey heard real sympathy in his voice.

A small door in the side of the warehouse took them inside, where Serinda was already waiting with Salim by her side. Majid Ayad cried out the boy's name at the sight of him.

"Salim! My boy…"

Ayad ran towards Salim, reaching for his son, but he hesitated and stopped as Salim stepped backwards and held up his hands as if to ward him off.

"Son, what is wrong?"

This was followed by a long string of Arabic that Grey could not follow. Salim replied in the same language, the soft words he spoke seeming to upset his father.

"My boy, what are you saying?" said the father suddenly in centra-English. "There is no evil in you!"

Again Salim spoke in soft words Grey could not understand, but this time the boy turned to him and Serinda as he talked and lapsed back into centra-English.

"... but these people, too, I do not believe are evil. They helped me when I was lost," said Salim. "But it is not right!" he shouted abruptly, as if trying to convince himself.

Grey looked from the boy to Serinda and Majid.

"What is he talking about? What is not right?" he asked.

"Sorcery," said Salim, looking Grey square in the eye. "It is wrong to allow the *Djinn* to work through you. It is *širk*. I think... I believed..." Salim turned to his father, tears appearing in his tired eyes. "I cannot bring this upon my family, upon my sisters," he finished, looking young and lost.

Salim did not try to keep his father back this time, as Majid knelt in front of his son and, holding one hand behind his son's head, placed them temple-to-temple. They stayed there, eyes closed, for one long breath before Majid once again opened his eyes.

"Salim, my son," said Majid. "'You bring nothing but happiness upon our family. Whatever this is, it is not sorcery, not *širk* nor *harām*, it is a gift from *Allāh*."

"It's Aether," said Serinda. "Salim came into it without understanding what was happening."

Majid nodded.

"I have heard of this. We have it in the Crystal Caliphate, of course, though I have been told that this is the one area in which your Federation leads us. And much of the world, I believe."

Salim raised his head to meet his father's gaze.

"How long have you been keeping this from me, Salim?" asked Majid. "Why did you not speak with me? I am your *father*, and you don't ever need to hide your pain from me."

"It started with the leaf rust last year," replied Salim. "When all those people came to the plantation, trying to save the crop. I kept seeing their dreams, seeing their desires and fears and... other things. I thought I could shut it out, learn to control it, but..."

Salim's words trailed off and he stared into the middle distance, replaying the trauma of the past year in his mind.

"So you ran," said Grey. "In a place so far away you thought it would keep your family safe."

Salim gave a shallow nod.

"We can help him," said Serinda, stepping away from Salim as his father took him in his arms. "Just in these past few days he has begun to control it, but…"

"But he would have to stay here, in this city."

Serinda nodded. Majid was a fast learner.

"No," said Majid, shaking his head. "No, he must come home. Now we know what this is, there will be help for him back with his family."

Majid crouched down and met his son's gaze once more.

"Will you come home, son? Your mother and sisters will be lost without you."

Salim looked from his father to Serinda, and back.

"You can control it now," Serinda said softly. "Remember the exercises we showed you."

She turned to the father.

"But he *will* need help. I don't know what it is like back in your home, but you must find someone who can guide him, teach him. There is still much he doesn't understand," she said.

Majid nodded.

"I will be sure to find him a teacher." He turned back to his son, kneeling to look at him eye to eye.

"Son, will you come home with me?"

Salim said nothing for some time, listening to some inner voice.

"*Aywa*. Yes," he said, eventually.

A weight lifted from Grey's shoulders, though tinged with guilt. After all, he was glad Mr. Ayad had found his son, but he also had an ulterior motive in ensuring this happened.

As if sensing what Grey was feeling, Ayad stood and turned to face him.

"I thank you, Mr. Grey. You did what I asked. But I feel maybe that the payment has changed, yes?"

A very fast learner, indeed.

"I need your help," said Grey.

"The kind of help someone with the diplomatic immunity of a foreign representative can offer?"

"Yes," said Grey, noting Serinda listening curiously to their discussion. He hadn't said anything of his intentions to the *Fallen*. "I need Salim to be staying at the Meridian for a while."

Ayad drew himself up to his full height, showing some of the build age had taken from him.

"I already said that Salim is coming *home*, Mr. Grey. I will not change that for you."

Grey nodded. "I know, Mr. Ayad. But I need it to *look* like he's staying. I need the room."

17

Reconstruction is impossible while the territories of the Reclamation remain separate. Equally, global instability makes the creation of a national authority an imperative. The very structure of the Reclamation demands the formation of a federated state capable of guaranteeing external security and internal economic prosperity.

Declaration on the Formation of the Federation, Reclamation Authority

It took some arguing to get Raphael to agree to let them go, but in the end she couldn't stop them without resorting to coercive means that Serinda would never approve of.

The reasons for getting away from the *Forever Fallen* were fuzzy even in Grey's mind, but he knew that eventually he would be forced to explain exactly what Fen could do. All they knew was that he was an Aether user, escaped from some kind of Far facility out in the Waste and now hunted by the agency like many others before him.

If they stayed, it was just a matter of time before they discovered how Fen could manipulate Mindfire. And he didn't know what the *Fallen* would do then. He'd already seen that they had heavy weapons, and were confident enough to take a group of RA forces head-on. Before doing anything else, he needed to use the Meridian as a place to regroup and collect his thoughts.

What finally made Raphael concede, though, was Fen. Something had happened between him and Blane – an argument of some kind, Raphael said, though over what she didn't know. Fen refused to talk about it, and Blane wouldn't come out of her room.

Grey went to see her in her room on the top floor before they left. Tapping the door-ring and showing his face to the camera, he was relieved when the lock clicked and the door swung open.

Blane was standing at her window, looking out over the city as she so often seemed to. Grey wondered what she saw out there. Was it something she'd lost, or something she hoped to find?

"Hi," she said as he drew up beside her, looking out at the view himself. The lights of the city reflected dully off the grey, polluted clouds hanging low overhead, a false twilight though the sun was still up, somewhere above.

"Hi."

"You spoke to Fen?" Blane asked.

"He's not talking. Something happen between you two?"

Blane looked thoughtful. Grey stared out over the city while he waited for a reply.

From where he stood he saw the vista of concrete that was Albores, grey buildings stretching outwards in all directions towards the distant brown smear that was the Waste. Clusters of skyscrapers in distant districts broke the monotony, and right in the heart of the city the spire of the Central Tower thrust like a spear into the sky.

"He... he is *angry*," she said after a pause.

Grey turned from the window and sighed.

"Yes, he probably is. He's been through a lot. Like you," he said.

"Did he really kill all those people?"

Grey froze.

"What people? What did he tell you?"

"He said he killed them. Far Agents. RA. Pan... Pan-Fed."

Blane's tongue seemed to stumble over the last word, though she quickly recovered.

"Is it true? How could he even do something like that?"

It was unclear to Grey if she was asking about the limits of ability, or morals.

"They were attacking him. Attacking *us*."

"Even the two he killed first?"

Grey was lost for words at first, not understanding what Blane was talking about.

"The couple that took him from the site? What are you talking about?" he asked.

"Well, they weren't *attacking* him, were they? They got him out."

Again, Grey didn't know what to say.

He replayed the story Fen had told him of his childhood and his escape from the site. Fen had said he thought their behaviour was strange...

"You didn't *see* it?" said Blane, incredulously. "Aren't you meant to be a detective?"

"They were... I mean, Fen thought they were taking him somewhere."

"Just the two of them? After letting him Read them, letting him know they were going to take him? Did you not *listen* to his story?"

"You think they were trying to save him?"

But, Grey realised, it made sense. It *was* possible.

But then who were they? *Forever Fallen?* But that at least clearly didn't make sense – Raphael would have known more about Fen if so.

"He enjoys the killing." Blane's words interrupted his thoughts as if she hadn't heard his question. "He was *proud* when he told me how he killed a load of Far agents, of… of Pan-Fed agents. He's so angry, I don't think he realises they're people too."

There it was again, a slight stumbling over her words.

"What is Pan-Fed to you?" Grey asked, softly.

"Home," she said, equally softly. "My parents both worked for Pan-Fed."

"But they're the *bad guys*," said Fen, sat in the re-painted Switcher beside Grey as the vehicle drove them to the Meridian. Serinda had convinced Raphael to allow them to take it, along with an anonymised thin-screen and a week's worth of spangle fabric. "They're the ones trying to kill *us*."

"They are," replied Grey. "You're right. But Blane's also got a point. Hell, some of them might not even know why they're hunting us."

"So I should just let them shoot you?"

Grey noted the way Fen said 'you,' not 'me' or 'us.'

"No, kid. You did right. But maybe be careful how you talk about it around Blane."

Grey thought for a moment.

"No, scratch that. Be careful how you talk around *anyone*. It's my fault, I should have said something. We don't know what the *Forever Fallen* want, not really."

"They want a world free from the oppression of the Reclamation Authority," said Fen, as if this was a fact so obvious Grey must already know.

"Do they now? And who told you that?"

"Well, that man Uriel for a start, and Raphael said something similar. She said the RA was just a modern form of old tyranny. The same old men in the same old shadows."

Grey could hear the boy only half-understood what he was saying, but he could also hear conviction. So they'd been indoctrinating him while Grey was elsewhere, had they?

"But Serinda said I needed to find the truth for myself," continued Fen thoughtfully. "Raphael was annoyed by that, I think.

Grey chuckled at this. He was by now convinced the two were in a relationship, but Serinda had shown she wasn't afraid to stand up to the *Fallen*'s leader when she disagreed with her.

"Serinda's smarter than the rest of us put together, I think," said Grey, shaking his head with a rueful smile.

The conversation stilled for a moment, the two of them watching the city pass by through the windows.

They were already out of the downtown area, and the number of pedestrians and the number of marked patrol cars had increased greatly. Grey tensed every time they passed a uniformed law enforcement officer, but they drove on without attracting any attention.

Loud signs and screens shouted their wares to the world in bright, lurid letters, as below them the inhabitants of the city went about their lives. The buildings on both sides of the road were several stories high, grey concrete almost buried beneath the posters, logos, and signs stuck all over. In many ways the street resembled the high streets of the past, though in a world where monthly Basic Allowances meant everyday goods were ordered directly from Requisitions the majority of stores marketed a limited number of higher-end products for those with the funds to pay.

Another major difference to the pre-Fall world was the large number of elevated walkways running between different buildings, practically blocking out the sky for those at ground level. Designed to protect shoppers from the clothes-staining, ashy rain that was so frequent, it was said you could walk across half the city without once stepping outside. At least, the better parts of the city.

"So what are we doing next?" asked Fen after a while.

"*We* are going to the Meridian, and then *you* are going to stay there while I figure this out."

Grey softened his expression as Fen's own showed both fear and frustration, determination to be involved in his own fate mixed in.

"Look, Fen…" continued Grey. "Let me look after you, ok? I know you want to help … lord knows you've already saved my life more times than I can count … but you can't put yourself in danger."

"I'm already in danger!" Fen protested. "I wasn't safe in your apartment; why would I be safe anywhere else?"

"The Meridian's sort of… special. As long as we keep our heads down, we'll be safer there than anywhere in the city."

"Isn't it just a hotel?" asked Fen. "Not that I've ever stayed in a hotel…" he finished with a hint of surliness.

Indeed, Fen was right. But it wasn't *just* a hotel. Grey had needed to check online to clarify the details, but he'd always known the Meridian had some kind of special status. Even the Far Agency didn't go there without invitation.

It turned out this was because of the building's history, and the city's. Though it seemed impossible to believe when you looked at it from the outside, the gleaming white building rising high above everything else in its section of the city was one of the oldest in Albores.

It had been built almost before Albores *was* a city, but most definitely after the economic potential of the area was realised. Not only that, but it had been used for the formative meetings of the Federation, when representatives of the cities of the Reclamation, the Reclamation Authority, and the Carib-Federation came together to debate and codify the various treaties, agreements, and under-the-table dealings necessary to allow talks of such a unification to even begin.

Ever since, it had sat apart from the rest of the burgeoning city, an unspoken agreement becoming unwritten rule. It was where Carib-Federation oligarchs and RA officials met to ensure the balance of power in the region remained stable, and, Grey would wager, where nameless suits exchanged the thick, plain envelopes that were so often the lubricant of society, where what shouldn't be done in the light of day was done in the shade of small, secluded conference rooms. Albores law enforcement and RA agencies most definitely did *not* have writ on its grounds.

Grey had only known half of this himself until recently. It wasn't exactly broadcast by the Reclamation Authority, and some of it he had to work out by inference, but as long as he and Fen stayed under the radar and under the auspices of Majid Ayad, he thought the Meridian would be a safe haven for them.

A sudden loud bang somewhere behind them reverberated through their car and made him jolt upright in surprise. Were they being attacked?

The next instant, the car's screen turned a bright red and the windows and doors made a sharp cracking sound. But they weren't cracking open, they were pulling tightly shut. A hissing sound Grey recognised as pressure canisters releasing their stored atmosphere into the cabin filled the air, and his ears popped.

Airborne pathogen detected. Please fasten seatbelts and assume safe seated position.

The message flashed upon the navscreen as speakers in the car blasted a sequence of warning tones and the same message, spoken.
"What's happening?" yelled Fen, over the noise.
The tires of their vehicle squealed as the car swung left, across the road into what would ordinarily be oncoming traffic. Instead, every vehicle on the road was heading in the same direction as them, some in reverse, directly away from the source of the explosion. Their vehicle slotted smartly into the line, moving at exactly the same pace as the cars in front and behind.
"Bio-terror attack," said Grey, trying to keep his voice calm for the boy. In fact, he realised, he *was* for the most part calm. A measure of relief was mixed in with the tension and shock he felt.
They weren't the targets of the attack.
"What's happening to them?"
Too late, Grey realised Fen was looking out the rear window as their car tore away from the area. Back the way they had come, people were falling to their knees, gripping at their throats and jaws.
"Don't look, kid. It's an attack. Pathogen. Another crazy slipped through the cracks."
But Fen was looking, wide-eyed, at the fallen figures. Even from this ever-growing distance, blood was clearly coming from the mouths and nostrils of the afflicted, red sprays fountaining through the air in front of them.

Safe distance achieved. Risk of contamination: nominal. Please proceed with caution.

Their car slowed suddenly enough to make the both of them lurch forward in their seats. The cars ahead and behind them did the same, pulling into the correct lanes, navigation algorithms already plotting new courses to their preset destinations.
"What happened? Why didn't we stop?" asked Fen.
"It's the way it is, kid. Someone set some kind of explosive with a

pathogen attached, then one of the cars nearer to the blast detected it in the air and broadcast an emergency evacuate signal to all other vehicles in the area. We got out, so... that's the end of it, where we're concerned."

"It was so fast..."

"Yeah, totally automatic. The computers in these cars are way faster than any human operator would be. Every one of them immediately sealing the cars shut, increasing air pressure inside to ensure that if there *is* a leak, air will always leak outwards. You saw how all the vehicles moved in sync, right?"

Fen nodded.

"What about the people back there?"

"Depends," replied Grey. "If the pathogen was known, was analysed quickly enough, there's a chance..."

But even as he spoke, several Rapid Reaction Vehicles sped past, flying down the road towards the source of the explosion. Quick Fix.

"Try not to worry about it, kid."

They sat in silence for a while as the car slowly drove onwards. Already, any traffic issues had been handled by on-board sequencers.

"Is it really that... normal?" Fen said, half-whispering.

"You'd be surprised what can become normal when you live it long enough," said Grey.

He watched the boy, staring out the back of the car the way they had come.

"...or, maybe you wouldn't."

18

The pre-Fall world was built upon concepts such as rights and dignity, tolerance and justice. While noble, these are not practical as the foundations of a stable global society. They saw the mirage of an oasis in the desert, and spent the currency of their lives trying to draw its water.

Chairman's Address to the 4th Assembly, *Assemblies of the Reclamation: Collected Speeches*

The Meridian was even more luxurious than Grey had imagined. From the moment they stepped into the marbled lobby he was sure they were going to be picked out as not belonging in such a place, and asked to leave.

But Ayad's credentials were solid, the thin, transparent pass-card he had given them instantly authorising their invitation and simultaneously pinging Ayad for confirmation. Somewhere out in the city, hopefully already approaching the airfield to the east, Ayad confirmed their right to be there.

All of this happened before the first attendant stepped towards them, eyes down the entire time.

"Would you prefer human or automated assistance?" the man asked.

"Uh, automated?" Grey answered, thrown by the question.

With a slight bow, the attendant or bellboy or whatever he was sidled away, returning to stand by one of the colonnades that bracketed the entrance.

The next instant Grey realised the pass-card he held in his hand was vibrating quietly. Drawing it out, he saw both room number and a map appear on the thin plasglass.

"I guess we follow it," he said.

They followed the map on the pass-card, the bright yellow icon that marked their location moving as they did. There were several people in the lobby, all smartly dressed and moving purposefully about their business, some entering and some leaving. Grey, taking a chance, decided to *Read* them as they passed, and the attendant.

The thought-images he could see showed nothing to make him concerned; contract details and meeting times and the occasional fantasy involving violence towards bosses or 'intimacy' towards co-workers - nothing out of the ordinary. The few he couldn't *Read*, their thoughts amorphous and built on sensation, not words, had nothing about them to make them suspicious. The worst thing he picked up on was the attendant's secret loathing for the clientele he served, a low-heat mix of resentment and jealousy.

The elevator took them silently but speedily up to the 38th floor, where the doors to their respective suites slid open as a welcoming chime played. Fen looked excitedly at the suite on the right, waiting only for Grey to make him promise to go nowhere without him before tearing off through the entrance and disappearing inside. With a low chuckle, Grey stepped into the suite on the left.

The suite reminded him of Francisco's apartment-stroke-safe house, the same maybe-faux-maybe-real leather furnishings facing another wide LEF wall, this one playing a soothing visual medley of soft colours and shapes, accompanied by gentle, inoffensive piano music. The colour scheme ran to beige and brown, but what immediately caught Grey's eye was the mini-bar.

That couldn't be right, could it?

He stepped closer to the small fridge, wiping his eyes to make sure he was reading the screen above it correctly. Tapping the screen rapidly several times to check it wasn't broken, he turned away from the mini-bar to find another, any other, screen. Then he had a thought...

"Room, what is the daily allowance for us here?" he asked loudly to the open air.

"The daily allowance for your reservation of two luxury suites is five thousand Carib-dollars, including tax," came the reply, a neutral feminine voice emerging from hidden speakers in the walls as the same message appeared in text at the bottom of the LEF wall.

Five thousand Carib-dollars.

Five thousand Carib-dollars. A day!

Grey had known Majid Ayad was a wealthy man from the moment he saw him, but this was beyond anything he had expected. Five thousand Carib-dollars was more than he could hope to make in a month, even if he managed three cases a week.

And a daily allowance was pre-paid. It was the limit of what you could spend *before* incurring an extra charge. There was no way he would be able to even make a dent in it, but he and Fen could at least make good use of it to escape some of their worries for a short time.

Flinging himself down onto the (amazingly comfortable, he

discovered) main couch, he grabbed a beer from the fridge and ordered the room service menu up onto the wall screen. He let out a long, deep breath as the tension he hadn't known he had been holding in escaped his body, and closed his eyes.

The wall rang.

More correctly, the wall beeped. But it was the beep that indicated an incoming call. "Main Desk," read the ID on the screen.

"Answer," ordered Grey, pulling himself up into a straighter seated position.

"I am awfully sorry to disturb you, sir, but we have been getting calls from someone who appears very much to want to talk to you. Of course, we respect our clients' privacy and we have not confirmed your presence here, but her description of you and the boy you are travelling with very much match your appearance."

The man on the screen wore the same outfit as the attendant had downstairs, smart and clean-shaven. He looked genuinely dismayed to be making this call.

"Ordinarily we would dismiss this sort of thing out of hand, but she is *very* insistent."

She...? thought Grey.

"And, well, you see sir, it makes no difference of course, should you request privacy, but she *is* a Far agent."

Grey put his hands to his temples and closed his eyes. How...?

"Put her through," he said, pushing his beer aside.

The screen beeped, and the image flickered and changed.

"Hello, Nestor," said Ritra Feye.

"Well now, you *have* been making friends and enemies in high places, haven't you?"

They were meeting on what was nostalgically called the Albores Hyperloop, though it bore only a passing resemblance to the pre-Fall transportation systems of the same name. The modern mode of transport had far more in common with a raised, enclosed highway than a sealed, airless system, though both moved through cylindrical tunnels. The speed attainable by the automated cabin cars inside was due more to highly efficient navigation algorithms and a lack of potential hazards such as pedestrians and manually controlled vehicles, rather than the removal of air-induced friction. It did not come close to the speeds of those few authentic hyperloops built before the Fall.

It was also incomplete despite a decade of work and decades more away from being connected to its nearest sister-city in the Federation. Construction was deliberately arranged to maximize employment, not efficiency, and for now it was simply a slightly faster way of travelling from one hub area of Albores to another, provided you didn't mind having to flag an auto-cab or walk onwards if your destination was elsewhere.

It was, however, excellent for ensuring you weren't being surveilled or followed. The cabin cars were small, pod-like vehicles made of semi-transparent plasglass, easy to check for hidden surveillance equipment and, enclosed on all sides, impossible to follow from above or below. Grey had used them before to meet with clients wary of discussing potentially valuable or incriminating topics in public.

Meeting Ritra Feye here, however, felt strange. Far didn't go in for 'clandestine'; like any other government agency, it was the one that *did* the watching, not the one that was watched. Still, she had agreed to meet wherever he proposed and promised to come alone.

"How did you find me?" Grey asked, sitting across from her in the round cabin as it sped along its route from one part of the city to another. Though no hub was more than ten or so minutes away from any other, they had set the cab to travel randomly between them for as long as necessary.

"It's good, whatever it is they gave you to change your face. *Very* good." Ritra leaned forward and reached out a hand as if to touch his cheeks, then thought better of it and sat back. "They call it Spangle fabric, right? Stupid name."

Grey gave a noncommittal grunt.

"We've heard of it, even seen evidence of it in action, but never got a sample. Throws recognition algorithms for a loop."

"So you figured out a way to beat it? That's how you found me?"

Ritra Feye gave a small smile and leaned further back, placing her hand between her head and the headrest.

"I'd like to say yes. It *can* be beaten; all we need is to confirm the identity of a person some other way, and then we know their new face." She looked across at him. "Hell, we could just round up anyone who *resembles* the guy we're looking for. But no, that's not how I figured you out."

She paused, gaze flicking slightly upwards for a second and giving a thin, knowing grin.

"You really can't help yourself, can you?" she said.

She seemed to think she was saying something funny, Grey could tell, like she was telling a joke he didn't get. So he said as much.

"Your head, Grey. On your head."

He slowly reached up, brow furrowing. There was something wrong with his head? But he felt nothing, just hair beneath his... oh.

"That damned hat, Grey. What is it with you and that hat?"

"It's very... convenient," he mumbled.

"Well, I've seen that damn hat every time I've seen you for the past ten years or more. You think I wouldn't be able to place it just because you've made your cheeks a little higher?"

Grey took the hat off his head and held it above his lap, staring down at it.

"So, Far spotted my hat. Great. And they haven't come for me because...?"

"Not Far, Grey. Me. Though that could still change, depending on what you tell me here."

So it both was and wasn't as bad as he'd worried. He sighed.

"What do you want to know?"

"I want to know what the hell is going on, Nestor. The entire Reclamation Authority seems to be after you, and won't say why. Then you've got that guy, what's his name, Francisco, running around with you..."

"The Spaniard?"

Feye looked confused.

"He's Spanish?" she asked.

Grey shook his head. "No, forget it. Anyway, I've been working with him for a long time."

"Yeah, but only under his guise as your friendly neighbourhood fixer. He's not made a move like he did with you in *years*."

"You know who he is?"

"Me? Not really. But I know enough that we don't mess with him. He's got the support of the Silicon Isle behind him. We mess with him, we mess with our Fabricator privileges."

"The Althing Republic? Francisco?" Grey didn't know what to make of this.

"Indeed. You've got a friend from the most technologically

advanced nation on this trashed planet. And another friend from the Caliphate of all places, I see."

"Ayad was a client. He's not involved with any of this."

"I should hope not. We let him go, anyway. He and his son took off this morning. Not taking a chance on *that* kind of diplomatic screw-up. Should be halfway to Makkah now, provided the suborbital doesn't have to detour because of a rad-storm or something."

Grey felt a surge of relief. The thought that Ayad and Salim could be further dragged into this made his stomach lurch.

"And then there's your bio-terrorist friends."

Relief drowned under the tidal wave of apprehension this comment pushed before it.

"Bio-terrorists?" he said, feigning incomprehension.

"The ones who gave you that nice new face; the only people with a line on them are anti-state groups. The kind who like to leave little packages of organ-eating microbes around for others to find."

She hadn't said the *Fallen*, Grey noted. She didn't know exactly who he had got involved with.

"I'm not working with bio-terrorists," he said flatly.

"No? I wouldn't be so sure, Grey. I've got a slagged Rapid Response convoy out in the Waste says otherwise."

Feye let out a long sigh, looking out of the car's small window for a moment though it showed nothing but white tunnel walls speeding by.

"Look, Grey, you were Far; not Pan-Fed, not RA. You dealt with Aether, and that's what you know. But don't think you know *anything* about the kind of groups who have access to the kind of stuff you've been given. Their support comes from all sorts of places, including overseas powers that would be *very* happy to see the Federation suffocated in its crib."

"And you're better informed?"

"I'm pretty high up in Far now. Inter-agency cooperation is part of what I do, so I'm authorised to know things ordinarily kept extremely compartmentalised."

"High up enough to meet a wanted man without back-up?"

"No one knows about this meeting, Grey. The only reason I'm here is because I know you. I know that whatever you've got mixed up in, *you* are not a threat. I need you to tell me why this is happening before the RA really does find you."

"Only you? No one else?"

"No one. My team had no idea what they found when they sent me the footage of your meeting with Majid Ayad. I followed the trail from there myself. I know it's something to do with this kid you're with. He was back at your apartment, too, right? Which, I might add, seems to have been completely levelled, though no one seems to know why."

"Are you high up enough to know anything about a Far agency site out in the Waste about eighty kilometres south of here?"

Feye looked puzzled.

"A Far site? Outside the city? What are you talking about?"

She looked genuinely puzzled. Grey once again wished she didn't have that damned lack of internal monologue. He wanted to *Read* her, to know how much of what she was saying could be trusted. If what she was saying was really true.

Taking the opportunity granted by Grey's hesitation, Feye pulled out her thin-screen and made an audio-only call.

"... yes, any kind of Far facility south of the city," she said into the phone. "Ok, send what you find to me." She hung up, placing her device on the arm of her seat.

They sat in silence for a minute or so, until her thin-screen vibrated. Feye picked it up, looked at the screen, and whistled.

"What *are* you involved in, Nestor?" she said.

"What is it?"

"Well, I don't know. My team got locked out of the system just for making the enquiry. Apparently the clearance is *way* higher than anything they can access."

She stared at him, a long, penetrating look that made him want to shift in his seat. He forced himself to stay motionless.

"Alright, Grey, you win. I'll leave you to whatever it is you're doing, for now. But Far *is* coming for you, and when we do, I will be right there too."

The screen atop the doors of the cabin car was flashing a twenty-second countdown to the next hub. Ritra Feye slid her thin screen into her pocket and dusted her suit pants down.

"You need to figure out who your friends are, Grey, and soon. Whatever you're mixed up in is *big*, and if you don't find a way to get off this ride you're gonna get *thrown* off. Here..." she said, passing him a thin-screen. "It's anonymised. Contact me when you figure out who you're with."

Ritra Feye stood as the cabin doors slid open, and stepped out onto the platform and exit beyond. Grey stared at the anonymised thin-screen in his hands as the doors slid shut again.

"I seem to be collecting these," he said to himself.

19

All those who wish the Reclamation to succeed realise that factionalism of any kind is harmful and impermissible, for no matter how individual groups may desire to safeguard the foundation of our new nation, factionalism in practice leads to the weakening of unity and intensified attempts by those who oppose us to destroy what we have built.

Ban on political factions and unsanctioned groups, *7th Assembly of the Reclamation*

They spent the next two days at the Meridian, living off the daily allowance and watching old movies from before the Fall. Grey tried to get Fen interested in the ones he liked, from Sergio Leone westerns to Warner Herzog epics, but they were too slow-paced for the boy. Instead, they watched the movies Francisco had turned him on to; giant lizards stomping through cities and massive apes climbing the towers of a previous age.

Grey had to admit that, despite himself, he quite enjoyed them.

On the morning of the third day, though, Grey made a choice, and made a call.

"How's Fen?"

Serinda wasted no time with niceties as the line connected.

"He's fine. Better than fine, actually. There's a pool here; turns out he can swim like a fish."

Grey didn't add that, as Fen had explained, he had been forced to ford any number of icy lakes and rivers during the survival trials he had been put through.

"Good. Are you coming back to us? I don't like the idea of him out there, no matter how secure you think that place is."

Serinda's expression on the screen was severe and disapproving, tinged with worry for the boy.

"Not yet. But... look, I need to speak with Raphael. She there?"

Almost before he finished speaking, Serinda's face was pushed aside by Raphael's. She had what looked like oil on her cheeks, and was flushed by some kind of exertion.

"We're doing maintenance here," she said. "If you're not coming back, then what do you want? This line isn't meant for free chat."

"I need to know if you have anything on a 'Doctor Caldwell.' Probably in Far, or definitely RA. You ever heard the name?"

Raphael's brow furrowed, and she gestured for Grey to wait. The line went mute and she disappeared from view, putting down her thin-screen and leaving the screen to show only a high concrete ceiling, cracks running through its surface. Another disused area of the city, no doubt.

Grey was beginning to think that somehow he'd been forgotten before Raphael's face reappeared, the oil smudges wiped away and a focused look in her eyes.

"Never heard the name," she said. "*But...*" she continued before Grey could say anything. "But, we do have a way to find out."

"You do?"

"We do," she nodded. "This time though, Grey, you're going to do *us* a favour at the same time."

He didn't like the way she said that, but there was little choice but to go on.

"Tell me," he said.

"Well now, this isn't something I can just tell you over the line. No, we're going to need to meet."

"When and where?"

"Now. Uriel will come get you. Meet him outside the Meridian's security gates, and he'll bring you the rest of the way. Oh, and bring Fen."

"Bring Fen? Why would I do that?"

"Come *on,* Grey," said Raphael as if he were a particularly stupid student. "You really want to leave him there alone? You trust the security there that much? You trust a *teenage boy* to stay there alone that much?"

Serinda's face reappeared on the screen as Grey found himself torn about what to say.

"She's right, Nestor," said Serinda. "He's safer with us, at least while you're not there. Don't worry, I'll look after him."

It was Serinda that decided it for him. Grey had major reservations about Raphael looking after Fen, but there was little doubt in his mind that Serinda was concerned only for the boy.

"Fine," he said. "But you don't let him out of your sight for a second. And if anything looks suspicious, you get him away, ok?"

"Ok." Serinda nodded, while off screen Grey could hear Raphael yelling for Uriel.

"We have a mole," said Raphael.

They were sat in a Scraper in a sub-floor level car park of yet another downtown residential block. Grey didn't bother to ask if this was another *Fallen* block, as the answer seemed obvious.

It was just him and Raphael. Uriel had brought him and Fen here and then driven off, while Serinda had taken Fen's hand and led him away. The last thing Grey heard before they entered the building entrance was Fen asking if Blane was there. He didn't hear the reply.

"What do you mean?"

"A mole. Someone in our organisation who's working for the RA."

"You're sure?"

Raphael nodded sharply.

"Too many coincidences. Some of our residences being raided, one of our clinics getting stormed. We can't even take our Scrapers out any more; too many of them getting pulled over and taken in."

"A clinic got stormed?"

Again, a short, sharp nod.

"Yes - by your old friends at Far. Our doctors only just got out in time. Serinda wasn't there, thank god."

The final comment was said with a note of fear and anxiety that was probably the most vulnerable Grey had ever heard Raphael be.

"What about the patients? The families?"

"Taken in," answered Raphael. "Of course they'll be questioned, but they don't know enough to be a real danger to us. It does mean we have to shut down the clinics, though. Until we know what this is, at least."

"When did this start?"

"A while ago. I only started getting suspicious a couple of months ago, but who knows how long it was going on before that..."

So, before Fen and I got involved, thought Grey. At least this wasn't directly related to them.

"Could they know about me? Know about Fen?" he asked.

"Who knows?" Raphael replied with a shrug. "But there's a reason I limited the number of people who interacted with you, and even fewer know anything about the kid."

So *that* was why she had kept most *Fallen* away from him? He'd assumed it was because she didn't want *him* to know much about *them*.

"Oh, of course I also wanted to keep you from being able to identify any more of us than strictly necessary," she said, once again doing that annoying thing where she seemed to read his mind. "I still don't think you're on our side, not really. But Serinda seems to be on *yours*, so here we are."

"Serinda knows about me and the kid. So does Uriel. Couldn't it be one of them?"

"It's not Serinda," replied Raphael, in words as definite and hard as diamond. "And if it was Uriel, we'd have been finished a hundred times over. He was part of this group before *I* was; we wouldn't be here today without him."

She leaned suddenly towards him, her face coming to within inches of his. Watching her severe expression, Grey felt a bubble of Thoughtscreen wrap around them, blocking all sound from getting in or out. It was always a weird experience, as if your head had been wrapped in miles-deep layers of cotton.

"We aren't secure enough already?" he said with a barked laugh. The clarity of sound inside a bubble, though, was always as crisp as the best earphones, like it was emanating from right beside the eardrum.

Raphael's expression didn't change.

"I need you to break into the Central Tower," she said.

That was certainly serious enough to warrant the bubble.

"You want me, a hunted man, to break into the most securely guarded location in the city?" he said, but he wasn't laughing now. He could see Raphael was serious.

"You want to know about this 'Doctor Caldwell', don't you?"

"What does that have to do with breaking into the home of the Federation government?" he snapped.

"Future home," she replied. "The inauguration isn't for another couple of months. But *before* that, the whole site is being readied for when our glorious leaders arrive. Which means they also have hard-coded lists of everyone on the RA payroll."

Grey sat back, moving out of the Thoughtscreen bubble. Sound returned, the soft background hum of the world that a person isn't aware of until it is taken away.

So now he knew what Raphael wanted with him, at least. She could have even been planning this from the start. He could see it clearly; what an opportunity he was.

If there really *was* a mole in the *Forever Fallen*, then she couldn't trust any of them to do this. The wrong choice, and the mole could simply alter or forge the list of names before bringing it to her. And, if the person they sent *wasn't* the mole, but was captured, then the whole organisation was in jeopardy.

He leaned back into the Thoughtscreen bubble.

"Let me guess how this plays; either I bring you the names and you root out the mole, or I get caught and you and the rest of the *Fallen* disappear off the face of the earth for a while."

Raphael nodded. "If I even *think* you've been caught, we go black. You won't be able to give them anything. We've done it before; we can do it again."

"That's why you wanted me to bring Fen, isn't it? I do this and don't come back, you take him."

"Would you rather he stayed in that hotel until the RA summons up the courage to go get him?"

He hated to admit it, but she was right. If Grey disappeared, then Fen had no one besides the *Fallen*. They would be the only people able to keep him from the Reclamation Authority, and whatever Far wanted from him.

"It's not all bad," said Raphael over his thoughts. "You will be able to find out who this Doctor Caldwell is."

"And you're sure this list is really in the Central Tower? It seems... irresponsible of the RA to allow something like that."

"The benefits of centralised power," she said. "Our brave *politburo...*" She spat the word. "... have to have everything right under their thumb."

Grey understood this, at least. The Federation leadership, elected by a select group of 'citizens' who earned their status through wealth, enlistment, or other achievements ordained sufficient, was still subordinate to the Reclamation Authority, and probably would be for a generation yet. Grey himself was a citizen due to his time in the Far agency, and could name maybe a handful of Federation politicians. The upper echelons of the RA, on the other hand, remained by large anonymous and out of the public spotlight. They truly did resemble a *politburo*.

The Federation led, but the Reclamation Authority ruled.

And though the Central Tower was to be the new home of the Federation executive, it was the Reclamation Authority who would occupy most of its many floors. In fact, were Albores *not* to be declared the official capital of the Federation in the next few years, against the predictions of most, the building would become purely for the use of the RA.

"Fine," Grey said, not quite believing it even as he said it. "How do I get this list?"

20

Neurologically speaking, there is no difference between a dream and reality. The same inputs are received, the same stimuli reacted to. If it is possible to control a dream, it must be possible to control reality. Aether is the tool to make this true.

Agency Handbook, Section 7.1 (Aether usage and practice)

The Central Tower stabbed into the sky like a needle of the gods, the pinnacle of it impossible to make out from where Grey stood. Though he was still several hundred metres from the centre of its base it dominated the skyline, making everything else pale into insignificance. Its glassy facade reflected the wan sun above and somehow made it brighter, as if a second, healthier star shone from within down upon everything around it.

Not that there was much around it, except more Central Tower. The body of the building rose out of a wide, square base that was itself five or six storeys high, filled with the offices and conference rooms a burgeoning bureaucracy requires. The base alone took up more than a whole city block and would be enough by itself to house the governmental machine. In fact, it already *did* house the city administration.

But the Central Tower wasn't meant to just be a centre of administration, but a symbol. A symbol of reconstruction and revitalisation, of Reclamation. It had to be the highest tower in the Federation, the highest tower in the new world, surpassed only in height by buildings now long since turned to rubble and dust in the Sudden War.

What the majority of its rooms would be used for was, like much of Albores, as yet undecided. Build it first, repurpose later, was the mantra of urban planning. Or 'if you build it, they will come'.

Well, thought Grey. *They've built it, and now I'm here. Only, I don't want them to realise this.*

His face still felt tight from the fresh piece of spangle fabric he had overlaid on the old one, though this served to make his face quite pock-marked, and older. It wouldn't fool any facial algorithms that were calibrated for his new features, but at least would change his appearance yet again to the human eye. He just had to hope Ritra Feye hadn't yet revealed what she knew to the agency.

He had run his meeting with her on the Hyperloop over again and again in his mind. Did she really trust him? Could he really trust her? What did she really know?

He'd left his hat back at the Meridian, and felt naked without it.

Ahead of him was a plaza, open to the skies until halfway across. There, the Central Tower rose above it, casting it in shade. Essentially, the whole ground floor of the structure was one wide open area, designed to be a public thoroughfare running beneath the entire tower. Escalators led up and into the overhanging ceiling at carefully spaced points beneath, and past these Grey could see all the way through to an identical open plaza on the other side of the building. People wandered through it, in groups or individually, some cutting through on their way elsewhere, others riding the escalators up into the tower. It looked open, and inviting, the way the Federation would like to appear.

The security posts scattered around said otherwise, however. At each one, and there were several, heavily armed guards stood and watched each person who passed by like bored but sated wolves eyeing a solitary lamb. Not hungry yet, but considering.

Anyone approaching one of the entrance escalators was stopped and scanned with the personal hand-scanners each guard carried, to have IDs confirmed and belongings checked for dangerous items simultaneously. Grey had left his own stun-lock behind with his hat and instead carried a smaller version given to him by Raphael that seemed somehow like plastic. Undetectable, she said, though with limited rounds.

Carrying any kind of offensive weaponry near the Central Tower was usually a sure way to get flagged; it wasn't only the guards scanning the area, he knew. *They* were for appearance. The true scans were being carried out every second by hidden sensors scattered throughout the floors, walls, and decorative greenery of the area. It seemed, however, that Raphael had been right about this strange, compact stun-lock; no alarms were tripped by his presence, no security teams descended on him.

Fortunately, as well, there was still no way to scan for Aether abilities. *That* could only be done by other humans, at least as far as anyone had been able to discover so far, and Grey was fairly sure none of these guards had any talents in that area. These looked like straight-up RA security, not Pan-Fed or any other agency, and certainly not Far.

The ID, though, was going to be a problem, because the instant he got scanned he was either going to be flagged as unregistered, or flagged as wanted for detainment.

So, he couldn't be scanned.

Fortunately, though, there *was* a way. He'd used it before, though never to get into a heavily guarded government facility. It was a tactic he used to get into parties, clubs, dinners or society events where there was a guest list on the door preventing him from getting inside to find whoever he was looking for. Using it to trick his way into the heart of the Reclamation Authority felt somewhat... amateur, but hey, you stuck with what you knew.

First, he needed a group. A certain kind of group, one of those with a large mix of people who all knew *some* of the other members, but not all of them. Usually, he'd just look for the most raucous group celebrating a birthday or something, where disparate groups of friends came together for a single person, but that wasn't going to work here. This was hardly a place for a party.

What it *was* a place for was gawking at the wonders of the modern world, and specifically the Federation. The whole building was designed to draw the attention, and that is what it did. There were, he could see, groups of actual *tourists* down there, thin-screen cameras clicking away beneath a sky grey with the ashes of past generations. Like Brownian particles, at times only a small number of these were simultaneously trying to access the inside of the building, but at other times they clustered and clumped together around the base of an escalator to the extent that the security guards had to shout them back into a more orderly line.

Perfect...

The most difficult thing about doing this was judging when such a cluster was going to occur; he couldn't exactly hang around an escalator without attracting suspicion. Then, he needed enough time to allow the effects of Unsettle to really set in on the guard before it was his turn to be scanned, making the guard twitchy and nervous. Finally, he needed to time his use of Distract and Slowtime just right, enough to make the guard place his attention elsewhere just long enough for Grey to step past and onto the escalator, the eager tourist behind him pushing forward for his own check before the guard could turn back and, shaking his inexplicably foggy head, get back to scanning what must be the next person in line.

It went perfectly.

Well, good job, Nestor Grey, he thought sarcastically to himself. *That wasn't even the hard part.*

He'd made it through the first checkpoint, which any ordinary inhabitant of the city could do without even thinking about. Fantastic.

The first floor was a wide, well-polished lobby turned into a maze of counters and help desks, signs loudly declaring the way to various departments of finance, housing, immigration, records, planning, and a multitude more. The air itself had that stale, heavy character that has been the hallmark of local government since the dawn of time, the one that caused people to shuffle their feet and talk in whispers.

Now things were going to get tricky. Everything up until now was open to the public, the base of the building designed for city administration. The tower section of the Central Tower, however, was anything but, and that was where he needed to go.

The most important thing to do in a situation like this was to move with purpose. Grey pushed past the clumps of people stood looking lost at the top of the escalator, each trying to work out exactly where it was they wanted to go, and strode confidently forward.

The lobby ceiling rose another three or four floors above him, with broad flights of stairs leading further upwards towards, as the signs stated, more departments whose purpose was to handle the various specifics of urban administration. Harassed-looking people moved up and down these, carrying the various forms that had to be completed and stamped and approved then stamped and approved again elsewhere just to open a case with the city. No digitised, automated processes here; everything was paperwork, to be filed in triplicate and rejected for every slightly misplaced cross or incorrectly filled out box.

Grey headed directly for the nearest set of stairs, following these up and looping around the next floor to head up a second flight, crossing the next level on his way higher up. With each floor the number of people around lessened, the size of the departmental offices becoming smaller, each one taken up primarily by shelves lined with boxes full of forms and documents visible through the windowed walls. Most were empty, or occupied by a single tired-looking civil servant in an ill-fitting suit. They barely registered him as he walked by.

The highest floor accessible here was practically deserted and gave the impression of dusty disuse despite the fact that the filters of the atmospheric circulators pumping air around the building made this quite impossible. Eventually, he came to a stop by a room labelled 'Exotic animal permit and licensing: Equine.' There was no one inside.

Well, as he was fairly sure there were no horses left within the span of a continent or two, this seemed as good a place as any. He stepped inside.

The office was cramped and musty, with a small c-shaped desk taking up most of the space, its touch-screen power cable disconnected from the socket in the floor. A stack of booklets labelled 'rules and regulations' stood in one corner, the pages frayed and yellowing. Clearly no one had used this place for some time.

There was, in fact, nothing of interest in the room. But Grey wasn't here for the room; he was here for what led *out* of the room.

The windows of the office were tall and wide, as if to taunt the bureaucrat trapped inside its cramped walls, and were fitted onto sliding rails that allowed them to be moved all the way across flush with the silvered walls of the outside of the building. A small ledge protruded out beyond these rails, a ledge wide enough to stand on, if you were sure enough of your footing not to slip and fall forwards to instant death on the concrete below. And if you were sure enough of *that*, then maybe you were even able to stretch up and, with a little *Push*, reach high enough to grab the lip of the roof above.

Grey struggled with the last part, his upper body strength almost not enough to get himself up and over the lip, but eventually he dragged himself up onto the flat roof of the base of the building. Panting, he lay there for a few seconds before pushing himself to his feet, keeping low.

The roof here was a flat, grey surface broken by numerous out-jutting air conditioning and circulator vents, spitting steam out into the atmosphere, and miscellaneous maintenance equipment. At various points, low, thin doors and hatches provided access back into the building, designed in such a way as to not interrupt the smooth, gleaming glassiness the building projected from a distance. Beyond that, thirty or forty meters away, the central spire of the tower rose before him. He made his way towards it, moving at a crouch.

The final stretch to the tower shaft was a sprint across open roof which he could only hope went unobserved by anyone above. Pressing himself against the silvered windows that wrapped around the tower from bottom to peak, he could just about make out a dark hallway beyond. He *Reached* out with the Aether, stretching his senses as far as they would go. Nobody nearby, at least. The tower should only be running with a skeleton crew until its official inauguration as the new home of the Federation, but that skeleton crew could still easily number in the hundreds. Fortunately, the area he approached was deserted, at least for now.

He found an access door a short way away, using Reach constantly to scout for anyone in the area. The door was, of course, locked from the inside, but Grey placed his hands and head close to the door and used Push to try to dislodge the lock from its position. It took several attempts, and his panic was just beginning to rise, but with a *click* the tumbler shifted and the door popped open. Just a few millimetres, but enough to get his fingernails in between and pull the door open, sliding through and pulling it closed behind him.

Alright, here we go...

Grey drew out the small grey box Raphael had given him. Once he hit the button, the jammer would search for and then block out any and all wireless frequencies it detected being broadcast in a 20-metre area. Perfect for disabling any security cameras nearby, though with the major downside being that someone, algorithm or human, was guaranteed to notice this moving hole in the security feeds eventually. The jammer also provided the additional benefit that any guards who spotted him would find their radios drowned out by interference, but the downside to *that* was that it meant he'd been seen.

He hit the button.

According to plans the *Forever Fallen* had, personnel files were kept somewhere on the sixty-second floor. There was no way he was getting up that high without using an elevator, but this also meant there was no way he was getting up there without putting himself through one hell of a bottleneck.

He met only a single person on the floor he'd entered through, a guard positioned near the elevator who he sensed with Reach long before the guard noticed him. It had seemed almost unfair to hit her with Flare while still hidden around the corner, using the momentary sensory overload to grab the guard's own stun-lock and turn it back on her. He left her slumped under a desk in an empty room nearby, though her absence would inevitably be noticed shortly. He just had to keep moving, and hope they didn't work out where he was going before he got there.

The elevator ran up the side of the building silently and smoothly, affording him an ever-widening view of the city spreading out beneath him. Though the sun still shone fitfully somewhere above the grey clouds, a low moon was also visible on the orange horizon. The sight of it as he slowly ascended made him feel like one of the astronauts in that *New Patriot* movie, the one where they flew cobbled-together shuttles to Lunar in a doomed attempt to supply the nascent colony with enough supplies to survive after the Sudden War. Indeed, somewhere on the face of that rock hung shining in the sky, the bones of the real astronauts still sat in cold, empty vacuum.

The chime of the elevator doors opening broke him from his thoughts. Standing in front of the doors as they opened were two suited figures, a man and a woman, who stepped aside for him to pass. Grey kept his eyes focused forward as he stepped out, hoping against hope that they would just get in the elevator and go about their business without...

"Hey, are you authorised to be here?"

Grey span and hit first one, then the other, square in the chest with the stun-lock. They slammed back against the rear wall of the elevator and crumpled. Closer range than he would have liked, and probably causing serious injury, but he had no time for anything else. In the same breath, he spun back and shot the guard stationed near the elevator once. Only using Slowtime on him had given Grey the time he needed to do this.

The elevator doors slid shut on the two fallen figures before Grey could do anything else, and he watched with despair as it headed downwards. Wherever it stopped next, those waiting were certainly going to raise the alarm.

Now he really *was* on the clock. He sprinted down the corridor, following a very helpful sign marked '*Departamento de personal*'. Sometimes you really had to love bureaucracy.

Another pair of confused-looking suits stepped out of a door to the left, stun-lock knocking them down and out practically before they had time to see the intruder running towards them. Out of time, and out of ammo, he sprinted onwards as somewhere behind him, shouting started.

Grey dived into the nearest room to his right as a bullet whizzed over his head. He thought he bent its path a little, or the shot was wide, but without Fen there was no way he was shielding himself from a sustained assault. This would have to do.

He slammed the drive-reader the *Fallen* had given him on top of the nearest desk, the in-built screen of the counter top flashing on and flickering as the small black box brute-forced its way into the files stored on the local network. No cables or anything were necessary; just getting the drive-reader within a few inches of any department computer would begin the transfer process, Raphael had said. Grey hadn't bothered to ask where they could have got such advanced technology.

More bullets came down the corridor outside, followed by the shouts of multiple people. It sounded like they were getting ready to make their assault.

A quiet double chime from the drive-reader told him its work was done. Already, it would be broadcasting its stolen data via encrypted link to an identical-looking box in Raphael's possession. Grey had succeeded.

But not the way he had planned. They weren't meant to react so fast. He'd hoped he'd have time to figure a way out in the confusion, not be cornered into a firefight. Still, he had at least one advantage; he could *Reach* and sense them.

There were three of them, gathered at the end of the corridor. Grey could feel their nervousness and confusion; the tension they were gradually forming into determination. If he could get into their heads, maybe he could Distract them long enough to get away, or Flare and push past. Three at once was more than he'd ever tried before, but...

There was a fourth.

They hadn't been there a second ago. Or rather, they had, but they hadn't allowed Grey to sense them. Now they did.

Grey barely had time to worry about what would happen to Fen without him before Aether poured through his mind and everything went white, then black.

21

Die on your feet, or live on your knees.

Graffiti atop Gate 17, Carib-Federation Southern Migrant Camp

The room was dark and cold, the floor beneath him hard. Something damp and sticky ran beneath his palms. Pushing himself up, Grey realised it was his own blood.

A nasty cut ran down the side of his head, making him hiss and pull his fingers back when he touched it. It felt like he'd been dragged through a trash compactor and left to rot.

Which, he began to worry, could be exactly what had happened. Even in the dark, he could *feel* this place wasn't one for people. Not for upstanding, right-thinking citizens, anyway.

"You're on the right lines," came a voice, deep, male, and filled with a sinister authority. Grey couldn't say where it came from, but it wasn't in the room.

Which meant he was being watched. And Read.

Warned to it now, Grey could feel the other person inside his head, watching his thoughts. It felt like a tick, burrowed inside his mind.

Well, there was nothing he could do about it for now. He was too weak and woozy to mount any kind of mental defence, and something seemed to be wrong with his legs, so he'd just have to get on with working out where he was.

"Go on," came the voice again. "You're doing *very* well."

So, a small, dark room, the floors hard and damp, not just with his blood but with moisture also. Pushing out with his legs, he felt his back hit one wall as his feet hit the other. Rough concrete.

He leaned to his left, stretching out a hand that soon found another wall. To his right, and a similar wall met hard metal, a heavy steel door that resisted his push. Locked.

The voice, he realised, had been coming from behind the door, the sound coming through some small space cut out somewhere above.

This was a cell.

"Oh, *good* job!" came the voice, the sneer that accompanied the words somehow audible. "But a cell *where?*"

Grey knew the answer the moment the voice asked, but he tried, futilely, to keep it from the monologue of his upper thoughts.

He, an Aether user, was locked in here, with another Aether user outside his door. A deep, dark basement room designed to keep those with extrasensory abilities isolated, and trapped.

He was in the Far Station.

"You really are a *detective!*" Grey heard the owner of the voice give a loud, slow handclap that slowly came nearer.

Sudden light as the door opened, a dull red LED strip that ran across one side of the ceiling flicking into life. Good enough to give definition, dull enough to hide the blood.

The figure who stood in the doorway, framed by the light of the empty corridor behind, was stocky and dark, with thick black hair flecked with white that ran down to meet short black stubble that stopped just short of being a beard. The face framed by it had deep, inset eyes and hard, granite-like features. Despite having few lines and no scars, at least as far as Grey could tell in this light, he looked somehow aged, as if years of violence and brutality had seeped into this man's very pores.

"Nestor Grey; the one that got away," said the man, stepping into the cell and perching himself on the edge of a small iron sheet that jutted out of the wall, what passed for a seat in this tiny space.

Grey pushed himself further up with his elbows until he was sitting straight with his back against the opposite wall. He still couldn't get his legs to move with anything more than a weak jerk.

"Good, isn't it? We're calling it *Tranquilize*. I preferred Paralyze, but you know how it is with people. The researchers who figured it out had been calling it that for months before it was even proposed for inclusion on the training list."

"And you are?" said Grey, trying to keep both his voice and eyes steady as he met the gaze of the man.

"I'm sure you can work that out, too."

Grey gave a groan half of pain, half of exasperation.

"Come *on*. You're one of those types who likes to play with suspects? Really? Gives you a little thrill of power, does it?"

This did not provoke the reaction Grey was expecting. Oh, the man seemed to get angry, but it was a *resentful* rage, not a prideful one.

"*I'm* the one who likes to play, am I? Me?" the man spat, face reddening even in this light. "When *you* left the agency to go and play private eye? Took everything we'd given you and *wasted* it all out there?"

Even thinking he was ready for it, Grey found himself drawing back into himself at the vehemence it this man's voice. He took note of the 'we.' This wasn't some thug with a propensity for violence abusing their authority, this was *personal*.

Grey decided to play the silent card. This could often lead to the person ostensibly in control of an interrogation revealing more than they meant to. He cleared his mind, using the old pink elephant trick to focus his thoughts elsewhere.

"I'm in your *head,* remember?" snarled the man. "You can't use your tricks on me. Hell, I probably *invented* them."

Grey smiled at that. The silent card *always* worked.

He saw the man's face grow angrier as he realised his slip, then suddenly he sat backwards and laughed.

"So you're *old* Far," said Grey, meeting the man's thin smile with his own. "Old enough to have been there in the early days, before everything was divided into techniques and strategies. Old enough to have been involved with opening the academy, perhaps?"

"A real Pepe Carvalho, aren't you?"

Grey *almost* gave a start. He didn't know anyone else who had heard of those books in this era, let alone read them.

"I do alright," he said, not allowing himself to be distracted. "So, what, you think I'm some kind of traitor?"

"I think you're an *ingrate*," the man said in long, drawn-out syllables. "I think we wasted a great deal of time and money on you, just to have you throw it out into the Waste."

"I gave my life to the agency for over thirty years," Grey replied.

"Your life *was* the agency's. From the moment we picked you out of that pestilential shelter and brought you here to the Reclamation, brought you into the Academy, you were ours."

"I think you have a severe misunderstanding of the term 'lifelong employment,'" Grey muttered, shaking his head and giving a cynical chuckle.

"Well, it doesn't matter anymore. You'd never have been allowed to leave if it wasn't for that damned woman, and we would have taken you in a long time ago if she hadn't kept interfering. But then you walked right into our arms!"

What woman? Grey knew this could mean only one person, but

that didn't make any sense…

"Yes, yes, you know who I'm talking about. I can see it right there, just under the surface of your mind."

Ritra Feye? But why…?

"Who knows why she does anything?" growled the man. "She's been a thorn in my side from the day she graduated the Academy. *But she at least fulfilled her potential, no matter how much she interferes with getting the boy back.* Now, where is he?"

Grey felt a second's cognitive dissonance at the seemingly abrupt change of track. Then, suddenly, two things were clear. He knew what this man wanted, and he knew who this man was.

"Took your time," said Doctor Caldwell.

22

Control of others begins with control of yourself.

Academy maxim

Grey didn't know how long it had been. Weeks, at least. Months, perhaps. Always the same cold, dark cell, the same hard floors kept slick with fresh blood.

Always the same cold faces, the same malevolent eyes and bruising fists. The same impassive reactions to the groans and screams that escaped his lips when he couldn't hold them in any more.

And then Doctor Caldwell would come.

But he didn't give him anything. No matter how much they beat him, how deep Caldwell scratched at the surface of his being, Grey refused to let thoughts of Fen surface. Caldwell hadn't even got the boy's name, not yet.

Not yet.

Grey knew he didn't have much left in him. Which would break him first, he didn't know. Caldwell's mental attacks were brutal and searing, fragmenting his senses and fragmenting his mind. The beatings, designed to soften him up, were less soul-rending, but every day the wounds piled up, the cuts and bruises and broken nose and broken teeth small fires of pain whose embers kept him from peace even when left alone. Though delivered by several different agents, the heaviest physical injuries he had received could be attributed to one specific person; the tall agent from Blane's apartment, in what seemed like another life. The one he'd hung from the balcony like a piñata.

That one *enjoyed* what he was doing.

With every beating the pain grew worse and the Aether drew further away, but at least Grey wasn't the only one finding it difficult. Caldwell's demeanour had shifted over the period of Grey's incarceration, moving from cold and sure to heated and frustrated. Today, he was almost wheedling, as if trying to persuade Grey to his side.

"But you surely see that controlling those who use Aether is the only way we survive, *agent* Grey," he was saying. "More than you realise, in fact."

Grey was crumpled in one corner, unable to pick himself up from the most recent of his daily beatings. The best he could do was push himself up against the corner, looking up at Caldwell much like the first time they had met. He'd spent so much time folded into this corner he was sure his spine was taking on the shape of the tiles.

"We almost destroyed ourselves in the Sudden War, and *did* destroy our planet. We came close to doing it countless times before that, too," continued Caldwell. "I'm simply trying to stop it happening again."

All the time he spoke, Grey could feel him crawling atop his thoughts, searching, picking through each one like a gull through flotsam, trawling for that one morsel it could consume.

Grey did his best to block him out as Caldwell tried to guide his thoughts, but it got more difficult each time. The man had tried detailing the experiments they had done on … Grey steered his mind away from that train of thought … and spoken at length about the potential of… the subject.

No, Grey shouted to himself in the fortress of his mind. Concentrate on what Caldwell was saying now; he seemed to have given up on forced recollection and was trying to reason with him.

"You were one of the first, you know," said Caldwell, looking down at the bloody, gently coughing shape of his prisoner without sympathy. "I remember seeing your file. One of the first students the Academy was designed for, the ones born into the Aether that we found young and tried to shape into true adepts."

Memories of his first day at the Academy floated up from the depths of his mind. He'd been so young, taken from the orphan centre only a year or so before by a group he would only later understand to be the Far agency. He was taken into a small, white room and told to wait, the woman leaving him there departing without a second look.

That was where he met the other 'rescues,' taken from the centres or camps where they were destined for starvation or… something worse. Emile. Dante. Trevan. Jem. And Ritra Feye, a year above them and tasked with their induction.

Feye was the only other one of that group that graduated. The others dropped out, or failed. To find their paths elsewhere, Grey had always assumed, until meeting Doctor Caldwell.

"Hmm, I wonder what happened to them?" said Caldwell, seeing the names flowing across Grey's thoughts like text on a screen. "Maybe I'll find out. Some of our failures actually *did* get to live another day. Some."

But the Academy had been some of the best days of his life. After a childhood swept along by the chaos and trauma of a displaced world he barely understood, the order and security and *purpose* of the place had been... a sanctuary.

And he'd learned to use the Aether.

"You see?" continued Caldwell. "We are the ones that gave you that, the ones that kept you safe. The ones that made you *strong*. That is all we do, for *all* our students."

He nearly succeeded with that one. Grey felt the face and image of ... the one Caldwell sought ... struggling to surface and forced it down under memories of his own childhood, his vague recollections of a frightened and frail-looking woman, old before her time, that he knew must be his mother. He could see the tents behind her, smell the caustic odour of the various cooking fires and burning garbage heaps that dotted this strange, terrifying place she had brought him to.

"Yes, she brought you *here*. All the way from the radioactive wastelands of Europe. She knew this was where she needed to bring her child. Not to the religious fools of the Caliphate, or those further east who have fallen back into imperial worship and satrapy. *Here*. And that is yet another reason we must learn to harness the Aether; to protect ourselves from them."

Grey had long ago resigned himself to the fact that he would never know why his mother had brought him all the way across the storm-churned ocean to the Carib-Fed camps.

Perhaps Caldwell was right; maybe her ultimate goal really was the Reclamation. It was possible, even likely; the promise of a new start in a land of boundless potential attracted many millions from the deadlands across the Atlantic. All Grey remembered was how she had changed after his younger brother passed.

The memory of his younger brother, long suppressed and constantly fighting to surface, was like a knife through the ribs. Grey had been just a child himself, and all he had now were half-remembered sounds and images, memories of how badly he had wanted to protect that sickly child; the small, frail child who held his hand and whose eyes burned brightly in defiance of the lot this poisoned world had given him.

Burned with the same defiance he saw in...

The sudden strike at the centre of his mind was like nothing Grey had ever experienced; everything Caldwell had done up to now paled into insignificance. It felt like a red-hot poker had been forced through his skull, his brain frying from the inside yet somehow maintaining its ability to think, to feel.

But it wasn't this pain that made it so powerful; it was the feeling of his mind being forced open like an urchin cracked out of its shell, as if his very being were being pushed and pulled out of the one place it could exist. Memories of the Academy flickered past his eyes, memories of the camps, of his time as a Far Agent. The faces of past lovers he'd thought he'd forgotten a hundred times over flashed across his mind's eye, mixed with clients and suspects and those he'd helped and those he'd failed and...

"So, you call him Fen, do you? Now that *is* amusing."

Caldwell laughed, a laugh that continued as Grey slumped sideways, eyes rolling backwards and body shaking violently.

"You left me no choice," said Caldwell, not caring if Grey could hear him or not. "The Forced Read technique is something we've kept secret for a *very* long time. Needs the victim to be deep in their memories, too, and even then it's too wild and chaotic to be used if other options are present. You left me no choice."

The cell door opened as if on cue, and the tall Far agent stepped inside.

"Dispose of him," ordered Caldwell, barely registering the agent's salute. Grey continued to shake and jolt, spittle frothing from the sides of his mouth.

"Pity, we could have still found a use for him, but he's going catatonic. He'll be lucky to survive long enough for you to put a bullet in the back of his head."

Caldwell stepped half out of the doorway before pausing and turning back.

"Put a sensory dampener on him anyway, though. No point taking any risks."

With that, he turned again and walked away.

"Now, what do we know about these *Forever Fallen*?" he could be heard saying to himself, as he stalked down the deep, dark corridor.

Grey wasn't sure when he regained consciousness. Perhaps minutes, perhaps hours. He expected pain, expected to feel his broken body and broken mind, but instead felt… nothing.

Sensory dampener, he told himself. Even his inner monologue sounded weak and tired. He had heard Caldwell's final words in some small part of his mind that was still aware of his surroundings as his body convulsed.

Yet somehow the sensory dampener was *helping* him. Before, it had felt like the Aether was trying to drown him, to tear him apart within its currents and flows until he was nothing but scattered motes of what had once been a mind. The soft, cool cloth over his head made him a single star suspended in an empty universe, something whole in a place where nothing could be broken because nothing else existed.

Part of him was scared to break the strange tranquillity of such isolation. Another part of him was screaming that even now the barrel of a gun could be being placed against his skull.

Think.

What was it Fen had said? Pain lessened the effects of the dampener. Well, Grey certainly had plenty of *that*. It was just that he couldn't feel it right now.

He reached tentatively out with his mind, stretching for the Aether. He had to force himself to do so; the feeling of it trying to pull him apart still echoed through his head, making him fearful.

There it was, just as Fen had described, like something soft but resistant lay between him and it. As if with a push of sufficient strength that resistance could be overcome, the barrier pulled apart to allow the Aether to come flooding back.

Only, it was getting weaker.

Shit, he thought. They were leaving the city.

So, they were going to shoot him and dump him in the Waste. After all, it was much easier to deal with a corpse beyond the boundaries of Albores; no one around to ask awkward questions. Shoot him, and leave him for the jackals[10].

---

[10] The descendants of old world, formerly domesticated animals such as dogs and cats had quickly learnt to adapt or die. They roamed every continent, opportunistic hunters capable of taking down even a healthy human with sufficient numbers.

Time to bite the bullet. He rolled.

At least, he thought it did. It was difficult, trying to convince a body that you could no longer feel to move. At first, he thought he'd got it wrong. Then, sensation. Dull at first, like a pinprick, then growing. His face, he thought, maybe his broken nose desperately sending muted signals of damage and injury through the fog. It felt… unpleasant, but it didn't *hurt*.

The Aether drew nearer, or he drew nearer it.

Lift your head, he told himself. The pinprick faded, only to flare back into life as he released his hold on his numbed body and allowed his face to crash into the floor.

The Aether lurched again.

Somebody was grabbing him. He felt it through the numbness, not a sensation of touch but a sensation of pressure, of movement. They were trying to pull him up.

Grey smashed his head forward with all the strength he could muster. Pain, and the Aether poured into him.

With a *Push*, the fabric over his head exploded outwards and tore apart. Now, with one set of senses Grey saw the tall Far agent standing over him, holding his bloodied nose from where Grey had smacked his temple into it, and with another set of senses he felt the Aether try to submerge him, to drown him in his own memories and what felt like the memories of others. Only the weakness of the flow out here, wherever they were, their distance from a population mass, allowed him to endure it.

In one movement, he pushed himself to his feet and leapt at the agent.

It was one of the dirtiest fights of his life. Several times, the agent nearly got the upper hand, but even in his weakened state Grey was more experienced at using both physical attack and the Aether to tackle an opponent.

Poor training, that's what it was. The agent met each punch with a more powerful punch of his own but flailed out with a fist or elbow at each mental assault. He seemed to have no instinctive reactions to meet Push with Push, or to block Flare with Thoughtscreen. This was a man who was used to using the Aether only against those who couldn't fight back.

In other words, a Far agent like so many others, and one of the major reasons Grey quit the agency when he did.

Now he stood rigid and still above the ridge of a drop to a dark pool below, kept from falling only by the grip of Grey's hand on the lapel of his shirt. Grey had to focus to keep himself from swaying, all the while keeping the barrel of the pistol he had wrestled off the man pressed into the agent's chest.

They were somewhere deep in the Waste, the ground around them dry earth and broken rock, the sky above black with the night. No stars could be seen through the clouds, and the only light came from the headlights of a nearby black van. An agency vehicle, no doubt, unmarked and nondescript.

"The entire agency will come hunting for you if you kill me," said the tall man, keeping the fear from his face but failing to keep it from his mind.

Grey smiled through bloody features.

"They're hunting me either way," he said. "I don't think you'll factor into the equation, whatever happens to you."

The truth of this statement was visible on the man's face.

"Now, why don't you tell me about Caldwell, and we'll see if I can't find some reason not to let go."

To emphasise his threat, Grey let his grip loosen a small amount. The agent gasped as his footing slid slightly back down the lip of the hole. Below, flakes of dirt and rock tumbled into the water with a thick 'gloop' that told Grey all he needed to know about the viscosity and contents of that waste-filled liquid.

"This is where you dump the bodies, is it? Some crater filled with industrial waste that no sane person would ever go near?"

The agent flinched as Grey tightened his grip again. Truthfully, Grey *had* almost dropped him. He was only holding on through force of will; his body wanted to collapse.

"He's from the RA!" cried the agent. "Caldwell. He's RA through and through. His credentials are all Far, and he's got rank enough to give orders to almost anyone in the agency, but he's not part of any of the usual chain of command."

"And that cell you kept me in? Is that part of the 'usual chain of command?"

"No!" cried the man again. "Well… yes. But only for the worst terrorists. The ones Pan-Fed brings in, the ones with information they need quickly."

"So Far provides 'enhanced interrogation techniques' now does it?"

"Usually we just Read them!"

The agent's terror bloomed again as his left foot slipped. Grey tried to pass it off as intentional, but actually his aching muscles had nearly given way.

"You need an off-the-books dungeon just to Read someone?" he growled.

"Well, we soften them up as well. They're terrorists!"

"I bet they are."

Grey stared into the man's eyes, watching him pant in fear. He was going to have to pull him back; letting him fall into the poisonous pool below would be as good as pulling the trigger of the pistol.

The agent must have seen Grey's hesitation, though, because *now* he used the Aether. And it *was* an opportunity; Grey knew he'd let his guard down, and by all rights he should have been overwhelmed by Flare, or Slowed for valuable seconds. He should have been Pushed back, or even... what had Caldwell called it? ... *Tranquilised*.

Only, this agent was a fool from start to finish. The compression-release he used was indeed powerful, smashing a good volume of the air between them down into an infinitesimal point before allowing it to explosively expand again, and it sent Grey tumbling backwards to smash against the van.

Unlike Push, however, this technique didn't project force in a single direction - you needed to be able to brace yourself when using it. Even as Grey went flying backwards, he could see realisation in the eyes of the man as he also was launched several feet back - right over the lip of the hole. He fell, tumbling, down into the waters below.

There was a 'gloop,' then silence.

"Well," said Grey, slumped against the side of the van. He had hit it hard enough to dent it. "What an asshole."

He passed out.

23

They may buy our food, but they will never again purchase our souls

Irumba Mbabzi, *On the Restoration of International Trade*

He had to be careful. All he had was downtown; anywhere else was simply too dangerous without any way to disguise himself. Even here, he couldn't guarantee he would be safe.

I wish I had my hat, Grey said to himself. The thought of it, sitting comfortably in a suite at the Meridian surrounded by luxuries he might never see again, filled him with a strange sense of despondency that nothing else had.

It was, once again, raining. Only this time it felt like a storm coming in, one of the big ones, powerful enough perhaps even to overwhelm the filters atop every building and bring in skin-reddening, cough-inducing droplets of toxins from the Waste. The van wipers were already struggling to keep the windscreen clear. Grey turned them off; they were unnecessary for the autonav, and the more he was concealed from outside observation the better.

He'd tried the *Fallen* buildings first, the one close by the riverside where he'd originally met Raphael, and the one in which Blane and Salim had been kept. As he expected, there was no sign anyone had ever used the locations for anything except temporary accommodation before moving further into the city.

It had been thirty-three days since his infiltration of the Central Tower, an infiltration both successful and a failure depending on the criteria you used. He'd learnt this upon climbing into the unmarked van the agent had taken him to the Waste in, date displayed both on the navscreen and the thin-screen the agent had left behind.

This was the second thin-screen that now-former agent had provided Grey, and he thanked the heavens for that; a more competent Far agent and Grey would currently be rotting at the bottom of a cold, glutinous pool.

Almost five weeks; plenty of time for the *Forever Fallen* to go dark, just as Raphael had promised they would. If they thought they could hide from the entire Reclamation Authority, then he had no chance of finding them on his own.

But did he have anyone else? In the entire city, he could think of only two who might be able to help him, and each had motives he couldn't fathom.

Jeder Francisco, and Ritra Feye.

Of these two, it was Jeder Francisco he sought out first. The man was practically the oldest resident of downtown, despite the mysterious comments Feye had made about his connections to the Althing Republic. He should be easier to find.

Easier, however, was a relative term. He hadn't realised it at the time, but somehow Francisco had managed to conceal the location of his 'safe house' from him without giving any indication of doing so. Whether this was through his general exhaustion at the time - an exhaustion that had only increased since - or through some other means, Grey couldn't say, but even though he could recall the view from the apartment windows he couldn't place it within the city.

The view had been high, high enough to see across a broad swathe of the city. High enough to see the Central Tower, he now realised... but he hadn't seen the tower from the window, had he? And, unlike the *Fallen* tower where he had met Blane and Salim, the section of the city it made the most sense for it to be in didn't have any building high enough to overlook all others the way the view in his recollection did.

So Francisco's safe house was in a location he couldn't place, in a building that didn't exist. Great.

DON'T PANIC.

Grey blinked at the message that had suddenly appeared on the navscreen, bold and unchanging. Words that looked exactly the same, in fact, as the words that had appeared on the personal fabricator in Francisco's apartment, back when Grey had needed stun-lock rounds.

DON'T PANIC.

"Well, yes, that is probably the first helpful thing anybody's said to me all day, but I actually *wasn't* panicking until mysterious words appeared on the screen of a vehicle I thought I was in control of," Grey said to the open air.

YOU HAVE BEEN BUSY.

Grey stared at the screen fixedly, not replying. When in doubt, wait and see.

SEE YOU SOON.

With those final words, the screen snapped back to normal,

displaying the same map of the city around him as always. Changed, however, was the final destination.

Timed for arrival in approximately fifteen minutes, it was labelled with only two words.

SAFE HOUSE.

The van drove him into the roofed parking lot of a plain residential building that *may* have been the one Francisco had brought him to, so long ago. It was just another one among a row of similar structures, with nothing to mark it as special. It certainly didn't extend high enough to provide the view Grey remembered.

GO TO THE ELEVATOR.

The message flashed up on the navscreen as soon as the van pulled to a stop.

LEAVE THE THIN-SCREEN.

Grey stopped his hand, already half-way in reaching reflexively for the device.

As soon as he stepped out of the van, it turned and pulled away.

"I guess they would be able to track it, eventually," he said to the air. His words echoed around the empty lot, leaving him feeling faintly foolish.

A short way away, a set of glass doors shone brightly, a small entryway to the building itself and to the pair of elevators visible behind them. He made his way towards them.

The doors to the left side elevator slid open as he approached, closing behind him as he stepped inside. This *did* all seem familiar, though he still couldn't understand how he could be about to find himself on a floor that didn't exist.

GOING UP.

This message appeared in the corner of the elevator display above the floor buttons. The elevator jolted, then whirred as it began to move. The floor number on the screen slowly began to rise.

GOING UP?

The message changed only slightly, adding the question mark.

Grey focused on the feeling beneath his feet as he stared at the floor numbers on the screen.

6… 7… 8…

But they were going *down*.

"*Hola, Señor Grey*! It is good, isn't it? Deceive the eye, deceive the mind!"

Francisco was there as soon as the doors opened, throwing his arms wide and giving Grey a swift hug with a strong slap on the back and stepping back before Grey could open his mouth.

Grey looked to the windows in the far wall of the brightly lit apartment. Warm sunlight streamed in, and visible beyond the city stretched out into the distance. Only...

"Only it's not *your* city, *si?*"

It was so obvious that Grey couldn't understand how he hadn't seen it before. The streets were less regular, the colours more varied, and the sky a gorgeous blue only visible after the largest of storms these days.

"Of course, I had the setting much dampened for your first visit," said Francisco. "*Mas cielos grises,* less *carnivale.* Don't kick yourself," he continued, a little more serious. "The mind sees what it expects to see."

"You called this *my* city. Are you really from here?" Grey asked.

"Oy *hijo,* I have probably been here longer than anyone else. I was certainly here long before the Reclamation Authority. But this city is too new to be mine."

"How old *are* you?"

Francisco stared at him for a moment, looking like he was weighing up answering or not.

"One hundred twenty-seven, *más o menos.*"

"Then you were around for the Sudden War!" Grey couldn't hide his shock.

"I was born while it raged, yes. But I was yet very young when it ended. I am more a child of *el hundimiento.* The Collapse."

Grey knew the term, though it was one that had fallen out of use in the public imagination. Today, the Collapse was just an early stage of the Great Migration, as the structure of society frayed and split under an avalanche of starvation, violence, and poverty.

"How did you find me? Could the RA find me the same way?" asked Grey. He still hadn't stepped out of the elevator.

"*No te preocupes.* I have access to... certain ways the Reclamation Authority does not."

"Then you really are from the Silicon Isle?"

Francisco laughed again.

"No, my boy, not in the way you mean. I am from much closer.

Though, yes, whoever told you was correct; I *am* a representative of the Althing Republic."

"It was someone in Far. Who told me, I mean. They know about you."

"Well, I would think so," replied Francisco, beckoning Grey to follow him into the apartment. "I was a part of the discussions at the formation of the Reclamation Authority. An observer only, of course, but I'd be upset if they had forgotten me so easily."

Somehow, Grey thought, Francisco seemed restless, full of more energy than he'd ever seen in him.

"How did you do that?" Grey asked. "To the van, I mean. How did you override my auto-nav? That's only meant to be possible for law enforcement, and even then they can only stop the vehicle, not reprogram it."

Francisco's eyes narrowed, and some of the energy seemed to leave him for a moment.

"That, unfortunately, I cannot tell you. That is something I am allowed to speak of with no one. No one on this continent, anyway."

Grey decided to leave it at that.

Something else caught his eye.

"The Fabricator. It's gone."

The alcove where the personal fabricator had been was empty, a hollow space that seemed designed to be no more than a storage area or pantry.

"Fabricator?" said Francisco, feigned incomprehension betrayed by the mischief behind his eyes. "I don't know what you mean."

The painting was also gone. In fact, most of the trinkets and models that had been displayed all around the room were gone.

"Going somewhere?" asked Grey.

"A good eye as always, Grey," answered Francisco, a more serious note in his voice. "Yes, I am leaving Albores for a while. Our little foray into the Waste drew more attention than my... *superiors* ... would like. I have explained all that shooting had very little to do with me, but I think I may need to explain this in person."

The way Francisco paused before choosing the word told Grey that 'superiors' was not the term he would ordinarily choose, but there was no hint of what he could otherwise mean.

"So you're leaving. Then, why bring me here?"

The smile and pent-up energy returned to Francisco's demeanour.

"Why, Mr. Grey, because I *am* leaving! I have a chance to help you in a way that will never get back to me, because as far as the RA and Carib-Fed are concerned, I've already left. Someone very much fitting my description is already far past the borders of the Reclamation. Again, people see what they want to see."

"The Carib-Fed are watching you too?"

"Grey, my friend, everyone is watching everyone else. This is something you must learn. In this world, a person is either the ruler or the ruled, the user or the used. When they involve children, though…" And again Francisco became serious. "… then, I think, we can break the rules ourselves."

"Can you get me in touch with the *Forever Fallen*? With Fen?"

Francisco nodded.

"I can. I will. For once, I can be *involved*."

This was why the man was so excited, Grey realised. He was energised by being able to do something.

"And I will give you this apartment. So long as you lead no one here, it will be the safest place in the city. Completely disconnected from the grid, and power and water are both self-sufficient. Untraceable to me, of course."

Relief flooded through Grey.

"Thank you," he said, not knowing what else he could say.

Francisco nodded again.

"Of course, Grey. But be aware; something is going on in the RA that even I can find nothing about. That boy, Fen, he is involved somehow, and they are willing to move on me for the chance to get him. That is unusual; risking the withdrawal of the Fabricators for the chance to capture or kill a child."

"I'll keep him safe." Grey's voice was filled with determination. He ignored the niggling question of *how* echoing in the back of his mind.

Francisco turned to take a last sweeping look at the apartment. Satisfied by whatever he saw, he turned once more towards Grey.

"I've stayed longer than I should have already. Stay here, and you will be notified when the *Fallen* are found. And for god's sake, get some rest. You look like some dead thing from the Waste."

With that, Francisco turned to leave, elevator door sliding open for him.

"How's your neck?" said Grey abruptly. Francisco turned back to him.

"I'm sorry?" said Francisco.

"Your neck. The more I replay your escape from that ambush in the Waste, the more I'm sure there's no *way* anyone could survive a snap like you experienced being yanked away by that drone."

Francisco grinned.

"A *good* eye," he said. "You may be right, Grey. Not anyone *could* survive that. But then, I am not anyone."

And with that, the elevator doors closed.

24

The pre-Fall philosopher Rousseau declared that liberty with risk was preferable to peace in chains. The Sudden War proved this a fallacy.

Coen Falwell, *Flames at the End of the World* (Sanctioned Publication)

The room woke him from the sleep of the damned. What Grey had experienced was not the peaceful slumber of a body recuperating, but the deep, dark abyss of unconsciousness caused by a body at the end of its limits.

He couldn't say how long he had slept; hours, days, he didn't know. All he knew on waking was that he was starving, and that the wall was singing.

Well, not singing, but playing a gentle melody that sounded almost vocal, ethereal and gentle. Designed to wake him gently? Grey wouldn't put it past a habitation that seemed to be so cutting edge you had to be careful you didn't get sliced.

He staggered into the living area, where the LEF was glowing softly with a small message icon flashing in the centre.

"Open message," he said groggily.

What actually opened was no message. Instead, it was a nav-link with a small map beside it, a bright red location marker dropped above a large building complex in the south-west of the city. Besides the both of these flashed a date and time.

Grey compared the date and time of the message with the date and time at present. He had several hours, it seemed. Apparently it was early morning, though the false windows showed the same bright city view they had when he'd first entered.

"Room, can you make the window images something more… consistent?"

That shouldn't have been enough, Grey knew. He was just still too tired to phrase an instruction clearly. Nothing should have happened., save maybe some kind of error message. You had to be as clear as possible with Reclamation-approved voice assistants, or they tended to go into capture failure and become non-responsive.

Yet somehow, when the images *did* fade to become a reproduction of an early dawn sun rising above a clear, distant ocean to bathe the now peaceful city in golden light, he wasn't surprised.

He headed to the kitchen to see what there was to eat.

Several hours later, he felt more human even if his broken nose, missing teeth, and dark bruising under the eyes made him appear less so. Holding a pack of ice that he had found in the blessedly well-stocked kitchen to his nose, he made his way via the elevator to the parking lot where he was unsurprised to see a car pulling up and opening its door to him.

The vehicle was sleek and black, low-slung and looked like it was speeding even when stationary. While an incredibly attractive piece of machinery, it was *not* what Grey would have chosen. He needed plain and unremarkable, not sleek and attention-grabbing.

Still, if this was what he had, he might as well own it. He slung himself into the driver's seat and hit 'confirm' on the already flashing navscreen. The car pulled away with a gentle acceleration that hinted at the horsepower beneath.

A pile of spangle fabric sat on the seat next to him. He stuffed it into his pockets. His face hurt too much to even consider putting it on, and anyway, he had difficulty even identifying himself in the mirror. He looked *awful*.

Still, Spangle fabric. So Francisco had a line on the material, too, and with what Grey now knew about the man's associations, certain suspicions about exactly where the *Forever Fallen* were getting their materiel from were reinforced.

He reclined the seat backwards, taking comfort in the soft, maybe-faux leather and closing his eyes. The drive time display was predicting forty minutes. Enough time to catch up on some more desperately-needed beauty sleep.

But tiredness was already being replaced with the tension he was becoming so familiar with. He lay with his eyes closed, images of rifles and rockets and dragons shaped of flame flickering across his thoughts like some badly-edited action flick, feeling the cold of the Far Agency cell and the heat of Mindfire on his skin, and the agony of Caldwell's mental assault in his very being.

It was a long ride.

He pulled his seat back up when the car announced the imminent arrival at its destination. It had brought him to another old area of the city, one more place of huge metal crates and hulking machinery. Unlike the old docks, though, this was designed for purely land-based work. Old bulldozers sat quietly next to caterpillar-tracked diggers, the first traces of rust apparent on their chassis. It couldn't be long before they would be worth nothing except as recyc.

This must be one of the old construction sectors, he thought. From here, giant machines would have fanned out and forced the earth itself to rise, scouring many metres of topsoil and poisoned surface layers from what would become the bedrock of Albores. The waste generated by this scouring was either used as raw materials for the Fabricators or, more frequently, simply dumped in the Waste until one or another of the penal clean-up-and-reclamation convict crews got around to the hazardous job of purifying it.

Now, though, the crates stood empty, and the old vehicles that once ravenously torn at the earth - insignificant in size compared to the pre-Fall terraformers that had long ago formed the world anew, but that were all the Reclamation had - crumbled slowly into dust.

The car drove slowly through a wide canyon formed by massive stacks of steel storage containers, piled up either side until they blocked out the light of the weak grey sun. The ground crunched under the tires, dusty grey-brown gravel untrodden for what seemed like years.

He spotted the first *Fallen* seconds later, standing atop one of the crates to the right-hand side. A young woman it looked like, possibly even someone he'd seen before, though impossible to tell from this distance. She ducked down almost the instant he saw her, though not before he glimpsed the long-barrelled rifle held to her chest.

A second one appeared on the other side, carrying a similar rifle. Then a third, and a fourth. Several more stepped out of the shade as his car came to a stop at what was effectively a crossroads in the middle of two perpendicular roadways through the stacks.

"Well, you couldn't have made me any less defenceless if I'd asked," he said to the vehicle as the figures encircled his car. And, *yes, of course*, one of them was holding a rocket launcher.

He popped the door.

"Grey!"

Serinda's voice came from somewhere behind the figures.

"Nestor!"

That was Blane's voice, coming from the same direction.

A moment later, and a gap appeared in the circle of rifle-toting *Fallen*. Serinda stepped through, Blane a short way behind.

"How the hell did you find us?" asked Serinda, looking furious.

Not the welcome Grey had been expecting.

"Good to see you too," he replied, wincing as soon as he smiled.

"We could have *shot* you," said Serinda, stepping forward and grabbing his jaw with one hand. "What happened to you?"

Grey winced as she held his jaw, before a strange feeling like cooling gel seemed to flow into his flesh.

"That should kill the pain somewhat, and increase the healing rate."

Grey simply nodded, though part of him even now wondered what else this woman could do with the Aether that the Academy had no idea of. There would be time for that later.

"There's no time," said Serinda, the weird synchronicity with his thoughts causing Grey a momentary disorientation.

"No time?" he asked. "For what?"

"It's Raphael," said Blane, stepping up beside Serinda. She looked... worried? Afraid? "She's going to do something stupid."

"It's the data you stole for us," said Serinda. "She thinks it proves there's a mole. But it doesn't make sense! Shiner wouldn't... would never..."

"Come on," said Blane, grabbing Serinda's hand and tilting her head to indicate for Grey to follow. "We've got to get back."

Blane led them down the right-hand valley, a long, straight passage that stretched away into seemingly endless rows of metal crates. The group of *Fallen* fell in behind them, seeming still wary of the newcomer but willing to go along with Serinda's word.

There was the unexpected sound of crunching gravel.

Everyone stopped and turned back. Several rifles were raised.

"Um, Grey, was there someone else in that car with you?" said Serinda.

Grey shook his head.

"No, just me."

"Then why is it following us?"

And indeed the car had turned, its wheels rotated in the direction they were heading and body halfway to facing straight towards them.

"I have no idea," Grey said.

He stepped towards the car, pushing past a *Fallen* who still had his rifle pointed at the vehicle.

"Um, stay?" he said, feeling the eyes of the group on his back.

The car gave no response.

Well, of course it didn't, Grey thought. He looked back at Serinda and Blane, and gave a bemused shrug.

The car didn't move when they walked away this time. Grey heard low, uneasy murmuring amongst the other *Fallen*. If he was honest, he was feeling a little unsettled himself.

"You will explain that later," said Serinda with a finality that made it clear this wasn't a request.

I hope I can, thought Grey. *I'd quite like to know what that's about myself.*

Blane led them to a gap between two stacks of crates, one that was almost invisible from any angle except directly in front of it. The thin passage led a short way down before coming to a sudden open area covered by a large sheet of corrugated iron acting as a roof about three or four meters above them. Several holes were cut out of this roof to let in a small amount of light, but most illumination was provided by LED strips stuck around the sides and along the ceiling. This was clearly a temporary place.

In the middle of this space stood Raphael, Fen by her side. Uriel stood to one side, while in front of her, bound and gagged, lay who Grey assumed was Shiner. He'd never seen the man's face, as he was always beneath some vehicle or another performing the necessary maintenance or stripping, but he'd heard the name several times.

"Nestor Grey? Alive and well, I see," said Raphael, taking her eyes from the figure at her feet. "Fortuitous timing, as always. You *do* have a habit of turning up in the middle of things, don't you?"

"Believe me, I'd rather not," he replied.

He met Raphael's gaze, then looked down at Fen. The boy's eyes were fixated on the man lying in front of them, though sensing Grey's gaze he looked up at him and waved. It was an incongruous gesture, totally out of sync with the ferocity in his expression when he looked at Shiner.

"What's going on here?" Grey asked. Demanded.

"We found our mole," said Raphael. "The damned *hijo de puta* has been giving up our clinics and safe houses for months."

"You don't *know* that," said Serinda, almost pleading.

"I *do*. I waited, like you asked. I told no one about the info Grey got for us. I changed nothing, except keeping our real movements from Shiner. And the *only*, *the only*, safe houses and clinics that got hit were the ones he knew about. He's been informing on us to the RA for who knows how long."

The figure on the ground was making muffled moaning sounds through his gag, struggling as if to deny the accusations against him. Grey saw his eyes bulging, face red, as he fought to speak.

"It's Shiner! He's been with us for years! There's no way..."

Raphael cut Serinda off with a raised hand.

"I'm sorry, Seri, I really am, but I know it. It's all that makes sense."

"It *doesn't* make sense!" Serinda yelled back, the first time Grey had ever heard the woman sound at a loss for what to do. "Even if it looks that way, you can't know for..."

"But I do," Raphael said, cutting Serinda's pleading off. "Not only in the files, but in my *gut*."

Raphael pushed a fist into her stomach in emphasis.

"People have *died* because of him," she snarled. "People are *missing*. We have no idea where most of those caught at the clinics have been taken."

"So you're going to *execute* him?" Serinda cried. "Sara, this isn't you..."

A look passed over Raphael's face at the name, and for a moment she seemed trapped. Grey, drawing on the Aether since the moment he had arrived, could *see* the confusion in her mind, caught between the pleading in Serinda's voice and the path she had already decided upon.

"Can't you Read him?" said Grey. He'd never seen such an odd mix of resolution and uncertainty exist so simultaneously in someone's mind.

"No inner monologue," Raphael replied, and even as she spoke he could see a renewed determination engulf and swallow any hesitancy. "Can't do it. And even if we could, we could never know for certain that..."

"He's RA! He needs to die!"

The whole room went silent, each and every person looking at Fen. The boy seemed unaware or uncaring of the reaction his words had elicited, still glaring at the prisoner on the floor.

"Fen..." said Grey.

When Fen looked at Grey this time, Grey almost took a step back in fear. There was fire behind his eyes, so intense Grey almost thought it was real.

"They need to be *punished*," snarled the boy.

Blane stepped forward, reaching out towards Fen.

"Fen," she said. "This isn't the right way. This isn't what you want…"

"You don't know what I want!" shouted Fen.

Grey could tell that Blane sensed the danger too. The boy's face was contorted in pure rage, and the Aether *pulsed*.

Grey had never felt anything like it before. It was like the surface of the Aether, usually so smooth and gentle in its flow, was disturbed by a leviathan passing beneath. He could tell the others felt it too, faces paling and rifles half-rising towards the boy.

Raphael waved them down.

"Fen is right," she said. "You knew what this was when you joined. You *all* knew…" she looked directly at Serinda. "This isn't a game. We're fighting a monolith that would think nothing of crushing us into the dust and using our blood for lubricant. We're in a war against Heaven. We all know we're risking our lives…"

She drew a previously-concealed handgun from her belt, pressing it to the back of Shiner's skull.

"…. so theirs are forfeit too."

She pulled the trigger.

25

The turn of tragedy to tyranny was and ever will be.

Songs of the Camps (Unsanctioned digital document)

Fen chose not to come with him. That's what kept playing over and over in Grey's head as he sat, staring at the hat in his hands as if it could give him the answers he sought.

Serinda and Blane sat with him in the living area of the safe house. It hadn't been a spoken decision to stay together; after Raphael's murder of Shiner, Serinda had just turned and left without a word. Blane had looked torn, and then run after her.

The boy stays with me.

That was all Raphael had said, not looking up from the sprawled form in front of her. Grey even then would have fought, futile though it may have been when outnumbered by armed and trained Aether users, but Fen had nodded and moved to stand closer to her.

Everything Grey had prepared for, everything he had expected or considered, came crashing down at that moment and left him rudderless and confused. He had resolved that he would protect the boy, but Fen had chosen a different path.

Leave.

At Raphael's words, the other *Fallen* lifted their rifles and pointed him away.

"Keep Serinda safe."

That was the last thing Raphael said as he walked away. He turned back to face her for a moment, but Raphael was already deep in discussion with Uriel. The dark, crimson patch coming from the body on the floor nearby slowly grew.

He was almost to the car before Fen called out to him from behind. It was a strange feeling, the paternal joy that stirred in him when he thought, for a moment, that the boy had changed his mind.

"I brought your hat," said Fen, softly.

Grey looked down, to see his wide-brimmed hat held in Fen's outstretched arms.

"I... I took it from the hotel when we left. I thought... Well, look, here it is."

Fen thrust it out in front of himself again as if it were burning hot.

"You can come with me, you know," said Grey, not taking the hat.

"I know," replied Fen. He looked calm now, the anger behind his eyes replaced with childlike sadness and, behind that, determination.

"But I want to hurt them like they hurt me," Fen continued. "And the *Fallen* can help me do that."

"That's Caldwell speaking through you."

"And it's him who left those scars on your face, and your mind," said Fen, suddenly projecting maturity beyond his years. "I can see them."

Grey looked down at the hat, still held out between them.

"Why'd you take it?" he asked.

"I thought...," and suddenly the boy in front of him was a confused child again. "...I thought it looked *cool*."

Grey laughed, a genuine laugh that echoed through the stacks around them.

"Keep it, Fen. It's yours," he said. "But keep it safe, you hear? And, if you ever need my help, you only need to ask."

"Thank you."

Fen's voice was almost a whisper. He hesitated for a moment, looking behind him and back, then abruptly shoved the hat towards Grey, forcing him to take it or let it fall, and ran back the way he had come.

Grey found Serinda and Blane at the car. There didn't seem to be anything else to say.

"She's planning something."

Serinda was looking at her hands as she spoke, though her eyes were unfocused as she stared within at thoughts that only she could see.

"Raphael," she said. "She's planning something *stupid*."

"I think she's as angry as Fen," said Blane, sat beside her. "She just hides it better."

Serinda gave a short, derisive laugh.

"I don't think she hides it at all. She just shows it in a different way. The whole damned *Forever Fallen*, for a start."

"She started the group?" asked Grey.

Serinda nodded.

"Sort of. The *Fallen* are entirely hers, though some of the older members came from older, smaller resistance groups."

"Resistance groups?" Grey looked confused. "I never heard of any resistance groups."

"Your side called them terrorists," she said bitterly. "Bio-terrorists, usually; it's a nice catch-all that means you don't need inconvenient things like 'due process' or 'evidence'."

There was a long pause, during which Blane leant forward and picked up one of the anon-spec thin-screens left behind by Francisco. She started playing with it, most likely aimlessly browsing the way most of the younger generation did when they were unsure of what they were supposed to do.

"She told me Uriel was in the *Fallen* before her," said Grey, moving on from an argument he had no idea how to counter. "How can it be hers, then?"

"She said that? I guess, in a way, he was," replied Serinda. "He was the one who helped her get the other groups to come together. He's 'old resistance,' back before spangle fabric and relocation schedules and so on. It was Raphael who figured all that out, allowing the group to expand so far in size and scope. I've never really understood why she trusts him so deeply, but I guess she planned the party and he brought the guests."

"Why? Why did she do all this? What does she have against the RA that she'd go this far?"

Serinda turned to Blane as Grey finished speaking.

"Blane, why don't you explore this place? We might be here a while, so which room do you want?" she said.

Despite the heavy atmosphere hanging over the room, Blane still seemed excited at the suggestion. She jumped to her feet and went at a half-run towards the bedrooms at the other end of the living area.

"It was her parents," said Serinda as soon as Blane disappeared from view through the nearest door. "The RA took them one day, and they just... were gone."

Serinda used her hands to emphasise the point.

"Vanished. All record of them, like they'd never existed. None of her neighbours acknowledged ever seeing them, and even the few family members she knew refused to speak to her about it."

Serinda sat back, pain evident in her voice but held back by strength of will.

"She was just seventeen. The only evidence of her parents'

existence, and barely a woman herself."

"They just disappeared?"

Serinda gave another short, sharp nod.

"They were involved with some of the earlier anti-RA groups. Just pamphlets and digital documents, you know, but technically illegal under the security regime. They must have annoyed the wrong people and... that was that."

"I see."

The words sounded empty even to his own ears, but what else was there to say? He knew this sort of thing went on - he'd even used his agency connections to help a number of clients get access to relatives who had been taken into 'non-disclosure' detention, as it was called. Hell, he'd only just recently escaped from an off-the-books prison himself.

Still, to hear practically first-hand that people could just disappear and never return...

The feeling of guilt rose like bile in his throat.

"Since then, she's dedicated herself to stopping anything like that happening to anyone else, ever again. It's why she's established so many safe sites across the city. But now I... I think..." Serinda tripped over her words. "...I think she wants to do *more*."

"And that guy? Uh, Shiner? Was he something to do with it? And Fen? What was that back there?"

"That's a long story..."

Raphael ordered the *Forever Fallen* to go dark the instant it became obvious Grey wasn't coming back. The data dump he'd sent came through strong, including the info on Caldwell. An RA man born and bred, who'd been a part of their research division for decades and apparently an integral member in establishing the Far agency and its Academy. Not much more than Grey already knew, back in the present.

What Raphael had been looking for, however, was more difficult to find. The list of operatives from various agencies operating undercover on assignments was easy enough to find, and incredibly long. It looked like the RA had infiltrated or established collaborators in almost every group in the city, from wannabe-unions to major corporate and financial institutions, to groups like the *Fallen*. The infiltration ran deep, with covert operatives even within the institutions of the Federation and the RA itself.

The data, however, was stripped of anything that could be used to identify individual agents. No pictures, no medical records or record of the pseudonyms they were operating under, just a brief collection of stats such as age, length of service, and supervising officer. It looked as if each agent possessed a unique encryption key that they used to encode and send information back to their superiors in the Reclamation Authority without fear of interception. They could use practically any terminal or thin-screen to do so, secure and unreadable, and none of the contents of these reports was included in the data Grey had stolen.

The data was, in fact, almost useless. Almost, except that the list included the year groups were first infiltrated. The year the *Forever Fallen* were first infiltrated saw a number of new members, but the closest to Raphael and the only one with access to the decision-making levels of the group was Shiner.

It was during the days that Raphael, Uriel, and Serinda were poring through the data to discover this that the first safe-sites went quiet. First to go was a building in the north of the city that housed several recent recruits to the *Fallen*, all demonstrating a limited degree of Aether abilities that, with training, could have been useful. The recruits were just... gone one day, and the remaining inhabitants of the site refused to say anything about what had happened to them. The RA had made clear what would happen to anyone who talked.

Next was one of the only clinics the *Fallen* were still running, one only recently set-up and that should have been secure from discovery for weeks yet. It housed those too sick to be sent home, and its location was known only by Raphael's inner circle.

Both of these could have been put down to bad luck, and a Reclamation Authority sweep inspired by Grey's assault on the Central Tower, but then another safe-site went, and another.

The only piece that fit the puzzle was Shiner. Raphael spotted the pattern first, waiting until she was sure of it, and Uriel agreed once she shared what she had found. They would have moved on him earlier, but Serinda convinced her to wait until they had incontrovertible proof.

So they began limiting the information Shiner received, feeding him false details within truths they felt they could safely reveal. And it worked. Not fully, perhaps because Shiner was becoming suspicious, but the majority of sites hit were ones the man knew about - ones Raphael had already begun evacuating. Then, three sites were hit in quick succession, all abandoned before feeding their location and false information about major *Fallen* gatherings to Shiner.

For Raphael that settled it. She and Uriel were on their way to confront Shiner when they were informed that the block housing Blane and Fen had been attacked.

"They went for Fen? Blane?" Grey was shocked. He'd had no hint of this.

"They nearly got them, too," replied Serinda. "A group of Far agents, trained in counter-Aether use and ready for almost anything."

"Almost?" said Grey.

"They weren't ready for Fen," said Blane, stood in the doorframe of her chosen room.

He slaughtered them, each and every one. Even when they were running, he pursued them, and Blane found it hard to blame him for that.

They came for her first, which was their first mistake. Their second mistake was to not silence her instantly.

Both she and Fen were staying in a small, repurposed building deep in the downtown area, a place that looked like it had once been a shop styled after the tiny stores of the pre-Fall era. Almost nobody knew about this place; it wasn't an 'official' *Fallen* site at all, just an old building Raphael and a few others knew about.

The relationship between Blane and Fen was still tense, but they were careful to avoid getting under each other's feet, and under each other's skin, and things became less fraught as the weeks passed. They spent most of the time practising Aether techniques, often with Serinda's guidance during her regular visits, though Fen almost always instantly grasped the few techniques he didn't know.

Sometimes they'd watch old movies together, something Fen couldn't seem to get enough of, and discuss what they would do if they were the main protagonist. They rarely agreed.

On the day of the attack Blane was in her room, eyes closed and breathing slow in the almost trance-like state Serinda had taught her for enhancing the connection to the Aether, when she heard the door swing open. Thinking it must be Serinda or another of the *Fallen*, she opened her eyes and began a casual greeting before the black-clad, helmeted figure fired off two quick stun-lock rounds.

The second round hit, but in the space of time afforded by the first stray one, Blane let out a cry and *pressed* the air between her and the figure as hard as she could. The subsequent explosion wasn't enough to stop the second round from hitting her square in the chest, but it sent the attacker flying backwards against the wall.

The next thing she knew, the sprawled figure was aflame. As she gasped for air herself, struggling to stay conscious, she heard screams rise as heat pulsed through the air and everything became vivid light and shadow. A second armour-clad figure half-ran, half-stumbled through her door while waving his weapon behind him and shooting wildly, but collapsed to his knees an instant late as Mindfire poured out of his every pore, engulfing him in a golden flame that incinerated the flesh yet somehow merely scorched the surfaces around him.

Fen stepped in behind the blackened form a second later.

"Are you alright?" he asked.

He barely waited for her answer, turning back as she began to nod. His features, briefly soft and concerned, became lined and wrathful as he walked back out the door.

More shooting, and more screaming.

"They didn't even come close to stopping him," said Blane, sat again beside Serinda in Francisco's safe house. "I saw two try to *Close* him, but he somehow turned it back on them. Neither of them knew which way to run when he came for them."

"They were using stun-locks?" said Grey. "They're back to trying to capture him, then, not just kill him."

Or there's two factions in play here, he thought. Caldwell had said something about Ritra Feye interfering with him capturing the kid.

But if Caldwell was the one trying to take Fen alive, did that mean it was Feye who wanted him dead?

"The way he uses the Aether, it feels different," said Blane, staring at something only she could see. "It feels *wrong.*"

Serinda reached over and placed a comforting hand on the girl's shoulder.

"What do you mean?" asked Grey.

"You've felt it too, right? Like he's not just floating in the Aether, but a part of it. Like it moves *with* him, not through him. Like…

like… like the Aether when he is around is *deeper*, and could drown you if you let it."

Grey considered his own experiences. He thought he understood much of what Blane was saying; the Aether did feel more potent around Fen, allowing him to perform techniques with a power and frequency he had never experienced. But it didn't feel like drowning, he thought. It felt like *flying*.

"I think he generates it," said Serinda suddenly. Grey and Blane stared at her, waiting for more.

"Well, we *all* generate Aether, of course. Every living organism does. But it's like sap in a tree, slow to form and slow to move. It seeps out over time, forming these pools we draw from when we need."

She took her hand from Blane's shoulder and sat back.

"I felt it when I first treated him. He was badly wounded, you know. A gut shot like that should have killed him, or left him out of action for weeks at the least. But it was like I was attached to limitless energy. I could sense every dying cell, every site of early infection. I saved him more quickly, more cleanly, than any patient before. And the Aether I was using was coming from *him*. Not from the city, but from him."

"I saw him stop *bullets*," said Blane.

It said something that Grey had almost forgotten that Fen's ability to freeze multiple projectiles in mid-air was something special. The boy had shown too many other abilities.

"You didn't tell us what he was," said Serinda, half-accusatory.

"What is he, then?" Grey challenged back.

"I don't know. But he's not just another runaway, is he." It wasn't a question.

"No. I'm not sure what he is." A thought struck Grey. "The, uh, the Mindfire…" he asked. "How did he use it?"

Blane looked at him quizzically.

"He just made them… burn," she answered. "Sometimes from meters away. How can he do that? Isn't Mindfire difficult to control?"

You don't know the half of it, Grey said to himself.

They sat in silence, each lost in their own thoughts. Eventually, Blane picked up her thin-screen again and began scrolling. Grey and Serinda just sat there, replaying the various regrets of their individual recent pasts.

No one spoke for several minutes, until Blane's expression abruptly changed, first thoughtful, then concerned.

"Uh, guys… I think I have an idea what Raphael might be planning…"

26

People disappear all the time. This world chews up and spits out those who get caught between the cogs of its wheels, and the machine continues to turn. It is the natural order of things. Where, then, is the moral failing in acknowledging that some must disappear to ensure the smooth running of a society?

Processes of Regulation and Order in the Reclamation (Sanctioned Digital Document - section redacted)

It made too much sense for her to be planning anything else. The moment Blane had shown them the image on her thin-screen, both Grey and Serinda knew it.

The image was that of the Central Tower, glistening in digitally-enhanced sunlight that would never be so warm in reality, and beneath that, the text announcing the inauguration of the building as the new home of the Federation. Not only that, but…

They were making Albores the capital. This made the inauguration an even bigger deal. There would be tens of thousands, hundreds of thousands, flocking to attend this birth of both city and nation. The Federation, and the world, would be watching.

And some of the highest figures of the Reclamation Authority would be there, emerging from the shadows to mark their presence at this birth and remind those watching that they remained.

What had she said? … *Their lives are forfeit too.*

It was too good a chance for her to pass up. And now she knew what Fen could do.

Grey had given her a weapon of mass destruction, and in two days she was going to use it.

Serinda had already left. None of the contacts she had for getting in touch with Raphael or any other of the *Fallen* were working, so she had taken a car and left in the probably futile hope that she could find them. Grey didn't entertain much hope of her success.

He, meanwhile, was left feeling like a bullet without a gun. He couldn't exactly march up to the Central Tower and demand they call off the inauguration. Hell, he'd be arrested before he got within a hundred metres of the place.

Which left him… with nothing to do.

It was a strange feeling, sitting in this luxurious apartment while knowing the single greatest act of domestic terrorism the new age had seen was brewing somewhere out in the city.

Blane, at least, seemed relatively unfazed by the problem. Youth, and a lack of understanding regarding the true extent of Fen's abilities, protected her from the frenzied thoughts that swam uncontrollably through Grey's mind. She even convinced him to train her.

Serinda didn't return until the next morning, and the look on her face told him all he needed to know.

He had no choice. He had to contact Ritra Feye.

They met once again on the Hyperloop, Grey cursing the lost time it took to set up their meeting. Lacking a way to contact Feye directly, he'd been forced to risk calling Agent Chau.

Chau had been… *concerned* … that Grey was now high up on their list of most wanted, but had agreed to contact Feye before anyone else. At the very least, he could get her orders on what to do next. She'd contacted Grey via the virtual dead drop an hour later, telling him she'd ordered Chau to keep quiet.

Now Feye was sitting across from him as the walls rushed by, taking another aimless journey across the city.

"So you're saying this kid is some kind of lab-rat of the RA? And *Far* were running the show?"

Feye had a look on her face that said she was having difficulty believing him.

Grey hoped he was hiding the growing disbelief from his own.

"The whole thing - the Academy, our training, finding us in the orphan centres - the whole thing has been a huge experiment in developing stronger and stronger Aether users. That guy, Caldwell, has been overseeing it from the start. He's been watching us, watching *you*, since before we began training."

Feye nodded to herself.

"Caldwell. I know him. Always thought he was a bit slimy. He's got friends in high places, though. I can't directly override anything he says."

"Well, there's got to be something you can do. After we stop the *Fallen*, maybe, but Fen should be all the evidence you need. If we can stop Fen now, we can get Caldwell later."

Again, the nod as if Ritra was factoring all this into some grand strategy in her head.

"I warned you about your terrorist friends," she said. "And this kid uses Mindfire? At a distance? It'll be dangerous if he spots us, then."

Grey nodded.

"But if you can catch them off guard, before they're aware of you, you can stop this. There's no need for anyone to get hurt."

Feye gave a wry smile at this, shaking her head.

"Nestor Grey, always the bleeding heart."

Grey didn't smile back, fixing her with a stare.

"*No one* gets hurt, ok? Especially not Fen. He's just a…"

"… just a kid. Yeah, yeah, you keep saying. Seeing yourself, are you, back in the early days of the Academy, all lost and alone? Or maybe Trevan? He never was cut out for this life."

Maybe she was right. Sometimes, Grey thought Feye understood his thoughts better than he ever could.

"Do you know what happened to them?" he asked. "The others from the Academy, I mean. Our group."

Feye gave a derisive snort.

"It was never *my* group," she replied, as she hit the button instructing the car to stop at the next station. "I just made sure you lot were doing what you were supposed to, even then. And no, I have no idea what happened to them. I was hardly going to start a chat group, was I?"

Grey guessed not. It didn't matter now, anyway.

"Don't hurt the kid, ok? It's not his fault."

"We'll do our best. Besides, you'll be there to keep an eye on things."

Grey jolted back in surprise.

"What do you…? What have you done?" he spluttered, looking around in panic.

The car was beginning to decelerate, the quiet hissing of the brakes reverberating through the air as he was pressed gently back into his seat by the fading momentum.

"You didn't think I would just let you go, did you?" said Feye, pushing herself out of her seat as the vehicle came to a stop. Shadows moved outside. "Come on, Nestor. You assaulted the Central Tower, and there's at least one Far agent missing who was last recorded overseeing your transfer."

"Transfer?" said Grey, almost shouting. "He took me out to the Waste to shoot me and dump the body!"

He reached for his stun-lock.

"Not a good idea," said Feye, reaching for her own, more lethal weapon. "There are ten agents outside this door who will kill you if you make a move against me."

As if on cue, the door of the car slid open to reveal several armed figures wearing the steel-grey and black uniforms of the Far Agency. They each had a rifle pointed at him.

Lacking any alternative course of action, he put up his hands.

On the plus side, he really *would* be able to keep an eye on things; Feye had been telling the truth about that.

On the downside, though, it would be with his hands cuffed behind his back and a Far agent at his shoulder.

They'd bundled him into a van as soon as they got him out of the Hyperloop, and taken him directly to the Central Tower. Ritra Feye had left him to the less-than-tender mercies of the agents on the journey there, but joined them again shortly after arrival.

They had brought him to a room near the centre of the tower, on what he thought must be the third or fourth floor - he'd been hooded on the way in. Not a sensory dampener, just a plain old black hood. Somehow it was just as disorientating.

The room was wide, with rows of desk-screens spaced evenly under the high ceiling. Flat counters when not in use, they could be tilted for ease of viewing when an agent sat at one. Most were occupied right now, agents tapping away at their screens or speaking to some contact unseen from the angle where Grey stood.

The entire front wall was yet more plasglass screen, numerous divisions on the display showing the view of cameras positioned everywhere both within and without the Central Tower. Each video feed was live; Grey had known the city was under constant surveillance, but the extent of it still astounded him. It was as if every single door and window was under a lens, each vehicle observed by a creature with a million eyes. Occasionally, a feed would pause and zoom in on the faces of someone caught in its view, providing a snapshot that remained until Grey gave a slight shake of the head.

"It's impossible," he said. He'd been at it for hours, and the number of images was only increasing. "Too many people."

He'd given the best description he could of Fen and the *Fallen* he knew, especially Raphael and Uriel, and these descriptions were being used by the algorithm to eliminate as many people as possible, but any person or group of people even slightly resembling their prey had to be confirmed or dismissed by Grey. The likely use of Spangle fabric meant they had to cast the net wide, though at least Fen's relative youth meant they could discount groups consisting of only older people.

"Keep looking," said Feye. There was none of the familiarity in her voice from their previous meetings; now, she was in charge and he was, if not a prisoner, at least a person of interest.

Grey had never really seen Feye in action, he realised. Not like this, at the head of a chain stretching across the city and beyond, a net laid out to catch those labelled enemies of the state. She was... superb.

It was like watching a juggler effortlessly keeping a hundred balls in the air, simultaneously responding to requests from subordinates both in person and through the e-pad in front of her, maintaining multiple group calls on both radio and thin-screen, all while making sure Grey was focusing on his task. Even if he hadn't been focusing on image after image, he would have found it difficult to keep up with half of what she was doing.

"You don't have anyone to help you with that?" he asked at one point, when an agent approached her with a request involving some kind of Aether incident northeast of the city.

"Focus, Grey. You just do your job." She bit her words off, signing off the e-warrant with a tap of her screen to the agent's own and turning to some other duty.

"Very top-down approach."

Feye flashed a glare at the sarcasm in his voice.

"I've had to move my whole damn base of operations here because of your bad choice in friends. Now, stop distracting me."

An image caught his eye just before he reflexively shook his head for the nth time. Something about the woman on the screen's features. Something about the man beside her. The way they moved.

Raphael and Uriel.

They were mixed in with a crowd of people making their way towards the tower from the streets beyond. At first, Grey was still unsure if it was really them, and couldn't see what had tripped the algorithm. Then the image panned out slightly to reveal a teenage boy a short distance away.

Fen. There was no doubt in his mind despite the darkening of his hair and alterations to his features. It was that air of... anger. Youth, and anger.

Grey opened his mouth to speak, and hesitated. He looked around the room, at the tens of agents all engaged in the search. In the *hunt*. Could he really...?

"That's them? Right."

Grey was suddenly aware of Feye staring at him, e-pad lowered to her side and all other duties put aside. She'd been watching him the entire time, he realised, even through everything else she had been doing.

"Tag those three. Squads *Rojo* and *Morado*, stand by. All others, move to the south sector."

Feye was all business again, but that laser focus was now trained on a single goal.

"Remember, don't do anything rash. Fen is just..."

Grey didn't even finish his sentence before Feye yelled over the top of him.

"Get *mister* Grey a seat out of the way, and don't let him interfere."

Grey could do nothing as the agent at his shoulder dragged him away, shoving him down onto a chair in the far corner. He watched the screens from afar as Ritra barked orders out, coordinating the movements of different groups of Far agents and gradually moving to encircle the three *Fallen* he'd identified.

The three came gradually closer to the Central tower, moving at the same sedate pace as the gradually increasing crowd around them. The tower itself was closed to public access for the inauguration, but the plaza around it was open and already full of people, with more trying to get in all the time.

Alcohol, and likely other substances, were clearly flowing freely amongst the crowd as city residents gathered for what was brewing into one huge street party. Even the rain had let up, and the wan sun was being assisted by several full-spectrum spotlights, giving the illusion of a warm, pre-Fall day. Grey had never seen such a demonstration of pride in the city before.

He knew how this was going to go. He'd seen enough movies,

from pre-Fall to *New Patriot,* to know that the hubris Feye and the Far agency were exhibiting was going to doom them all. It was the same cliched approach as the one-note villains of modern historical dramas denying the possibility of nuclear annihilation moments before the Sudden War broke out. They underestimated Fen, underestimated the *Fallen,* and for that others were going to pay. And there was nothing he could do.

Which was why he was surprised when the operation went off without a hitch.

Fen went down first, a plain-clothes agent Grey hadn't known was there putting a stun-baton to his back and scooping him up from the crowd before Raphael or Uriel even noticed he was gone. Uriel went down next, silenced stun-lock round picking him off from some rooftop perch on a surrounding building, grabbed almost the moment he fell by another agent.

Raphael had maybe a handful of seconds to react before she too fell, then it was over. The people around her were concerned for no more than a moment before being relieved to see someone else take responsibility for helping this maybe-sick-but-probably-just-drunk stranger. The Far agents made off with their prey unmolested and without drawing attention, carrying them out of the crowd.

"Operation complete. All squads, stand down," he heard Ritra Feye say. "Good job everyone. Now, bring them here."

27

We stand together or die alone

Ian Mateo Sosa, *First Congress on the Formation of Federation*

They were brought up only a short while later, each cuffed and flanked by three Far agents with weapons primed both physically and mentally. Grey could sense the Aether flowing from the agents to surround their prisoners in a way reminiscent of Thoughtscreen, though at first he couldn't tell what they were doing.

"We call it Locking," said Feye, to the three as they were brought before her. "You won't be able to reach the Aether for as long as we maintain it. Which, I imagine, will be a very long time."

Grey could see first confusion, then anger, on their faces as they attempted to reach for the Aether. Another technique developed since he'd left the agency, it seemed, and the first one he'd seen that required multiple users to work in tandem.

It was like each agent provided a section of impenetrable shell which wrapped around their target, blocking them from the Aether. Of course, it wasn't really a shell, but more like a sphere of interference. A powerful technique, he could see, though it was also clear that if just one of the agents was knocked out of the ... link? Chain? ... then the whole barrier would be rendered useless.

If Grey had thought he saw anger on Raphael's face before though, the instant she noticed him he saw pure rage.

"You? You sold us to the RA?" she growled.

Her voice stayed surprisingly low and calm but held blades so sharp they cut.

Feye didn't let Grey answer.

"You will not speak until spoken to," she said, and at a nod one of the Far agents holding Raphael gave a sharp twist of the prisoner's arm.

Grey reflexively stepped forwards in protest, before his own arm twisted painfully behind him. Looking back, he saw his own Far agent escort slowly shake her head.

"I assume," continued Feye, "... you were told your rights before being brought here, but to confirm; you have the right to a state-appointed legal representative; you have the right to request specific nutrition based on dietary requirements both physical and cultural; you have the right to request clarification of meaning before answering when questioned."

"Spare me this pantomime of justice," spat Raphael.

"I will take your statement as acknowledgement," replied Feye in a neutral tone. Then she turned to Uriel, who just nodded, locking eyes with her. He didn't look phased.

"What have you done to Fen?" asked Grey, unable to wait any longer.

Fen was stood a small distance behind Raphael and Uriel, equally surrounded and shielded by three agents. However, his eyes were unfocused and he seemed to be standing only because the agents on either side of him were holding him up by the shoulders.

"A sedative," answered Feye, not looking at him. "Locking should be sufficient, but from your description of this child's abilities *should be* and *is* are often two very different things."

Feye stepped closer to the boy, who swayed slightly and struggled to focus on her, eyes half-closed and head bobbing as if fighting sleep.

"So you're the one this whole thing is about, are you?" she said. "You know, there's some in the Agency who want you destroyed…"

She looked at Fen thoughtfully, making Grey tense.

Grey would never know what she was going to say next, though it would haunt his thoughts, because at that moment a mass of black-clad, body-armoured figures came bursting into the room, rifles raised and barrels flitting from agent to agent as they spaced themselves out along the walls. Grey counted seven, then eight.

Confusion reigned for a second, Far agents spinning their own guns to meet this unexpected threat, before a voice came from back where the Quick-Fix troops had entered.

"Anyone wanting that is going to be extremely disappointed," said Doctor Caldwell as he strode into the room, flanked by two of the largest people Grey had ever seen, dark helmets occluding their faces but not their air of mercenary competence.

"Caldwell," said Feye, turning to meet him. If she was surprised at this turn of events, she gave no sign. "And what exactly do you think you're doing here?"

Caldwell met her stare with one of his own.

"Why, Agent Feye, I'm here to collect RA property."

Caldwell looked to Fen as he said this, making it clear what he meant.

"This is a counter-terror operation under my supervision," replied Feye, not taking her eyes off the man even as a number of the Quick-Fix troopers swung their rifles towards her.

"And you're doing very well," replied Caldwell. "I hope you continue to do so, because the inauguration will be starting shortly and there's still plenty of potential threats out there. In the meantime, I will be taking the boy."

"He's a suspect in an active investigation…"

"… who you were no doubt just about to have taken to the Far Station for processing, as procedure dictates. And I, as a ranking officer in the Agency, can take him for you. After all," and Caldwell sneered as he said this, "You are so *very* busy."

Feye maintained her cold stare for a moment, before sweeping her hand around the room to encompass the surrounding Quick-Fix troops, all still holding weapons at the ready.

"Well, as you've no doubt already discovered, the boy is extremely dangerous, and Far is hardly equipped for this kind of situation. I thought a Rapid Reaction Force would be useful in the case of… unexpected eventualities," Caldwell said in answer.

"So you're here in your capacity as both Far *and* Reclamation Authority? You really *have* pulled out all the stops."

Grey didn't understand the small smile that curled around Feye's lips as she said this.

"Fine, take him."

Grey jerked forward with a yell of protest, only to find the agent to his side tightly holding him back.

"Quiet, Nestor," snapped Feye. She turned back to Caldwell. "And the other two?"

Caldwell looked at Raphael and Uriel for a moment, as if weighing their value to him.

"Keep them. I will, of course, need your agents to maintain the Lock on the child." He pointed at the three Far agents surrounding Fen, then at himself, before turning to look at Grey. "And I'll take this one, too. We have some unfinished business, and I would truly like to know how he is standing here after our last… discussion."

"I'm sure you would," said Feye. "But he isn't a part of this operation. You have no authority to take him; he's not even being detained."

Caldwell's voice finally cracked, showing irritation and impatience. "Not being detained? The man's in handcuffs!"

"Release Mr. Grey," Feye said in curt tones to the agent behind him. Grey felt the cuffs pop open.

Feye raised a warning hand to cut off Grey as he went to speak.

"I'll remind you, Mr. Grey, that you are here at my forbearance. You will speak only with my permission, or find yourself *actually* detained for interference in an ongoing operation."

Grey was going to argue despite her words, was even readying himself for a futile attempt to free Fen himself from the grip of the two Quick-Fix members who were even now stepping towards the boy to grab him, when he paused.

Something he had never experienced before was happening. Ritra Feye was allowing him to Read her.

Wait, her mind said, clear as if projected in a beam of light on the ceiling. *Wait, and you'll have your chance.*

And it was more than words. The Read on her showed her absolute belief in these words, no trace of deception or subterfuge, just hard certainty.

"Nevertheless, I will take him," said Caldwell, failing to notice the sudden coalescing of Feye's mind. "He is an escapee under my jurisdiction, and implicated in the disappearance of a Far agent assigned to his case."

"Interesting you should say that," replied Feye, flicking across unseen screens on her e-pad. "There *is* a warrant out on him, yet the filing is extremely… haphazard. For instance, there is no actual record of where he was being detained, nor any details of incarceration or transfer authorisation."

Feye looked up and smiled a serpent's smile at Caldwell.

"Of course," she continued, "All you need to do is file the relevant documents right now, and you can have him."

She held out her e-pad, inviting him to perform the tap-transfer there and then.

Caldwell bristled.

"You know full well we don't file when taking prisoners to…"

He paused, looking around the room. Feye raised an eyebrow, waiting for him to continue. Despite himself, Grey settled back, rubbing his wrists where the cuffs had bitten into his skin.

She's calling his bluff, he thought. There was no way Caldwell could say outright that he'd been holding Grey in an off-the-books cell. Far agents, and the Reclamation Authority itself, were willing to do many things in pursuit of their duties, some of which would shock an ordinary citizen, but it all had to be filed. Paperwork was the foundation upon which RA legitimacy was based. That this paperwork might never be seen by anyone ever again was beside the point.

"Fine," snapped Caldwell, drawing himself up to his full height. "Keep him for now. We'll discuss this, though, Feye. You are overstepping your authority these days."

Raphael, stood almost forgotten to the side, suddenly exploded outwards. She lunged towards Caldwell, attempting to use teeth and shoulders in place of her constrained hands to attack the man. Caldwell was forced to take two steps backwards before one of the Far agents assigned to her knocked her to the floor with the butt of a rifle to the back of her head. Raphael fell to the floor and lay still.

Uriel, meanwhile, continued to do nothing except watch. Something about his attitude this whole time didn't sit right with Grey. Where Raphael had displayed disbelief and anger at their predicament, Uriel seemed to radiate resignation and... confusion? Expectation? Grey was unsure, but the confidence and surety the man usually exhibited had disappeared, though whatever had replaced it was not fear.

Perhaps that was just the result of being captured by the group he'd spent a lifetime resisting. Regardless, it wasn't important now.

Grey watched with painful uncertainty as Caldwell led Fen and the two huge Quick-Fix escorts away, the boy seemingly too sedated to comprehend what was happening. The two Quick-Fix troops walked either side of the boy, practically carrying him, while the three Far agents assigned to go with them walked behind, maintaining the Lock.

As soon as they stepped out the door, the remaining members of the Quick-Fix team filed out themselves.

"He brought a hit-squad into *my* operation," growled Feye, speaking aloud but talking to herself. For an instant, Grey saw fierce rage and indignation under her usually cool mask. The next instant, she was back in control.

"Reset watch reports, and let me know any priority comms I missed because of our unexpected *visitor*," she barked at a nearby subordinate, who snapped to attention in an exaggerated way that betrayed how unsettled the agents had been by the encounter. Then Feye dismissed her and turned back to the screens.

"What are you still doing here?" she said suddenly.

It took Grey a second to realise she was speaking to him.

"I already said; you aren't being detained," she continued. "You're free to go."

"Sir, this is a secure area. He isn't authorised to be…," broke in one agent nearby. The look Feye flashed him made him go quiet, and probably reconsider a number of life decisions made up to this point.

"He. Is. Not. Being. Detained." The agent who had spoken up gulped as Feye fixed him with her stare, each word the blow of a heavy hammer. "I have already made that clear. What he decides to do now is his decision, as a citizen of the Federation."

Grey looked from her to the doorway where just moments ago Caldwell had gone.

"Oh, and give the man back his gun," Feye said, as if an afterthought. Grey's stun-lock was shoved into his hands a second later.

Taking one more look at Raphael on the floor and Uriel stood cuffed close by, he turned and sprinted for the elevator.

28

In the pre-Fall era, many societies claimed that freedom of expression was fundamental to liberty, and liberty fundamental to human progress. The end result was the blighted world you can see outside your window.

Maryon Torres, *Choice after Apocalypse*

The Quick-Fix team were already gone by the time Grey got to the row of elevators, leaving no trace of where they were going. He dived into the nearest one as it opened, smashing the button for the ground floor. The doors slid shut with frustrating slowness, as the elevator lurched into motion.

Up. The elevator was going up.

"No!" Grey shouted, punching the button pad in frustration as the number began to rise.

GOING UP?

The words on the display screen above appeared there between one blink and the next, the same hard font Grey had come to recognise.

GOING UP.

Grey paused and stared at the words as the elevator rose and rose, passing floor after floor as behind him the view of the city grew. It became apparent that this elevator was going to take him to the very top of the building, high above the city.

Ok, time to take stock, Grey told himself, closing his eyes and drawing in a deep breath, feeling the Aether beneath him. The flow seemed to jump to meet him, the potency of it telling him Fen was still near.

So, what do I do now?

He opened his eyes to stare at the words on the screen again.

No, stop it. Focus on the things you can *explain.*

If Caldwell really was taking Fen upwards, not down, then that meant aerial transport. Heli, or VTOL drone. Which meant the instant they took off, they were gone. They could go anywhere, far beyond the possibility of finding them again.

So, he was going into a situation where he was outnumbered and outgunned, with no time to prepare. What advantages did he have?

The only one he could think of was that he had the Aether, while

Caldwell seemed to be relying on gun-dependent Quick-Fix goons. The only other Aether users were the three holding Fen's Lock, which would require all their focus, and Caldwell himself. Which made Caldwell the greatest threat, though Grey wouldn't leave himself open to anything like a Force Read again.

What was it Caldwell had said? That Grey was 'born into the Aether'. Well, he'd have to hope that made up for the gap between himself and a man who'd made a lifetime study of it.

First though, of course, he had to get through the armed guards. He wouldn't be able to test himself against Caldwell if he got shot beforehand.

He could feel them now, as he *Reached* out far beyond his ordinary limitations, further than he had ever before. It seemed as if the Aether flowed even more powerfully than normal around Fen, like the energy he had access to had somehow grown.

No time to think about that now, though. The eight Quick-Fix agents were just a few floors above him, rapidly coming closer as the elevator ascended. Beyond them, the three Far agents and two other guards. He could feel the Lock around Fen, a strange vortex in the Aether that spun around a darkened sphere, cutting off anything inside from reaching out. And there, besides the vortex, another Aether user, their threadlike connection to the Aether marking them out as Caldwell.

GET READY.

Grey nodded at whoever or whatever it was that was sending him these messages. As unsettling as it might be to have an unknown hand guiding him, right at this moment it provided at least some reassurance that he wasn't entirely alone.

Oddly, the only thing he was sure of was that it wasn't Francisco. His thoughts briefly flickered to the personal Fabricator, long ago in the safe house.

SHOW ME THE WEAPON, it had said.

The time for thinking ended as the doors slid open.

It turned out Grey had one more advantage: they had no idea he was coming. Still, the initial fight was a terrifying one.

The elevator doors opened to a small area completely enclosed in glass, a circular waiting area no more than six or seven meters in any direction. It had a few flimsy-looking tables and chairs, and pitifully little cover. Beyond these, a double-door exit led out onto the rooftop proper, where a wide landing pad stood. On it waited his quarry. There was no sign of any aerial vehicle yet, but he could hear the roar of jet engines coming closer. VTOL drones then, not helis.

The wind outside was strong and the light weak, which gave him precious seconds before the three Quick-Fix standing guard at the exit to the landing pad noticed him. They were on the other side of the glass and didn't spot him as he stepped out of the elevator, but he knew it would only be moments before they did.

He knocked the first one down with Flare before slamming Tranquilize down on another. He'd picked that technique up from Caldwell himself, back in the cell, and Grey was gratified to see the Quick-Fix trooper sprawl on the ground, limbs no longer communicating with spinal cord.

The third, though, was fast. She spun and drew her weapon, opening fire in rapid bursts. Grey thought he was dead.

That thought was swiftly swallowed by a flood of relief when the glass between him and the woman splintered and cracked, but did not break.

Ballistic glass! He sent prayers of thanks to the RA or whoever had designed this building. Overengineering, the watchword of the upper echelons of society, came to his rescue. Why use standard glass, when you can quadruple the price to *really* demonstrate your power?

This was possibly the best outcome he could have hoped for; to use Aether you only needed to see or sense an opponent, and with the extended reach afforded him by Fen's presence physical obstacles had little meaning. He could see the Quick-Fix agent realise her predicament at the same time as he did.

She went down to Flare without getting off another burst, as further away a commotion amongst the rest of the group told him his presence was now common knowledge. More bullets came smacking into the glass, chipping away at it without piercing.

Now Grey could see the VTOL drones, sleek silver things half-hidden against the grey clouds behind them. They were two specks growing rapidly larger, though he knew they could carry multiple passengers; he thought he had maybe only a minute or two before they landed.

The rest of Caldwell's group were still too far away for him to be able to do anything but sense them, so Grey pushed himself flat against the edge of the exit and used Push to swing the closest side of the double-door open. Instantly, bullets started peppering the inside of the room as well as the glass outside, sending wood and plastic chips flying where they hit floor and furnishings. Several fizzers hissed by, unable to find space for a decent angle and wasted.

Keeping as low a profile as possible, Grey pointed the barrel of his stun-lock around the edge of the doorframe and fired several shots off. He wasn't expecting to hit anyone, but at least force them into cover.

His hopes were dashed, though, as he saw two figures stand up from their crouched positions and start to walk towards him at a calm, steady pace. Covering fire from their compatriots continued to pepper the space around Grey, forcing him back behind the glass.

They knew his stun-lock rounds were ineffective against body-armour, then. Barring a luck shot, he wasn't going to be able to take any of them down with just his weapon.

It seemed, however, that the Quick-Fix team still didn't understand quite how amplified his abilities had become. The two figures advancing on him slowed as they approached, crouching and taking cover behind a couple of air filtration units as they neared, and ordinarily the several metres they had left between him and them would be more than enough to stay clear of an Aether user's abilities.

But the key word was *ordinarily*.

The compression technique ripped both units from their bases and sent the heavy metal boxes flying, the Quick-Fix agents behind carried along with them. They were sent tumbling into their teammates, knocking one off their feet and forcing a break in the shooting. Grey used the confusion to dive out of the waiting room and take cover behind another unit himself, a much larger and sturdier-looking one that stood taller than he did at full height.

"Where'd he go?"

Electronic filters removed any trace of emotion from the voice, but Grey would bet a Carib-dollar it would be tinged with surprise. He *Reached* to locate the source of the voice, at the edge of his limits, and reinforced that surprise with Unsettle.

"What are you doing, fools? Keep it together!"

This was Caldwell's voice, and there was nothing disguising the worry in *his* words.

Grey supposed his worry was warranted. He'd successfully taken out five of the Quick-Fix agents in quick succession, a single man taking out half of Caldwell's team in an instant.

His momentum now, though, was gone. The element of surprise had been key to his success, and he'd only got half. Now they were ready. He could feel their minds, alert and aware of his presence, becoming less susceptible to his influence with every second. Even as he thought this, he felt the Quick-Fix agent mentally shake off the effects of his Aether attack.

Why didn't Caldwell join in the defence? Could the man really be so reliant on his mercenaries that he didn't even think to support them with his own abilities? Surely he should be using the increased potency of the Aether as well.

Bullets smacked into the opposite side of the filter Grey was covering behind, drawing him back to more immediately pressing issues. He felt the remaining Quick-Fix move to flank him from either side, one of the two who had been with Fen joining them, meaning two moving along either side. They had adjusted for Grey's increased reach, and were keeping far beyond it along the sides of the rooftop.

Grey looked around, searching desperately for more cover. There was nothing nearby, just flat ground, the waiting room too far to get back to without opening himself to their rifles.

He was trapped.

Gunfire opened up, making him wince, thinking one had got around without him noticing. Another burst, then a thud.

"Report."

The flat-tone voice came from his right. Only silence came from the left.

Suddenly Caldwell yelled.

"There, you idiots! Someone's there!"

Grey heard running footsteps from where the voice asking for a report had come, then a sudden thud.

"Who the hell are you?" shouted Caldwell.

Another burst of rifle fire, then silence.

Grey tentatively peered around the side of the air filtration unit.

"Blane? What are you…? How…?"

Blane was standing mere metres away from Fen and Caldwell on the landing pad. At her feet, two Quick-Fix figures lay unmoving.

She turned her head and smiled at him as he stepped out from behind his cover.

"I think that's what we'd like to know," said Serinda, stepping out from the right. She held a rifle slung over her shoulder, barrel pointed directly at Caldwell and the three Far agents holding Fen's Lock, which explained why each of them had their hands up.

"How did you do it?" she asked.

"Do what?"

"Get us here. You know, the whole TAKE THIS DOOR, USE THIS CODE thing."

Grey could practically *hear* her speak in upper case.

"Not me," he said.

Serinda paused, looking confused.

"Not you? Then who?"

"*That* is something I'm going to find out," Grey answered. "But not now. Now, we deal with this guy." He gestured to Caldwell.

Caldwell stood behind Fen, grasping both shoulders of the boy and keeping him between himself and them.

"What the *hell* is going on?" he demanded, face reddening. "How did you do that? No one can use Aether like that! No one!"

He looked from Grey to Blane to Serinda and back, the anger apparent in his expression growing with every moment.

He didn't know. How could he not know? Could he not *sense* it, feel how the Aether seemed to leap and flow in Fen's presence?

"It's not Fen," said Blane. "Well, not the Fen we see."

Grey looked from her to Serinda, not understanding. Serinda seemed equally questioning.

"You can still feel it, right?" continued Blane. "Like something in the Aether is moving. It can't be the boy standing in front of us; he's cut off from it."

Understanding dawned.

Blane was right. He could feel the block surrounding Fen, a dark sphere of emptiness in the Aether at the centre of which he saw the sedated boy, barely able to stand. Even the unconscious Quick-Fix agents still left ripples on the surface, the ripples every living thing created as they slowly released their generated energy into the pool beneath. Fen left nothing, disconnected from all that.

Grey reached out with his senses, probing the flow of Aether beneath him. It jumped towards him as if alive... and as if disturbed.

Grey thought back to the old storage site where Raphael had

executed, no, *murdered,* the mole, Shiner. He remembered how the Aether had pulsed in response to Fen's anger, had lurched as if... as if there was something underneath.

"There's something there..." he said breathlessly.

Blane nodded.

Serinda's eyes widened as she sensed the same thing.

"What is that...?" she whispered.

"Stop this at once!"

Caldwell's yell snapped them back to reality, the leviathan retreating.

"Enough!" he yelled, sounding on the edge of hysteria. "Enough! I have the boy, and I am taking him. Put down your weapons, and you might just live!"

As if on cue, two VTOL drone carriers rose behind him, the roar of their vector-thrust jet engines filling the air as they moved to hover behind and above his head. An automated turret revolved on each of their undersides, turning to point directly at the three of them.

Caldwell hair blew wildly in the jet stream as he held up a hand, and laughed.

"I don't care what tricks you think you have, you can't stop a 50 calibre machine gun. I drop my hand, and you all will be riddled with holes."

Grey raised both his hands above his head.

"He's right," he shouted over the roar of the engines. "We can't do anything about those jets."

Blane and Serinda looked at him in disbelief, ready to fight despite impossible odds.

Grey smiled.

"... but *he* can."

He hit the three Far agents with Flare, and the Lock around Fen collapsed.

29

While the vast majority of Aether 'techniques' involve the interaction of two or more living beings, the development of varieties including compression-expansion techniques and forms generally termed 'Push' imply an ability to affect the physical world through Aether usage. All such discoveries are to be immediately reported to a superior officer

Agency Handbook, Section 7.6 (Aether usage and practice)

Caldwell dropped his hand the moment he sensed Grey hit the three agents with his mental attack, and the bulbous turrets hanging below the huge drones opened up with a hail of ammunition louder even than the jet engines.

Too slow, too slow.

Grey gazed at the stream of bullets frozen in mid-air, a thick metallic clump floating together just feet away from where they stood, trailed by a line leading back almost to the barrel they had been fired from. The drone turrets swung left and right on their axis as if bewildered that their targets remained standing.

"Welcome back, kid," said Grey.

Fen was glaring at the drones in front of him, the feral look on his face sending chills down Grey's spine though he had seen it before. *Because* he had seen it before.

Fen's eyes narrowed, and Grey felt the Aether pulse.

To Grey, it felt something like a compression technique; he could sense the Aether condensing, forcing the physical world to react to it. Only, this wasn't the instantaneous press-and-release of air. This was far more powerful.

The drone on the left went first, canopy cracking then buckling as if grasped by a giant invisible hand closing into a fist. The second followed shortly afterwards with the sound of crunching alloys, engines rising to an unnaturally high pitch as they underwent stresses it had never been conceived they would face.

Fen gave a wave of his hand and *Pushed* the machines away. They flew backwards, engine screams becoming even louder as they spun out over the city, rolling and turning until they were obviously unable to restore aerodynamic stability. They began tumbling through the air, curving downwards.

With a final surge of Aether from Fen, they exploded.

The shockwave reverberated across the city and down the Central Tower, shaking the superstructure. Alarms began wailing below, and Grey thought it was possible he heard screams from the distant ground; though that could just be the ringing in his ears.

At some point in the chaos Fen had pulled away from Caldwell and now stood facing him besides Grey and the other two. Now, the feral look of rage was focused on the man who had held him captive all his young life.

Caldwell's mouth opened and shut a few times, a look of shock on his face.

"Incredible, boy!" he said suddenly, drawing himself back up. "Incredible. Now, release the Aether."

The look on Fen's face grew, if anything, more hateful.

"Now, subject," said Caldwell, failing to keep the fear from his voice. "I said, release the Aether."

Grey felt the Aether lurch again the moment Caldwell said the word 'subject.' He could see Blane and Serinda felt it, and from the widening of his eyes he thought Caldwell did too.

It felt like something *huge* was moving in the depths. A leviathan, stirring.

Caldwell lashed out, a mental assault designed to cut Fen off from the Aether, but it was clear it was futile. It had taken three Far agents to maintain a Lock even when Fen was drugged and only half-conscious; Grey didn't think the technique could be completed by a single person even if the target was far weaker. The attack did nothing, its Aether dissolving into Fen's own.

The next moment, energy boiled outwards from Fen. Anyone unable to use Aether would merely have seen Caldwell abruptly fall to his knees, crying out at a pain with no apparent source. Grey, though, saw the energy pour out of Fen and wrap itself around the man, pressing and crushing in a way resembling how Fen had handled the drones. This time, though, there was nothing physical about it.

Grey could see the man's mind spark and flicker as energy poured through it, could feel the Aether scorch and tear both inside and outside of his skull. Caldwell's skin turned red and blistered, as if frying beneath the hidden sun, and wisps of steam rose around him.

Suddenly, the Aether snapped off. Caldwell swayed on his knees, panting and gasping for air through seared lungs.

Whatever the hell that was, Grey knew it wasn't Mindfire. Not the uncontrolled release of energy, but almost the reverse – like Fen had poured Aether *in*to Caldwell, until his cells were unable to take any more.

"I am not your subject."

Fen's words were almost a whisper amid the strange silence that descended. Even the wind had died down, and the wailing of alarms seemed somehow further away. There was only Fen, and Caldwell.

There was a strange, rough, bubbling sound.

Grey didn't know what it was at first; it didn't sound human. Then he realised it was Caldwell, laughing.

Through cracked lips and ruined throat, Caldwell took several painful, dry breaths, wincing behind his smile. Fen stepped closer to hear what the man was saying.

"You... are... an... *apocalypse* ..."

Fen stepped back again, flames of rage returning to his eyes.

Caldwell laughed harder, flecks of blood flying from his wheezing mouth.

Now Grey felt Fen prepare Mindfire, sensing the rising, burning tension in the Aether he now recognised from previous times Fen had used it.

"Read me..." spluttered Caldwell, meeting Fen's stare with his own.

Somehow, now all was lost, Caldwell seemed without fear. Though his body blistered and bled, and his lungs rasped, his eyes were cool and composed.

"Read me," Caldwell gasped, "...and see what you are when I am not there to control you..."

He began choking, wracking coughs that caused him to double over. Despite this, Grey felt him open his mind to Fen.

Fen stared at the dying man, uncertainty flickering across his face beneath the rage.

"Don't do it, kid," said Grey. Whatever Caldwell was up to, he knew it was a trap.

Caldwell drew himself up again, forcing down the ragged coughs and pushing himself to his feet. He stared down at Fen, a burnt and flayed escapee from the fires of hell.

"Do it," he said. "You can see it already, can't you? Just take it, and realise exactly what you are. See that I was *right*."

"Stop, Fen," said Blane, reaching out a hand towards him.

"Whatever he wants you to see, it's not for you. It's for him."

More hesitancy appeared on Fen's face, the flames of anger tempered if not extinguished. He looked from Blane to Grey, and Grey saw pain in the boy's eyes.

Finally, he looked at Serinda, eyes softening further.

"It's ok," she said, stepping forward as if to hold him, this boy who could sear a soul. "We can leave."

"No," said Fen, his eyes hardening again. "We can't. I can see it, there in his mind. I don't know what it is, but he *wants* me to see it. And... and he knows I need to."

With that, Fen turned back to Caldwell.

Grey felt the Aether move as Fen willed it, at first just the soft, thin tendrils of a Read reaching from the boy to the man, sensed not seen. Then, a wail, a thin, mournful thing that seemed to come from somewhere deep inside Fen.

The Read grew, the Aether leaping at Fen's demand, growing and pouring towards Caldwell's mind.

"No!" cried Fen, denying whatever he was seeing.

Grey fought the desire to try to Read Caldwell too. Simultaneous Reading was impossible, he knew, and dangerous. Minds could be lost when such a thing was tried. All he could do was watch as Fen's face twisted, first into an expression of pain and horror, then once more into a thing of rage and hate.

"Yes," Caldwell said through gritted teeth. The Read was clearly draining him as Fen probed deeper. "Now you see."

Fen just growled, a primal sound, and Grey felt the Aether surge again.

Caldwell grunted as Fen tore deeper into his mind, then collapsed to his knees. Then he began to scream.

Grey knew what was happening because he had experienced it himself. Fen was using a Forced Read, drawing out everything from the man's mind.

A cry tore from Fen's lips, a scream of rage and frustration that slowly built as he continued the mental assault. Fen didn't stop even when Caldwell's broken body tumbled forward and began to shake. Still the energy he drew increased, pulling in everything the man was and had been. He drew and drew, screaming and tearing at the essence of man fallen in front of him until Serinda placed a gentle hand on his shoulder.

"Get off me!" Fen yelled, spinning and pushing her hand away. "Get away from me!"

Serinda stood with her hand outstretched, tears in her eyes.

"Fen," she said softly. "It's ok. We're here for you…"

"No!" Fen's cry was filled with fear and sadness as he backed away from her, from them. "Stay away! You mustn't… you mustn't come close. I… I'm…"

His words trailed off and he stared at his hands as if he didn't know whose they were. He stood there, breathing gradually slowing, as the others looked at him, not knowing what to say.

"Get away from here," he said suddenly, voice cold and emotionless. "I'm going to burn them. All of them. Get out."

When he looked up, it was directly at Grey.

"Thank you," he said. "Thank you for… for everything. For rescuing me. For taking care of me."

Grey stepped forward then paused, warned off by the flash of flame in Fen's eyes.

"You were wrong," the boy said. "You shouldn't have saved me. I don't deserve to be saved."

Grey held out a hand to block Blane, who was trying to step past him. Somehow he knew it was dangerous to approach Fen now.

As if in response, the Aether roiled beneath them. He felt it flow into Fen, *something* rising with it.

And now he could feel that both Serinda and Blane had been right. There was something, some part of Fen, that existed beyond his corporeal form. Yet he did generate the Aether, far more than anyone else Grey had ever met. He could feel it, pouring out of the boy to meet the thing rising towards him.

And he could feel the heat rise with it.

"Run," Grey said, turning and pushing Blane back. Serinda looked torn, looking between Fen and Grey, but she must have sensed what was happening too. She ran, sprinting beside them as they made for the elevator.

They weren't going to make it. Even if they did, whatever Fen was going to do was going to hit anything inside the elevators, anything inside the whole tower, and they were far too high for there to be any other escape.

Something hit him from behind, sending him falling forward. Blane and Serinda fell too, some huge force picking them up and tossing them like leaves…. and not letting them go.

The ground never came. Instead, Grey found himself spinning out over the edge of the building, vertigo instantly setting in as the city stretched out before him a hundred stories below. Terror forced his eyes closed.

But he wasn't falling. Through the horror and nausea, some part of him was aware that he wasn't falling. Oh, he was going *down*, but not in the way gravity usually demanded. The wind was but a strong breeze.

He forced himself to open his eyes; it was one of the most difficult things he'd ever done.

The glass walls of the Central Tower stretched out both above and below him, growing gradually narrower as the distance between them increased. Blane and Serinda were nearby, Serinda slowly tumbling over and over; Blane, meanwhile, could almost have been stood on solid ground, staring back up the way they had come.

"It's Fen!" she shouted upon seeing him regain his senses. "I don't know how, but he's doing this!"

Forcing himself to look down now, he saw the crowds of people all gathered around the base of the tower. Tiny, dark-uniformed figures seemed to be herding them away, scars running through the surrounding buildings and ground where the debris of the exploding drones had crashed.

They were falling towards a nearby building, a tall one perhaps half the height of the Central Tower. As its roof loomed larger, it became apparent to Grey that, even if they weren't falling at the rate gravity would have preferred, they were still falling *very* fast.

He smashed into the top of the building heavily, the jarring jolt of hard concrete meeting limbs leaving him with what he thought was probably a broken wrist. Heaving himself up, he dashed across to where Serinda had landed.

Blane was already there, crouched over her with a look of concern.

"She's breathing," said Blane as Grey arrived. "But she hit her head pretty hard."

Grey saw a thin red trail of blood running from somewhere beneath the woman's hair. He leant down to get a better look, and a groan came from her lips.

"I just had the most horrible dream that we fell off a skyscraper" she muttered.

"We did!" Even with all the seriousness of their situation, Blane could hardly contain her excitement. "Fen knew a way to catch us. I think I figured it out too, at least a little. It's not flying, it's more... it's like... it's like *Pushing* off the air. You can't go up, but you can stop going down. A bit..."

Grey felt a half-smile on his lips at the girl's enthusiasm. Then he turned and looked at the Central Tower. Blane and Serinda fell silent as they did the same.

From their perch on the edge of this building they could see almost the entire Central Tower, from base to spire. A golden tint bathed it, as if it were reflecting the dawn light of the city in Francisco's false windows.

As they watched, the tint grew stronger, coalescing and solidifying in whorls and lines that winked in and out of existence, each time coming back deeper and more concentrated. The pattern swam and spun around the tower, sparking and glinting against its silvered glass, forming and splintering before returning in new, unfathomable patterns.

As if it had been there all the time, not invisible but somehow unnoticed, a serpentine form of blazing golden fire was suddenly curling and uncurling around the tower, wrapping itself around it one moment and then disappearing within the next.

This was no longer the dragon Grey had seen Fen conjure before. No, this was far longer, a scaled, eel-like body that stretched further and longer than the tower itself, a spiny mass that undulated as it moved like some nightmare from the deepest ocean. Its head was larger than a truck, with two eyes that burned brighter than the blinding flame that formed their sockets. A colossal jaw hung open to reveal sharp, curved teeth longer than a man, a mouth that seemed designed to swallow the world.

Giant wings unfurled as the creature spiralled around the tower, rising towards the heavens until they formed a new sky, a golden cover that lit everything beneath.

A deafening creaking sound filled the air, like the tower itself was screaming. More glass splintered and cracked, shards breaking off and falling with sharp lethality to the ground below. The screeching grew louder, the entire structure buckling under impossible pressure.

There was a powerful boom, and the tower blew apart in a rain of silver fragments, sparkling and flashing in the light as the entirety of the tower's shell came apart. Left in its place was the skeleton of a building, interior scarred and torn and as thoroughly destroyed as if hit by a bomb. The leviathan lifted its head to the heavens and roared, though the roar was the sound of roiling flame and not the sound of any creature that truly lived.

Then, with a sudden snap, the creature was gone. Silence filled the world, punctuated by distant sobs and screams.

30

As Seigfried was blind when he sowed his own destruction through his pact with Gunther, so pre-Fall societies were blind to the folly of seeking stability through cooperation with natural foes. It is from Etzel, the Hun, that we must learn.

Niclas Hölderlin, *Lessons for the New World*

They made their way down the stairwell of the building at a frustratingly slow pace, bodies that were already close to their limits pushed past them. They had to break several times, legs becoming spongey and hardly able to support the weight of their owners.

The silence of the dark, narrow space was an unsettling blanket that covered everything, with only the sounds of their heavy breaths and the occasional pained cough to break it. The place was deserted, either officially evacuated or simply emptying out naturally due to the events that had occurred beyond its walls, and the power was cut. Only dull emergency lighting lit their way.

Blane, the least hurt or possibly just the one with the most stamina, insisted several times that she should go ahead to get help, but both Grey and Serinda told her to stay with them. Who knew what they would encounter at the bottom?

After perhaps an hour, maybe more, they finally emerged into the lobby of the ground floor. The false daylight of the full-spectrum spotlights outside hurt their eyes, even weakened as it was by the toppling of several of the tall posts.

"Alive, then."

The voice made Serinda and Blane start, though Grey just sighed.

"How'd you know we'd be here?" he said exhaustedly, leaning against a wall.

Ritra Feye smiled, that same knowing smile he'd seen so often recently, directed at both himself and others. Calm and in control, even amongst the rubble and rising dust of a major catastrophe.

"I have my ways," she said. "Quite a lot of gadgets can detect three people staggering down the stairs of a deserted building."

He noticed she didn't say this was actually how she had found them.

"What do you want?" he said.

He saw Serinda tense, moving to stand between Feye and Blane.

"Don't worry," Feye said, eyeing both the woman and Grey. "I'm not here to take you in."

She gestured back towards the exit, wide grey-tinted doors beyond which the last of the crowd could be seen being ushered away, dust-covered wounded sat hunched over as they waited for emergency responders to get to them.

"I'm going to be quite busy for a while. Though you shouldn't wait around too long,"

Again, that damned smile.

"Once I get everything under control, all bets are off."

"So why are you here?"

Despite his exhaustion, Grey's still felt the annoyance push through his words.

"The boy. Fen, you call him? He's not with you?"

Grey spread his arms wide, gesturing to encompass his bedraggled companions.

"You see him?"

"Right. So he's still on top of the Central Tower?"

Grey sighed again, letting his hands drop.

"I… don't know. Maybe. Something happened to him, something…"

"Something that made him destroy the whole damn building? Yes, I noticed."

"Leave him alone!"

Blane pushed passed Serinda in one quick action, moving to stand square in front of Feye.

"This is *your* fault. You and your agency. What you did to him, what he's become, that was *you*."

Feye raised a single eyebrow.

"And you are…? No, I remember. The runaway. The one who…"

Thinking better of it, Feye stopped speaking, looking up from Blane to Grey.

"Still the saviour of little lost children then, Grey. Even after all this?"

And again, Feye gestured to the destruction outside.

"Caldwell's dead," said Grey, ignoring her words. "He pushed Fen too far, and paid for it. I don't know what he did though, to make Fen do all this. Let him Read him, showed him something that sent him… That made him lose control…"

"I might have an idea what that was," said Feye.

She lifted up a hand which until now had hung at her side. In it was an e-pad, maybe the one she had carried with her in the tower. She held it out towards him.

Grey stared down at it.

"What's on it?" he said.

"You should look at it yourself," Feye replied. "I didn't have access to all the details myself until very recently. Took a lot of piecing together."

"Piecing together?"

Ritra pushed the e-pad at him. He still didn't take it.

"Caldwell was more than just Far," she said. "I told you; friends in high places. I've been looking into him for years. Thanks to you, though, he made himself visible; made a few misjudgements. So now, because it was thanks to you, I'm giving you this."

She thrust the pad at him again.

"Give you some closure," she said with a heavy finality.

Grey took the tablet from her.

"Okay," said Feye, clapping her hands together and once again all cool professionalism. "Get out of here before I really *do* have to arrest you. Not that way..." she said as they began to move towards the main exit.

She pointed behind them, towards a small hallway that led to the left.

"That way. There's a service entrance round the back. I have a feeling you'll have an easier time getting out of here if you go that way."

Serinda and Blane turned to look hesitantly at where Feye was pointing, then looked at Grey. He nodded.

They began walking towards the hallway, but Grey stopped just before the turn that would take them out of sight of Feye. He looked back towards her, where she was watching them leave, still smiling.

"A feeling?" he asked.

She nodded.

"You've attracted a lot of attention, Grey. Some of which comes from places you can hardly imagine. There seem to be a lot of... *people* invested in your success."

With that, she turned and walked away, heading for the main exit and the chaos beyond.

Grey turned and headed after the others, too tired to do more than wonder what the strange emphasis on the word 'people' had meant.

When they stepped out into the back street, the same sleek black car from Francisco's safe house was waiting. Grey barely had anything left in him to be surprised.

"But we didn't leave it here," said Blane, turning with a questioning look to Serinda and Grey.

Grey stepped past her as she hesitated and stepped inside as the doors swung open for him. After a moment, the other two did likewise.

"This is how you got here?" he asked.

Serinda nodded.

"We thought it was you. Didn't know how you did it, but every security checkpoint and door was just open to us. All we did was follow the words that kept appearing on every screen, and they took us into the tower and up there."

A spark of anger flickered in him, even now, at the thought that whatever hand was guiding the vehicle had brought Serinda and Blane into the firefight.

They all instinctively leaned forward to take one final look up to the peak of the ruined Central Tower as the door shut and the car began to move. The navscreen showed a route through the city simply marked SAFE HOUSE.

Then Grey leant back and closed his eyes, letting out a deep, long breath. The peace of the car felt alien.

"What's it say?" said Blane.

Grey opened his eyes again, following her gaze to the e-pad on his lap. He turned it over in his hands, taking in the silvered back and blank, black screen. For some reason the thing felt like a puzzle, not the answer to one.

Serinda and Blane stared at the tablet along with him, saying nothing. Eventually, he tapped the screen and it sprang to life.

The home screen was empty save for one single folder, which upon a tap opened to show three separate files. The first was labelled 'Subject Records.' Grey tapped this.

A processing icon span in the centre of the screen for a while, conveying the size of the file being accessed. After this pause, the display changed into a long list of dates and times, often with an additional 'location' tag in the file name.

Video recordings.

"That is... That's *years'* worth of recordings," gasped Serinda, as Grey scrolled down a list that seemed never-ending.

"His whole life, probably," Grey replied.

He tapped a selection at random, one without a location tag.

The video that appeared showed Fen sat at a desk in a small, pale-cream-coloured room. He looked to be about eight or nine years old, still recognisably the same child but smaller, more fragile, the only thing out of place in the sterile, plain room.

He was sat at a tablescreen, images and text flickering across the display in rapid succession. Anatomical descriptions changed to chemical formulas changed to mathematical equations, and all the time a dull, electronic voice droned quietly on; a teaching program of some kind.

The camera angle was to the back of Fen's head, his shoulders hunched forward over the screen, so it took a while for them to realise he was sobbing.

At one point, he must have closed his eyes, because the images on the tablescreen paused, and a pre-recorded voice played out over the speakers.

"Incomplete studies will result in the revocation of evening meal privileges, subject."

The cold, imperious tones of Caldwell's voice were recognisable even through the tablet's small speakers.

"How long is this?" asked Serinda.

Grey flicked the timeline up onto the display.

"Hours," he replied.

He ran his fingers along the timeline, skipping the recording ahead at random. Fen seemed to barely move for the entirety of the video except to complete activities on the touchscreen, the constant stream of information pouring from the display only stopping when the recorded warning message rang out across the room again.

When the recording ended, Grey selected another one.

Another video with an even younger Fen, this time perhaps a further year or two younger than the previous recording. The room was the same; Grey couldn't identify even a single change in the layout or sparse furnishings.

This time, however, a woman in a white lab coat sat across from Fen. She held a tablet in one hand, the other holding an e-pen above its screen, ready to take notes at any moment. Fen sat awkwardly on his chair, watching her with wide eyes and clearly trying not to fidget under her impassive gaze.

"I need you to focus on me, subject. On what you can *feel* as well as see. We call this Reading. Now, I am allowing you to Read me. Tell me what you see."

The woman barely blinked as she spoke, fixing the child with her stare. At first, Fen met her gaze with childish incomprehension, unable to understand but realising he would be in trouble if he didn't.

Then, slowly, his face changed. His eyes refocused on some spot just beyond her temple, and his expression changed from one of nervous fear to curiosity and wonder.

"Excellent," said the researcher. "Tell me what animal I am thinking of."

Fen looked puzzled.

"You aren't thinking of an animal," he said, head tilting to one side. "You're thinking about… about me? About this place? You don't like it here…"

"Alright subject, that's enough," she said, flicking a nervous look to the camera.

"You're *scared* of me," said Fen, puzzlement and disbelief clear in his childish voice. "You're scared of me, and you're planning on leaving. You're going to run away…"

As Fen continued speaking, the woman's composure collapsed. She pushed her chair back and stood, looking from Fen to the camera, to the door. The tablet tumbled from her hands as she took two steps towards the exit before the door slid open unprompted.

Now the researcher stepped backwards, in fear, as two armed figures stepped into the room. Rendered androgynous by their dark uniforms, their visors hid any expression. Their body language, however, was enough for Grey to know they weren't here to escort her out. At least, not as a willing companion.

"Good job, subject," came Caldwell's voice from the speakers in the room. "You did very well today. Now, go to your room, please."

Fen seemed torn for one moment, curiosity vying with obedience as he watched the armed figures advance towards the now-cowering woman.

"*Now*, subject," came Caldwell's voice again.

Fen turned on his heel and marched swiftly to his bedroom. The door slid shut behind him, and Grey wondered if it was enough to drown out the screams of the woman as she was dragged away.

"Jesus."

Grey just nodded at Serinda's words. There wasn't really much else to add.

The car had pulled into the parking lot of the safe house building at some point while they'd been watching the videos; Grey thought the other two hadn't noticed until the clip ended either.

They made their way to the elevators and down to the apartment in silence, each lost in their own thoughts about what they'd witnessed.

"This still doesn't explain what Fen saw when he Read Caldwell, though," said Serinda once they reached the living area. "He *lived* this; I can't see Caldwell's memories of it making him become... like that."

The false windows of the apartment were showing the same view of the city and distant ocean as before, only this time the colours of the buildings were rendered duller and more uniform by dark clouds that towered above them, blotting out the sun. Blood-red light spilt over the ocean through cracks in the cloud cover, and the wind whipped up sprays of wild ocean and mixed it with the droplets in the air that spoke of an oncoming tropical storm.

Grey paid little heed to the image.

"What about one with a location?" said Blane, pointing down to one of the video file names including a location tag.

Before Grey could say anything, her finger darted forward and selected the file, marked after the date and time with the letters 'PARIS.'

"It can't mean *the* Paris, can it?" asked Serinda, leaning over from where she sat across from him to see the screen.

Grey tapped the e-pad once on the table in front of him, using a well-practised flicking motion to send the image on the tablet onto the LEF screen that made up the wall in front of them.

The view that filled the screen wall before them was that of a broken and blasted city, collapsed and collapsing buildings fallen into streets still filled with the wreckage of civilisation even over a century later. The remains of a great river ran across the top of the feed, the thin waters that remained thick with muck and poison, and beyond that, the fallen, blasted remains of a wrought-iron lattice tower toppled and lying broken on the cracked and weed-strewn ground.

"My god," said Serinda. "They took him to one of the dead cities."

Practically every city of the pre-Fall world was destroyed in the Sudden War, but none more so than the old capitals. In its bloodlust to burn and destroy itself, not a single one of humanity's great cities was spared. Not even the capitals of the African continent, least scorched of all the world's regions in the nuclear fires, escaped that fate.

And of these, the hardest hit were the cities of the old global powers; the targets of tens, if not hundreds, of automated retaliatory 'defence' systems, rendered into radioactive dead zones where nothing good could live. The dead cities.

The video feed on the screen panned forward, zooming onto a cracked boulevard lined with rusted vehicles and the refuse of a city caught practically unawares by its doom. At the end of the street stood Fen.

The video feed seemed to be coming from some sort of camera drone, steady but swaying slowly in the breeze. It closed in on the boy as he moved down the street, carefully making his way over and across the ancient vehicles, forever frozen on their futile, incomplete journeys.

Fen stared at the camera as it approached, apparently warned by the sound of it, though there was no audio on the recording itself. He looked almost as he had when Grey found him, a young teenager made older by harsh experience.

"Even with iodine tablets, you can only last a few hours down there. At most."

Serinda bit her nails in horror as she spoke.

"Survival tests, he called them," said Grey. "To force him to develop his abilities."

As he spoke, something moved near the bottom edge of the camera. The image span, swinging to focus on a group of small, dark spots moving swiftly among the decaying vehicles.

"Jackals," said Blane.

She was right. The canine forms were all sizes and shapes, though even from this distance it was obvious most were large. Several were misshapen, and most were scarred and bloody from a life where even being the fittest was no guarantee of survival.

They ran in a frenzy towards where Fen stood, now with his feet planted firmly atop a high, solid-looking truck roof.

As the first dog leapt for Fen, he looked up at the camera and smiled. The attacking beast was slammed backwards abruptly, as if hit by a giant's unseen hand, as the animals behind it leapt also.

Fen let out a shout, the feral look of rage Grey knew well appearing on his face, and raised his hands towards the camera.

The screen went black.

They sat in silence again, staring at the featureless wall on which until a moment ago the images of a distant ruined city had shone.

"What was in the other files?" said Blane after a while.

Grey swiped back on the e-pad, the screen mirroring itself on the wall as he closed the video list.

There were two more icons, besides the one they had already opened.

'Acquisition,' and 'Containment Breach'.

Grey tapped the one labelled 'Acquisition.'

The open file was not a list of recorded videos. Instead, it was a database of several documents, varying in format and size. None of the documents, however, was very large; no more than a physical page or two, the thumbnails of each one revealing a mixture of images and documents.

Grey opened the first one, dated the earliest of them all. Thirteen years ago, or thereabouts.

The document was made up primarily of text, with a square section near the top that upon tapping opened up a sequence of photos; images of a migrant camp, the flimsy structures and ragged clothing iconic of such locations. It reminded Grey of his own early memories, the smell of open cookfires rising up from somewhere deep in his mind.

The next few images were similar, taken from various angles centred around a cluster of shelters, each remaining standing only with the structural support of the equally fragile-looking shelters pressed in around it. Grey remembered this well, too; how everything built was makeshift, the temporary becoming long-term, the long-term becoming permanent as the inhabitants held on desperately to their dreams of a better life across the water.

The final image was of a couple holding a toddler between them, a tiny child of perhaps one or two years. They were outside one of the shelters, sat across from one another and clapping as the boy made its faltering way from the lap of the mother towards the father. Joy was apparent through their tired eyes, even at this distance.

Grey returned to the attached document, reading through the text. Details of location, of dates and times and patterns of behaviour. Some kind of test results were frequently referred to, though what these tests were was left unsaid.

The final lines, however, left Grey cold.

Approach made through usual channels. Offer refused.

An addendum was appended to these words, popping open in the corner of the screen when selected.

Acquire the subject regardless. Authorisation; N. Caldwell, Section Chief.

"They *stole* him."

All worry and fear was gone from Serinda's voice, replaced by a cold, hard anger Grey found somehow more dangerous than Fen's.

"They stole him from his parents, from his family. Took him, and locked him up as their lab rat for his entire life. No wonder he was angry."

But ever since seeing the image of the couple on the screen, Grey had felt a deep, dark void growing in his soul.

"It's… It wasn't that," he said, barely able to speak. "Not that. I think… I…"

He stared at Serinda, whose own anger faded into confusion and then concern at the look of torment Grey couldn't keep from his face, nor from his mind.

"What is it?" asked Blane, looking from one to the other. "What's wrong?"

Serinda kept staring at Grey, not saying a word. A hint of wary premonition crossed her expression, and she held out a hand.

"Here," she said. "Let me do it."

Grey passed her the tablet with trembling hands, hardly able to breathe.

Serinda stared down at the device, gave a deep, wavering sigh of her own, and opened the final file. The file marked 'Containment Breach'.

"Oh, no!" cried Blane, hand covering her mouth in shock and tears brimming from her eyes as the video filled the screen.

There they were, clear as if they were standing in the room with them. The feed from the dashboard camera showed them both, the tall, dark man dressed in the black uniform of a facility guard, the pale, fair-haired woman in the plain dull white of a caretaker. They watched the road ahead anxiously, but frequently turned to peer behind them. There, in the back of the van, was the sprawled and hooded figure of Fen.

"They weren't taking him…" said Blane, voice filled with horror. "They *were* rescuing him."

The man and woman smiled as they looked back to the road, the woman reaching out to tenderly take the man's hand in hers.

Soon, they would be safe. Soon, they would stop the car and free him. Soon, they would be free from any chase.

Soon, they would free their son, and escape.

Grey stared at the faces of the couple as they contemplated a future that would never come. The faces, now older and more lined, of the man and woman from the camp. The man and woman who had smiled with such joy at their child's first steps.

The dark hood around Fen's head exploded outwards, and the screen went dark.

Epilogue

In the event of an existential threat to the Federation, supreme power will be restored to the Reclamation Authority for the duration of the emergency.

Federal Emergency Regulation 1.17

There was a dark room. It didn't need to be dark, yet nevertheless it was. Some things are better done away from the exposing light of day.

Within the room a man sat, features obscured by the gloom so that only his ice-sharp eyes were truly visible. Everything else about him was shade and silhouette.

A line of light pierced the gloom as two large doors swung roughly open, and the man known in the *Forever Fallen* as Uriel strode into the room like the wrath of kings. He marched up to the edge of the wide mahogany desk that the man sat behind, as from somewhere behind him a worried voice demanded he leave.

"It's fine, Ms. Kondé. Mr. Hawkross is just here to clear up a few... complications. Aren't you, Hawkross? Or should I call you Uriel?"

The voice spoke slow, considered words in a smooth baritone that radiated authority; and the expectation that this authority would be heeded. The indignation on Uriel's face faltered for a moment, before returning.

"Complications? *Complications* isn't the word for it. This is decades of work, thrown into chaos at the last minute."

He smacked his palms down on the desk to emphasise the point. The man sitting behind it looked slowly downwards to where the hands rested and furrowed his brow.

The anger seemed to drain from Uriel at this look, replaced by a cold fear that verged on terror. Slowly, and ever so carefully, he removed his hands from the wood.

A sliver of brighter light filled the gloom, and the sound of hurried footsteps came up behind him, making the clip-clopping sound of high heels from an era long past. Pushing past him, the secretary the man had called Ms. Kondé rushed over with sanitising spray in hand and scrubbed the places Uriel had touched, before retreating back the way she had come and leaving the two of them once more shrouded in darkness.

Uriel cleared his throat.

"Ahem... Look, Caldwell's interference was bad enough, constantly trying to get the kid back like that, but I want to know what the hell *she* was thinking. Having her agents take us in like that, in the middle of a major operation. We only achieved our aims through luck, and I've lost the *Fallen* figurehead I use to control the whole damn lot of wannabe-freedom fighters."

"Your unsuspecting little pet terrorist will be released on a legal technicality in a few days."

Uriel's head whipped around in surprise to face the corner of the room where Ritra Feye stood, hands calmly folded behind her back.

"I, uh, I didn't see you there, Agent Feye," he said falteringly.

Feye smiled back at him.

"No, you didn't."

"Ms. Feye and I were just discussing the outcome of recent events," said the man in the chair, making Uriel's eyes snap back to focus on him. "Tell me, Hawkross, how do you think they went?"

Uriel looked from the man to Feye and back.

"Honestly, now, Hawkross. You know the Committee demands the unsullied truth," said the man.

"Yes, sir," Uriel replied, eyes flicking once more towards where Feye stood, that unsettling smile still fixed on her lips.

"Well, uh, as I said, uh, our main goal *was* achieved," he said, fighting the stammer that had appeared in his voice.

"Indeed," replied the man. "Explain what you mean by *achieved*, please."

"Uh, well, the inauguration of Albores as the capital is on hold, and the chaos has probably set back any possible handover of power to the Federation by years. Um, and the emergency law is in place, meaning..."

"Meaning the Reclamation Authority is once again the final arbiter in all decisions regarding the running of the Reclamation," finished the man.

"Yes, sir, that's right. But, uh, many of the Federation heads *did* escape the tower before it was destroyed. Uh, the Federation as a body still exists."

Uriel saw Feye's smile grow almost imperceptibly wider as he spoke.

"And you think it would be better if they had *all* been eradicated, do you?" asked the man.

Puzzlement crossed Uriel's face.

"Sir, that was always the plan. By eradicating the Federal executive, we ensure a restoration of power to the RA, and ensure the running of the state is not poisoned by discredited sociopolitical ideologies."

"And those that survive are still a threat to us, are they?"

The puzzlement on Uriel's face did not lessen but transformed as he sought for an answer.

"Um, well, not so much now. The attack must have shaken them, now they realise how exposed they are without... without the RA's protection..."

Uriel's words trailed off as he looked at Feye in disbelief.

"You *planned* this? You *wanted* some to survive?"

Feye gave a small nod.

"A tame Federation dependent on the RA is easier to control than whatever might spring up in its place."

Uriel turned back to the man in front of him.

"Then why wasn't I informed?" he asked.

"I was unaware I was required to run my decisions by you," Casco said with a smile that held only menace.

Uriel involuntarily began to raise his hands in fearful refutation before catching himself. Instead he froze, only a slight twitching beneath one eye indicative of the turmoil within.

"Still," said Casco, apparently satisfied with this reaction. "Things do appear to have been rather chaotic, Feye."

"I was... adapting to changing circumstances," said Feye, stepping smartly forward to stand beside Uriel and turning to face the man at the desk. "I could hardly risk a message to other departments breaking confidentiality now, could I?"

Uriel glared at her.

"And all this had nothing to do with your little feud with Caldwell then, did it?"

He didn't try to hide the resentment in his voice.

"That's enough for now, Hawkross. Uriel. Agent Feye has successfully reduced the likelihood of groups springing up outside of *your* influence, too. Now, you should return to your little band of terrorists, and maintain silence until we contact you next."

Uriel opened his mouth as if to protest, then thought better of it.

Casco's tone brooked no objection.

Uriel spun smartly on his heels, and headed out of the room.

"It *was* somewhat unkind of you, involving him in your political games like that," said the man. Though his voice was still cool and hard, it somehow seemed just the slightest bit more... casual. As if he were now speaking to an equal, or at least a not unimportant subordinate.

"It was no game and you know it, Casco. Sir."

In the gloom, the man smiled.

"Well, you won either way."

"Caldwell bugged Far agents. *My* agents."

"And you knew he would. It's how you drew him out, isn't it?"

Feye nodded.

"Correct. I knew he'd be listening in when Agent Grey contacted Agent Chau."

"*Agent* Grey? I believe he is no longer a part of the agency?"

Feye chuckled.

"There is no leaving Far. I never even rescinded his clearance; he's as much my tool now as he was when he was officially an agent."

"And you used him to great effect. You even got that *thing* in the Silicon Isle to make a move."

Feye's expression became serious.

"That was... unexpected. I had thought they'd leave it all to their monitor, the one who calls himself Francisco now. For it to actually show itself all the way out here..."

"The result of your excellent work, agent; a result the Committee has noted. And, more importantly, a result that underlines the necessity of what we are doing here."

The man sat back in his chair, looking up towards and past the low, dark ceiling before he continued.

"A war *is* coming," he said. "And we will not be found unready. Other nations may have a head start on us, but we will overtake and outdo them all. Even that *thing* in the Althing Republic."

Feye nodded and turned to go. The tone of the man called Casco's voice made it clear she had been dismissed.

"Uh, one more thing..."

She turned back, looking questioningly at her superior.

"Your agent, uh, the one called Grey. Does he know?"

"Know what, sir?" She asked.

"About the Sudden War. How it began."

Feye shook her head.

"No sir, I don't believe he does. He should believe it began in nuclear fire, just like it ended."

"You're sure? It could be... *problematic* for our pursuits if the real cause of the Sudden War were made public."

"I see no way he could know, sir. That is information I kept beyond his reach."

Now, the man looked questioning.

"And you're sure it will remain so? He has been *very* resourceful. Maybe more resourceful than you expected."

Feye stood and locked eyes with Casco for a moment, before nodding once more.

"He doesn't know. And if he does find out, I will deal with him like anyone else. He's not *that* useful a tool."

"Very good," said Casco, reaching down and pulling open a small drawer set in the desk.

Whatever he was looking at, it was clear that *now* Feye really was dismissed.

She left the dark, quiet room that was the centre of a web those trapped in couldn't even see, and made her way back to the Agency. There was much to do.

ABOUT THE AUTHOR

Luke Houghton (1984-) was born in the UK and has lived around the world, living in Spain, Saudi Arabia, Taiwan, and Japan. He now lives in Fukushima, Japan, with his wife and three crazy cats, dreaming sci-fi dreams. He is the author of, among other things, *Hidden Trials, Stars Above, Corporeal Forms,* and *The Pack.*

Printed in Great Britain
by Amazon